ASHTON SCOTT

NINA LEVINE

ISBN: 9780994585820

Editing by Becky Johnson at Hot Tree Editing

Cover Design by Letitia at Romantic Book Affair Designs

Cover Image by Wander Pedro Aguiar

For my #AssholeMonday lovers

You'll never know what your support meant to me while I wrote this book, episode by episode.

Thank you.
N xx

1

LORELEI

THERE AREN'T MANY MOMENTS I'VE REGRETTED IN my life, but this one would have to rank high on that short list. Doing the walk of shame through one of the most exclusive hotels in Sydney is not something I ever thought I'd do, but yet, here I am doing exactly that. I blame Rodney Stein. If he had just turned up to his own damn wedding yesterday and married his fiancé—my friend—none of this would have happened. She wouldn't have insisted on getting drunk last night, and I wouldn't have had to match her drink for drink. *And* I wouldn't have come back to this hotel with the guy I met and made a fool of myself.

Oh, God.

My head hurts.

Yeah, well a lot more is going to hurt if you don't get your ass home and then to your office in the next forty minutes.

I pick up my pace in an effort to achieve my goal. At the same time, my phone rings and I rummage in my bag for it.

Please God, don't let anyone I know see me this morning.

"Lorelei, where are you?" It's my best friend, Sienna, and the urgency I hear in her voice concerns me. She never takes that tone with me. Sienna is one of the most laid-back people I know.

"I'm on my way home and then to the office. What's up?" I keep my eyes down, focused on the marble floor while doing my best to avoid anyone's gaze.

There's a long pause where neither of us speak. When she finally replies, the urgency has given way to confusion. "Wait, did you hook up with that guy last night?"

I sigh. Admitting what I did is the last thing I want to do. "No... but I did go back to his hotel room. I'll fill you in later."

"Who are you and what did you do with Lorelei Winters?"

"I know... I know. Stupid."

"No, it's not stupid, but it's not you. You don't do sex with strangers."

As she speaks, I push through the front doors of the hotel—*finally*—and step outside into the warm sunshine. It's only eight in the morning, so this weather is unseasonably warm for a winter day in Sydney. The early morning hustle and bustle of Sydney fill my senses, and I breathe it in. I love everything about this city, even the cranky cab drivers who honk at anyone who dares get in their way and the people who shove past you in their hurry to get to work.

"Sienna, can we go over this later when my head isn't throbbing, and I'm not madly trying to get home so I can take a shower and get to the office before my appointment?"

"Oh, shit! That's what I'm calling for. Your appointment has been changed. The guy will be here in fifteen minutes."

Today is going to be a bad day.

It can't be any worse than last night.

"Wanna make a bet," I mutter to myself as I bend my head so I can balance my phone between my cheek and my shoulder. I then fumble in my bag to make sure I have supplies on hand to fix my face now.

"Huh?" Sienna asks on the other end of the phone.

"Ignore me. I'm talking to myself," I say as I find my make-up bag. Thank goodness I always travel prepared.

"How far away are you?" Sienna asks.

"I'm close, but this traffic is a bitch by the looks of it. Can you stall him if I'm running late?"

"Sure. I'll sell him some financial services."

I laugh at her while hailing a cab. Sienna is a financial adviser and can sell anything to anyone. I don't doubt the guy will have hired her before he leaves our office.

"Thanks, babe. Gotta go." I hang up and give the cab driver directions before sinking into the back seat. This day is just beginning, but I'm ready for it to be over. I can cope with most things, but hangovers are not one of them. Drinking is something I usually avoid for this very reason. I haven't felt this ill in three years—not since the killer hangover I ended up with from my twenty-fifth birthday celebrations that Sienna organised. A girls' weekend away at a winery in the Hunter Valley with ten of your closest friends will do it to you every time.

I attempt to make myself presentable for my appointment. Five minutes later, I've removed the mess of yesterday's make-up from my face and have applied new foundation, all the while cursing Rodney Stein. Who has a Sunday wedding, anyway? He was the one who pushed for that day and then he didn't even have the hide to show up. Sarah had been devastated. Naturally. Six years of her life with that man, gone.

"And to not have the fucking balls to tell her in person…," I mutter as I apply eye shadow.

"Did you say something, ma'am?"

My head jerks up at the cab driver's question and I make

eye contact in his rear-view mirror. "Sorry, talking to myself," I reply before looking back down at my compact.

Not bad.

My make-up skills have come in handy. I may be able to pull this off.

Except for the dress you're wearing that screams, 'I spent last night in a hotel with a guy I just met'.

I smooth the red satin material of the dress I'm wearing—the dress that shows just a little too much cleavage for a business meeting. I would have preferred to meet Ashton Scott looking anything but a woman who has just completed her first walk of shame. The guy is a legend in the business world and I want to make a good impression. The day his assistant phoned asking if I'd see him to discuss something that would benefit both of us, I jumped at the chance.

I'm going to kill Rodney Stein if I ever see him again.

The cab jerks to a halt and the red lipstick I'm applying ends up all over my cheek.

Worst. Morning. Ever.

Fuck you, Rodney Stein.

"Lorelei!" Sienna stands as I enter our shared office. Her brown eyes widen in the way they do when she's pissed off but doesn't want to show it. "I'll leave you and Ashton to it," she says. As she brushes past me, she mutters, "Good luck with that arrogant asshole. I'll bring you back a toasted caramel macchiato. You're going to need it."

She breezes out of the room and I turn to find Ashton Scott watching me from where he's standing near the window.

Sweet baby Jesus, the man is something else. Dark hair, chiselled jaw, tanned skin and fit—he's the kind of man pretty much any woman I know would kill to have in her bed. The thing that's getting my panties in a twist? The way he's wearing his five o'clock shadow first thing in the morning. Not to mention the way he's teamed jeans with a black dress shirt and black jacket. It's like a 'fuck you' to the business world he inhabits—a fuck you that I like.

His gaze travels the length of me, resting for a moment on my cleavage, before finding my eyes again. A bolt of heat hits me and I swallow hard.

Switch your damn brain on, Lorelei.

I want to impress him with my business savvy. Lust has no place here.

I move to where he's standing and extend my hand. "It's good to meet you, Mr. Scott. I'm Lorelei Winters."

Really?

He knows who you are. He came to you, remember?

He shakes my hand. "Lorelei."

No smile.

No pleasantries.

Just one word.

But hot damn if that one word didn't slide through his lips like sugar. His voice is a God-given gift; one I'm sure could cause a woman an unhealthy addiction.

My brain misfires and I hold his hand longer than I intended. It's not until he finally lets my hand go that I realise this.

"Sorry!" I say in more of a shriek than my preferred business voice. "Would you like a tea or coffee?" I am so damn flustered that I have no clue what might come out of my mouth next.

The corner of his mouth twitches. "No, thank you." He takes charge of the meeting—because clearly I'm in no shape to do this—and indicates for me to take a seat.

The office I share with Sienna is a room we've rented off a

friend on his company premises. It's a modern space rather than a traditional business office. We have one large round glass table that we both work at in the centre of the room. There is usually a large vase of flowers in the middle of the table, but being Monday, neither of us has filled the vase yet. Cream paint on the walls is covered by a selection of art prints we love, including a large canvas I painted with some of our favourite inspirational quotes. A floor-to-ceiling window takes up one wall and we've hung a sheer, pale pink curtain that allows light to filter through.

Ashton takes the seat right next to me. His leg brushes against mine as he leans forward to speak.

Damn you, round table.

I should never have convinced Sienna to get this table.

"I heard you were selling the building you own," he says. "I've come to make you an offer."

My business senses finally kick in. "Which one?" I only own one building, but he doesn't need to know that.

He quirks a brow. "The one on Willow Street."

He totally knows I'm lying. But he's humouring me. I'm not sure which is worse.

"No, it isn't for sale." My grandmother would roll over in her grave if I sold the building she left me when she died.

His lips pinch together. "I've heard it is."

How strange. I wouldn't have thought the building he's referring to would even be on his radar. Ashton is a property developer who deals in high-end properties from what I understand. My building doesn't fit into that category at all. And it's definitely not for sale.

"I think perhaps whoever told you that has mixed up the information. There are three shops in my building and one has just come up for lease, but the building isn't for sale."

"The person who told me never mixes up their information, Lorelei." The sugar disappears from his voice and it's clear I've said something he doesn't like.

I straighten in my seat, slightly annoyed at the tone he's taking with me. "I'm not sure who you've been getting your news from, but I can assure you it's wrong." I remove the friendliness from my voice to match his.

His gaze remains steady on me and it's only because I'm watching him so closely that I see the tiny flare of his eyes. He seems shocked, but I'm not sure at what. That his information is wrong? Or, that I had the gall to tell him that? I bet Ashton Scott is used to always having the right information.

"Lorelei, I'm not a man to be screwed with. If you're trying to play me to get more money out of this deal from the other party, I'll make you regret that."

Whoa.

My hangover collides with the anger bubbling up at his threat. Standing, I say, "You can leave now. I don't appreciate you asking for a meeting and then coming here and threatening me. I'm not a woman who lies about anything. You want to know something from me? Straight up ask me and I'll give you an honest answer. When I tell you that my building is not for sale, you can be assured that it's *not for sale*. And I don't respond well to intimidation. You can take your threat and go back to whoever fed you this bullshit and tell them to get their facts straight. *And* I would suggest hiring more capable staff."

My pulse beats hard and fast as I catch my breath.

How dare he come here and insinuate I'm a money-grabber? Or, that I would lie?

He stands, his gaze still pinned to mine. His jaw clenches as he stares at me with infuriation. "This isn't the end of this. I want that building and I always get what I want."

No more words are exchanged before he stalks out of my office.

I take a few moments to get myself together. Angry thoughts explode through my mind and I struggle to think straight.

The absolute nerve of that man.

Ashton Scott can kiss my ass.

2

ASHTON

"Jessica!" My voice ricochets around my office, intensifying the headache taking hold of my head as I call out for my assistant. The meeting with Lorelei Winters I've just returned from has completely fucked with my mind.

"I see Asshole Monday has returned," she says as she steps into my office.

Scowling, I reach into the top drawer of my desk and yank out a box of Advil. "What the hell is Asshole Monday?"

Passing me the glass of water she's holding, she says, "You're welcome."

Jessica can read my mind. It's the reason she's worked for me for five years. I down the pills before demanding, "Are you going to enlighten me?"

She sighs as she takes the empty glass from me. "You had a bad weekend, didn't you?"

"No."

She places a hand on her hip. At just over five feet, she's tiny compared to my six foot two, and yet she's fierce when she wants to be. I know she's about to have her say by the way she flicks her dark hair—it's a mannerism of hers that indicates her annoyance with me. "Ashton, you've just barrelled your way in here with that shitty look on your face, barking at everyone along the way and generally being an asshole. It's become a common occurrence around here over the last few months, but then you went back to being nice Ashton and we had some peace." She spreads her hands out in front of her and adds, "Like I said, Asshole Monday has returned. And the fact it always happens on a Monday makes me think you must have had a shitty weekend."

There are only three people in my life who get away with speaking to me this way—Jessica, my sister, Alessandra and my friend, Jack Kingsley.

"For the record, I did not have a bad weekend. But I will tell you what has been bad about my day so far—Lorelei Winters."

She frowns. "Really? That's surprising. From all the stuff I dug up on her for you, she sounded like a good person. I didn't read one bad thing about her. Hell, she dedicates hours every week to women at a local nursing home giving them beauty treatments."

"She was rude and she lied to me," I snap, not wanting to hear what an amazing woman she is. The fact I will have to deal with her again irritates me, but I want her building more than I want never to see her again.

Jessica cocks her head to the side. "Tell me what happened, because maybe your Asshole-Monday mood got in the way."

"Oh, for fuck's sake," I mutter. "I wasn't in a bad mood until *after* I saw her."

Crossing her arms over her chest, she gives me a blank look that says she's waiting for me to talk.

I walk around the desk and sit on the edge of it, resting my hands either side of me. My chest is so damn tight with annoyance. I can't recall the last time a woman managed to rile me up to this extreme. Men often, but not women. "She told me her building is not for sale and after I suggested she was playing me in an effort to get more for the sale, *she* suggested I employed idiots because I had the wrong information."

Jessica's eyes narrow at me. "Are you more pissed off that you thought she was lying or that she took a shot at your ego?"

"Are you sure *I'm* the one being an asshole today?"

"I just call it as I see it."

"For a start, I don't hire idiots. If the woman knew anything at all about me, she'd know that—"

She cuts me off. "Ah, see there's that ego I was talking about. You naturally assume that everyone knows all about you. From what I read about her, Lorelei isn't your standard businesswoman. She inherited everything she owns from her grandmother a year ago and has been stumbling her way through the business world since then. She probably doesn't know that much about you at all."

Jessica has this way of pulling my ass into line and it would appear she's doing it again this morning. I blow out a long breath as I rake my fingers through my hair. "Well, that may be the case, but she still lied to me."

She shakes her head. "Ashton, for a smart man, you're obtuse today. Give me one good reason why she'd lie about it? Don't you think that if she really wanted to squeeze anyone for more cash, she would have let you make an offer and then she would have worked from there to get more for the sale?"

As much as I hate to admit it, she's right.

Where the hell is your brain today?

"Where did we get the information from that the building was for sale?" I ask.

"Didn't Alessandra tell you your father had made an offer on it?"

Pushing off from the desk, I nod. "Get her on the line for me."

She doesn't move, but rather stays where she is and watches as I walk around my desk to take a seat behind it.

"What?" I demand.

"I'm just trying to assess where we're at with Asshole Monday. Are you good now, or do I need to get you a cup of *Get Over Yourself?*"

I purse my lips. Jessica will be the fucking death of me. "Just get Alessandra on the phone," I snap, my temper fraying.

She nods. "Good." And with that, she sashays out of the office.

"What's up, Ashton? I'm in the middle of a meeting with a supplier, but Jessica said it was important." Alessandra sounds distracted, but my sister is exceptionally good at multi-tasking.

"Who told you that building on Willow Street is for sale?"

She's silent for a moment. "Dad. Why?"

"I just had a meeting with the owner and she told me it isn't. I'm trying to figure out why she'd tell me it isn't if it is."

"Ashton…." Her voice holds a warning, one I'm not interested in hearing.

"I want that building, Alessandra."

"I know you do, but I worry it's for all the wrong reasons. Just because it holds sentimental value to—"

I cut her off, not needing or wanting to hear what she is

about to say. "It holds nothing for me. I want it purely to expand my holdings."

"Bullshit, little brother. You want it to piss Dad off *and* because it holds meaning to you."

I throw the pen I'm holding down onto my desk and stand. Ignoring what she said, I ask, "Did he give you any other information about the sale?"

She sighs. "No." After a brief pause, she adds, "Let this go, Ashton. There's too much hurt tied up in all this. It's eaten you up for years and if you buy that damn building, it will keep eating you up."

I've made my way out to Jessica's office and motion for her to stop what she's doing. Ignoring Alessandra again, I mutter, "I'll see you tonight, Aly." Before she can reply, I end the call and give my attention to Jessica. "What meetings have I got today?"

"You're back-to-back from ten until three, and then you're free to go and apologise to Lorelei." The look of expectation on her face makes it clear she wants me to do what she has said.

"Block off the rest of my day," I direct. "And phone Lorelei to arrange another meeting, please."

"Are we sure your mood will have improved by then?"

I turn to head back into my office. Calling over my shoulder as I leave, I say, "No one likes a smartass, Jessica."

Her laughter floats through the air between our offices. "You do or else I wouldn't still be here."

The knots I've felt in my neck for days ease a little. If there's one thing Jessica does well besides organising me, it's snapping me out of a bad mood. And God knows I could do with it today. After the weekend I've had and Lorelei Winters putting me off my game this morning, I need Jessica to work her magic.

3

LORELEI

Resting my head on the table, I squeeze my eyes shut and try to block the world out. Over the course of seven hours, this day has gone from bad to worse. First, I discovered one of my Willow Street tenants is going through a nasty divorce, and her ex is causing her all sorts of trouble, including vandalising her shop. Today we had to deal with graffiti all over the building. Then I found out the roof on the building is in urgent need of repair. The storm we had two nights ago revealed some damage and the repairs can't wait. After that, I had Ashton Scott's assistant harassing me to hold another meeting with him. The highlight of my day was telling her no. And now I've just discovered some of my shares took a dive overnight.

On top of all that, I never made it home to shower and change, so I'm still wearing the red dress from the wedding that flashes my cleavage in a very unbusinesslike manner.

"I want a do-over," I mutter to myself while I wallow in self-pity.

"Bad day?"

My head snaps up at the sound of that voice.

Sugar… sweet, delicious sugar.

Bad, bad sugar.

Ashton Scott stares down at me with amusement in his eyes, and I don't fail to notice the way his gaze sweeps over my dress.

As much as I want to stand and tell him where to go, I can't summon the energy to do that. "If you've come to issue threats again or to call me a money-grabber, I don't want to hear it."

He holds his hands up as if he's surrendering. "I wouldn't dream of it." Nodding at the chair next to mine, he says, "Mind if I join you?"

I exhale my frustration. "I told your assistant that I didn't have time for another meeting."

Ignoring me, he sits. "Looks like you can squeeze me in."

"So when you asked whether I minded if you joined me, what you really meant to say was that you *were* joining me."

His eyes capture mine in a way that doesn't let go. "I'm not a man who usually asks, Lorelei."

There's no denying the dominance surrounding this man. Everything about him declares control and power— from the way he stands tall with his shoulders back, to the deep, commanding tone of his voice, to the way he watches me with complete self-assurance. I imagine he doesn't ever have to ask for anything.

"I bet you aren't."

He doesn't react to that except to wait a moment before saying, "I want to apologise for the way I spoke to you this morning. I was out of line with what I said and I'd like us to begin again."

His voice is oh-so-smooth as if he expects for this to go his way. "I also bet you don't usually apologise."

Again, no reaction.

Except for the vein that twitches in his temple.

His emotions are contained; it makes me want to push him to see if I can provoke a response. I don't cope well with people who hide what they're feeling or thinking. They make me second-guess myself more than I already do.

"You're not going to make this easy for me, are you?"

"I'm not a woman who makes things easy for any man, Ashton."

The hum of the offices around us fades into the background as a new tension settles in the room. Ashton's body tenses and he takes a deep breath. His eyes never leave mine, and I do my best to hide the way he unnerves me. I might have said what I did, but that doesn't make it true. As much as I don't make things easy for men, I've never met one like Ashton Scott.

I've never met a man who turns me on, frustrates me and flusters me all at once.

After a few moments of silence, he leans forward and murmurs, "It's a good thing I like a challenge."

Desire curls through me and I want to rant at the injustice of this world. Who decided that men should be granted bodies and voices and faces and—*oh my God*—eyes that have the ability to screw with women's mental capacities like this?

I need a moment to collect my thoughts so I stand. Smoothing my dress, I say, "I need a coffee. Do you want something?"

He rises, and I notice his gaze taking in every inch of my dress again as he does. "Black coffee, no sugar, thank you."

His eyes on me have only flustered me more. I wish I'd had time to go home and change out of this damn dress before having to see Ashton again. The fact my boobs are practically hanging out has put me off my game.

"You can stop judging this dress," I snap, my ruffled state finally getting to me.

"That wasn't judgement, Lorelei." His deep voice moves through me as heat flushes my skin.

Oh dear Lord, is there no end to his assault on my senses?

Focus.

Deep breaths.

He can kiss your ass, remember?

"What do you want, Ashton? I've already told you my building isn't for sale, so I'm not sure why you're here." I load the Nespresso with a coffee pod as I speak, doing my best to ignore the war of emotions rushing through me.

"Everything in this world is for sale for the right price."

If there's one thing my grandmother taught me, it's manners. Those manners are the only thing holding me back from telling him what I really think about that statement. Instead, I face him and calmly say, "It would seem you've found something that isn't."

He rests against the counter and casually crosses one ankle over the other as if he's settling in. "You're attached to that building." It isn't a question, but rather, a statement.

"Yes. My grandmother owned it for years while I was growing up. She loved the opportunity it gives people."

Frown lines etch his forehead. "What opportunity?"

I shake my head in annoyance. "You know nothing about that building."

"I know there are three businesses that you lease space to in it and that it's a piece of prime real estate in Potts Point. I'm guessing the opportunity you're talking about is the exposure its location gives those businesses."

It's moments like these I truly question my chosen path of building a business. The Willow Street building is all those things he mentioned, and yet it is so much more. However, the other things aren't likely to rate high on any list that a man like Ashton checks off when considering acquiring an asset. The fact that I *would* include them on any list I make has me wondering at my ability to survive in the ruthless business world.

"No, the opportunity I was referring to was that the people she leased to, and that I now lease to, aren't your standard business-type people. Pearl Winters established the Willow Street Fund to help people who have great business ideas, but who can't afford to action them. The fund takes applications once a year and distributes money and works with the chosen businesses for a period of three years to get them up and running. If we have a lease available in the Willow Street property and they need a shop, we make it available to them at a deeply discounted cost." I pause for a moment before adding, "There's no way I'd ever sell that building. It's too important to these people."

He's staring at me with a look I'm not quite sure of. If I had to identify it, I'd say it's possibly confusion. "I knew about the Willow Street Fund and I knew your leases were too cheap, but I didn't realise the two went together...." His voice drifts off as if he's thinking about something else.

"It's not something we make known. My grandmother figured that if people knew they could get cheap rent, she'd have everyone applying for funding. When someone signs a lease, they also sign a non-disclosure agreement stating they won't share that information with anyone."

"So what you're saying is that anyone who has ever had a business in that building was helped by you or your grandmother. They wouldn't have had anyone else helping them. Financially, I mean."

"That's correct."

He continues to stare at me and doesn't say another word, until he mutters, "That bastard."

I frown. "Who?"

Without answering me, he pushes off from the counter.

"I'd like to be the first to know if you ever decide to sell." His phone is already to his ear and his attention has left me even though he's still watching me.

I truly dislike his style of business.

As he walks towards the door to leave, I say, "No."

He comes to a halt and turns back to face me. "Give me a minute," he says into the phone before holding it to the side so he can speak to me. "No?"

I nod. "I told you it's not for sale and never will be."

"Yes, well, we all know how business goes, Lorelei. Times get tough and assets need to be looked at. Call me if that time comes."

I watch him leave, and I feel a sense of accomplishment when my gaze stays firmly on his back rather than sliding down to take in that magnificent ass.

Ashton Scott would have to be the most arrogant man I've ever met.

And I have no intention of ever calling him.

4

ASHTON

"WE MISSED YOU THE OTHER NIGHT," ALESSANDRA says over the phone two days after I missed the dinner she'd asked me to attend.

"I'm surprised I haven't heard from you already." I'd texted her to say I wouldn't be there and hadn't received a message or call in return. Not my sister's usual mode of operation.

"Some of us have better things to do than chase Ashton Scott around." Her tone is cutting—unusually so for her.

"And what the fuck does that mean?" I throw the towel I'm holding over my shoulder and take a long drink from my water bottle. After a demanding day in the office, I've just spent the last hour running on the treadmill in my home gym.

She sighs. "Fuck, just ignore me. I'm in a bitchy mood and wine isn't working as well as it usually does. I ran into Cassia today, or should I say that *she* ran into me, and she's still carrying on about you." She stops talking and I hear her drinking. "You really need to put her out of her misery."

Wiping the sweat from my forehead with the towel, I

groan. "What would you suggest I do, Aly? I was extremely clear with what I wanted a year ago when I broke up with her, and I've been nothing but clear every time she's approached me since. I can't help it if she's choosing not to listen to what I'm saying."

"I can't believe I am going to say this, but you're too nice to her."

"So, what, you think I should be an asshole to her just because I didn't love her the way she loved me?"

"Well, you're an asshole to everyone else. Maybe it will force her to listen." There's no love lost between Alessandra and my ex. From the day I introduced them to the day I left Cassia, they were at odds with each other. Cassia's socialite status and refusal to work rubbed my sister the wrong way. Alessandra doesn't share Cassia's belief that an inheritance is a reason to sleep in most days and spend the rest of your time socialising.

"Aly," I chastise.

She takes another loud sip of her wine. "No, don't give me that. Cassia has you fooled. She's a bitch who plays to your good side and as a result, she gets away with things that others don't where you're concerned. You're blind to it, Ashton."

I leave my gym and take the stairs up to my bedroom, two at a time. "I'm not blind. I just have no interest in confronting it. The thing with Cassia is if you give her an inch, she'll take a mile. If I start a conversation with her, fuck knows what she'll make of it and where it'll all end up."

Alessandra sighs again. "I don't want to talk about her anymore. I want you to tell me why you didn't make it for dinner on Monday night." I hear a loud noise on her end, and then—"Shit, can you give me a minute? Sadie's just bloody smashed a vase and Malcolm is nowhere to be seen."

The sounds of her yelling at her daughter for breaking her

prized possession and then of her yelling through the house for her husband fill my ears. Alessandra has two sides to her personality: the in-control businesswoman I deal with during the day and this frazzled, wine-guzzling wife-slash-mother at night.

While I wait for her to sort out her domestic chaos, I take the opportunity to stretch. My shoulders are tight, even after having a massage a few days ago. I'll need to have Jessica schedule another appointment to get these knots sorted.

"Jesus, don't ever get married or have children," Alessandra mutters into the phone. "Although, you'd have it easy because you're the damn man. Ugh. I should have become a lesbian."

"I'm concerned about you. Your level of domestic disorder seems to have escalated. What's going on?"

"Malcolm is going on, that's what!"

"Aly, you've been married for nine years. Surely you two have your shit together by now."

Another long sip of wine. And then she lets loose on me. "You have no idea about marriage. I'm beginning to think that it wouldn't matter if we'd been married for a hundred fucking years. He'd *still* be clueless about how to make his wife happy. Do you know what he had the hide to say to me today?"

I shudder to think. "What?"

Another long sip of wine. *Surely that glass is nearly empty.* "He suggested I take some defensive driving lessons. Can you fucking believe that?"

I can, but no way in hell am I admitting that to her. Not in the state she's in. Malcolm adores her and he's a good husband. Alessandra just loses sight of that every now and then.

Before I have a chance to form a reply, she continues,

"Don't answer that because I know what you would say. Just take note—never say shit like this to your woman."

"Duly noted." I can't see myself ever settling down with someone for the same length of time Alessandra's been with Malcolm. Not because I don't want to, but rather because I can't seem to find the right woman.

"So where were you on Monday night?" She returns to her earlier question.

"I decided that with the mood I was in Monday, I was no good to anyone, so I just spent the night at home." *Stewing over what I'd learnt that day.*

"You're pursuing that Willow Street building, aren't you?"

I ignore the disapproval in her voice. "It's not for sale, but yes, I'm still pursuing it."

"How strange…. Dad definitely said he was putting an offer in on the Willow Street property."

"I'll get to the bottom of it."

"Oh, I have no doubt," she mutters. "Now, the reason I actually called you…. Please tell me you're still good for tomorrow afternoon. If you say no, I may just kill you. Or send little humans around to hang out with you. Either would be punishment enough."

"You fail to recall my love for your little humans. You've nothing to worry about—I'll be there."

Her relief is clear in her voice. "Thank you, Ashton. And now I will leave you so I can refill my glass before thinking up ways to show my husband just what I think of his idea for me to take those lessons."

She ends the call and I throw my phone down onto my bed. I pull my sweaty T-shirt over my head and dump it in the laundry basket before stripping out of the rest of my clothes. It's just turned nine and I'm going to have a shower before dinner and then work for a few hours. A deal I'm trying to close in Los Angeles has hit a problem so I'll be on the phone with them until the early hours of tomorrow morning.

As I head into the bathroom, my phone rings again.

Fuck.

I just want some peace and quiet.

I snatch it up. "Don't tell me…. You've cut Malcolm's dick off."

A chuckle filters down the line. "No, I can't say I have."

I rake my fingers through my hair. "Thank Christ it's you. I've just had Aly on the phone."

"Ah, say no more, my friend."

Jack Kingsley is my oldest friend. And any day I hear from him is a good day.

Sitting on the end of my bed, I rest my elbows on my knees and drop my head forward. "You're awake early." Jack lives in LA.

"Yeah, I can't sleep. Too much shit taking over my mind. How the hell do you do it?" Exhaustion threads its way through his words, and I wonder what's going on with him. I haven't seen Jack for a good three months, which is unusual for us. Between my trips overseas and his, we normally manage to see each other every month.

"Do what?" I ask.

"Juggle all the balls in your court without going crazy or blocking it all out with an unhealthy addiction."

Fuck.

Jack has a long history with drugs, and I've lost count of the number of times I've worried he might not wake up in the morning.

"You forget, work is my unhealthy addiction." I tread carefully; we've had more than one bad argument over his vice.

"Ah, yes, well, I've tried to take that addiction up and all I feel is ten-fucking-times worse." He blows out a harsh breath. "I'm coming home. I've had enough."

"For how long?"

"I'm done, Ashton. I'm coming home for good."

"Jesus, Jack. What the fuck is going on over there?" As much as I want him back in Australia, I know it's not where he needs to be. Every time he comes back here, he spirals further down the abyss of despair he lives most of his life in. Jack lives and breathes LA; he has no place living in Australia.

"Directors who are trying to kill my soul and actresses who use me on their way up and throw me away the minute I no longer serve a purpose. That's what's going on over here." His words are sour and he spits them out as if they are causing him extreme discomfort.

"But what's different, because you've been doing this for fourteen years now. And fuck knows, you've been dealing with asshole directors and fame-hungry bitches for a long time. What's happened this time to make you want to quit?" He's actually been acting for a lot longer than fourteen years, but that's how long he's been doing it professionally.

"What's the point to it all, Ashton? Why the fuck do I do what I do? *I'm* different this time…. It's me. If I have no point —*no reason*—for putting up with all this shit, then I have no reason to continue."

My head jerks up and I push up off the bed. "Have you booked a flight?" I'm fucking concerned about him now; more concerned than I've ever been and the only thing I want to focus on is getting him home. The rest can be dealt with once I have him here safe.

"Yeah, I leave tonight, just before midnight."

Thank fuck.

"I'll pick you up when you get in. And you'll stay with me."

"Always trying to save me," he murmurs and I feel his attention slipping away. "You're a good friend."

"Are you using at the moment?" I bite out, unable to stop myself anymore.

He sighs. "Nothing more than the occasional joint." A brief pause before he continues, "I'll see you soon, my friend."

And then he's gone.

I don't waste a minute. Dialling a number I know off by heart, I wait impatiently for the call to be answered.

"Fuck, Ashton, do you know what time it is over here?" Bruce Nielson's groggy voice filters through the phone.

"Yes, I know what time it is over there," I snap. "Do *you* know that your client's mental state is fucked up at the moment?" If he doesn't come back with the right answer, I swear to God I'll find ways to hurt him. Jack's manager has never impressed me; tonight my tolerance for him has hit rock bottom.

"What? So he punched his director and then went and got himself into a brawl with his ex's new boyfriend? It isn't like that shit hasn't happened before where Jack's concerned." This must have just happened because it's news to me.

"You're a piece of shit, Bruce, and I'm going to make sure Jack finally sees that. And then I'm going to ensure you don't work another day in Hollywood."

I rip the phone away from my ear and stab at it to end the call before quickly looking up another number. She answers much faster than Bruce and is awake just as I knew she would be.

"Ashton, to what do I owe this pleasure?" she purrs down the line.

My dick stirs at the sound of that voice. Josephine Thorne and I go way back and I briefly imagine the lips that voice escapes from. Those lips have given me many hours of bliss.

At one moment in my life, I thought they'd bring me decades of happiness, but she walked away before we could go down that path. We remained friends, though, and she's never let me down.

"Jack's not doing well. He's on a flight home tonight, your time, but I'm concerned about what could happen in the hours between now and then."

Josephine loves Jack just as much as she loves me. Hell, the three of us have a past that is entwined together in ways three people shouldn't be. She was the reason for one of his famous breakdowns after she walked away from him, too.

She doesn't hesitate. "I can go over to his place now. I'll be there in half an hour."

I exhale the breath I've been holding. "Thank you."

"Ashton, I've got this. You don't need to worry. I'll make sure he makes that flight. You just get our boy better, okay? God knows I've been trying."

I frown. "What do you mean?" It's been a good six months since I've spoken to Josephine.

"He started going downhill about four months ago. It was hardly noticeable at first, but I know his signs as intimately as I know his body. I've spent so much time with him over the past few months trying to help him, but nothing has gotten through. I really think he needs you. You're the only one who he's ever really listened to."

I grit my teeth. I'm an asshole. My best friend has been suffering for months, and I've been too damn busy to notice. "Thanks, Josephine. I'll make sure he gets the help he needs."

I can't get off the phone fast enough. The urge to inflict damage on everything in this room explodes through me, and I punch the wall.

Repeatedly.

I lash out, trying to rid myself of the anger coursing through my veins.

Anger at myself.

Jack needed me and what the fuck was I doing? Screwing my way through Sydney and London, and pushing deals through faster than I could keep up half the time, rather than being there for someone I love more than myself.

Jack's right.

What the fuck was it all for?

The foreign feelings I've been experiencing lately rear their ugly heads and I realise I'm going to need to take this anger and confusion back to the gym. Punching holes in my wall isn't going to cut it.

5

LORELEI

"Have you heard from the dude you tried to have sex with after the wedding?" Sienna asks me late Thursday afternoon.

It's been three days since I scurried from the guy's hotel room, and I am more than thankful that I haven't heard from him. I close my laptop and run my fingers through my hair while stretching my neck. "No, and I don't want to."

"Really?" The look she's giving me tells me that she thinks I'm mad. "Lorelei, that guy was hot. Like, off-the-charts-I'd-do-him-in-a-heartbeat hot. Did you at least get his phone number?"

"No, because I'm not interested. The only reason I went to his room with him was because I was so drunk I wasn't thinking straight. And then to fall asleep while he was... well, while he was doing what he was doing"—my cheeks flame while I recall what happened—"I was so embarrassed when he told me the next morning. I couldn't get out of there fast enough and honestly, if he called me, I would probably die of embarrassment."

Her mouth twitches and a moment later, she bursts out laughing. "You are too much, babe."

I narrow my eyes at her. "Why?"

She attempts to get her laughter under control, failing miserably. But she manages to splutter, "You can't even say the words, 'giving head'. God, you make me laugh."

Pursing my lips, I say, "Clearly." My cheeks still feel hot.

"And, who the hell falls asleep while a guy's eating her out? Unless he was really bad at it?"

"Well, I'm obviously not the right person to ask about that because I can't bloody remember." I glare at her. "Can we please change the subject? I don't want to rehash this disaster anymore."

Her laughter subsides and her features soften. "Oh, babe, it's not that bad. Why are you so embarrassed about it?"

I look down at my laptop for a moment, trying to ignore the feelings of not being worthy that are pushing their way into my head. Looking back up at her, I say, "You know how I don't do one-night stands?" I wait for her nod before I proceed. "It's because I feel dirty about them. Being a product of one, and not ever knowing who my father is turned me off them as soon as I understood what they were. Sex means more to me than a quick lay with someone I don't care about. I'm embarrassed at my behaviour that night—not because I judge one-night stands, but because I did something I don't believe in for myself." God, I hope she understands where I'm coming from because I don't care that other people—including Sienna—have casual sex. It's just not for me.

I shouldn't have worried, though, because she gives me a smile. After eleven years of friendship, she knows me better than anyone. "I get it. And for the record, you are the least judgy person I know."

"Thank you," I murmur.

"Okay, changing the subject, highs and lows. My high is that I've scored six new clients this week, and by the end of the week, I'm hoping to add at least one more. My low is that the guy who lives in the apartment next to mine *still* hasn't noticed me. Not even when I was wearing the tightest dress ever yesterday. Ugh. Do you think he's gay?"

She looks so depressed over the fact the guy hasn't noticed her that I can't help but laugh. Sienna's a gorgeous woman with her always-immaculately-styled, long blonde hair and a body she works hard to keep in shape. She also spends hours on beauty, so she's always dressed well with a full face of make-up. Either the guy is blind or gay. Or just not into hot blondes.

"Probably. I mean, who wouldn't want you?"

Her depressed expression gives way to a huge smile. "This is why we are best friends. Now, hit me—give me your highs and lows."

"Well, besides waking up in that hotel room on Monday, my encounter with Ashton Scott does not rate as a high. You know I hate doing lows, though, so I'm not going to call it as one. My high would have to be the fact I booked my flight to Hawaii." I've wanted to visit Hawaii for as long as I can remember. The trip I have planned will tick a few items off my bucket list.

"You haven't heard from Ashton again, have you?"

"No, I think perhaps he got the message." Just thinking about him stirs feelings I don't want. Damn him. As much as he annoyed me, I've thought about him a few times this week, and some of those thoughts have been about his ass and his eyes and that voice…. Argh!

Enough.

Focus, Lorelei.

Sienna's watching me intently. Pointing at me, she accuses, "You were just thinking about him, weren't you?

And I'm talking about an I-wanna-jump-his-bones-kind-of thought."

I groan. "How do men manage to do this to us? I mean, I know I have no desire to date a man like him, and yet I can't help but think about him."

She mimics my groan. "I feel ya, sister. I think God wanted some fun so he dreamt up ways for men to irritate women and now he just sits back and has a good laugh at our expense."

Her phone rings, interrupting us, and I listen as she has what appears to be a pissed-off conversation. When she ends the call, she looks at me with that look she gives when she wants something. "You love me lots, right?"

"What do you need?"

She grins. "I'm supposed to be taking my nephew to soccer practice this afternoon, but my mum just called and she needs someone to pick her up from the hospital. I'm the only one who can do it. I would love you forever if you took Tony to practice."

"What time?" It's nearly four already.

She pulls a pained face. "You'd have to leave in the next ten minutes. You'd just have to pick him up from my brother, get him there and then stay until I arrive after I get my mum home."

I stand. "It's no worries. I'm finished my work for today."

The relief is clear on her face. "I'll shout you dinner after practice if you're up for it."

"If I'm up for it?"

She laughs and says with a wink, "The kids all go to McDonalds afterwards, so it'd be a burger. Or you could just skip that and go straight for a sundae."

"I haven't had a sundae for years. You can shout me dinner."

We make it to soccer practice five minutes late. I'm stressed because running late for anything always knots my stomach with worry. Tony, on the other hand, just shrugs and thanks me for bringing him. He then runs ahead of me so he can join his team on the field.

I wander to where the parents are standing to watch their kids. It's an under-nines' game and by the looks of it, most of the parents are settled on chairs they've brought with them. Probably old hands at this by now. They're all engrossed either in watching their child or on their phone.

That is, except for one mother.

I eye her and bite back a laugh. I'm guessing from what she's wearing and her perfect blonde hair and face that she just came from the office, but she's projecting frazzled vibes. A young girl, probably about four or five, is doing laps around her refusing to conform to the woman's wishes.

As I move closer, I hear the woman shriek, "Sadie, if you don't sit down now and stop making all that noise, there will be no McDonalds tonight!"

Sadie immediately stops what she's doing. Her bottom lip quivers and her face crumples. "I want McDonalds, Mummy. I want to go there with Uncle A—"

Her mother appears to be all out of patience and cuts the child off. "Well sit down and be quiet."

Sadie finally does as she's told and as the woman lets out a long breath of relief, she sees me watching. Grimacing, she says, "Unfortunately bribery is my chosen method of parenting. Please don't judge me."

Something that doesn't happen often occurs—a memory of my mother flashes through my mind. I picture the two of us laughing at McDonalds after she took me to netball practice. I suck in a breath. This was right before she died.

I let the memory consume me, the world becoming non-existent in that moment. It's not until the woman touches me on the arm that I realise I got lost in my thoughts.

"Are you okay?" she asks, her voice full of warmth.

Smiling, I nod. "Yeah… I just got lost there for a second. And I try never to judge anyone, especially parents."

"Happens to the best of us. Some of us get lost for full nights at a time."

I frown, not quite sure where she's coming from with the last part of that.

She waves in the air and says, "Kids. Husbands. You'll understand one day."

I hope so.

I nod towards the field. "Your son's playing?"

"Yes. Bradley loves his soccer. I love the peace and quiet I get when my two children are separated." *I love her honesty.*

"This is my first time here. I'm with my friend's nephew, Tony."

She chuckles. "Oh, I could tell it was your first time, honey. And that you weren't here with your own child."

"How?"

She sighs. "You still have that youthful glow that announces to the world that you haven't been sucked into the parenting vortex yet. And you're hardly dressed for mummy duty." Her gaze travels to my heels that are sinking into the grass as we speak.

"You're not dressed for it either. And you don't look much older than me." She doesn't. Even up close, there's hardly a wrinkle on her face. And her slim body could easily pass as someone way younger than me. This woman is your classic blonde bombshell with her tousled bob, heavily made-up eyes and lips, and a sexy aura that clings to her even in the frazzled state I found her in.

Her brows rise. Looking down, she puts a foot forward to

show me the flats she is wearing. I hadn't noticed them before. I'd been so transfixed by her beauty and personality that I hadn't taken in the rest of her.

I bet this woman has men falling all over her.

She holds her hand out to me. "Alessandra Spencer. We can be friends because you say all the right things. For the record, I'm thirty-five, and I only tell people I like that."

I shake her hand, but before I can introduce myself, a whistle sounds loudly from the field and the commotion happening there attracts our attention.

The coach has obviously made a call that upset one of the parents because he's involved in a heated discussion with a father. Both men appear enraged.

As their voices filter my way, my senses go into overdrive.

I know that voice.

"Oh, God...."

"What?" Alessandra asks.

"*He's* the coach?" To say I'm stunned that I'm standing here staring at Ashton Scott is an understatement. I would never have picked him for a soccer coach.

"Yes. He's not a crowd favourite, though," she replies as she watches another couple of parents circle Ashton, all giving him their opinion on whatever he did.

"It's no wonder—he's an arrogant ass."

She turns to face me. "You know him?"

I meet her gaze. "Well, I wouldn't say I know him, but I've had the pleasure of meeting him, if you could call it that, and let's just say I was less than impressed."

Alessandra stares at me for a couple of moments and then her face breaks out into a huge grin. "I can just tell that you and I are going to be great friends. Anyone who is that honest about my brother is someone I need in my life."

Her brother?

Well, shit.

I swallow down the small amount of remorse I feel for insulting her brother. Holding out my hand, I say, "It's great to meet you, Alessandra, sister to the most arrogant man I've met. My name is—"

A deep voice cuts into our conversation. "Lorelei Winters."

I spin around to find Ashton Scott standing less than three feet away, his eyes boring into mine.

Oh, God.

Those eyes.

I straighten. "Ashton."

"Lorelei."

Oh, God.

That voice.

Tension swirls around us.

A delicious tension that I hadn't noticed the last time we met.

As we stand in silence watching each other, Alessandra says, "Oh, my, this is going to be fun."

Neither of us move.

Neither of us shift our attention from the other.

And when his smouldering gaze travels the length of me before finding my eyes again, my legs feel weak, and I know this could get messy.

6

ASHTON

"You're at McDonalds?" Jessica's disbelief blares loudly. I might not be standing in front of her, but even over the phone, I can picture the look of shock I know is on her face.

I continue watching Lorelei as she stands in line to order food with Tony and her friend. "Yes."

"Well, I'm going to call it because I've heard it all now."

"Call what?"

"You've finally lost the plot. What the hell has possessed you? I mean, can you even remember the last time you were in a McDonalds?"

My gut tightens as I consider what has possessed me. "I'm pursuing a deal."

"Bullshit, Ashton. You don't close deals in fucking fast-food joints." She pauses for a second. "Fuck me, are you chasing a woman? Because there're only two reasons a man like you does shit—for work or for his dick."

Lorelei's laughter floats through the air.

Jesus Christ.

I've never been entranced by a woman's laughter before, but Lorelei's laugh causes me some pain as my cock hardens.

"You should go home," I direct Jessica.

"And you should stop bossing me around."

"I'm your boss, Jessica. That's my job." I crane my neck to watch Lorelei bend to retrieve something off the floor. A child has partially blocked my view, but I manage to catch a glimpse. Her fitted black dress barely covers half her thighs, and I watch as more of those toned legs are revealed to me.

"And you do it so well," she says. "I just called to make sure you're all set for your meeting tomorrow morning with the Brentley Group."

"Fuck, I meant to get you to reschedule that meeting. I'm picking Jack up from the airport in the morning, and I'll need to keep my day free to spend with him. Do I have anything else on tomorrow?"

She takes a minute before coming back to me. "Nothing I can't postpone. You want me to do anything for Jack?"

I push my fingers through my hair as knots form in my shoulders. "Yes, can you phone Dr Winthrop and have him on standby. I'm going to convince Jack to see him in the next couple of days."

"Shit, is he bad again?" Jessica knows all too well the history here.

"Yeah, I'm worried this time."

"I'm on it. And, Ashton?"

"What?"

Her voice softens. "You can only do so much for him. You can't force someone to change and get better. That's on Jack."

"Jessica, there aren't many people in this world that I'd give everything up for. Jack's one of those people and I'll move heaven and fucking hell to get him better." My tone is a little harsher than I'd meant, but fuck, every word I said is true.

"I know," she says. And then—"I'll leave you to your vagina hunting now."

I shake my head as we end the call. Jessica has a way with words. She would have to be the crassest woman I know, but then again, she does think of women in the same way as most men do.

"Are you going to order something to eat?" Alessandra asks as she and the kids come back to the table.

"You should get nuggets," Sadie says as she sits next to me. She immediately begins unpacking the meal Alessandra has bought her.

"Why nuggets?" I'm always interested in Sadie's reasons for things. She has a mind that works in such an abstract way.

"So I can share them." She shoves a fry in her mouth and grins at me.

I return her smile and ruffle her hair. "Of course, makes perfect sense to me, pumpkin."

"So much like her uncle," Alessandra says with mock exasperation.

Directing a grin at her, I stand and say, "And her father."

Alessandra rolls her eyes. "Go, before that line gets too long."

She's right—the line is almost out the door. On my way to the end, I catch Lorelei's eye. Actually, I catch her watching me and take in the blush that spreads across her cheeks and down her neck when she realises I caught her.

Fuck me.

I can't recall the last time I made a woman blush.

It's fucking hot.

She quickly turns away and engrosses herself in conversation with her friend again. I take my place in the back of the line and continue watching her.

I've dated my fair share of women but not once have I

dated a redhead. Lorelei's long red hair was the first thing I noticed about her on Monday. Right before I got a glimpse of her eyes—beautiful green eyes that I'm sure see everything. I may have met her on a day she'd clearly come straight to work from the night before, when she wasn't at her best, but I could see the sharp workings of her brain.

My mind wanders, not for the first time this week, to thoughts of where she'd come from that morning. It's almost killed me not looking into whether she's involved with anyone, but I've spent the better part of my time talking myself out of pursuing her. She infuriated me enough on Monday morning to never want anything to do with her, but by the time I left her office the second time that day, intrigue had settled in. My feelings on the matter have alternated all week. And now I find myself back on the side of wanting her.

She places her order and makes her way to where the team is sitting once she has her food. I wait with only shards of patience for my turn to order. When I finally have nuggets, fries, and two milkshakes, I head back to Alessandra's table.

Sadie eyes me expectantly and I grin as I hand over the nuggets. When I place the milkshakes in front of her and her brother, Bradley, Alessandra glares at me. I simply shrug.

"I can't wait for the day you have children," she mutters. "I'm going to be the most favourite auntie in the whole damn world."

I chuckle as I reach for a nugget. "I would expect nothing less, Aly. Until then, I'm going to continue being the most favourite uncle in the world."

We finish eating and I forget my infatuation with watching Lorelei while I dedicate my complete attention to Sadie and Bradley. The time I have with these two is sacred time. No deal or meeting comes before them. Hell, they're the only people in the world I'd eat McDonalds for.

"So," Alessandra says after we've all finished eating, "are you able to fill in for coach again next week?"

I eye her. The way she's asked is as if she expects this to be a hard sell. I jumped at the opportunity when she asked me last week to fill in; I'm hardly going to say no this time. "I'll clear my diary. Any Thursday afternoon is yours."

Her eyes widen before narrowing at me. "What's the catch?"

"For God's sake, Aly, I'm not a fu—" I catch myself before swearing in front of the kids. "I'm not a monster. There's no catch."

"You *have* been pretty assholey for the last few months, Ashton. I hope you know that."

"What does assholey mean?" Sadie asks.

Alessandra turns her attention to her daughter. "It means he's been really cranky and treating people badly. But you can't use that word. It's an adult only word."

Sadie takes that in and nods. "So it's a daddy word?"

I smirk. Malcolm has a tendency to use many words that Alessandra would prefer he avoid. It's a constant source of irritation for them.

Alessandra glares at me again for a moment. "I shouldn't have said it, darling. Your uncle inspires me sometimes."

I wink at Sadie as she smiles up at me. Wanting to change the subject, I say, "Who wants to come over and hang out with Jack this weekend?"

Both Sadie and Bradley's eyes light up. They adore Jack. "Me, me!" they both exclaim with delight.

Looking at Alessandra, I ask, "Can I have them for a few hours one day?"

A smile twitches on her face. "You seriously think I'd say no to that?"

"Well, assholey runs in the family, so you do have your moments," I deadpan and fight the urge to give her more hell when she rolls her eyes again. But Alessandra has her limits and I try never to reach them.

"Okay, it's a date. I'll let you know which day once Jack gets settled," I say as I stand.

"Thanks for today," Alessandra says, her voice softer. Her gratitude is clear. My sister doesn't ask me for much, so when she does, I know she really needs me.

I bend and place a kiss on each of the kids' heads. Nodding at Alessandra, I say, "I'll talk to you tomorrow. Try not to commit bodily harm on your husband tonight." Then, I turn to Bradley. "Great game today, mate. We can kick a ball around on the weekend. Jack will be up for that, too." The huge smile he gives me is all I need to know I'd clear every Thursday for the rest of my life for him if need be.

I head out to my car and am welcomed by the sight of those toned legs that I'm beginning to think would look spectacular under me.

Lorelei's reaching into her car for something, and when she leans back out and straightens, I'm standing next to her. "Shit, Ashton, way to shave a few years off a woman's life," she says.

"I won't tell you what you do to a man's life expectancy," I murmur. I can imagine she's inflicted hurt to many men's hearts in her lifetime.

My words seem to confuse her and lines wrinkle her forehead as she frowns. "I don't know what you mean by that."

I lean in so our faces are close. "It means that you'd only have to give a man a skerrick of attention, let alone treat him to that sharp tongue of yours, and he'd be in danger of deadly damage."

Her sudden intake of breath is the only sound I hear. The effect I have on her is intoxicating.

"I have to go, but it was good seeing you again," she mumbles.

"Really? I wouldn't have thought you'd want to see me again after Monday."

"Well, I was using my manners." Her no-bullshit approach impresses the hell out of me.

"Manners are always a good way to go."

Her lips quirk. "It would seem you don't always practice what you preach."

"That is true, but I do like to practice things until I get them right."

Her shoulders loosen and she shifts on her feet as if she's settled in her spot. As if she's suddenly invested in this conversation. "I agree—practice makes perfect."

"Maybe you could help me with that?"

"I don't think I'd be much help."

"I beg to differ."

"In my experience, it's kind of hard to teach an asshole how to turn over a new leaf."

Jesus, I'm going to need a long shower after this.

I fight the urge to move closer to her. "I'd imagine it would take a woman with your experience to get the job done."

"What did you have in mind?"

"First round of practice tomorrow night."

She doesn't miss a beat. "I'm busy tomorrow night. But I'd be happy to give you some free advice."

"Free advice is worthless. I'm more than happy to put the hours into a proper education."

"I'm sure you'll be able to snap your fingers and make that happen."

Oh, baby, you have no idea.

"I could. But I only want the best and I have a feeling I'm looking at her right now."

She stumbles with her comeback and I taste victory.

And then she schools me. "For a smart man, you have a

bad memory. I told you the other day that not everything is for sale. There are no lessons to be bought here, Ashton."

Her declaration only inspires me. I take that step closer to her. Bending my mouth to her ear, I make a promise. "Although some things aren't for sale, I'm not a man who gives up. Ever. You seem to have a bad memory too, Lorelei. I told you the other day that I always get what I want, and I wasn't lying." I move my face so I'm looking into those beautiful green eyes. "I'm a patient man, but make no mistake, this *will* happen, and it will happen soon."

7

LORELEI

"So this *was* a good week... until today," Sienna says as she slumps into the chair opposite me in our office late Friday afternoon.

I drag my attention away from my computer and eye her. She looks defeated, and Sienna *never* looks defeated. "What happened?"

"I was so close to gaining a new client—a guy who would have brought me a lot of business—when he decided to go with another company. He would have been the equivalent of about three clients with how busy he would have kept me."

"There's no way you can try and talk him around?"

She shakes her head. "I tried. He's sold on this other company because they seem more solid to him. I guess my being a one-woman show doesn't project the kind of image some people want."

"And yet you are more than capable of looking after your clients just as well as the big boys." I can't hide my annoyance. Sienna and I come up against this time and time again. It's frustrating.

She sighs. "Do you ever feel like it's all too hard?"

"If I'm honest, yes, some days I feel that way. But then I give myself a talking to and figure I'll show the doubters just what I'm capable of by proving them wrong."

"I wish I was more like you."

My eyes bulge. "What do you mean? You're one of the few women I know who are super switched on and always positive."

"Ugh, no. I pretend to be, but on the inside, I'm wailing like a baby. I listened to you all those years ago when you drilled into me that we needed to fake it until we made it. I just can't help wondering how much longer I'll be faking it for."

"I know what you mean. Thirty is just around the corner, and I always thought I'd have my life more together by then."

She's quiet for a moment. "Do you wish things had turned out differently between you and Boston? Have you heard from him recently?"

My heart constricts at the sound of his name. *The guy I thought I'd marry... until the day he asked me to marry him and I said no.* "I want to say no, and that I've made peace with the way things went, but that would be a lie. I don't know why I said no. I think I panicked. And, no I haven't heard from him since he left." Five months of radio silence from the guy I spent over three years of my life with. The guy who waited around for three months hoping to change my mind after I said no to his marriage proposal.

"Do you still love him? Because you know, I have a theory about you and men."

"What's your theory?" Sienna is always coming up with theories for everything in life.

"I think you have this overwhelming fear of loss after losing your mum at such a young age. You're a hopeless romantic, but when men get too close, you push them away before they can leave you."

She's right. I've put hours into analysing myself and yet I can't seem to change. I pushed Boston away by fighting with him for three months. "I ruined what Boston and I had, Sienna. We fought so much those last three months and then we had that huge fight that ended it. There's no coming back from that."

She gives me a wistful smile. "There's always coming back from things, babe. If he's who you want in your life, you just need to tell him. Boston Haynes adores you. He only left town because he was hurting too much."

"Well, he did have a job come up overseas he could hardly turn down. Let's be honest, Boston's career is in America. He doesn't have half the opportunities in Australia that he'll have over there."

She lifts a brow. "And you don't think that man would give all that up in a heartbeat for you?"

"I wouldn't want him to."

"You didn't answer my question. Do you still love him?"

I've thought about this a lot over the last five months. The heartache I felt when he left was extreme enough for me to know I did truly love him, but the thought I've been left with is—if I love him, why don't I still think about him every day? "I will always love Boston. He was my first real experience of love. But I don't know if I am still *in love* with him."

Just as she opens her mouth to speak, we're interrupted by the sound of a deep voice at the door. "Lorelei Winters?"

Turning, I find myself looking at a man who reminds me so much of Ashton Scott that it can't be a coincidence. Even his voice has that same kind of deep, husky sexiness to it that Ashton's has.

I stand. "I'm Lorelei. I presume you're Mr Scott."

His eyes glitter with subtle amusement as if he's humoured by me in a condescending way. That does not start us off on the right foot, because as good-looking as he is with his silver-fox sexiness—that goatee he's sporting is hot—I refuse to be swayed by anything other than his personality. He walks to where I'm standing and extends his hand. "Gregory Scott."

Sienna excuses herself, leaving me alone with Ashton's father. Damn her. I would prefer not to deal with this man alone.

I hold my hand out towards the table. "Please, make yourself comfortable. Can I get you a drink at all?" God, my need to use manners irritates me sometimes. I do not want to give this man any reason to stay longer than necessary.

With a shake of his head, he says, "No. I'll just get straight to the point, Miss Winters. I've come to make you an offer on your property at Willow Street."

What is with these men trying to buy that property?

"I'm afraid you've wasted your time then because that property is not for sale."

"Oh, I think we both know that everything is for sale, Lorelei, if the price is right." So damn arrogant. I see where his son gets it.

"That may be the case in your world, Mr Scott, but it's not in mine."

"You haven't even heard my offer yet."

"I don't need to hear it because I'm not selling. I'm sorry, but no price can convince me."

"Three million," he says, his gaze steady on mine.

I don't blink. I don't show my surprise in any way, shape or form. But holy hell, that figure is about one million more than the property is worth.

He desperately wants this.

But why?

I stand a little straighter. "No."

Gregory Scott maintains his own poker face. We watch each other silently for a while before he eventually says, "I'll leave you to think about it, Miss Winters." He hands me his business card. "Contact me when you change your mind." With that, he turns and exits my office.

Jesus, what's with these Scott men?

Call me when you change your mind. Not if, but when. So bloody presumptuous.

Well, they can think again if they believe I'm an easy sell. I'm not.

8

ASHTON

"I love you, Ashton, but seven on a Saturday morning is taking our relationship to a whole new level," Jessica mumbles into the phone.

"It was urgent."

Silence.

"Oh, you should have said that sooner, boss. I mean, hell, why didn't you call earlier? I could have done urgent at three this morning."

"Smartass," I murmur, but my mouth curls into a smile. Jessica's snarky ways endear her to me. They hands-down beat the way most people pander to me in an effort to get closer and potentially gain something from a relationship.

"Ugh, Ashton, you could have at least sent me over some coffee to wake me up."

"It's on my list. Although, I'll have to get my assistant to organise that," I say with a grin, making a mental note to send coffee over as soon as this call is over.

"My, you're unusually fun this morning, Mr Scott. Did your vagina hunting pay off?"

I lean back in my office chair. I've been working in my home office for two hours this morning and the time has flown by. A strange occurrence around here on weekends lately. I've felt adrift recently and this feeling is only magnified on weekends when I'm alone. The fact I haven't felt the pull to socialise much hasn't helped. "The way you master the English language is astounding, Jessica."

"I'm glad you've recognised that. I look for new words to impress you with daily. Now, what is so urgent you dragged me from the best sleep I've had all week?"

"Have you managed to track down Lorelei's schedule yet?"

She groans. "Honestly," she mutters, her voice drifting off. "Okay, Monday afternoons between one and four she usually visits that nursing home I've already told you about. She goes to spin class at the gym five minutes from her office on Monday, Wednesday, and Friday at five. Sunday mornings are usually spent at the local farmer's market. She also does salsa dancing, but this appears to be an irregular activity. It's at that dance studio around the corner from Willow Street. Oh, and on Saturday mornings she often visits her Willow Street property."

"Impressive. You got all this from Facebook?"

"See, if I told you my sources, you wouldn't need me anymore. Let's just say, my investigative process involves more than Facebook. Now, you owe me. Make it a double shot and make it snappy."

"Mornings aren't your strong suit, are they?"

"Pay attention, Ashton—they *can* be with caffeine."

I chuckle. "Enjoy the rest of your weekend."

"Wait, before you go. How are we looking for Asshole Monday? Do you think it'll be on next week or not?"

"Goodbye, Jessica," I say as I end the call.

After I order coffee to be sent to her home, I make my way into the kitchen. Jack surprises me when I find him in there.

"Morning," I say. "I thought you'd be asleep after last night." After his long flight, he slept for hours yesterday and as a result was wide-awake at midnight.

"I slept for about four hours. Been tossing and turning for two hours, so I figured I may as well get up. I'm going to visit Mum today."

I narrow my eyes to take in his appearance. He still looks as bad as he did when I picked him up from the airport yesterday morning. This is the worst shape I've seen my friend in for years. He's lost weight; his hair needs a good cut and he's wearing don't-give-a-shit clothes.

"You want me to drop you off at her house?"

"That'd be great."

We haven't had a chance to talk yet. I'm hoping his mother might talk some sense into him, but in the meantime, I need to know he's travelling okay. "I'm concerned, Jack. What the hell happened in LA?"

He watches me for a beat. "You want coffee for this?"

I nod and he pulls another mug from the cupboard. "Do you ever wonder how you ended up where you are in your life, Ashton?"

I think about that for a moment. This is important to Jack and I want to give him the most honest answer I can. Finally, I nod. "Yeah, some days. Actually, a lot more lately than ever before. Not to do with my work, though. That has been a carefully planned strategy. But the rest of my life feels a little empty these days."

He passes my coffee, and I slide onto one of the stools at the kitchen counter while he stands on the other side.

"Do you remember back when we finished school? You

and I had so many plans. I don't feel like we achieved any of the important ones."

I frown. "What haven't we achieved, Jack? We're both doing work we set out to do and, hell, we're both successful at it."

He shakes his head. "No, not work. We always said we'd give back once we made our millions. We always said we wouldn't become our fathers, and yet we both have. We're workaholics who are too fucking busy to look beyond ourselves. Well, I'm done, and I'm ready to get back to basics."

"I give time to a business group and donate to charity. What else can I do?"

"I'm not talking about giving cash here. I'm talking about changing the fucking world."

Fuck, he's on about this again.

Jack always did have aspirations to change the world, and he's right—I wanted in on that endeavour when we were younger. These days I live in reality and understand that concept is futile. "You can't change a world that doesn't want to be changed."

"Fuck, Ashton, when did you become so negative?"

"When I realised the truth in life."

"And what's the truth?" His voice is full of scorn and I do my best to ignore it, but I'm feeling agitated with this conversation. I just want him to work on himself first, and then I don't give a flying fuck if he dedicates the rest of his life to being the next Mother Teresa.

"The truth is that the challenges facing humanity are insurmountable unless people open their eyes and take a long, honest look at it all, and sort the bullshit from the facts, all without being led by powerful people with hidden agendas. And then there's social media that drains people's attention and encourages superficial engagement with life. Shit, these days people think that supporting a cause is as easy as giving a fucking like on Facebook or sharing a post. If you want to change the world, you better be ready to yell long and loud just for a few to hear you."

He stares at me as if I've got two heads. "So much cynicism, my friend. I'm not talking about reaching billions all at once. I'm talking about changing one life at a time."

I lean forward. "Well, I know one that you can work on first," I say softly.

He processes that and then nods. Draining his coffee mug, he rinses it and places it in the dish rack before saying, "I'm working on it."

I watch as he leaves the kitchen. "Fuck," I mutter under my breath. Not the way I wanted to start the day.

After I drop Jack off at his mother's house, I steer the car towards Willow Street. It's just after nine and I'm hoping to catch Lorelei there. It takes me nearly half an hour in traffic to reach my destination, and after I cruise the street a few times looking for her, I decide to park my car.

The street is busy today and it takes me a good ten minutes to find a park. By the time I'm standing in front of her building, my patience is fraying. But one glance at the empty retail shop I know so well soothes my irritation as the memories come flooding back. It's been a good fifteen years since I've been here, but it feels just like yesterday.

"That shop isn't for lease anymore," a woman says from behind me. "I'll be opening a florist there in a few weeks."

I turn to see a plump middle-aged woman eyeing the shop with excitement. When her eyes finally meet mine, I say,

"What about the shop next door?" Lorelei's building houses three retail shops, of which two are currently vacant.

She shakes her head. "Nope, it's taken too. A café I think, which is a perfect match for the hairdresser on the other side and me."

I have to agree. Grouping businesses together that women frequent, rather than slotting in a male orientated business, should give them a fighting chance at success.

"Thank you," I say and take a step in the direction of the café I passed earlier. This is an older area of Willow Street, still untouched by corporations who have swooped in and knocked down the buildings to erect shopping centres in their place. The café I saw looked quaint and welcoming, and I have a hunch they'll know how to make good coffee rather than the shit pumped out at the coffee chains.

"Sorry there're no shops left for you," the woman says as I walk away.

"I don't need a shop," I call back over my shoulder. *I just need the woman who owns the shops.* I haven't been able to get Lorelei out of my mind since I made that promise to her two days ago. And I meant every word I said—she *will* be mine. She'll be the best sex I've ever had because sex you have to work for is a sweet victory.

Fifteen minutes later, I'm sitting in the corner of the café, drinking what is perhaps the best coffee in Sydney. *Mental note—tell Jessica about this place.* The owner is a lively Italian woman, probably about forty and possibly the mother to a challenging brood if her frazzled state is anything to go by. She reminds me of Alessandra in this respect. Either her business is giving her hell or her family is. The café is a cluttered mess of knick-knacks and tables pushed too close together, but the customers seem more than happy to be here. With coffee this good, I can see why.

"Lorelei! Bless you for coming," the owner says loudly while I'm getting lost in my thoughts.

My head snaps up at that name, and my gut tightens when I catch sight of the stunning redhead I'm slowly losing my time to.

Fuck, can she get any more beautiful?

She's wearing skin-tight leather pants that show off her long legs with a black biker jacket. Her feet are encased in stiletto boots. While I love the outfit, it's her windswept hair and flushed face that pulses desire through my veins. It's her lack of fake polish that screams at me. I inhabit a world of perfectly put-together women and I'm bored with the superficial perfection.

She swoops in and pulls the woman into a hug before kissing both her cheeks. "You know I'm here for you anytime, Francesca."

Francesca hits her with a smile that communicates her extreme relief and happiness to see Lorelei. I watch as Lorelei moves to join the woman behind the counter. She grabs an apron and secures it around her waist, and then she gets to work helping serve customers.

The two women work hard for the next hour until a man joins them. I assume he's Francesca's husband by the way he kisses her and slips his arm around her waist. Then the three of them spend another half hour serving the remaining customers. This café is one of the busiest I've ever come across.

The couple thank Lorelei profusely before she slings her handbag over her shoulder and exits the café. I leave my table and follow her.

When I catch up, she's waiting at a bus stop. Her gaze falls on me and she blinks her surprise. "Ashton."

"Lorelei."

Her brows furrow. "What are you doing here?"

"Looking for you." Honesty is my preference at all times.

"You don't beat around the bush, do you?"

"No."

"Did you have a plan in place for when you found me?"

"Of course. I'm not the kind of man to act without a plan."

She shifts her weight onto one foot and crosses her arms over her chest. "What does this plan involve?" As much as she's trying to project indifference, I'm hearing enough interest in her voice to know she's into this.

I move a little closer, invading her personal space just enough to fluster her. "It involves me taking you to lunch and getting to know you. It also involves me showing you I'm not the asshole you think I am."

"What about your arrogance? Does your plan have a clause in there for dealing with that?"

"I'm known as a closer, Lorelei. Anything a deal needs to make it go ahead can be arranged."

"Oh, I bet." She uncrosses her arms and points her finger at me before resting her fingertip against my chest. "I have to say, I'm not a fan of the way you do business."

My hand wraps around hers. I love the sudden breath she takes. "That's because you don't fully understand my way of doing business, but I can tell that you are more than intrigued by it. Give me an hour and I'll show you how good business can be."

She takes a moment. "If I give you an hour and decide I'd rather stick to my way of doing business, do you promise to leave me alone after that?"

Lorelei Winters is a tough negotiator, but just as she believes, I'm arrogant as hell. Letting her hand go, I nod. "I do."

"Okay, your hour starts now," she says.

I don't waste any time. I indicate the way to my car and place my hand on the small of her back, guiding her.

I'm cocky enough to believe she'll be giving me more than an hour today, but I'm going to make the most of every minute I have with her.

9

LORELEI

I sit across from Ashton in the expensive restaurant he's brought me to for lunch and stare at him, wondering how the hell he got me to agree to this. I'm fairly sure he brainwashed me. He smooth-talked me for sure. And then this whole other woman inside of me said yes. As for her, she's a traitor and I'm ignoring her right now. Because right now, she's hanging off every word Ashton says.

"So, I know your business imports home décor and you sell online. Do you work in the business or do you have a team who do that?" he asks.

"You've looked into my business?" I'm surprised a man as powerful as Ashton Scott has bothered to spend the time looking my tiny business up.

He raises his Scotch glass to his mouth. "Lorelei, I've looked into *you*."

The traitor inside me does a happy dance and butterflies flutter in my stomach. I ignore it all. "I'm not involved in the day-to-day running of the business. I have a manager for that. He runs the warehouse and the internet site. And honestly, he does a fantastic job, which allows me the time to put into other business ventures."

"What other kinds of ventures are you interested in?"

"At the moment I'm looking over a proposal to invest in a pub. The deal also includes the property."

His lips purse for a moment. "How many investors?"

"Four."

How much each?"

"Half a million."

"Have you had your accountant look it over yet?"

"Yes." Does he think I'm a complete idiot?

"And?"

"He thinks it's a solid investment."

His lips purse again. "I don't."

"Ashton, you know nothing about the property for goodness sake. How can you even make that kind of judgement?"

"Because four partners in not only a property deal but also a business running a pub is a recipe for disaster. There are too many options for disagreements if you all have a say, and if you're silent partners instead, there's too much potential for the business to fail. My advice to you would be to walk away and also to find a new accountant."

It's my turn to purse my lips now. "How dare you say that about my accountant? You don't know him."

He finishes his drink and places the glass on the table. "No, but I do know business, Lorelei. You need to think with your head and not your heart. Tell me something? Is the person who brought you this deal a friend?"

Even as my answer forms, I know he's going to tear it to shreds. And the stupid thing is that I knew this. I freaking knew this but didn't want to face it. "Yes." I refuse to show him the frustration I feel with myself. Instead, I hold my head high and choose to project confidence. When my grandmother left me her money, she believed in me—it's time I do too.

"I thought so. Never go into business with a friend. And never bring emotions into your deals." His tone is matter-of-fact and overly confident. It feels like he's lecturing me and I don't appreciate it. Solicited advice is one thing, but I didn't ask for this.

I want to wipe that look off his face—the one that says he knows everything. Instead, I stand. Looking down at him, I say, "You might know a lot about business, Ashton, but you know nothing about me and my life. In my opinion, your people skills also need some work. You might be able to control people and boss them around in your world, but out here in mine, you have no say. I know I've got a lot to learn about business, but I don't want to learn it from a man like you. And the other thing? We all have different goals in life and business. Before you start lecturing someone, perhaps you should ascertain what their goals are so you can advise them accordingly." I grab my handbag before adding, "I'm going to the bathroom. When I come back, I'd like a Moscato to be waiting for me, please." With that, I move as quickly as I can towards the bathroom. I need a minute to get myself under control because this man is causing all manner of confusion inside me.

It takes a good ten minutes to sort myself out. Ashton brings out all kinds of emotions in me. I want to simultaneously punch and kiss him. By the time I'm calm enough to head back to the table, I wonder if he'll still be waiting for me. I wouldn't be surprised if he's decided I'm more of a handful than he wants, but as the table comes into view, so does Ashton.

I slide into my seat and find a bottle of Moscato chilling next to the table. Ashton reaches for it once I'm seated and pours me a glass. I take the opportunity to appreciate his good looks while he's busy with the wine. He's sporting a fairly casual look today with dark blue jeans and an untucked dark grey button-down shirt. The five o'clock shadow I loved on Monday is still in place and his blue eyes are still sexy as hell. I actually think it might be his eyes that trip me up. The way he watches me so intently makes me feel like I'm the only person in the world to him. So while the words coming out of his mouth annoy the hell out of me, his eyes completely captivate me.

"I think we should start over, from the very beginning," he says once he's finished pouring the wine.

Reaching for my glass, I say, "And how do you propose we do that?"

He smiles. Holy shit. *Holy freaking shit.* When Ashton Scott smiles the world lights up. And my butterflies go into overdrive. Extending his hand, he says, "Hi, I'm Ashton Scott. I'm thirty-two, a property developer, and I travel a lot with work. In my spare time I play golf, sail, watch motor racing and visit art galleries."

My heart beats a little faster. For the first time since I met him five days ago, Ashton looks a little unsure of himself. He's maintaining a confident expression on his face, and his body language is strong, but there's a new tone in his voice —vulnerability.

I shake his hand and return his smile. "Hi, I'm Lorelei Winters. I'm twenty-eight and began my own business two years ago when I inherited my grandmother's money. Before that, I was studying business part-time while selling travel with Flight Centre. I love anything outdoors—skiing and surfing are my favourites. Making art is my therapy. When the world gets all too much, I lock myself away and paint. And travel is my ultimate goal. I've spent a lot of time in the States and have seen a little of Europe. One day I want to be able to work from anywhere so I can travel anywhere, anytime."

He listens with complete focus and his eyes sparkle with obvious interest. "Did you finish your degree?"

"No, I wasn't loving it. I always would have preferred to be doing rather than learning theory. My guess at the time was that I could learn on the job just as well as I could learn on paper."

"And now? Do you still believe that?"

I take a sip of wine. "To a certain point, yes. But I'm now figuring out that while I'll learn on the job, it can be a painful lesson. I wonder if learning some more theory first might shorten the learning curve I'm facing now."

"I never studied business. I was like you and impatient to get out there and *do*. So straight out of school I went to work for a property developer, and I spent five years learning everything I could from him. Those years were invaluable, because not only did I learn from a highly successful developer, I networked and made contacts that still benefit me to this day. My parents were angry with me for not going to uni, but as far as I'm concerned, I could have spent years studying and not walked away with half the knowledge and contacts I did from five years of on-the-job experience."

"See that's exactly what I think. I probably should have found someone to work for and learn from before I threw money and time into my own business, though."

He shakes his head. "Not necessarily. I would have done the exact same thing as you if I'd had the money behind me. I spent five years saving, and the only reason I was able to eventually get a foot in the industry was thanks to my friend, Jack, who backed me with cash."

I frown. "Your family didn't help you get started?" Ashton's family is one of the wealthiest in Australia.

He scowls. "My father is a cold man and refused to help

me because I didn't go to university. And then when I chose a developer to work with, who he didn't approve of, it just cemented his refusal to have anything to do with my work. We'd always had a hard relationship while I was growing up, but this was a slap in the face."

I'm surprised he's so open with me, but I like his honesty. My heart hurts at the thought of his father treating him that way. "He must be so proud of you now, though."

"I wouldn't know what he thinks. We hardly talk these days. In fact, the last time I saw him was a good six months ago, and that was only because we ran into each other at a charity gala. A year ago, I decided I'd had enough of him and the way he treats his children, so I stopped intentionally seeing him."

"What does that actually mean?" I can't imagine choosing not to see a parent. When you grow up not knowing who one of them is and losing the other at a young age, you spend a lot of time envying those who have both in their life.

"It means no family dinners, no Christmas together, no holidays together. I refuse to put myself in any situation where he can try and destroy my belief in myself." His voice wavers and I can feel his pain. I can also see it in his eyes. They've lost their sparkle while he's been talking about his father.

I'm not sure what makes me do it, because it's not something I blurt out to people I've just met, but I share a piece of my soul with him. "I don't know who my father is, and my mother died when I was eight. I grew up with my grandmother. I can't imagine what it's like having a parent who doesn't build you up because my grandmother dedicated her life to helping me become an independent woman with a good dose of self-belief."

The sparkle returns to his eyes and he smiles again.

"From the little I've seen this week, it appears she succeeded."

When Ashton Scott switches off his inner asshole, he's the kind of man who could charm every woman in sight without breaking a sweat. I've heard mixed things about him. Some say he's a player. Others mention the long-term relationship he ended last year, noting that his ex still pines for him. They believe this shows he's a good guy. I always prefer to form my own opinion of people, so I'm withholding judgement. It would seem, though, that my earlier assessment of him might have been a little hasty if this new side he's showing me is anything to go by.

I drink the rest of my wine and decide to see how far I can push him to open up. "Tell me one of your favourite childhood memories."

He refills my glass as he speaks. I'm impressed that he doesn't hesitate to share the memory with me. "I was fourteen and on holiday with my mother and sister in France. Family holidays usually consisted of the three of us visiting some exotic beach destination. My mother would spend most of it by the pool with a cocktail while Alessandra took me exploring. This particular holiday, though, we went to France for three weeks and did a lot of sightseeing. Mum didn't spend it drinking—she spent it with us. But on one of the days we were in Paris, she was ill, so Alessandra and I spent the day on the Metro and saw many parts of the city we probably wouldn't have if Mum had been with us. To this day, Paris is one of my favourite cities in the world. Every time I visit, I'm reminded of that day." He leans forward and says, "Tell me one of your favourite memories. I want to know what a beautiful woman like you remembers from her childhood."

I take a longer sip of wine. He's making me nervous.

Because as much as he thinks he's looking at a self-confident woman, I feel out of my depth with a man like him. *A man who is so at ease in his own skin and who knows exactly what he wants and believes he will always get it.* "I was nine and with my grandmother while she was visiting the Willow Street property. She liked to check in weekly with the business owners and make sure they were doing okay. If they were struggling for money or anything, she'd do her best to help them out. Anyway, it was a year after my mother had died and I was still feeling lost. I mean, my grandmother did everything she could for me, but sometimes you need someone outside your family to get you through. I don't know if that makes sense to you, but it seems to be how some of the pivotal moments in my life transpire. So, while she was with one of the shop owners, I wandered into the newest shop there. It was a furniture store and the man who owned it, Victor, spent hours restoring the furniture before selling it. I didn't spend that much time with him over the years, but the time we did have was some of the most important in my life. That particular day, he invited me in and showed me how to sand a wooden table. We sat there for an hour sanding and talking. It was the first time since my mother's death I remember not feeling so lost. He didn't know my history, so he didn't look at me with sad eyes like everyone else in my life did. We talked about the world. He'd done a lot of travelling, and he told me stories that made me want to see the world. Victor's the person who gave me the travel bug."

Ashton has been listening intently to everything I've said, but now he's staring at me like he's seen a ghost. The waitress interrupts us before I can ask him why. By the time we've given her our orders, he's recovered and watches me with warm eyes rather than that haunted expression.

"What's the next trip you have planned?" he asks, and we

lose ourselves in a long conversation about travel destinations.

I manage to consume three-quarters of the bottle of Moscato during lunch. For a woman who doesn't really drink, this is not good, and I can't believe I've done this again in the space of a week. I'm more than tipsy—I'm on my way to being plastered. Wine goes straight to my head. When I asked Ashton to get me a Moscato, I didn't mean a whole bottle. But my nerves got the better of me and I just kept sipping.

The bathroom is calling and as I excuse myself and stand, Ashton eyes my wobbly state and looks at me with concern. He also stands and says, "Are you okay to get there by yourself?"

"Absolutely," I say as I wave him away, full of fake alcohol-induced confidence.

The concern in his eyes doesn't ease. "I'll get the bill while you're gone and then I'll take you home."

"No!"

He quirks a brow. "You don't want to go home?"

"I meant don't pay the bill. I'll pay for my share."

Amusement flickers across his face and he jerks his chin in the direction of the bathroom. "Go. I'll get this one."

I place a hand on my hip and attempt a stern glare. "No, you won't. I'm a woman who can pay my way."

The amusement on his face gives way to a full grin and oh, how I love that grin. I want to kiss that grin right off his face. Oh, shit... no, I don't. Oh, but I do.... Damn you alcohol for making me want things I don't want. He moves his face closer and murmurs low, "I know you're a woman who can pay her way, but you're also the sexiest damn woman I've ever had the pleasure of eating with and this is going to be the first of many meals I pay for."

When he moves his face away from mine and gives me a

look that says 'Don't argue with me', I do what I've been told. Even my addled brain can figure out it's not worth arguing with him over this. I'm beginning to grasp that Ashton is a man who gets his way often and if we're going to keep doing this dance together, I'll need to choose my battles wisely.

10

ASHTON

I settle into the driver seat of my Aston Martin and glance at Lorelei sitting next to me. She consumed a lot of wine at lunch and is pretty messy now. Unfortunately, it means we're going to have to cut this date short so I can take her home. A shame because we were finally getting somewhere. I'm hoping it wasn't just the alcohol that loosened her up.

She meets my gaze and smiles. "Thank you for driving me home." Her words are a little slurred.

"I would hardly leave you to catch public transport alone." She informed me that while she can drive, she prefers public transport or cabs. I wouldn't have left her here sober, let alone drunk.

Her head lolls back against the headrest and she continues to smile. I'm fairly sure I could say anything at the moment and she'd give me that drunken smile. Lorelei is a happy drunk.

I turn the key, but before we exit the carpark, my phone rings.

Jack.

"What's up?" I ask as I answer it.

"Assshhhton." He's drunk, too. I hear the sounds of a noisy pub in the background. "I need a lift. You far?"

I lean my head back. "That depends on which pub you're at, Jack."

"Oh, is it that one… No, it *is* that one near your office," he says, laughing at his own mix up with his words.

I check my watch. "I'll be there in about fifteen minutes, depending on traffic. Try to stay away from the alcohol."

"Yes, boss." He's still laughing, clearly amused at himself.

"We have to make a slight detour," I say to Lorelei after I end the call.

She shrugs. "I don't have anywhere to be."

We drive in silence for most of the way to the pub. Lorelei seems content to stare out the window, taking in the busy Sydney streets. My mind has wandered to Jack, concerned at his mental state.

"Who are you picking up?" Lorelei asks.

I glance at her. She's still watching me with that beautiful smile. "My best friend, Jack. He's in town for a visit and by the sound of it, he's spent a fair bit of time today at the pub."

Her eyes narrow at me. "You sound disappointed by that."

I grip the steering wheel tighter. "I am."

"Because?"

I come to a stop at a red light. Turning to give her my full attention while I have the chance, I say, "Because the last thing Jack needs right now is alcohol."

She's quiet, thinking. "I like that," she murmurs.

I frown. "What?"

"I like what I can hear when you talk about your friend. You obviously care deeply for him because it's right there in your voice."

A horn blares, diverting my attention from the conversation momentarily. When I turn back to Lorelei, she's smiling at me. Jesus, this woman could get herself into trouble while out drinking. Her beauty is intoxicating, and the way she loosens right up with some alcohol in her could lead men to try and take advantage of her. I make a mental note to keep track of her at all times going forward.

We sit in silence, each simply watching the other. When the light turns green, I miss it, but she doesn't. "Light's green," she murmurs. My gaze lingers on her lips for a second too long. The car behind honks to express their frustration.

I finally drag my gaze away and concentrate on the traffic, which isn't as bad today as I thought it might be. We arrive at the pub where Jack is within ten minutes. He's waiting outside for us, leaning against the brick wall of the building. He eyes us instantly and stumbles across.

"Ashton never told me he had a hot date today," he says to Lorelei as he spreads out across the back seat.

Facing him, she says. "And he never told me he had a hot-as-hell best friend either."

I glance in the rear-view mirror. He's watching her like he wants to fuck her, but I know he never will. Jack and I share the same taste in women, and we've shared one before, but it's not something we'll ever do again. Lessons from the past guarantee that.

"Do tell… how long have you two been seeing each other?" Jack asks.

"We're not seeing each other. It's more of a situation where Ashton thinks he's going to get some, but he's living in fantasyland."

I raise a brow at Lorelei. "Me and fantasyland have never been friends."

"Well, I think you've recently taken a detour."

"It's a dead-end there and I'm not looking at a dead-end right now."

Her hand absently moves to her collarbone and she fiddles with the necklace she's wearing.

Jack chuckles. "Hate to break it to you, sweetheart, but from where I'm sitting you two are one step away from fucking." He leans forward and shoves his hand at her. "I'm Jack."

She shakes his hand. "Lorelei. And I hate to break it to you, Jack, but I don't enjoy casual sex, so it's not going to happen."

"Ah, you're more the commitment type?"

"I'm more the find-a-man-who-is-satisfied-with-one-woman kind of woman."

"And you don't think my friend here could be satisfied with one woman?"

"I've only just met your friend. I don't know him well enough to make that call, but he's smooth as hell and that makes me think he's a pro at wining and dining women."

"You might be pleasantly surprised, Lorelei," Jack says. His eyes meet mine in the mirror. He always has my back.

"So I can hear a slight accent there, Jack. Where are you from?"

"I'm Aussie but I live in LA at the moment."

She's silent for a moment and I glance at her to find her squinting at Jack. "Are you that actor?"

I can hear the grin in his voice when he answers her. Jack's ego loves recognition. "That would depend on which one you're thinking of."

She clicks her fingers as if the name is on the tip of her tongue. "Shit, I have it… help me out, Ashton." Before I can reply, she exclaims, "No, wait! I have it. Jack Kingsley." She swivels her body to look at him. "Am I right?"

"I think I should perhaps be a little offended that you're still not absolutely sure."

"Oh, God I'm sorry. It's the damn alcohol. I never drink…. Well, clearly that's not entirely true because this is the second time in a week I've been drunk. And let's just say the last time ended up far messier than today." It seems alcohol really loosens Lorelei. I have a feeling we're about to learn more about her than she'd perhaps prefer if Jack has anything to do with it. He has a way of getting women to reveal their innermost thoughts.

"What does messy look like on you, sweetheart?" he asks, proving me correct.

"You do not want to know."

"Try me."

I glance at her again. Her hand covers her face as she remembers. Jesus, I need to know what it was if it's causing this reaction in her.

"Let's just say I embarrassed myself by agreeing to something that, in the end, I didn't go through with. The next morning was one of the most mortifying mornings of my life."

"And here I thought you don't do casual sex," Jack says, echoing my thoughts.

"I didn't end up sleeping with him."

"Ah, but you had the intent if you woke up with him the next morning."

"I was so damn drunk I didn't know what I was doing." And that right there proves my earlier thoughts correct— Lorelei drunk is a recipe for disaster.

I've reached her apartment and pull the car into a space that is conveniently empty right outside the complex.

As I switch off the car, she says, "How did you know where I live? I didn't tell you."

Jack chuckles. "Lorelei, sweetheart, you and I need to sit down and swap notes on Ashton. If you don't think he knows everything there is to know about you, *you're* the one living in fantasyland."

I exit the car and walk around to her side. She opens the

door before I reach it, and I place my hand on her back to steady her after she stands.

Her eyes find mine. "I can manage on my own."

"I'd rather make sure you don't fall."

"I might be drunk, Ashton, but I'm still capable of looking out for myself."

"I have no doubt," I murmur. My hand stays where it is as I walk her in.

Jack comes with us, clearly attached to Lorelei already. When we reach her front door, she fumbles in her bag for her keys. I take the bag out of her hands and locate the key for her, ignoring the irritation she levels on me.

She puts her hand out and says, "Can I at least open my own door?"

My lips twitch. Her fight turns me on more than I've been turned on in a long fucking time. I hold up the key and she swipes it from my hand. A moment later, she opens the door, and I step into an apartment that is as different to mine as you could get.

Lorelei's home is colourful and cluttered. But not cluttered in a messy way; rather it's immaculately tidy, just packed full with books, art, photos, plants, pillows on couches, candles, and more colour. So much colour.

She leads us into her kitchen where I discover more plants, along with recipe books. Large windows line one wall in here and a window seat scattered with cushions sits under the windows. Lights hang low over a long wooden island bench, and I can picture her cooking here. I imagine Lorelei to be an amazing cook from what I see.

Jack whistles as he takes it in. "When are you having us over for dinner?" At her frown, he adds, "Tell me this isn't all for show. You do cook, right?"

"Oh, that…. Yes, I love to cook. Nothing for show here." She looks genuinely confused as to why anyone would bother to put on a show in their home. She hasn't met the people Jack and I usually associate with.

I track Lorelei's movements while Jack wanders off and leaves us alone. She fusses for a few minutes, tidying the books and papers on the island bench.

When she looks up at me, I'm surprised to see uncertainty in her eyes. I've not seen this emotion in her—Lorelei always appears confident and sure of herself. "Thank you for lunch," she says softly.

I close the distance between us. "It won't be our last."

She stills and her breathing slows. "I'm beginning to think you aren't the man I assumed you were."

"What did you assume?"

The uncertainty disappears from her gaze. "I thought you were an asshole. An arrogant asshole who pushed people around until you got what you wanted."

My lips quirk. Her honesty is refreshing. Most women just talk dirty to me. I'm all for dirty but this is far more interesting. "And now?"

She cocks her head as she considers that. "Now I think you're just a man who knows what he wants, and your laser focus on it means you don't always realise the things you say or do brand you as an asshole." She steps closer, which means our bodies are almost touching because we were already damn close. Her hand lands on my chest a second later, and I take a deep breath to steady myself. "*I* think that although the world thinks you're this put-together man with more money than he'll ever need, you're actually a man with issues just like the rest of us who can't actually use that money to buy the things he needs in his life."

Our eyes lock. Those beautiful green eyes of hers see so much. I feel more exposed than I usually allow myself to be. "Do you want to know what I thought of you the first time I met you?"

That damn uncertainty flares in her eyes again. "Sure, knock yourself out."

I shake my head. "Don't do that, Lorelei."

She frowns. "Do what?"

"Don't doubt yourself."

Her chest rises as she takes a breath. "I don't doubt myself."

"Yes, you do. But you have no reason to."

"Ashton, the day we met was not a good morning for me, so I can only imagine what you first thought."

"I'd love to see what you consider a good morning because what I saw that day was a sexy woman who stands up for what she believes in and who doesn't waver from her convictions."

She grips my shirt. I doubt she realises she's doing it. "And now? What do you think now?"

I lean my face a little closer. "Now I want to get to know you a hell of a lot better."

I dip my face so I can experience those lips of hers that have been driving me crazy in one way or another since I first saw them. I expect her to resist, but she doesn't. Instead, she opens herself up to me.

I sweep my tongue across hers and she moans as her body angles towards mine. I slide my hand around her waist and pull her hard against me while deepening the kiss. When her hands move to my neck and then up into my hair, I groan into her mouth.

Lorelei's lips are demanding. She can protest as much as she wants, but she's in this as much as I am. She ends the kiss, breathless, and I know she's full of shit when she says, "I don't think we should get to know each other better."

I hold her close when she attempts to step out of my embrace. "Bullshit. You want this just as much as I do."

Her hands push against my chest. "I won't deny I'm

attracted to you, Ashton, and that kiss was something else, but I told you where I stand on casual sex."

"You think that's all I want from you?"

She pauses, confused. "Isn't it?"

I tighten my grip on her waist and slide a hand down over her ass. "Lorelei, the last thing I want from you is casual sex. I can get that anywhere. I can't get *you* anywhere. I want you in my bed just as much as I want you in my life." I claim her lips again before adding, "I'm not taking no for an answer. You will learn that while I'll allow you to fight me, I'll never allow you to deny me when I truly want something."

11
———

LORELEI

I AM NEVER DRINKING AGAIN.

Sliding my sunglasses on, I enter the markets and scan the crowd for Sienna. The sun is shining too brightly for me. I don't have a hangover, but I don't feel my best, and the sun is not helping.

"Lorelei!"

I turn at the sound of my name and find Sienna walking my way. "Morning," I greet her. "Don't even go there," I mutter when she scrunches her face at my appearance.

Frowning, she says, "What happened to your face?"

"A face mask."

"You had a reaction to it?"

"Yeah. I was drunk, though, when I put it on. It tingled, but in hindsight that was probably a burn I was feeling without realising."

She stares at me in shock. "You were drunk?"

"I know, I know. So unlike me."

She grins and grabs my arm. "Girl, we need to talk. Something has clearly happened here that I am unaware of and I wanna know what it is."

A couple of minutes later, after pushing her way through the busy market, she finds us a table to sit and chat at. I dump my bag on the table. "I had lunch with Ashton yesterday and drank almost a full bottle of wine. After lunch, he took me home and kissed me. It was hot and that's a whole other story, which I'll get into in a moment. In my drunken state, I decided a facial would be a good idea after he left." I point to the rash on my face. "And now I have this."

"Putting Ashton aside for a moment, is your face sore? It looks it."

"Yes, it's really tender. I wasn't game to even attempt foundation to try and cover some of the nastiness."

She leans forward, resting her elbows on the table. "What the hell possessed you to do a mask while you were drunk? Most people would just pass out or some shit."

"I couldn't pass out because my mind wouldn't stop thinking about Ashton. The man kissed me!"

Sienna laughs. "You make it sound like he fucked you."

"He practically did! You have no idea."

Her eyes widen and she turns to look behind her for a moment. "We need coffee for this! I'll be back."

She's out of her seat before I can blink. When she returns, her eyes hold excitement as she exclaims, "Now, tell me everything."

"He's different to what I thought. I mean, he's not a complete asshole from what I can work out. And he has this awesome best friend. You can't have a great best friend if you're a dick, right?" At her nod, I continue, "So they took me home and walked me in. When Jack left us alone, Ashton kissed me after telling me he wants more than just a casual hook up. And let me tell you, that kiss was the best kiss I've ever had."

She holds her hand up. "Wait, I'm a little confused here.

Jack is his best friend? And he was at lunch, too? How did this lunch eventuate?"

I fill her in on what happened yesterday, adding, "His friend is that actor, Jack Kingsley. You know him, right?"

"Oh, wow." She nods. "Yeah, I've seen some of his movies. You know me, though, I'm not really up on movies or actors so the name is familiar, but I might not recognise him if he were to walk past us right now."

"I didn't recognise him at first, but that could be because I was drunk."

"So this kiss? On a scale of one to ten, what would you rate it?"

"A twenty."

"It must have been good. You're a hard woman to please."

"You have no idea. It wasn't just the kiss… it was the way he touched me and spoke to me, too. Goodness, the man is lethal."

She laughs. "This is gonna be fun."

"What?"

"Watching you deal with a man like Ashton Scott. You're no pushover, so for him to have you all worked up like this tells me a lot. When are you seeing him again?"

"We have no plans."

"Right, well I want updates. I need to know the minute he calls you."

I run my fingers through my hair and take a deep breath. "I'm totally out of my depth here, Sienna. I've never dated a man like Ashton. Hell, I've never *met* a man like him. Until yesterday, I didn't want anything to do with him, but now he's all I can think about."

"What do you mean by 'a man like Ashton'? You dated Boston for three years."

"He wasn't anything like Ashton."

"Sure he was. Well, except for the asshole bit, he definitely wasn't that. But he was confident and sexy as hell."

I shake my head. "Boston was many things, but he wasn't as…. God, I don't even know what the right word is. Ashton is so in your face. He's—"

"Bossy?"

I laugh. "Yeah, bossy. But so much more than that, too. He's the kind of man you can't help noticing the minute he walks into a room. He's powerful. I can't do powerful."

She grins. "Well, powerful can definitely do you."

I drink some coffee before admitting what I'm truthfully scared of. "I don't want to be consumed by a man. You know what I'm like." I have this way of losing myself when I'm with a man and I don't want to do that again.

"I do. Your inner hopeless romantic does tend to take over sometimes and lead you astray. But you won't know unless you try, babe. I say give him a go. And honestly? I think you need a powerful man like Ashton in your life. You're too strong and independent yourself to have anyone less. Boston walked away when he should have fought for you. I have no idea what is down the track for you and Ashton, but if you guys get serious, I could never see him giving up without a fight."

"Oh, God, he'd just bulldoze his way through. That's a whole other problem with him. I don't want to be pushed into anything."

"Okay, let's calm down and be rational here. You're thinking too much. Just have sex with the guy and see if you like it. He might suck in bed and then all this worry would be for nothing."

I pull a face. "You seriously think Ashton would suck in bed?"

Her eyes sparkle with humour. "I'm not the one who he fucked with his mouth, so I have nothing to base my opinion on, but I'd say no, I don't think he'd suck in bed. One has to test these things, though. Am I right?"

"You know I'm not a fan of jumping straight into bed. I want to get to know him first."

She rolls her eyes. "Of course you do." Her sarcasm fills the air.

"There's nothing wrong with slowing things down," I mutter. We've had this discussion many times. I'm pretty sure we'll never agree on it.

"And there's nothing wrong with taking a test drive."

As I sit thinking about what she's said, I wonder if she's right. And the fact I'm even considering sleeping with him so soon stuns me the most. Ashton is already bulldozing his way into my life and I'm beginning to think I'm helpless to slow him down.

A few hours later, I stare at myself in the mirror and grimace. Gently touching my cheek, I wish I could go back to yesterday and not apply that facemask. My face is so red from the skin reaction. And sore. I can barely touch my face without it hurting.

I head out to my lounge room. An afternoon in front of the television sounds like exactly what I need. Some quiet time away from people.

I've just settled on the couch with a travel documentary when a knock sounds at my front door. I ignore it. Mostly because I don't want to move off the couch but also because I'm not expecting anyone. It can't be important. However, they don't leave. The knocking only grows more insistent so I eventually give in and make my way to the door.

I'm surprised to find Ashton on the other side of the door. "You don't give up easily, do you?" I say, recalling my conversation with Sienna today. *I could never see him giving up without a fight.*

"I can't say it's in my nature, no," he replies. He frowns. "What happened to your face?"

My hand absently moves to cover a cheek. "A mask and I had a fight. The mask won." I cock my head. "What are you doing here?"

His intense eyes lock onto mine. "Organising dinner for tonight."

I quirk a brow. "You couldn't do that over the phone?"

"No."

His intensity flusters me. I don't know what to say to that so I take a moment to try and figure out a response. I mean, who doesn't just pick up the phone to organise a date?

He doesn't wait for me to reply. "I'll pick you up at seven."

I bite the inside of my lip, still flustered. "Do you organise all your dates like this?"

A flicker of amusement touches his expression. "If you're asking whether I knock on a woman's door and tell her what time I'll pick her up, the answer would be no. I usually just phone or have my assistant send flowers to organise dinner." He pauses for a moment. "I also usually give women the opportunity to say no."

His meaning is not lost on me and my breathing slows. "Oh." Again, lost for freaking words.

He takes a step closer to me and drops his gaze to my mouth. "Do you like Italian?" He drags his eyes from my lips after he asks this. The heat I see there causes my knees to weaken. I can't recall the last time a man looked at me the way he is. In fact, I'm not sure a man has ever watched me like Ashton does.

"Yes, it's one of my favourites. But we'll have to make it seven thirty."

He continues to watch me with the intensity that causes my pulse to quicken. "I'll see you at seven thirty."

As he's leaving, I call out, "I'm good with a guy calling to organise a date. Just so you know."

He halts and looks back at me. "I'm not. I can't see you over the phone."

And then he's gone.

And I'm standing here more confused by my own reactions than ever.

12

ASHTON

I EXIT MY CAR AS I REACH INTO MY POCKET TO GRAB my ringing phone out. Placing it to my ear, I say, "Alessandra. What's up?"

"I'm just calling to let you know Bradley left his coat at your place today. Malcolm will drop by tomorrow morning to collect it because Bradley's being a pain about wanting it back."

"I'll leave it with Roberta."

"I'll get Malcolm to bring her some fudge. Your house-keeper is one of the only people alive who loves my fudge."

"Why are you cooking?"

She groans. "School bake sale. Bane of my fucking existence."

I enter Lorelei's complex and jab the button for the lift. The fact I can enter her apartment complex without any issues concerns me. The front door is secured with a keypad, but the door is never fully closed. I make a note to mention it to her.

"Bradley seemed a little off today."

"I think he's getting a cold. He loved hanging out with you and Jack today. So did Sadie."

I enter the lift and press the number for Lorelei's floor. "They should come over more often."

"What are you doing? You seem a little distracted."

"I'm on a date." *Almost.*

"Where'd you meet this one?"

"Fuck, you say that as if I've got a different woman every night, Aly."

"You have to admit you've come close."

"I will admit I've dated a lot of women, but not a new one every night." I step out of the lift and head to Lorelei's door.

"Well, okay, maybe I'm a little off there. I'd like to see you settle down again. With a good woman. And not someone who only wants you because of who you are."

I've reached my destination. "Goodbye, Alessandra." I end the call and knock on Lorelei's door. She doesn't take long to answer it and I stand,, staring at the most beautiful woman I've ever met.

My gaze sweeps over her body, taking in the black dress painted over her curves and the heels that accentuate her toned legs. *Heels I'd like to remove slowly before making my way up those legs.*

"You're early," she says.

I check my watch. Quarter past seven. "No, I'm late. I said seven."

"And I said seven thirty."

I close the distance between us and place my hand on her hip before snaking it around her waist. "We both know you had nothing on between seven and seven thirty."

She grips the bicep of my arm that I have around her. It's like she's trying to push me away while at the same time keep me close. "I might have."

"Are you ready? Or do you need fifteen minutes?"

"Just let me get my bag," she says before turning to leave me.

I want to follow her.

I want my lips on hers again.

But I don't. Instead, I wait with patience I don't possess for this woman. Patience that I know I am going to have to work on, because Lorelei has made it abundantly clear she doesn't want just sex—that she wants to spend time getting to know me first. And as much as I want so much more from her than sex, my need for her body is intense.

She doesn't take long to return and a minute later I'm tracking her steps as we make our way to my car. When we hit the footpath and she sees the car, she turns in surprise. "A double date?"

I eye Jack leaning against my Aston Martin and shake my head. "No, I don't share, Lorelei."

Jack pushes off from the car and grins at her. "We definitely don't share, sweetheart. I'm only along for the ride because my best friend thinks I'll spend the night drinking or taking drugs if I'm alone."

Surprise flares in her eyes as she glances at me. "Really...." Her voice drifts off and I wonder what she's thinking. One of the things I like about her is that I can't always figure her out. She keeps me guessing.

Jack shrugs. "He's right. I do have a problem with those things. This is a little extreme, though."

Before I can respond, Lorelei speaks. "No, I don't think so. I hope my friend would look out for me like Ashton is for you if I had a problem."

Jack mutters something under his breath about me taking things to the extreme as we all settle in the car, him in the back, Lorelei next to me. The argument he and I had before leaving tonight is long forgotten, though, which is our way. We've always had our say and then moved on without holding onto shit. He didn't want to come tonight, but I forced him. I refused to take no for an answer.

I listen as Jack and Lorelei laugh over a story he's shared about an embarrassing moment he had at the Oscars once. The sound of Lorelei's laughter hits me in the gut. And not for the first time. It seems every time I hear her laugh I'm affected this way.

"Ashton, just drop me off on the way to Lorelei's. No fucking way am I getting in the way of you guys tonight," Jack says from the back seat of the car. We've just left the restaurant.

I meet his gaze in the rear-view mirror. He mouths, "Take me home."

I decide to do as he's asked and steer the car in the direction of home.

Lorelei turns to face him. "You won't be getting in the way of anything, Jack. Ashton knows the score."

My lips twitch.

I know the damn score off by fucking heart.

"Sweetheart, were we at the same dinner tonight?" Jack asks.

"Yes," she replies hesitantly.

"You two couldn't keep your eyes off each other. If I hadn't been there, you probably would have spent the night sitting on his lap."

I glance at her in time to see her hand move to her throat. She catches me looking and sucks in a breath before facing the road again.

We drive in silence the rest of the way to my place, all lost in our thoughts. When I pull into the driveway, Jack jumps out and rounds the car. I roll the window down when he taps on it. "I won't wait up for you," he says with a grin.

"Keep out of trouble."

His grin fades. "I can control myself, Ashton."

"I won't be long."

He straightens. "Like I said, I won't wait up. Don't hurry back."

I watch him walk inside before shifting the car into reverse. As I back out of the driveway, Lorelei says, "How worried about him are you?"

I glance at her. "Tonight, not so much, but in general, I worry a lot."

"Why not tonight?"

"His mood is easy tonight. You put him in a good mood."

"Really?"

"You sound surprised."

"Well, I hardly know him so I wouldn't expect to have an effect on him."

"Lorelei, not many people know the real Jack. He has hundreds of so-called friends, but I could probably count on two hands the number of people who know him better than you."

She's silent for a beat. "I find that so sad."

"Yeah, it is."

Shifting in her seat to face me, she says, "You surprised me again tonight."

"How?"

"By bringing Jack with you. I don't know many guys who would have done that."

"Trust me, I wanted you all to myself."

"But you didn't let that stop you from looking out for him."

I pull up at a red light and look at her. "Jack is one of the only people I would do that for, so I'm perhaps not as good as you think."

She smiles. "Well, I'm reserving judgement."

The light turns green and I continue towards her apartment. We arrive five minutes later, and I make my way around to her side of the car to open the door. She exits the car before I hit her side, though, and frowns at my expression when she meets my eyes.

"What?" she asks.

I ignore her question and guide her inside. I've never been a man to open car doors for women before, so my actions are perplexing to me also.

The elevator ride is excruciatingly long. Being so close to Lorelei and not touching her takes all my control. As I step out of the lift and follow her, my gaze is drawn to her ass and down her legs. I groan inwardly; this will be the hardest part of tonight.

She turns the key in the door, pushes it open and then turns to face me.

Our eyes meet.

"Thank you for dinner," she says softly.

My eyes drop to her lips.

I need to taste those lips again.

Hooking my arm around her waist, I pull her close. "You're mine again tomorrow night."

Her eyes widen a touch and her breath catches. "What if I'm busy?"

I don't let her go. "Are you?"

She hesitates for only a second. "No."

"I'll pick you up at seven thirty."

"I'll be ready at seven."

Fuck.

My arm tightens around her and I bend to kiss her. She leans into me and loops her arms around my neck while kissing me back. A moan escapes her lips and my cock jerks to attention. Hell, my dick has been semi-hard all night.

Suddenly, her arms leave my neck and she pushes against my chest while she ends the kiss. I pull away and look down at her, questioningly.

"Sorry," she says, a pained expression on her face. "It hurts my face to kiss you."

"Fuck," I mutter. I've completely forgotten about her face. "Sorry."

"Yeah, it sucks. I won't be doing one of those masks again in a hurry."

"Good to hear. They're a hazard to men," I murmur, my arm still around her, my eyes not leaving hers.

She stares up at me, her breaths slowing down. Then she surprises the hell out of me. "Do you want to stay for a drink?"

I lift a brow. "As in a real drink?"

Her lips curl into a smile. "Yes, an actual drink. I'm sorry I don't have alcohol, but I do have tea, coffee, water, mil—"

I press a finger to her lips. "I'll have a coffee."

Her smile fills her face and she leaves me to head into the kitchen. I rake my fingers through my hair. This taking it slow business isn't something I've ever had a woman request. But fuck if it isn't making me want her all the more.

13

LORELEI

"So you've lived here for two years?" Ashton asks while I fiddle with the coffee machine. It's unnerving that he knows so much about me.

"Do you do that with everyone in your life?"

He moves closer so he's standing less than two feet away. Resting against the counter, he casually crosses one foot over the other. It's as if he feels at home in my kitchen. His eyes meet mine, the usual intensity shining from them. "Do what?"

"Make a point to know everything about them like that?"

"I don't know everything, Lorelei."

I finish making his coffee, black with no sugar, and pass him the mug. "I beg to differ. You seem to have made it a point to know most things."

"I always take the time to learn about the people impor- tant to me." He lifts the drink to his mouth and takes a sip while I process what he's told me.

The people important to me.

"We've known each other a week," I remind him.

"Your point?"

The kettle finishes boiling water for my tea and I turn to reach into the fridge for the milk. When I face him again, I look up into his eyes, finding his gaze still focused intently on me. "My point is that I hardly think I could become someone important to you in the space of a week."

"That's not true. Time doesn't dictate that kind of thing for me. I knew Jack would be my best mate within days of meeting him, and my assistant wormed her way into my life within two weeks." His voice deepens when he adds, "I have no idea what will happen between us, but I know I want to learn absolutely everything there is to know about you."

I stare up at him, unable to move. My breathing slows and I fight my way through the thoughts filling my mind, trying to figure out exactly what I'm thinking. Trying to work out exactly what I want to happen here as my inner conflict settles in.

Before I can speak, he leans even closer to me, almost taking up all my personal space. "Lorelei—"

I place my finger against his lips, quietening him. "I want to take this slowly."

He takes hold of my hand and moves it away from his mouth. "No, you don't. And even if you do, I don't ever take things slowly."

I fight the effect his dominance has on me and attempt to stand up to him. Because as much as I'm turned on by the way he's assuming control here, I don't want to give him all the power in whatever this relationship might become. "I can tell that about you, but I won't be controlled, Ashton, so if that's the kind of thing you're used to in your relationships, this might not be what you're looking for."

He moves so he's standing in front of me with my back against the counter. Placing his hands on the counter either side of me, his body presses against mine as he dips his mouth to my collarbone. I suck in a breath when his tongue traces a line along my skin, and a shiver runs through me as he kisses his way slowly up my neck. He stops when he reaches my jawbone and lifts his face so he can make eye contact again. "Controlling you is the furthest thing from my mind, Lorelei."

I stare at him, bewildered, and know that as much as he may not be trying to control me, simply being in his presence is enough to give him all the power. Ashton owns his world and converging his with mine only increases his dominion. Whether I like it not, he has that effect on me.

He watches me for a moment before lowering his gaze. Trailing his finger down my neck, he stops when he hits the material of my dress. I chose a dress for tonight that doesn't reveal much of my cleavage. It is short and fitted, but it gives nothing away up top. He slowly runs his finger down my dress between my breasts, his focus completely on my chest. "Do you have any idea how much I want a taste of you?"

God, I wish I hadn't used that facemask yesterday. If my face wasn't so sore from the reaction, I'd kiss him right now. I halt the progress of his hand and hold it in place between my breasts. "I want to kiss you, but it seriously hurts way too much."

He moves his free hand to the hem of my dress and his fingers slide under. "I wasn't talking about a taste of those lips."

His eyes find mine as he pushes my dress up. Unable to form a reply, all I can do is breathe through every sensation his touch evokes. I'm practically panting by the time he kneels in front of me.

"This is as slow as I'm willing to take us," he says before placing his lips against my panties and kissing me. His hands grip my ass and a moment later, he slides my panties down.

My fingers tangle in his thick dark hair as he brings his mouth to my pussy. His tongue circles my clit and a moan escapes my lips. I steady myself against the kitchen counter because my legs feel weak. It's been five months since I've had sex and every single inch of me is alive with need. If Ashton is as skilled as I think he is, this won't take long.

He continues to bless my clit with his tongue before kissing his way to my entrance. As he pushes his tongue inside me, he lifts my left leg and rests it over his shoulder. Burying his face in my pussy, he then shows me just how skilled he is at making a woman come.

Ashton brings me close to orgasm—*so damn close*—before backing off and letting my release tease me while he shifts his attention to my inner thighs. He kisses me there and runs his hands over my ass and down my legs before finally returning to the place I want to beg him never to leave again. His eyes meet mine. "I knew one taste would never be enough," he growls before his tongue enters me again.

I grip the counter hard.

One taste will most definitely not be enough.

He doesn't rush this, but rather, takes his time. I ride the waves of pleasure he gives me, losing track of my thoughts along the way. By the time he brings me close to orgasm again, I'm completely consumed by him. I'm unaware how long he's had his mouth on me; all I'm aware of is that he has the most talented lips and tongue I've ever had the good fortune of being treated to.

When I'm just about to come, he stops what he's doing and trails kisses across my skin above my clit. My eyes blink open and I look down, meeting his heated gaze. I try to push his face back to where it was, but he resists and shakes his head.

"Please," I beg, wanting this more than I realised.

He shifts my leg off his shoulder and stands. Without saying a word, he spins me around and unzips my dress in one swift movement. His hands ghost across my back and he removes my dress, letting it drop to the floor. He then flicks my bra open and slides his hands up my back and over my shoulders, pushing my bra off. By the time he turns me to face him again, I'm naked.

"Fuck," he rasps as his gaze sweeps over my body. "So beautiful."

I flick the top button of his shirt open and attempt to undo the next one. He stops me and I meet his gaze with a frown.

"No." His tone is as commanding as his touch. "I'm not going to fuck you tonight, Lorelei."

Confusion collides with disappointment at his words. "Really? You're just going to get me all worked up and then leave?"

He moves his mouth to my ear. "You will come before I leave tonight, but it will be because of my mouth, not my cock."

My frown deepens. I thought I wanted to take this slow and he proved me wrong. I can't figure him out now. "Why won't you sleep with me?"

"You're not ready for me yet. But you will be by the time I'm finished with you tonight." His voice drops to a growl. "And then I'm going to schedule a day to spend fucking any remaining hesitation out of you."

His words send a thrill through me. Oh God, I need that day already. "We could just skip ahead to that day now."

"No, we couldn't. Because what I have planned needs you to be well rested."

He dips his mouth to my neck and kisses me while he takes hold of one of my breasts. Pressing his erection against me, he moves his mouth lower to take my breast between his lips. At the same time, his free hand glides down my body and a second later, he pushes two fingers inside me.

Gripping his hair, I open my mouth and his name escapes. "Ashton...."

His fingers reach deep inside and expertly hit the spot I need them to. Closing my eyes, I allow the pleasure to consume me once more as his mouth, hands and fingers work their magic. When I think he can't possibly intensify the pleasure, he kneels again and shows me that when Ashton Scott makes a promise, he delivers.

With his face buried deep in my pussy again and his hands cupping my ass, I finally—*finally*—come. Wave after wave of bliss pulses through me. I grip the kitchen counter with one hand and Ashton's head with the other to hold myself up. The sensations are so intense, unlike any other orgasm I've ever had, that I'm almost sure my legs are going to give way. But Ashton makes sure I don't collapse. His strong arms circle me as he stands, holding me close while I abandon myself to the release.

I never want it to end.

It's the best I've ever had.

And I haven't even had his cock yet.

Clinging to him, I open my eyes and attempt to get my breathing under control. His heat-filled eyes stare down at me. "You weren't kidding, were you?" I say.

"I never kid, Lorelei."

A smile touches my lips. "I can see that." Of course, I already knew this about him. Ashton is the most intense man I've ever met. "I now also know some other things about you."

He cocks his head. "And they would be?"

I place my finger against his lips. "That these lips know what they're doing."

His arm around my waist pulls me tighter against him and his hand slides down to take hold of my ass. "You have no idea what these lips are capable of, Lorelei."

I love the sound of my name coming from his mouth. Even more than that, I love thinking about his mouth and what it might do to me in future.

"I look forward to you showing me."

He pushes against my ass so that my pussy tilts forward. At the same time, he presses his erection against me. "Block Tuesday off. You're mine for the day." His actions combined with his words and his growly voice shoot heat to my core.

Ashton has completely changed my mind.

I don't want to take this slowly anymore.

I don't care what I have in my diary on Tuesday. It's about to be rescheduled so I can spend the day in his bed.

14

ASHTON

JESSICA STARES AT ME IN SHOCK. "CANCEL everything for tomorrow?"

I lean back in my chair and nod. "Yes, everything. I don't care how you manage it, but I won't be in tomorrow." The thought of what I *will* be doing causes my cock to twitch. The image of long red hair splayed out underneath me only builds my anticipation.

Today is going to be a long day.

Jessica takes a step closer to my desk. "Have you lost your mind, Ashton? You're meeting with Marc Brentley in the morning."

Fuck.

"What time?"

"Nine. After that you've got back-to-back meetings and let me just say, it took weeks to schedule in your eleven o'clock with Aaron Steele. *Weeks.*"

I take in her glare. She's pissed off and rightfully so. Aaron Steele is notoriously difficult to nail down for a meeting. Raking my fingers through my hair, I say, "Okay, let me take a look at the calendar and see what I can move around and what I can't."

Her eyes widen before narrowing at me. "Is this your new form of Asshole Monday? Finding ways to give me heart palpitations? Because if it is, I'm stating right now that I'm not a fan. I'll take your moods over this any day."

"It's one day, Jessica."

She huffs out a breath and shakes her head at me in disgust. "One day in Ashton-land is the equivalent of a week in most people's lives. You don't cancel appointments, let alone entire fucking days. What the hell has gotten into you?" A look flashes across her face and her eyes widen again. "Jesus, is this for pussy?"

I stand. "You're being melodramatic now."

She doesn't take her eyes off me as I walk around the desk. "Fuck me, I never thought I'd see the day that Ashton Scott cancelled work for a woman."

Grabbing my phone off the desk, I ignore her. "I'm heading out for about an hour. I'll take a look at the calendar and let you know what I want moved around."

Frown lines crease her forehead. "You're leaving? You just got in. It's only just past eight—"

"I'll be back in an hour."

I exit my office to her yelling after me. "I'm getting to the bottom of this when you get back."

Her words filter through my thoughts but are quickly replaced with images of Lorelei.

Naked.

In the throes of an orgasm.

Fucking beautiful.

I'll meet with Brentley and Steele tomorrow, but no other meeting will take precedent over seeing Lorelei.

~

"What can I do for you, Ashton?"

I eye the real estate agent standing in front of me, taking in the unironed fabric of her dress and the dishevelled appearance of her hair and face. *So unlike the Margie Brown I know.* It would seem the rumours I've heard are correct. Margie is losing her touch. Disappointing because she's the best agent I've ever worked with. It'll be hard to replace her. "Can you tell me what properties you have available on Willow Street currently?"

"In Pott's Point?"

I nod.

"There's only one at the moment, and I doubt it's a property you'd be after."

I ignore the irritation her statement stirs. "I didn't ask you to think for me, Margie. Which building is it?"

Her nostrils flare at my hard tone, but she doesn't acknowledge her annoyance. "It's the rundown dress shop on the corner of Willow and Blair. Tiny building that no one seems to want. It's been on the market for three months now and only one other person has shown any interest."

"Who?" I demand.

"You know I can't divulge that, Ashton."

"It's never stopped you before."

She takes a deep breath. "Well, it's stopping me this time."

"It's my father, isn't it?" I watch closely for her tell. When Margie lies, she runs her fingers through her hair.

"No, it's not your father." Interesting. Her tell is nowhere to be seen.

My phone buzzes with a text.

Jessica: Aaron Steele just rescheduled his meeting to

Wednesday. It would seem the universe is onboard with your quest for pussy.

I look back up at Margie. "Email me the info on that property. And the second anyone makes an offer, I want to know. Also advise me if any other properties on Willow Street become available."

She nods. "There's plenty of other properties for sale in Pott's Point. I can email the best listings to you."

"I'm not interested in anything else. Just send me what I've requested." Without waiting for her reply, I leave her office.

Placing my phone to my ear, I wait for Jessica to pick up. "Did you get my text?" she asks.

"Yes. I also just discovered I require a new real estate agent. Can you compile a shortlist?"

"What happened to Margie?"

"If the gossips are to be believed, her drug habit has kicked up a notch. I wouldn't be surprised, but I don't really care what it is. She's not on my side anymore and I need someone on my side." I've worked with Margie for five years and not once in that time has she refused to divulge any information I need.

"Don't you think that's being a little rash? Maybe she ju—"

"Jessica, I don't fuck around. You know that. Find me someone I can trust. And reschedule every meeting for tomorrow except the one with Brentley."

"I've already started. Oh, and Jack dropped by. Said his appointment with Dr Winthrop was a waste of fucking time and he's finding a new doctor. You might want to track him down because he didn't look the best."

I rake my fingers through my hair. Today is slowly turning to shit.

~

I find Jack at home.

"What do you want, Ashton?" He scowls at me from the sofa before raising his drink to his mouth and draining the glass.

I move further into the living room to join him. "Whisky so early in the morning? I thought you usually reserved that for late night drinking."

He stands and I don't fail to notice he's wearing the same clothes he wore yesterday. "I reserve whisky for when life really fucks me in the ass."

I watch as he refills his glass and downs half of it in one go. "Jesus, Jack, what's going on?"

Raising his drink, he says, "Cheers, mate. My manager just informed me he's no longer my manager and that the movie I was supposed to start filming in a couple of months is no longer mine."

I frown. "I thought you wanted out anyway?"

"I did. Turns out I didn't know what the fuck I wanted until it was taken away from me."

"And Dr Winthrop? Jessica told me—"

He scowls again. "Dr Winthrop is a fucking asshole. I'm not seeing him again."

"Because he tells you things you don't want to hear, or because he's an asshole?"

He finishes his drink and slams the glass down on the coffee table. Glaring at me, because he knows I'm the only person in his life who won't let this shit slide, he says, "Do you really think he's telling me something I don't know,

Ashton? *I fucking know*. I live and breathe this shit every day of my goddam fucking life."

I push him harder. "So, what, you know, but you don't want to hear it at the moment?"

His chest pumps furiously as his anger rises. "Is that a crime? Would you want to hear that shit every time you went to the good doctor?"

"No, but I wouldn't want to be fed fake hope, Jack. You're bipolar. You can't fix it, drink it away or get rid of it. It's here to stay for life. And it's about time you fucking dealt with it once and for all."

We stare at each other in silence. My words sit between us like a gaping wound that needs to be healed. The kind of wound no one wants to go near because it's too nasty and filthy to even know where to start fixing it. *Or how.*

Finally, he says, "I'm tired, Ashton. I'm tired of my own damn mind. And sometimes it's easier not to hear how I keep fucking shit up." All his fight is gone and that sends a chill up my spine. I need him not to give up. I need him to keep fighting.

"Let me find you a new doctor then." My words come out in a ragged beg as I plead with him to let me help.

Still staring at me, but now through vacant eyes, he exhales a long breath. Waving his hand in the air, he says, "Fine. But make this one a woman. If I'm gonna spend my hours talking to someone, I at least want some tits and ass in the room."

"I'll book you an appointment for this afternoon. You need to shower and change into clean clothes between now and then." No fucking way am I allowing him to surrender to this disorder.

"I'm going back to bed first," he mutters as he walks past me into the hallway. I watch as he heads to his bedroom.

Once the door closes behind him, I pull out my phone and call Jessica.

"Did you find Jack?" she asks, answering my call.

"Yes, and I need you to come over and babysit him today."

She groans. "Really?"

"Yes, really," I snap. "I'd do it myself if I could get out of work today."

"You're lucky I like you, Ashton. Jack is hard fucking work. You want me to come over now?"

"Yeah, I'll wait here until you arrive."

There's no way I'm leaving him alone again until we get his mental state under control. Jack is far too important to me to lose.

By the time Jessica arrives, Jack has wandered back out into the kitchen where I've spent the last fifteen minutes searching for a new psychologist.

He glances at Jessica as she enters the kitchen to join us. "Hello, beautiful. I see Ashton has called in the big guns."

She rolls her eyes before wrapping her arms around him and pressing a kiss to his cheek. "Ashton is lucky I like him and *you're* lucky I love you."

He doesn't let her go when she tries to pull away. Rather, he slides his hands around her waist and rests them on her ass. "Why did I ever let you go?"

"Because you were dumb."

A smile lights up his face and he chuckles. "I was. And now you're into women so I have no chance at fixing my mistake."

"Jack, I'm into women *and* men, but trust me when I tell you that I would never let you break my heart again. One doesn't simply get over Jack Kingsley. My scars still hurt."

His smile disappears and he lets her move out of his embrace. "Fuck, I'm a bastard."

She nods. "Yes, you are. But somehow you still make us all love you." Turning to me, she says, "You should get going. I've got this from here."

I nod as I scribble an address and time on a piece of paper. Eyeing them both, I instruct, "Your appointment is here at four this afternoon." I direct my next question to Jessica. "I'll be home by seven, maybe earlier. Are you good to stay until then?"

"Yes." The way she clenches her jaw, though, lets me know this isn't something she really wants to be doing. I can't blame her. Jack threw her love away five years ago and took a chunk of her heart with him. While I know she'd do anything to help him, I also know that being with him is hard. It reminds her of everything they had and everything he did to kill their life together.

As the door to my home closes behind me, I hear her bossing Jack around and can't help but smile. *He deserves that.* Thank fuck she agreed to today. I only hope she'll be good for tomorrow as well because giving up my plans with Lorelei isn't something I want to do.

15

LORELEI

"Lorelei!" Jack greets me with enthusiasm as Ashton shows me into his living room. "Another double date."

I smile at him as I take in Ashton's house. It's the first time I've been here. His home is the most masculine home I've ever set foot in. From what I've seen so far, it's a mix of browns and greys with a hint of black in places. All cement, marble, glass, and sleek furniture. "Jack," I greet him in a more subdued manner but am equally happy to see him. Ashton's hand brushes across my back as he guides me to the sofa. Lust pools in my belly at his touch. *Tomorrow can't come fast enough.*

"Sorry Ashton had to cancel your dinner plans for tonight. I tried to tell him I'd be okay on my own, but it seems my friend thinks I'm going to do something stupid with my life."

I take a seat and look up in time to see Ashton scowl. "Jack, don't—"

Jack cuts him off. "Don't what, Ashton? Tell her how fucked up I am?"

The air is thick with tension between these two. I decide

to cut straight through it. Turning to Jack, I ask, "Is he right to think that?"

Jack stares at me. "To think I would kill myself?"

I nod. "Yes, that." My heart beats faster at the topic of conversation. This hits a little too close to home.

He continues to stare at me and I wonder if perhaps I have misread him. Maybe he doesn't prefer upfront and honest after all. However, when a grin fills his face, I relax. Glancing up at his friend, he says, "I fucking love her, Ashton." And then to me—"I would never end my life, Lorelei. That's a coward's way out."

I narrow my eyes at him. "But you'll find other ways to fuck with it."

Jack rubs the back of his neck, clearly bothered by that statement. Leaning forward, he says, "You just say it like it is, don't you, sweetheart?"

I swallow hard. "Not usually, Jack. Usually I have more manners than this, but let's just say this is a topic close to my heart, and I don't like to see people going through what you're going through."

"How do you know what I'm going through?"

I'm not sure exactly what illness he has, but it's clear his mental health is suffering. "I can see the signs. I lived with them for most of my life," I admit softly. This isn't something I tend to discuss very often.

He cocks his head. "A parent?"

I nod. "My mother and my grandmother were both bipolar. Mum didn't look after herself, whereas my grandmother did. A car accident ended up taking my mother's life, but that was after two failed suicide attempts."

Ashton, who has sat next to me, places his hand on my leg as I speak, and I'm thankful for his touch. It calms me, and my heart rate slows.

Jack leans back and blows out a long breath. "Fuck, I'm sorry to hear that. How old were you when she died?"

"Eight. My grandmother raised me after that and gave me the stable life I'd never known. Mum had always been all over the place, going from one guy to another and one job to the next. I think she was always trying to find a way to make herself feel better. She wasn't a bad mother; she just wasn't there emotionally for me."

Jack's eyes glaze over; he seems lost in his thoughts. "Sometimes it's just about making yourself feel *something*. *Anything*. Because some days, when stuff happens to you that you know you should feel, all you have is this nothingness. There's just this fucking dark void, a blank space. And all you want is anything but *that*." He stands and gives me one last glance before looking at Ashton. "I'm gonna check out your gym."

Ashton nods. "Let me know if you need anything."

We watch him leave and I can't help but think how scruffy he looks in his worn dark jeans, faded grey T-shirt, and day-old stubble. Turning to Ashton, I say, "Is he seeing someone about this?"

"Yes, I found him a new psych today and he saw her this afternoon. He seemed to get on with her and they've scheduled appointments for the rest of the week."

"Thank goodness. He doesn't look great. I mean, compared to yesterday he seems to have gone downhill overnight."

He leans forward and claims my mouth in a long, deep kiss. A kiss that causes me to struggle for air when he ends it. "Your face is better today," he murmurs, his eyes searching my face.

I touch the skin there. The pain is gone, as is the redness. "Yes, thank God."

Leaning back against the sofa, he says, "I don't want to

talk about Jack tonight." I hear the exhaustion in his voice and even though I hardly know him, I sense how much this is affecting him.

Shifting sideways on the sofa, I place a hand on his chest. "Tell me about your day instead." When he'd called me earlier to cancel our dinner and ask me to come over instead, I'd heard the conflict in his voice. It was pretty clear the last thing he wanted to do was change our plans, but seeing Jack now, I'm glad he did.

His eyes find mine and I see surprise there. "It was the kind of day I'd rather forget. Tell me about yours."

"What was that surprise in your eyes just then?"

He spreads his arms across the back of the sofa and my eyes are drawn to his chest. Ashton is still dressed in what I presume he wore to work today: a black suit with white dress shirt. His jacket is open and his tie is loosened around his neck. Suits are my downfall and when he casually spreads his arms wide, his powerful body on full display, excitement flares deep inside me.

He's mine.

Well, not really, but we've a hot date for tomorrow so I'm claiming him for the moment.

He answers my question while I drool over his suit. "You asked me how my day was. It's been a long time since a woman has asked me that—since one cared enough to enquire."

I want to ask him how any woman he was with could not care enough about him to ask that, but it feels too soon for such a personal question. Besides, I'm not sure I want to hear about his past relationships just yet. I like to think of myself as a woman who doesn't experience jealousy, but the thought of him with someone else causes weird feelings I'd rather not think about at the moment.

When I hesitate to say anything, he moves his hand and places it on my knee. "What are you thinking?"

Because I don't want to tell him what I'm thinking, I push up off the sofa and straddle him. Surprise flares in his eyes again. He wasn't expecting this and I love that I've done the unexpected.

I slide my hands over his chest and bend my face to his. "I was thinking how I don't want to wait until tomorrow for your cock." My words make me feel bolder than I really am. I love sex as much as any woman, but I'm not really an initiator. And on top of that, I'm not experienced with dirty talk. What I just said wouldn't be dirty talk for many, but for me it is. I hope I don't look as flushed as I feel.

His eyes hold mine. He cups my ass with one hand while his other arm remains spread out across the sofa. "I don't believe you."

I blink and try to sit back a little so our faces aren't as close. That wasn't what I thought he'd say and it confuses me that he didn't take the lead and run with it. He doesn't let me shift back, though. His hand remains firm on my ass, keeping me close. "You don't believe I can't wait until tomorrow?" I practically stammer my words out. I'm feeling stupid for even attempting to talk dirty to him.

"No, I don't believe that's what you were thinking."

I push against his chest in an attempt to move off his lap. This has gone from bad to worse because I really don't want to admit the truth. When he refuses to allow me to move, I say, "Ashton, let me off."

He holds me tight. "Tell me what you were really thinking."

Heat flushes my skin again and I push even harder against him. The vein in his temple pulses as both his arms circle me. He then stands, taking me with him. My arms and legs instinctively wrap around him even though all I can think about is how much I want to escape his hold.

His eyes flash with determination. "I'm not letting you go until you tell me what I want to know, Lorelei. So start talking, baby."

I suck in a breath at both his use of that word and the command he wields. But I meet his gaze and dig my heels in. "Put me down first."

His brows rise. "You're going to challenge me?"

As determined as he is, I hold my ground. "I'll tell you what you want *after* you put me down."

"No. You'll tell me now."

"God, you're infuriating, Ashton. Put me down."

He's silent for a moment. "Why are you all flustered? Did I say something to cause that?" His position isn't as hard-line as it was a moment ago, but his tone is still demanding.

I sigh and all my fight leaves me. "If you really must know, I was feeling weird about discussing your past relationships, and then I tried sexy talk with you, and it's just not something I'm good at, and then it all went to shit from there. Now, can you *please* put me down?" Warmth fills my cheeks yet again. I'm kind of wishing I hadn't said yes to tonight.

He finally sets me down but right when I think I'm escaping his clutches, he sits on the sofa and pulls me onto his lap again. "Let's go over all that."

"Let's not," I mutter as I hold his arms to steady myself.

His lips twitch as amusement flickers in his eyes. "First, let's set something straight—I need more sexy talk from this mouth." He runs his fingers across my lips before brushing his lips over them. "Understood?"

My fingers dig into his biceps as I nod. "Yes." *God, yes.*

"Do you want to discuss my previous relationships?"

"No, not really.... No." I stop talking because really it's

the only thing I should be doing right about now. The words coming out of my mouth sound confused even to me.

His eyes search mine. "I've had two relationships in my life that lasted more than a couple of months. The first one was for a year and the second one lasted four years. That one ended about twelve months ago. I'm won't lie, I've dated a lot of women in between." I love his honesty and his willingness to share that information with me.

"It wasn't that I necessarily wanted to know all that, Ashton. I was just wondering how any woman you'd been with wouldn't want to know how your day was. But I didn't want to ask that because it felt too soon to bring up a discussion on your women. And—" My mouth snaps shut before I admit what I was about to and I pray he lets it go. Of course, he doesn't.

"And what?"

"God, why do you have to be so demanding?"

"Because I want to know everything going on in that beautiful mind of yours. You can tell me anything, Lorelei. There's no judgement here."

I still at his words. "How do you do that?" I ask quietly.

"What?"

"Get inside my head like that."

"You blushed repeatedly. It was a guess. Getting inside your head is something I'm still trying to do because believe me, you're one of the only women I've ever met whose head I can't seem to get in." And there he goes again—impressing me with his honesty.

My body relaxes and I loop my arms around his neck before my mouth finds his. His lips part and my tongue sweeps over his as I shift closer to him. He deepens the kiss and runs his hands down my back to settle under my ass.

I could kiss Ashton for hours.

I could get lost in him.

And I'm sure I would except for the fact someone knocks on his front door.

"Fuck," he mutters when he ends the kiss. He lifts me with him when he stands, and deposits me on the floor. "Don't move. I'm getting rid of whoever it is and you're going to practice your sexy talk."

My eyes remain glued to the wide expanse of his back as he walks away. I sigh. *That suit.*

When I can no longer see him, I take a seat on the sofa and attempt to get my thoughts and emotions under control. Tonight has not gone the way I thought it would. Not even close. But I feel like in all my awkwardness we made some headway. Ashton managed to put me at ease, which is something not many men achieve. I might be a hopeless romantic and always searching for my soul mate, but I guard my heart ferociously, essentially closing a part of it off. *The part that allows me to be completely vulnerable with a man.* I'm pretty sure Ashton is going to attempt to demolish that wall.

He returns to the living room with Alessandra in tow. Her eyes widen when she sees me. Smacking her brother's arm, she says, "I knew you had a woman. And thank fuck she's a good one this time." She pauses before adding, "Now, get me a drink, Ashton. Lorelei and I have a lot to catch up on."

I can't help it; I burst out laughing. Ashton's sister is a breath of fresh air in life. I have no idea why she's here, but I do know that tonight's about to get really interesting.

16

ASHTON

As I watch Lorelei with Alessandra, it strikes me how little I know about her. *And just how much I want to know about her.* I might know all the superficial things that Jessica dug up, but not the important stuff. Things I've never really cared to know about a woman before.

What inspires her to strive for her dreams?

What wakes her up in the middle of the night in a sweat?

What is her greatest regret in life?

Who she gave her heart to the first time?

"Ashton, did you hear what I just said?" Alessandra asks, drawing me from my thoughts.

I drink the rest of the Scotch sitting in front of me and give them my full attention. "No."

"I said I want you and Lorelei to come for dinner this week." She looks at me expectantly and I know I have no hope of avoiding this. Alessandra has never taken it upon herself to become involved in my relationships; she clearly wants to with this one. And stubbornness runs in our family.

"Next week," I fire back. *I want Lorelei to myself this week.*

Alessandra's mouth spreads out in amusement. "Oh, you

didn't hear the part where she said yes already? To *this* week."

I place my hand on Lorelei's leg. "I'm sure you two will have a nice dinner, but I can't do it this week."

Lorelei's hand lands on mine. "Next week is good."

Alessandra smiles as she takes that in before holding her empty wine glass out to me. "Next week it is. I'll have another drink, Ashton."

"You've already had two, Aly."

She stares at me. "Your point?"

"Are you planning on staying here the night?"

She shrugs. "I might."

"Does Malcolm know?" It wouldn't be the first time she's spent the night after an argument with her husband, but I'm not in the habit of encouraging it.

Her shoulders tense before she lets out a frustrated breath. "He's the one who suggested it."

"Jesus," I mutter. Usually she's the one who calls time out. "What happened?"

She moves off the sofa and begins pacing. "He's being an asshole, Ashton. This isn't all my fault." I have to give her credit; she's self-aware enough to understand her contribution to their arguments. Most of the time.

I don't reply, but simply wait for her to continue.

She finally stops pacing. "He's always at work. *Always.* Nights, early mornings, weekends. And when he is home, he spends most of his time arguing with me. I can't take it anymore."

There's something off here. "None of this is unusual. What's *really* going on?"

Her eyes are everywhere but on me and her posture isn't as confident as usual. I take in the dark circles under her eyes that I missed noticing earlier. She bites her lip and when she speaks, her voice lacks the certainty it usually holds. "He's got a new assistant…"

I stand and move to her, placing my hands on her shoulders. "Aly, Malcolm adores you."

Her eyes find mine and I see so much doubt there that it hits me in the gut. *This* is not my sister. *Where the fuck has she gone?* "He used to adore me. I feel like we're strangers half the time these days. We're both so damn busy with work and the kids." She glances down for a moment before looking back up at me. Her voice cracks on her next words. "What if I've fucked it all up?"

I don't let her go. "How would you have fucked it all up?"

"I'm not who he married. And I don't think he likes the person I've become."

Lorelei clears her throat behind us. "Do you want me to go, Alessandra? So you two can talk this through."

Alessandra shakes her head. "No. We don't need to talk about this. I just need to get a good night's sleep and—"

I cut her off as I let her go. "No, what you need to do is talk this out. You're not going anywhere until we do that."

Her shoulders sag. "God, I should never have opened my mouth." She eyes Lorelei. "I don't want you to go, but I understand if you don't feel comfortable staying."

"I'll make tea." Lorelei makes her offer as I turn to face her.

"Thanks," I murmur. She's never been to my home before, but she leaves us without any further questions. Her take-charge attitude impresses me and I spend a moment watching her go, before turning back to Alessandra. "Are you seriously worried about his new assistant?"

She hesitates for a moment. "I trust him, Ashton, but at the same time, I'm not sure how strong we are anymore."

I nod at the sofa and once she takes a seat, I sit on the

coffee table in front of her. Resting my elbows on my legs, I lean forward and speak the only truth I know. "Aly, you've been married to Malcolm for nearly a decade, and you've been with him for longer than that. If anyone knows how difficult you can be, besides me, it's him. But that man loves you more than I've ever seen a man love a woman, and I hardly think he'd throw what you two have away for a quick fuck with an assistant."

Her eyes are wide as she takes that in. "Yes, but yo—"

I shake my head. "I wasn't finished." She closes her mouth and sits back a little, waiting for me to go on. "For a smart, accomplished woman, you have insecurities a mile wide. It's time you sorted through them and started to believe in yourself where Malcolm is concerned. He's going to grow tired of always having to prop you up."

She swallows hard and I'm certain tears aren't far away, but she manages to blink them away. "He doesn't always prop me up."

"Yes. He does. And you know it."

"God," she mutters, standing. "You are such a bastard. I came here for your support and you say this shit to me."

I watch her as she reaches for her bag, and I stand as she takes a few steps in the direction of the hallway. "Aly, you know it's true."

Spinning around, she glares at me. "No, what I know is that you never have my back where Malcolm is concerned. You've always sided with him when we've fought. I thought this time you might let me talk and listen to my side, but I was wrong. You never change, Ashton."

I grip her arm and halt her progress as she tries to leave. "There aren't sides in this. There's you and Malcolm—two people trying to make a marriage work, and all I'm interested in is helping you do that. I don't want to see you struggle in your marriage, and to do that you need to face the facts."

"And what are the facts?" Tension settles over us and it

would be easy for me to mistake it for anger, but I know that it's really fear.

"You're afraid to give yourself completely to Malcolm. You don't let him all the way in, Alessandra, and it's time you did. Because not letting him in is what's causing all these fights and doubts in your marriage."

She yanks her arm out of my grip. "You don't know what you're talking about. God, you haven't even been married or hardly had a real relationship, so how do you even get to say that stuff to me?"

"I get to say that stuff because I'm your brother and no one else says it to you. Everyone else in your life just panders to you, but what you really need to hear is what I just said."

"Yeah, well I've changed my mind. I don't want to stay here tonight." With that, she stalks out of my house, slamming the front door behind her.

Lorelei joins me in the living room after Alessandra leaves. I sigh as I take in the expression on her face. "If you're going to give me hell for what I just said, I don't want to hear it."

She shakes her head. "No, I'm not going to give you hell. You just said all that to her for two reasons, didn't you? Because you believe it to be true, and because you knew it would force her to go home. To her husband."

I snake my hand around her waist and pull her close. "You're a smart woman, Lorelei." I press my mouth to hers and kiss her, before adding, "I'm not waiting for tomorrow to fuck you."

A sexy smile settles on her face. "Those are the best words that have come out of your mouth tonight."

"No, the best words to come out of my mouth are these— take your clothes off."

17

LORELEI

A SHIVER RUNS THROUGH ME AT ASHTON'S WORDS and I suddenly feel shy in front of him. Weird, because the man stripped me last night and made me come. But the way he's looking at me now is making me self-conscious and all kinds of confused.

I move out of his hold and take a step back. "I'm not stripping for you in here. Jack could walk in at any moment."

"True."

He guides me out of the room and down the hallway to a flight of stairs that are encased in glass. Indicating for me to go first, he follows closely behind as I do my best to ignore the butterflies in my stomach.

Why am I so damn nervous?

It's not like I haven't slept with a man before. But there's something about Ashton that I've never experienced with a man, and right now it's crashing into me in a big way.

He's so dominant.

I'm beginning to think that Ashton might be the kind of man I could lose myself in, because if he doesn't give me space now to keep him at arm's length, he's sure as hell not going to give me space once I've handed him my heart. I'm not sure I can survive him if this relationship turns into something that consumes me like that.

We enter what I presume is his bedroom, and as he closes the door behind us, I turn and face him. "This room is stunning."

Ashton has expensive taste. Floor-to-ceiling windows fill one wall of his room, the view a jaw-dropping panorama of Sydney. The city lights up his space in a beautiful wash of colour, highlighting the opulence that even his minimalist style can't hide. Only a few pieces of furniture occupy the room—a bed that I'm pretty sure is larger than a king, bedside tables, and a leather armchair—with a couple of lamps scattered around. He has a preference for the rich tones of brown; various shades of the colour are splashed throughout. But it's the large pieces of art adorning the walls and the textured grey paint that really make this room.

He doesn't stop or acknowledge what I've said, but rather keeps moving towards me. The hard set of his jaw and shoulders, coupled with his stride causes my heart to beat faster.

I swallow hard.

I'm not sure I can do this.

I need more time to figure this out.

I'm not ready for this man.

"Why are your clothes still on?" His words are a demand that match the flare of command in his eyes.

My mouth is so dry.

I need water.

Oh, God, I need a lot of things. Number one is to get my head together.

When I don't reply, he growls, "Lorelei. Clothes off. Now."

"I'm not ready," I blurt out and instantly feel the flush of embarrassment stain my cheeks. He's going to think I'm some naïve little woman now. *The last thing I want Ashton Scott to think of me.*

"Yes, you are." My words don't even slow him. He just keeps on coming. "It would seem, though, that you need some encouragement."

"Ashton, I'm more than ready for sex, but—"

Before I can stop him, he reaches his arms around me and unzips my dress. As he slides it down, he says, "I told you I would fuck any remaining hesitation out of you, and that's what I intend to do." My dress drops to the floor. "So, stop talking and start doing what I say."

I stare at him as I make a mental note to stop wearing dresses with zips when I'm with him. His eyes meet mine and his hands move to undo my bra. When my breasts are bare, I draw a sharp breath. Maybe it's the way Ashton's attention remains fixed on my face. Where any other man I've ever been with would be moving this forward, he's finally stopped and appears to be waiting. For what, I'm not sure.

He looks so intent.

So driven to make this happen.

Without shifting his eyes from mine, he runs two fingers down the front of my panties. His thumb rubs my clit through the silky fabric and my back arches.

It feels so good.

I can do this.

I won't allow him to consume me.

Pushing my reservations away, I reach for his tie. Once I've removed it, I slowly unbutton his shirt, revealing chiselled muscles unlike any I've ever seen.

His lips claim mine in a searing kiss as he steps closer, pressing his hard body up against mine. Strong arms circle me before he takes hold of my ass and pulls me in close.

His lips leave mine before he demands, "Do we have a problem?"

I frown. "With what?"

His intense eyes bore into mine. "With me burning my name into your memory forever."

"We never had a problem with that, Ashton."

His eyes continue to search mine for a few moments before raking over my body. He lets me go and removes his suit jacket before moving to the armchair in the corner of the room and leaving it there. He then finishes unbuttoning his shirt so he can deposit it on the chair also. When he stands in front of me again, his belt is undone.

I reach for his zip and our hands meet. His skin scorches mine and I lick my lips in anticipation. This man turns me on more than any man ever has.

I'm in over my head here.

His hand wraps around mine and he helps me push his zip down. A few moments later, we've shed every last barrier between his body and mine, and I sweep my gaze over his muscles. Ashton must spend hours working out because his body is a work of art.

"Lorelei." His deep voice snaps me out of my inspection and I meet his gaze again. Such a shame, because I was drooling over his cock. *His larger-than-I've-ever-had cock.* While I imagine all the things he could do to me with it, he surprises me by wrapping his arms around my body, picking me up and walking me backwards.

He's caught me completely off guard and I scramble to hold on tight. My back hits the wall and without giving me even a second to prepare, his mouth crashes down onto mine.

Any last lingering thoughts about not being ready for him are forgotten. Ashton has asserted his power over me and I'm helpless to fight him.

Tonight, I'm his.

As his mouth dominates me, he reaches down between

us to slide his finger into my pussy. Dragging his mouth from mine, he growls, "You are more than ready for me, Lorelei." Pressing his mouth to my ear as he pushes his finger inside me, he continues, "But just so there's no left-over doubts, I'm going to finger-fuck you until you're screaming for my cock."

His dirty words cause my core to clench.

While I love what his fingers are doing to me, I *need* his dick inside me already.

My hands glide up his neck so I can grip his hair. "It's not your cock I'm unsure of, Ashton. It's *you*."

He reaches deep inside me while his eyes remain firmly on mine. "I know." He adds another finger. "I'm going to show you there's nothing to be unsure of."

I arch my back, pressing myself against him and tighten my hold as he builds my pleasure. Each second he's in me is a sublime promise of what's to come.

We watch each other while he fucks me with his fingers.

No kissing.

No talking.

It's the most erotic experience I've ever had. The sounds of our breathing only intensify this feeling. I'm almost panting and Ashton's breaths are coming harder.

When my orgasm hits, I squeeze my fingers tighter in his hair and moan a bunch of words I don't even recognise myself. The orgasm takes over, rendering me useless. It's a burst of light and emotion and intense bliss that I never want to end.

Ashton's lips find mine and he kisses me hard before a deep growl cuts through my thoughts. "Watching you come is something I need to do more of."

I blink, trying to catch my breath and my thoughts. "We could make that happen."

He trails kisses up my neck. The way his teeth graze my

skin is hot; I want more of that. When he reaches my ear, he rasps, "I'm going to make it happen right now."

Depositing me on the floor, he strides to his bedside table and searches the top drawer. After he locates what he's after, he returns to me, condom in hand.

Ripping the foil packet open, he takes hold of his cock and rolls the condom on. Then his eyes settle on mine again as he reaches an arm around my waist, pulling me close while at the same time, kicking my feet apart. Bending his knees slightly, he pushes his dick up against my entrance. He doesn't enter me fully, just teases me by pushing in and then out, over and over until I'm a hot mess of desire.

"Ashton," I moan, gripping his biceps. "Just fuck me already."

Heat glazes his eyes. "I see you're practicing your dirty talk."

"I want to be practicing a lot more than that."

He thrusts up into me on a groan. "Fuck."

Oh, God, I've died and gone to heaven.

Seriously.

His cock fills me and I loop my hands around his neck while he holds my ass. He pulls out and when he pushes into me again, he grips me harder, pulling me close at the same time. All while keeping his eyes firmly on mine.

He then begins the dance of sex, and our bodies move together in a perfect rhythm of slow, sensual thrusting. And once again, Ashton shows me just how erotic this can be. Everything about him, from the way he watches me, to how he takes charge, to the way his powerful body moves effort-lessly is sexual. The man commands every second of my attention, and in return gives me sex I won't ever forget.

He was right when he said he was going to burn his name into my memory.

His rhythm picks up and he enters me with more force.

The look of determination in his eyes heightens my arousal, and I dig my nails into his skin as I reach desperately for my release.

Our slow dance turns into a rough chase of pleasure and Ashton switches it up when he pulls out of me and spins me around. Taking hold of my hips, he orders, "Hands on the floor." I do as he says without hesitation. I've never had sex this way, but I'm pretty sure that if Ashton is demanding it, it's going to be good.

He holds my waist and enters me in one quick motion.

Oh.

God.

He's so deep.

And it's so damn good.

Before I can catch my breath, he pulls out and thrusts deep again. This isn't going to take long. With this angle, each thrust causes the delicious friction I need.

And then he blows my damn mind.

Keeping one hand firmly around my waist while he continues to thrust in and out, he reaches his other hand around so he can rub my clit.

Beautiful circles of bliss.

Around and around.

Thrusting in and out.

Over and over.

Ashton delivers me straight into his own little piece of nirvana, and all I can do is squeeze my eyes shut and pant in ecstasy.

My mind explodes.

It's like a glorious sunset, colours colliding behind my eyes, painting a masterpiece of pleasure.

I'm adrift, floating along that rush of joy.

And then he grips me harder and climaxes, and we're joined in our pleasure.

I lose track of time.

I don't know how long we stay connected like that. It's not until Ashton pulls out and turns me to face him that I gather myself again. Blinking, I find him staring down at me. "That was amazing." My voice sounds all breathy, so unlike me.

His expression is still serious.

Intense.

"That was just the beginning, Lorelei. You won't be leaving this room tonight." He's growly, forceful.

Sliding both arms around him, I lean against his body. I'm still floaty and breathy. *Thoroughly fucked.* "I don't want to leave this room tonight."

He removes my arms from around him. "I want you on my bed. On your back."

My eyes widen. "I think I need a breather, Ashton."

He stares down at me. "On my bed. Now."

His words are an order and this time I obey.

I'm figuring out pretty fast that when Ashton Scott demands something of you in the bedroom, you don't argue. I'm also figuring out that I like relinquishing control to him here.

18

ASHTON

I SHAKE MARC BRENTLEY'S HAND. "I'LL BE in touch."

He nods. "Are you free on Thursday night? We're holding our annual charity gala. I'd like you to be there."

"I'll make it happen."

"Good."

As he leaves my office, my mind wanders to his proposal. It was a good one, and I'm almost certain we'll do business together.

"He looked happy." I glance up to find Jessica entering the office.

"He should be."

"You think you'll say yes to him?"

"I'd say so from what I've seen today, but we'll do the research and see if it pans out." Marc's group is heading a multi-million dollar development in the heart of Sydney.

"I heard it would be the tallest building in Sydney if it goes ahead. Is that true?"

"It is." I hand her the documents he left with me. "Can you get the ball rolling on this?" Jessica will begin the research, and after she presents me with her findings, I'll finalise it. In the years we've worked together, I've trained her to know what to look for. And she's damn good at her job.

"I've already started." Of course she has.

I check my watch. The meeting with Marc ran over, so I'm more than ready to get out of here. Giving Jessica my attention again, I ask, "Anything urgent come up this morning?"

"Alessandra called and asked for you to phone her back. And your new real estate agent returned your call from yesterday."

I reach for my phone and car keys. "Did you finalise my plans for today?"

"I did." She grabs my phone off me and presses the button to light up the screen and check the time. "Lorelei will be receiving her first delivery right about now."

I take the phone when she hands it back. "Call me only if absolutely necessary."

"And you still want me to work from your place today so I can be with Jack?"

"Yes."

"What about tomorrow? How long do you envision this gig will last?"

"Let's play it by ear. I'll assess his frame of mind tonight and let you know. We might need to work from home tomorrow, too."

"You do know that at some point you're going to have to ease up on this, don't you? You can't spend every minute of your life watching him, Ashton."

I purse my lips. "I'm going to be there for him as long as he needs it, Jessica."

"Yes, but—"

"No buts. Don't argue with me on this because you won't win."

She sighs. "No one ever wins against you."

My phone rings, interrupting us. I glance at it to find Alessandra's name flashing on the screen. "I need to take this. Was there anything else?"

"No, you go. And don't worry, I'll take care of Jack."

"I was never worried, Jessica. As much as you say you disagree with me, we both know you'd be there for him at any time of the day."

She lifts her chin in the direction of the door. "Go."

I place my phone to my ear as I head out of the office. "Aly. I see you're still talking to me."

"Only just."

"What's up?"

"I wouldn't be calling unless this was important." She pauses and I wait for her to continue, intrigued as to what would cause my sister to ask for help that she clearly doesn't want to ask for. "I need a babysitter tonight. Are you free?"

I reach the lift and stab at the button. "I am."

"Oh, thank God."

"What's going on? You sound stressed."

"That's because I bloody am stressed." She blows out a breath. "Malcolm and I are booked in for marriage counselling tonight."

"Good."

"What do you mean, good?" she shrieks. "We had another huge fight after I left your place last night and he told me that if we don't get counselling, he'll be considering his options."

I ride the lift alone down to the car park. "Have you two discussed counselling before?"

"He brings it up every now and then."

"But you refuse?"

"Of course I bloody refuse. Talking stuff out with him only causes us to fight more. This is the last thing I want to be doing." Her fear is laced through her words. My sister would be one of the only women I know who doesn't want to talk about this kind of stuff.

"So you'd rather continue on, not knowing what he's feeling? That makes no sense, Aly."

She's quiet and I have to prod her. "Aly?"

"I'm honestly scared where this will end up, Ashton. I think Malcolm wants to leave me."

The lift reaches my destination and I exit it to head towards my car. "No, if he wanted to leave you, he would have done that. When a man wants to talk, he wants to stay and fix it. What time's your appointment?"

"It's at seven. Can I drop the kids off at about six?"

"I'll make sure I'm home by then. And Aly?"

"What?"

"He loves you. Remember that."

"It's kind of hard at the moment when all I can think of is the way he looked at me last night—"

"No. Forget that. People say and do things they don't necessarily mean when they're angry. Think about the fact he cares enough to want to do this with you. If he didn't love you, he wouldn't bother."

She's silent for a beat. "I'm sorry I was a bitch to you last night."

I unlock the car and slide into the driver seat. "Were you? I don't recall you being any different to usual."

"Smart-ass," she mutters.

"I'll see you tonight."

I end the call and start the car.

Finally.

Lorelei is waiting for me less than fifteen minutes away and my cock is hard as hell thinking about her.

I call her and she answers on the third ring. "Ashton."

"I'll be there in about fifteen minutes. Did you receive the delivery?"

"Yes. I'm staring at it. What exactly do you want me to do with it all?"

"I want you to choose your favourite. Another delivery is about to arrive. You can open it but then put it aside for me." I adjust my pants as my dick pushes against them.

"Okay." I can tell by the way her voice drifts off that she's already deep in thought about those deliveries.

"I want you to get yourself ready for me, Lorelei."

"What? As in, you want me to… ummm—"

Fuck.

I love her inhibition.

I'm going to fuck that out of her.

"As in I want you to touch yourself and get that tight pussy wet for me."

She sucks in a breath.

I grip the steering wheel hard.

When she doesn't reply, I growl, "Lorelei, I want your fingers inside you for the next fifteen minutes so that your pussy is dripping for me when I get there. Are we clear or do I need to stay on the phone and direct you?"

"We're clear. And Ashton?"

"Yes?"

"My fingers are already inside me."

Fuck.

19

LORELEI

I OPEN THE DOOR OF THE HOTEL ROOM AND WAIT silently for Ashton's response. He asked me to get myself ready, so I did.

His eyes flare with heat as they roam my body. "You surprise me," he says when he meets my gaze again.

I tilt my head to the side. "You thought I'd choose something a little less revealing, didn't you?"

Stepping inside the hotel room he sent me to this morning, he closes the door and runs his finger along the top of the black crotchless lace thong I'm wearing. Besides the sheer thigh-high stockings attached to it with suspender straps, and heels, it's the *only* thing I'm wearing. He nods in response to my question. "I certainly didn't imagine you'd choose this out of everything I had delivered."

Ashton's first delivery had consisted of an assortment of lingerie. He told me to choose my favourite, but I struggled to pick between them all. The man has exquisite taste and I fell in love with each item. So I decided to go with what I thought would be *his* favourite.

"This one allows you easy access." I hold his gaze while I lick my bottom lip and work myself up to saying what I want to say to him. My heart beats faster as the words fall out of my mouth. "It's time for your fingers to be where mine were a minute ago."

He loosens his tie with one hand while his other one glides over my hip and around to my ass. "How wet are you?"

My heart practically bangs in my chest as my pussy clenches. Having no experience with dirty talk like this, I'm a contradictory mix of turned on and self-conscious. I step closer to him and run my hand down his chest. "So wet that you could easily slide more than one finger inside me."

His face angles down so he can press his mouth against my ear. "Let's test that."

He turns the heat up when he moves his hand from my ass and brings it around to my front so he can push two fingers inside me.

I bite my lip and suck in a breath while placing one hand on his shoulder to steady myself.

His eyes meet mine again as he strokes my G spot. "Did my other package arrive?"

"Yes."

"And you opened it?"

"I did."

He reaches deeper inside me. "Did you go through the box?"

I steady myself against him with both hands on his shoulders because I'm not sure I'll be able to stand much longer with the pleasure he's giving me.

When I don't answer him straight away, he pushes me. "Lorelei." The dominance in his tone is enough to get me off. Add to it what he's doing with his fingers and the images flashing through my mind of what's in the box, and an orgasm teases me.

I grip his shoulders hard and moan louder than I've ever moaned. Ashton brings that side out of me. He makes me feel pleasure in a way I wish I had before. Because this kind of pleasure is the kind a woman would beg a man for.

"I went through the box," I finally answer him.

He slides his fingers out of me and I instantly miss them. "Did you see something you liked?"

Letting go of his shoulders, I move my hand down to the top button of his shirt and undo it. "There were so many things in that box I liked, Ashton." I undo his second button. "The question is, which one are you going to use first?" The third and fourth buttons pop open before he places his hand over mine and stops me.

His mouth crashes down onto mine and a shudder runs through me at the force with which he kisses me. When he scoops me up into his arms and stalks into the bedroom, I quickly loop my hands around his neck and hold on while need burns in my veins.

God, how I want this man.

I was stupid to think I could slow him down last night. Ashton is not a man to be slowed. And regardless of where this ends up between us, I'm ready to take a chance.

After he deposits me on the floor in the bedroom, he sits on the edge of the bed. Circling his arm around my body, he pulls me between his legs. Pressing his lips to my bare stomach, he then trails kisses down my body while circling his finger inside the entrance to my pussy.

Around and around.

It's divine.

But I want more.

I want his fingers all the way inside me.

He teases me by pushing in a little deeper and then licking along my slit. But right when I think he'll give me more, he lifts his face to look up at me. "Was there anything in the box you've never used before?"

I grip his hair. "Seriously, you're going to stop what you're doing to have a conversation about *that*?"

He moves swiftly, pulling me to straddle him. His intense eyes demand my complete attention. "I'll stop everything until you tell me what I want to know."

My pulse races.

God, I love this side of him.

A little too much.

I relax in his hold. "I've never used most of the things in that box."

Ashton is good at concealing his thoughts and emotions, but I catch the flare of approval in his eyes at my confession. I'm a little shy to admit I don't have much experience with sex toys, but he appears to like that fact.

He grasps my hair and angles my head back to expose my throat. He then dips his face and licks a line from my collarbone up the side of my neck before sucking my skin and nipping at it with his teeth.

When he's finished with my neck, he meets my gaze again. "I'm going to explore every inch of your skin today, but first I need to fuck you."

Finally.

I press my body against his. "I'm down with that."

He pulls my hair. Rougher. "It's not going to be slow, Lorelei," he growls and I hear the need in his voice. It matches my own.

I dig my nails into his back. "Like I said, I'm good with that."

A moment later, after he quickly rolls a condom on, I'm on my hands and knees on the bed, and he thrusts his cock inside me from behind. He grips my hips and increases his pace until he's slamming into me hard and fast.

I was so damn wet and ready for him that it doesn't take me long to orgasm. I ride the pleasure while he chases his own orgasm, and as promised, it doesn't take long before he thrusts in one last time on a deeply satisfied roar.

Dropping my head, I try to catch my breath and refocus. When he pulls out and leaves the bed, I collapse onto my stomach. Rolling onto my side, I watch as his ass disappears into the bathroom.

I love his ass.

I want to spend hours with that ass.

He re-enters the room, and I run my gaze over his body as he walks towards me. Ashton is built with muscles that scream power and strength. I watch, transfixed, as those muscles flex when he sits on the edge of the bed.

"Are you ready?' he asks, confusing me.

I drag my eyes from his chest. "For what?"

His eyes darken. "To play."

I've died and gone to heaven.

Surely.

I crawl into his lap and lace my arms around his neck. "I'm pretty sure that playing with you is something I would never say no to. Not after you convinced me last night."

He holds up a silk scarf. "I'm going to put this on you and then I want you to lie on the bed on your back."

I'm confused again, wondering where he got the scarf. Staring at it, I ask, "Where did you get that?"

He ignores my question for a moment while he secures the scarf over my eyes. Once it's in place, and I can't see anything but darkness, he murmurs against my ear, "I always come prepared, Lorelei. You will soon understand that about me."

Goodness, if I thought I'd died and gone to heaven a moment ago, I was seriously mistaken. His warm breath and his touch collide with my temporary blindness, sending a new wave of anticipation through my entire body. Every single nerve ending is buzzing with want for him.

The bed shifts as he stands. I lie back and wait for his next move. When he does nothing, I say, "Ashton?"

He doesn't respond and I wonder where in the room he is. Not being able to see during sex is something I've never experienced, and I have to admit it's hot not knowing what will happen next.

I slow down my breathing in an attempt to hear him, but I can't make out his breathing.

Maybe he's left the room.

My toes curl at the thought of what he's doing. The box of toys is on the counter in the kitchen. I imagine he's looking for something in there.

All thoughts of what he's doing are soon forgotten when ice hits my stomach. My back arches up and I squeal out his name, unprepared for the cold sensation on my skin.

He places a hand on my stomach and holds me in place while he runs the ice over me.

Exploring every inch of my skin.

The bed dips as he positions himself on it between my legs. A moment later, his tongue circles my clit and I arch up again.

"Ashton...." His name escapes my lips on a moan. It's the only word I get out, though, because my brain can hardly process a thought.

He doesn't reply, just simply continues to circle my clit with his tongue and run ice over my stomach and hips.

And then he stops everything.

I try to get my breathing under control, but I only manage to draw one ragged breath in before his mouth presses to my clit again.

Oh. God.

My arms fling out to the side and I grip the sheets.

He sucked the ice cube before he went down on me. My attempt to control my breathing flies out the window as I hold my breath.

I can't.

It's too much.

Way too much.

"Breathe, Lorelei." His deep voice cuts through my thoughts.

I take a deep breath. "Are you trying to make me come fast? Because I'm pretty sure that's what is about to happen."

I might be unable to see him, but I can feel him as his body moves over mine. My mouth is quick to respond when he kisses me. His tongue sweeps over my lips before pushing inside. He deepens the kiss, dominating me completely; totally wiping away any ability I have left to process what's happening.

"You won't come fast. I'm going to take you close, over and over, until you're begging me to fuck you."

Before I can respond, he moves back down my body to lick my clit again. And then he flips me onto my stomach. His strong hands make their way up my back to massage my shoulders as he positions his legs either side of me.

Cold liquid hits my back, and my breathing slows again as he massages the oil into my shoulders and back. His hands move slowly, gradually making their way down towards my ass.

His movements are deliberate and designed to drag me closer to the edge of release. Every so often he slides his hands over my butt or down and around my side to massage my breasts. But it's the moments when his fingers glide through my pussy that really light me up.

By the time he's finished the massage, every inch of my body thrums with need. When he flips me onto my back and starts his erotic massage on my front, I want to beg him to stop and just fuck me. But I don't. Instead, I reach for him, trying to find his face so I can pull him close and kiss him.

He avoids my hands and breaks our silence. "Tell me what you want me to do to you."

"I want you to kiss me."

"No. Tell me where you want my fingers," he demands on a growl.

"I want them all over me, Ashton."

His warm breath hits my ear. "If you could only choose one place, what would that be?"

My pussy clenches. *There*. I reach for his hand. "Let me show you."

He grabs hold of my hand instead. "No," he orders. *"Tell* me. I want to hear you say it."

Oh for the love of God. "I want your fingers inside me."

"And?"

And? "Deep inside me." Heat flames my cheeks and I pray it isn't visible to him.

He slides a finger inside me slowly. "Do you want me to go slow or fast? Tell me exactly how you want me to touch you, Lorelei."

Fuck it. If he wants me to talk dirty to him, I will. "I want you to find my G spot and stroke me there. Slow to start with and then I want you to go faster until you make me come."

At my request, Ashton moves so fast I hardly have time to realise what's happening. Flipping me onto my stomach again, he positions himself on top of me and rubs his cock over my ass while pinning my hands to the bed above my head. He pushes my legs apart to give his cock access to my pussy. "Do you want this?" he demands as he slides through my wetness.

I moan into the mattress. "Yes." It comes out like a whimper, revealing just how desperately I want that.

"You're going to have to work for it. And that means I want you to tell me your dirtiest fantasy."

Heat floods my face again, and I'm relieved he can't see it because I'm sure I couldn't hide my embarrassment.

When I don't reply, he pushes his cock inside. Just the head, but it's enough to make me want more.

"I fantasise about being a stripper," I blurt out.

He stills, his cock resting against my slit. "And what else?"

"That's it."

"No. Everyone has more than one fantasy." His cock enters me again and he teases me once more by only pushing in a little before pulling back out. He then flips me onto my back and removes the scarf.

Once my eyes adjust to the light, I reach for his dick but he's too quick and stops me. Bending, he takes one of my nipples into his mouth and sucks. He then begins a maddening assault on my pussy by pushing in and then out with his cock. Far enough to drive me wild, but not far enough to get me off.

I take hold of his neck and drag his mouth to mine. After I kiss him hard, I hold his gaze and say, "I want to fuck you in public. I want everyone to watch as I ride your cock and make you come harder than you ever have in your entire life. *That's* my real fantasy."

Heat flares in his eyes and his lips crash down onto mine.

His kiss is savage.

Demanding.

Claiming.

A growl rips from his chest as he ends the kiss and moves off the bed. "Stay there. I'll be back," he orders before leaving the room.

It doesn't take him long to return and when he does, he's wearing a condom and watching me like he wants to eat me.

Moving between my legs, he places his hands on the bed either side of me. "Legs over my shoulders," he orders, his gaze focused on mine. There's a determined glint in Ashton's eyes that sends a ripple of pleasure through me.

I grip his arms and do as he says right before he thrusts inside. He does this so hard that I slide up the bed.

"Fuck," he roars as he pulls out.

I feel the same way.

Ashton is a man who knows what he's doing. I'm not sure whether it's his confidence, his bossiness or his skills that turns me on more. All I know is I can't get enough. And I can't get it as fast as I want it.

He slams into me again.

Deep.

So fucking deep and hard that I feel like he's going to slam right through me.

I shift my arms so my hands lock around his neck. "Don't stop," I beg. "Fuck me so hard I can't walk out of here."

"Jesus, you're perfecting that dirty talk," he rasps.

"Well, I figured I have to. You seem to like it."

He stares down at me as he pushes me closer and closer to another orgasm. His muscles flex as he holds his powerful body over mine, giving me what I asked for—the kind of sex a girl doesn't recover from fast.

I grip him harder when his pace picks up even more. Our bodies move in perfect rhythm together until my orgasm finally tears through me.

Takes me high.

So high.

And then I'm gliding.

The pleasure wraps itself around me.

All I know is that bliss.

It shatters me.

I come completely apart in Ashton's arms.

Time stands still.

When I eventually come to, he's stopped moving, his cock still fills me, and his head has dropped to my shoulder.

I slide my hands across his shoulders and down his arms. Ashton has the biggest arms I've ever seen on a man and I take a moment to touch them. My mind is still righting itself after that orgasm just wiped all sense from me, and I linger in this moment for a beat.

Just him and me.

He lifts his head and finds my gaze. I'm not sure what I see in his eyes, but he watches me with an expression I haven't seen from him yet.

Catching my lips, he kisses me. "For the record, I *do* like your dirty talk. I'd planned hours of exploring your body before I fucked you again, but you pushed me over the edge faster than I thought you would." He drops his gaze to my lips. "This mouth is full of surprises."

I trail my fingers over his lips. "You like surprises?"

"No, I don't, but it seems you have a way of challenging everything I know and turning it on its ass."

I have no idea what he means by that, but I don't have the energy for a deep conversation right now, so I simply smile up at him. "I like surprises. Just so you know."

He pulls out of me and pushes himself off the bed. "I'll keep that in mind," he says before leaving the room.

I roll onto my side and wait for him to return. My entire body is worn out and sleep beckons, but I'm determined not to fall asleep.

I came here to spend the whole day with Ashton; there's no way I'm spending any of it sleeping.

20

ASHTON

HOLDING THE PHONE AGAINST MY EAR, I WATCH Lorelei sleep. She passed out after I fucked her the second time and she hasn't woken up since. That was a couple of hours ago. I'd been just about to wake her up when Jessica phoned me with an urgent issue I needed to take care of. So I let her sleep.

"You're heading into the office now?" Jessica asks over the phone.

"Yes, I need to sort this out before it escalates." It's a million-dollar-at-least problem if I don't fix it today so I have no other choice.

"Is Lorelei pissed?"

"I doubt it."

"You haven't told her you're leaving yet?"

"I haven't spoken to her for a couple of hours."

"Fuck," she mutters. "You wore her out, didn't you?"

"You could say that."

"I am so jealous of you right now."

"You—"

"Nuh, uh… stop talking. I haven't been laid in weeks so you need to shut the hell up about your sex life."

"You were the one who brought it up." Lorelei stirs, blinking up at me. "I have to go, Jessica. Can you email me the information I need for when I get back to the office?"

"Will do. And just to keep you in the loop, Jack's spent most of the day in your gym. I have no idea what he's doing down there, but at least he's not drinking."

We end the call and I take a seat on the edge of the bed.

Lorelei frowns. "Why are you dressed? And how long did I sleep for?"

Fuck, she's beautiful when she's just woken up.

"You slept for a couple of hours."

"Why didn't you wake me?"

"I've had some problems at work to take care of while you slept."

"And now you have to go to work?"

I wait for her to complain, but she doesn't. Instead, she surprises me once more by not giving me hell about it. She's so unlike the women I've dated in the past who took issue with the number of hours I chose to work.

I nod. "Yes."

She sits up and her arms circle my neck. A sexy smile spreads across her face. "I think you should leave your toys behind so I can play with them. We didn't get to test any of them out."

"They're not mine. I bought them for you." I steal a hungry kiss from her before adding. "I'll call you later for an update."

"An update on what I tried out?"

"No, an update on how wet you are."

I stand before I lose the shred of control I have left. Lorelei has me so damn hard for her that I'm concerned I'll fuck up the business deal I need to fix. This is new territory for me and I'm not comfortable with it.

However, as much as I don't want to be in this predicament, the only thought in my mind as I exit the hotel room is how soon I can have her under me again.

My thoughts drift to Lorelei as I listen to my sister later that night. It's been a few hours since I've spoken to Lorelei. She was on her way out to dinner with a friend after leaving the hotel and promised to call me when she got home.

"Ashton, are you even listening to me?"

I turn my attention back to Alessandra and take a swig of my Scotch. "What was the outcome of the session?" She's just arrived back to collect the kids after the counselling session with Malcolm. I'm surprised he isn't here with her.

She exhales a long breath. "Well, we ended up having another huge fight afterwards, and he told me to get in my car and pick up the kids while he calmed down."

"Did the session go okay, though?"

"It was bloody awful. I hated every fucking minute of it. And I think he did too."

I lean forward and rest my elbows on my thighs. "I imagine that's how this is going to go for a while, Aly. At least while you two get all the shit out into the open."

"I know! And it's why I didn't want to do it. What if he decides he hates me and can't live with me?"

"How could anyone decide that, Alessandra?" Jack asks as he enters the living room and sits next to me on the sofa.

Aly rolls her eyes. "You only say that because you've had a crush on me your whole life, Jack. This is my husband we're talking about. The man who shares a house with me and puts up with all my shit. There're no rose-coloured glasses there."

Jack chuckles and I drink some more Scotch. "It's all true. I have had a crush on you for that long. Maybe if Malcolm leaves you, I could finally have a shot."

My phone buzzes with a text message and I leave them to their conversation so I can check it.

Jessica: Your father is doing the rounds on Willow Street trying to buy up property.

Me: Where did you hear this?

Jessica: I just had drinks with your new real estate agent, Sian. It only took me three drinks and some sweet talk to get it out of her.

Me: Leave it with me.

Jessica: Oh, I was planning to. I've got better things to do now. You're not the only one who's getting lucky today.

"Was that Lorelei?" Jack asks.

I glance at him before directing my attention to Alessandra. "No, it was Jessica who has informed me that Dad is trying to buy up properties on Willow Street. What do you know about this?"

She sighs. "God, Ashton, let it go. I keep telling you this. It's not good for your mental health."

My shoulders tense. "You knew about this?"

"I heard rumours, yes, but I haven't spoken to him about it yet."

I push up off the sofa. "Fuck, Aly. You knew I wanted to be kept up-to-date with this."

She stands too and glares at me. "I did. And I also know that you should stay well clear of anything he's got going on. You two are toxic when you get mixed up in this stuff."

My phone rings and I stab at it without checking caller ID. Holding Alessandra's gaze, I bark, "Yes?"

There's a pause before Lorelei's voice sounds. "Have I done something to piss you off?"

I rake my fingers through my hair. "No, I thought you were Jessica."

"And you answer your phone like that to your assistant?" She sounds less than impressed with me.

"No. You caught me in a bad moment."

"What's going on?"

"It's nothing. Are you home?"

"Ashton, it's hardly nothing. You practically bit my head off just now."

Forcing out a harsh breath, I say, "I just discovered something about my father that irritated me."

"Oh, God, your father. He came to see me."

I frown. "When?"

"Last week."

"And you're just telling me now?" I snap, instantly regretting it, but unable to stop myself. My father always brings out the worst in me.

"I didn't realise it was that important. But if it's that important to you to know, he offered me three million dollars for my property."

I still. That amount is about a million more than it's worth and in my experience, people don't turn down money that comes that easily. "Are you going to accept his offer?"

She doesn't reply.

"Lorelei," I demand, "are you going to accept it?"

"You know what, Ashton? I'll tell you what I told him. *And* what I told you when you wanted to buy it. Not everything is for sale."

The line goes dead as she ends the call.

"Fuck," I mutter as I stab at the phone to dial Jessica.

She answers almost straight away. "This better be important, Ashton. I was just about to go dow—"

"Find out everything you can from Sian tonight, and then first thing tomorrow, I want an estimate of how much each property on Willow Street is worth. And I want an appointment set up with my father."

"Done. Now can you please leave me in pussy heaven?"

I end the call and throw my phone down on the coffee table.

Alessandra stares at me. "What are you doing?"

I stare back at her. "I'm buying up Willow Street. No fucking way is he getting his hands on that street."

Her eyes widen. "Oh, God. This is not a battle you want to fight with him, Ashton."

"This"—I stab in the air at her—"is not a fight he should have waged. He fucking knows what it means to me. I won't allow him to have it."

My phone buzzes with another text and I snatch it up off the coffee table.

Lorelei: I think we made a mistake. I'm going to send these toys back to you.

I exit the living room as I phone her, wanting privacy for this call.

"Ashton, I don't want—"

"Lorelei, you want me. You can't deny it."

"I might want your body, but I forgot that I don't like the way you do business. And that's a huge part of you, so I think we should just stop this now before it goes any further. We're just too different to be able to make anything work between us."

"Bullshit. You told me last night you weren't ready for me and I knew what that meant, but I also know you just need some time. And now you're using this as an excuse to pull away."

"That's not true."

"Yes, it is. And I'm not taking no for an answer."

"Well, you're just going to have to for once in your life, because I'm not saying yes to you."

"I'm coming over."

"No, you're not."

"I'll see you in twenty." I end the call before she can argue with me anymore and stalk back into the living room.

"I have to head out. Are you good to get the kids into the car?" I ask Alessandra.

"You go," Jack says. "I'll make sure Aly's okay."

"Thanks."

As I'm leaving, Alessandra yells out, "I'm calling you tomorrow morning to try to talk some sense into you."

I ignore her, my thoughts completely on Lorelei.

There's no way I'm letting her walk away from this. As much as she thinks she can say no, it's not a word anyone ever says to me.

21

LORELEI

FIFTEEN MINUTES AFTER HE HUNG UP ON ME, Ashton bangs on my front door. The man is infuriating. I told him not to come over for a good reason, and he just barges right on over. I know if I let him in that door, he'll convince me to change my mind. And goddam it, I don't want to change my mind. He may have given me the best sex I've ever had, but he's too much in every other way. My heart isn't ready for what I know he'll demand.

He bangs harder. "Lorelei, open the door."

I give in, expecting him to stride through the door, but he doesn't. Instead, he stays where he is and watches me, waiting. It unnerves me. Just being in his presence is enough to do that, but the way his eyes hold me captive, and the way his body screams desire completely messes with my thinking.

Not to mention the fact my body remembers every inch of his from earlier today.

Pointing my finger at him, I say, "Stop that!"

His brows lift. "I haven't done a thing yet."

His deep voice stirs butterflies in my stomach. *Damn you, Ashton Scott.* I wave my finger in the air. "Yes, you have. You came over here when I told you not to and now you're just standing there staring at me...."

His lips twitch. "Staring at you isn't doing anything."

"Well, you're talking to me, too. So just stop it all, turn around and go home. We had fun and now it's ove—"

With one purposeful step, he enters my home and invades my personal space. His arm easily slides around my waist, pulling me hard against his body. "It is so far from over, Lorelei. I know that, and as much as you're trying to convince yourself otherwise, you know it, too."

My heart races so fast I can feel it all over my skin. My core is begging for him. *Traitor.*

He holds me tighter and forces his way further into my home while closing the door behind him. Once the door's closed, he turns me and backs me up against it. Pressing his erection into me, he growls, "Tell me you don't want this and I'll leave."

My hands go to his chest and I attempt to push against him, but my effort is weak at best. I open my mouth to reply, not even sure what I'm about to say. When no words come, I snap my mouth shut.

His eyes search mine. "I thought so."

A second later his mouth crashes down onto mine. The traitor that it is, my body responds without hesitation. My arms circle him and my hips rock against him while my lips show him just how much I want this.

No, no, no.

Unwrapping my arms from around him, I push on his chest. Breathless, I manage to get out, "I don't... I can't.... You need to go." I'm scattered and still fighting to think straight, but I need to end this.

"Why?"

I blink, staring up at him. Again, he didn't do what I

expected. I assumed he would continue to try and force his way in, but he's not. And that only bewilders me more.

"I told you on the phone, we're too different for this to go anywhere."

"Leaving aside the fact I don't agree, why do we have to know where it will go before we begin?"

"Because I like to have a plan and know where I'm going."

"Bullshit."

My eyes widen and angry heat flushes my skin. "You've said that to me twice tonight, Ashton. I won't put up with it again."

"Someone has to say it to you. I suspect not many get the chance to challenge you."

I fold my arms across my chest. "And what does that mean?"

"It means you run hot and cold, and I can see that you close yourself off at the first sign of trouble. But what you need to know about me is I don't give up easily. I want you and I will have you."

I exhale a harsh breath. "And I keep telling you that sometimes you just can't have what you want."

He dips his face to mine and traces my lips with his finger. "Baby, you can keep fighting me if you want, because trust me, I fucking love a good fight. But what I'd really love you to do is let me fuck that fight out of you. I thought I'd done that today. Clearly I need to up my game."

My legs sway.

Ashton does not need to up his game.

Far from it.

But I'm finished playing his game.

I drop my arms, straighten my shoulders and take a deep breath. "No. I want you to leave."

His face is still close and he doesn't shift away fast. He

holds my gaze for what feels like forever before finally taking a step back. "This isn't done, Lorelei. Not by a long shot."

With that, he leaves and I close the door behind him. His scent lingers, and I close my eyes and inhale it as I sag against the door. The tension knotting my shoulders eases, but not by much, because as much as I don't want to admit it, Ashton was right. I do run at the first sign of trouble. Usually, though, that trouble takes a lot longer to find me. Usually, I don't fall this fast.

"Why do you look like you've been hit by a truck?" Sienna asks the next morning over coffee in the office.

I sigh and place my mug on the table. "Because I'm pretty sure one hit me last night."

She frowns. "Come again?"

"Ashton. He may as well be a truck with the way he rams into people's lives."

She raises her brows and her lips form an 'O'. "Tell me more. The last I knew, he'd rammed himself into things other than lives, and you were smiling about it. How can a man fuck shit up that fast?"

"Oh, trust me, he can," I mutter before filling her in on what happened last night.

Once I finish, she says softly, "I don't think Ashton's the problem here."

"What the hell does that mean?"

She holds her hands up defensively. "Hear me out, okay?"

I lean back into my chair and cross my arms while scowling at her. "Fine."

"I think you're having a hard time letting yourself fall for him. From everything you've told me, he's as alpha as they come, and you've never dated a man like that. He's pushing for a lot straight away, more than you've ever had to give at first."

Fiddling with my pen, I stare at her. "It's true. He is pushing."

"And you're resisting."

I nod.

She leans her arms on the table. "Do you want him?"

"Yes, but—"

"No buts. I'm not letting you get away with that this time."

"Sienna, I might want to screw him, but that doesn't mean we should date." I stand and gather the documents in front of me. "I appreciate what you're doing, but Ashton's not the man for me."

"So that's the end of it? Just like that?"

"Yes. I've got his sex toys here to give back to him and then we're done. And now, I have to get ready for my meeting. Stan will be here in about five minutes."

"That's the guy who wants you to invest in his resort?"

"Yeah, the one he's building on the Gold Coast."

She stands and places her hand on my arm. Meeting my gaze, she says, "I doubt you've seen the last of Ashton, babe. Like seriously, he doesn't seem like a man who just gives up. I hope you're ready for that."

"I know he won't, but I'm ready. I think the main thing with Ashton will to always be one step ahead of him and to try to catch him when he's not expecting me. That's why after my meeting I'm going to actually go to his office and drop those toys off."

She grins. "You're playing offence."

I return her smile. "I'm pretty sure it's the only type of play when your opponent is Ashton Scott."

A deep voice sounds from the doorway. "It's a smart move, but when your opponent is Ashton Scott, you need to remember one thing, Lorelei. He's the one playing offence."

His voice hits me first and then his smell.

And as I turn to face him, catching the three-piece suit he's wearing, and the good looks he couldn't hide even if he tried, I know he's right. While I wanted to be the one who was a step ahead, Ashton is probably about five steps ahead already.

He watches me intently as he moves closer. "Shall we get started?"

I frown. "Started with what?"

"With the meeting." He checks his watch. "I know I'm a minute or so early, and that Stan isn't here yet, but you and I can get started."

My heart beats faster. "You're part of the deal?"

A slow smile spreads across his face. "Stan didn't tell you? I signed up this morning."

I stare at him.

For a long few moments.

Goddam it.

I am so far from playing offence it isn't funny.

22

ASHTON

LORELEI GLARES AT ME LIKE SHE WANTS TO strangle me. "This wasn't what I agreed to with Stan." Christ, her fight turns me on. I would have paid double what Stan needed on this deal just to ensure I could work with her.

I run my gaze down her body.

Slowly.

Deliberately so.

It's a bad move because today she's opted to wear the tight black leather pants I love on her and stilettos that may keep me hard all day. The mental image of fucking her in nothing but those shoes will be difficult to remove from my mind.

When I meet her gaze again, I'm pleased to see heat there. She might be telling me no with her mouth, but her eyes and body are telling me exactly what I want to know. "Stan's looking forward to working with you. Don't disappoint him by backing out now."

She continues to glare at me. "I'm not backing out, but I'd like you to reconsider your involvement. Unless you're planning on a silent investment?"

"I don't ever invest silently." Our hands almost touch when I step closer to her. Again, my movements are deliberate when I don't allow any contact. That will come later, once I've worked her up to it. "I'm not reconsidering. This is a good investment."

Sienna coughs. "I've got an appointment, Lorelei. Are you good, babe?"

Lorelei's eyes don't leave mine as she answers her friend. "You go. I've got this."

I fight the smile forming on my lips.

She's going to give me one hell of a chase.

Sienna says her goodbyes and leaves us alone.

I note the exhaustion in Lorelei's eyes. "You didn't sleep last night."

"I was busy."

I quirk my brows. "Playing with the toys I gave you?"

"No. Planning a holiday."

"For when?"

"I leave in a week."

"Where to?"

"I'm going on a cruise to the Pacific Islands."

"That's your way of playing offence? Running away?"

Her glare returns after easing for a few moments. "I'm not running away. I haven't had any time off in ages and I want to get away from everything, so a cruise is perfect."

Stan interrupts us. "Good, I see you two have met."

With one last glare, Lorelei turns to greet him, a smile fixed on her face. "We have." Gesturing for him to take a seat, she adds, "I didn't realise you were bringing Ashton on board."

As we all sit, Stan replies, "I was as surprised as you, Lorelei, but when he phoned this morning to discuss it, he solved some problems I was having."

Her eyes widen as she looks at me. "This morning, huh?"

Stan glances between the two of us before settling his attention on her. "Yes, as a matter of fact, it was about half an hour after my other major investor pulled out, so Ashton saved my ass. After I promised you I had everything sorted, the last thing I wanted to do was attend this meeting and have to tell you I didn't."

I lean forward, checking my watch. "Can we get started? I have another meeting after this one."

She purses her lips. "Absolutely, Ashton. I'd hate to hold you up."

While Stan runs through his presentation, I watch Lorelei. And listen to her. She's smart and asks the right questions. The way she handles Stan impresses me and I realise where her talents lie. Lorelei is good with people; she's firm, yet knows when to be soft, and she has this ability to direct a person to her way of thinking while allowing them to believe they came up with it by themselves. In the process, it makes them feel confident not only in themselves but also in the idea—the idea *she* wanted to make happen.

We discuss our next steps and then Stan summarises everything before saying, "I think this is going to be one of the best developments I've been involved with. You two have a wealth of experience behind you and the fact we all agree on so much should help this run smoothly."

Lorelei glances at me. The glare she started the meeting with has disappeared. "I don't have anywhere near the experience that Ashton does. I'm looking forward to learning from both of you."

I stand and shake Stan's hand. "Contact Jessica if you need anything. I'll get the ball rolling on what we've discussed."

"Thanks, Ashton. I'd like the three of us to meet once a month if that works for you."

"It does." I glance at Lorelei for a brief moment. "This

project is a top priority for me, so whatever you need, you've got."

His phone rings and he excuses himself to take the call. I watch him leave and then face Lorelei again.

"You just broke a few of your own business rules," she says.

"I did." My eyes drop to that exquisite body of hers. I've had a taste and it was far from enough, but this new tension between us is intoxicating, captivating me more than I imagined possible. Lorelei Winters means more to me than a casual relationship. I want this woman by my side just as much as I want her under me. Meeting her gaze again, I continue, "It seems you bring that out in me, Lorelei."

"I'm just concerned for Stan. This project is everything to him and you're treating it like a game."

I close the distance between us. "I may have broken some of my rules today, but I never treat business like a game. I'm here for two reasons, the main one still being to make money."

"And what's the other one?" Her breathing is a little shaky as she asks this question and I know this is my moment to push her.

Placing my arm around her waist, I pull her to me. Moving my mouth to her ear, I growl, "I'm here to show you just how I do business so we can move past the standstill we're at."

"And what if you fail to change my mind?"

I draw back so I can look her in the eyes. "I won't. I'm good at two things in life, Lorelei: business and sex. I've shown you one. Now I'll show you the other. And when I tell you I'm better at business than sex, that should mean something to you, because we both know that even though you're saying no to me, your pussy is begging you to change your mind."

Her eyes burn with lust, but she doesn't disappoint me by giving in easily. Instead, she steps out of my hold and says, "You should leave now."

"I am. Jessica will be in touch."

"What for?"

"I thought you missed that point in the meeting. I really need to teach you to listen more carefully when I'm involved in a business deal."

She places her hands on her hips. "What damn point?"

"The one that put me and you in charge of the interior design."

"I didn't miss that. I just thought we'd be overseeing a team who did that."

"Welcome to my way of doing business. I believe in being hands on. This is going to be the most luxurious resort in Australia by the time we're finished with it. To ensure that happens, you and I need to check out our competition."

Her eyes narrow at me. "And what exactly does *that* mean?"

"It means cancel your cruise. We've got resorts to visit."

"Oh, my, God, you sneaky bastard."

"I told you this wasn't over and I meant it, Lorelei."

"I'm not a pushover, Ashton," she calls out as I exit the office.

My lips curve into a smile.

Baby, I'm counting on it.

"I've scheduled this weekend and next for you, and shuffled your Friday meetings to free you up on those days," Jessica says over the phone a couple of hours later.

I enter my father's building as we talk, ignoring the

tension that has settled into every muscle of my body. "Let Lorelei know. And don't allow her to say no."

"Will do. She sent a box over with a note. You want me to open it and tell you what it says?"

"I'm fairly sure I know what it says, but humour me." I wait for the lift to take me up to the top floor.

A moment passes before Jessica's laugh sounds through the phone. "Oh, I love this woman. No wonder you're chasing her all over town even after she's shot you down a million times."

"Tell me what it says," I mutter.

"She says she's keeping the toys you sent her except for the one that's in the box. She'll need all the rest because she's decided to take a break from dick for a while. And she thinks you should stick the toy she sent back in the same place you should stick your idea for her to go away with you."

"She sent the butt plug back."

"She did."

Stepping into the lift, I smile. "Change of plans. Don't contact Lorelei about this weekend. Leave it to me to handle."

"You ruin all my fun," she grumbles.

"Goodbye, Jessica." I end the call as I reach my destination. Taking purposeful strides, I make my way to my father's office.

This meeting has been a long time coming.

"Ashton, to what do I owe the pleasure?"

I stare at my father as he stands and moves towards me from behind his desk. He's hardly aged in the six months since I've seen him. I doubt the flecks of grey hair he's sporting have even increased in that time. His rugged good looks are only enhanced by his tanned skin and immaculate style. My mother doesn't work, but she spends a great deal of her time ensuring her husband looks good when he appears in the gossip columns.

"Let's cut the bullshit, Dad. What's your plan for Willow Street?"

He clenches his jaw as he glowers at me. "What makes you think you have a right to come here and ask me that after you cut me out of your life a year ago?"

"You know damn well what right I have."

"Whatever you think you have, you don't, son. Now, is that all you came here for today? Because if so, I've better things to do than stand around squabbling like children over a business deal. I suggest that if you want to play with the big boys, you grow the fuck up."

I step closer to him and lower my voice as I spit out, "I know what you did back then, and I've held onto that knowledge all these years. Don't make me use it."

He never saw that coming and he flinches. But I'm still left with nothing but anger.

Fuck.

I've wanted to say those words to him for years.

Why the hell don't they make me feel good?

As I stalk out of his building, I curse myself for coming. I should have known better. My father *always* manages to get under my skin. The only thing different about today is that this time, I managed to get under his, too. The fact I'm not leaving feeling victorious confuses me.

What the fuck is wrong here?

23

LORELEI

THROWING MY HOUSE KEYS ON THE KITCHEN TABLE, I sort through my mail. Besides a phone bill, there's not much of interest, so I dump it on the table and grab some cold water from the fridge. The spin class I just returned home from kicked my ass and every muscle aches. Or maybe that was the sex with Ashton yesterday that did that.

Just thinking about the man causes my blood to boil. When he turned up to the meeting with Stan this morning, it threw me. To then discover he'd forced his way into the project irritated me, but when he dictated to me that we'd have to spend time away at resorts together, that just pissed me off.

Why can't he take no for an answer?

I finish my drink and head into my bedroom to take a shower. The class ran over tonight and it's now past seven thirty. I've got a stack of work to get through, and the fact I'm home late and tired doesn't give me confidence that I'll get it all done.

A knock on my front door slows me as I trudge into the bedroom. I wouldn't answer it except for the fact I told my neighbour she could bother me for help anytime. She's a single mum of two rowdy boys and I figure she needs all the help she can get.

Swinging the door open, I'm surprised, as well as annoyed, to find Ashton standing on the other side. I don't know why I'm surprised, though. I should have expected it. He *is* playing offence after all.

"Ashton, it's late and I've got work to do."

The determination in his eyes softens a little and concern flashes across his face. "It's not late, Lorelei." With that, he enters my home and leads me into my lounge room before I manage to stop him.

I pull out of his hold. "Do you do this with everyone in your life?"

"No."

The way he watches me with such intensity as he answers my question, along with the answer he gives me, unleashes a wave of desire I don't want to deal with.

When I don't reply, he takes charge again, settling me on the couch. "Have you had dinner?"

Oh, God. I realise how I must look after my spin class. I didn't even wear my good gym clothes today because they were all in the wash. Looking down at my old T-shirt and tights, I cringe. "No, but I'm not hungry." Pushing up off the couch, I say, "You need to go so I can have a shower and get my work done."

"No, I'll order dinner while you have a shower."

"Ashton—"

"Lorelei," he bosses, "shower, now. We'll talk after."

I stare at him. And I just know he's not going anywhere.

I huff out a breath. "Fine." I wave my finger in the air at him. "But make sure you order me something good. And a cupcake. If I have to deal with you tonight, I want a bloody cupcake." With that, I stalk into my bedroom without waiting for his reply.

Bloody infuriating man.

After my shower, I find Ashton engrossed on his phone at my kitchen table. When he hears me enter the room, his gaze sweeps slowly up my body before settling on my face. Jesus, the man has perfected the art of sending a woman from zero to one hundred in one second flat. By the time he finds my eyes, my body is panting. Well, it would be if it could.

"Dinner is on its way. As is your cupcake."

I feel a tinge of guilt about my irrational request for that cupcake. But damn, he listened and ordered me one. "Thank you." I join him at the table. "So, what did you want to discuss with me?"

"That can wait. We'll go over it while we eat. Tell me about your day first."

I raise my brows. "You really want me to detail my day for you?"

His lips twitch. "I do."

I cross my legs on the chair, getting comfortable. "Well, let me see…. It started off with a bang this morning when the guy I said no to last night forced his way into a business deal that had nothing to do with him. Then I discovered my building had been vandalised. *Again.* And after that, I found out the council is looking into noise complaints at that address. So I've had a pretty craptacular day really."

"Let's start at the beginning. You have to admit I bring a lot to the table with that deal."

I don't want to admit he's right, but it's the truth, so I begrudgingly give him that one. Sighing, I nod. "You do. But seriously, you managed to get someone to back out at the last minute just so you could spend time with me?"

That intense look returns to his eyes. "I did. And I'd do it again, and *will* do it again if I need to."

I'm not sure whether to yell at him to stop or to simply give in now. Our dinner arrives, saving me, and I take a moment to pull myself together when he leaves to answer the door.

Surely he'll give up soon. He must have hundreds of women who'd happily go out with him. He doesn't need me.

Returning with dinner, he passes me a white paper bag. "Your cupcake, in case you want it first."

I track his movements as he searches my cupboards and drawers for plates, cutlery, and glasses. He's still wearing his three-piece suit. *His pinstripe suit.* Those things are dangerous to womankind.

Stop looking at the damn suit.

Ashton Scott is not the man for you.

Dragging my attention away from him, I open the cupcake bag. He's right. I do want it first.

My eyes widen as I look at what he had delivered. "Jesus, Ashton, are you trying to kill my hips?"

He joins me at the table. Eyeing the four cupcakes in front of me, he says, "You're going to need more than one tonight."

"Oh, God, what have you done? Tell me now!"

He smiles, and I do my best to ignore it. *And the lust that hits me.* "Let's just say your next few weekends are now booked, so I'm preparing for backlash. The cupcakes might help."

My eyes narrow at him. "You've already booked those resorts, haven't you? I could be busy those weekends."

"You're not busy," he says calmly, as if he knows for sure. I want to throttle that arrogance out of him.

Then it hits me. *"You know my schedule?"* My voice is practically a shriek.

He holds my gaze. Doesn't give me an inch. And he sure as hell doesn't allow me to look away. "Lorelei," he starts, his voice deep, "you should know me well enough by now to understand that I have made you my priority."

I should tell him where to go.

I want to.

Really, I do.

Instead, my core clenches and I simply stare at him.

And I don't say anything.

He stands and moves around to where I'm sitting. Placing one hand on the table and one on the back of my chair, he bends so our faces are close. "This is the last time I'm going to tell you that you will be mine. You can run and you can say no, but I'm not a man who will accept either of those things. I will be patient, Lorelei, and I'll do whatever you need to believe in me, but I won't give you forever. And in that time, I won't stay away." His voice drops to a growl. *"You* are not a woman I can stay away from."

I thought Ashton had taken charge already.

I was wrong.

This is him taking over.

And if I ever thought I had a hope of holding him at arm's length, I was wrong about that, too.

When Ashton Scott wants something, he gets it.

He made that promise to me and he's keeping it.

Right now, I'm certain that whatever he asks for in this moment, I will give.

I'm also certain my life is about to change.

24

ASHTON

"Jessica!"

She appears in the doorway, irritated. "What?"

"Have you got those numbers for the Steele proposal yet?"

"No."

My head snaps up. "Why?"

Crossing her arms, she says, "What crawled up your ass this morning?"

I narrow my eyes at her. "More to the point, who pissed you off? You've been traipsing around here all day in a foul mood."

She settles a glare on me before huffing out a breath of irritation. Dropping her arms, she enters my office. "It might have something to do with the fact Jack is hell-bent on ripping open old wounds suddenly."

"Fuck." I lean back in my chair. Jack revisiting the past is not something any of us need. Too many ghosts reside there with the potential to wreak havoc on everyone involved.

"Exactly." She drops down into the seat across from me. "He called me late last night and wanted to talk about what happened between us." Hurt flashes in her eyes. It's an emotion she does her best to avoid, so it surprises me. It shouldn't, though, because what went down between them wasn't pretty. When I look closer, I realise there's exhaustion to go with it. "I can't do this with him again, Ashton."

"Jesus, Jessica, you need to shut him down now. That shit was five years ago, and it's not helpful to either of you to rehash it."

"You know him better than anyone. I don't think he's going to let it go."

She's right; when Jack wants to drown himself in misery, he always finds a way. "I thought he was doing okay yesterday. Clearly I was wrong. Have you spoken to him today?"

"No. You?"

I shake my head. "No, I left early for work." Pushing my chair back, I stand. "I'm going to check on him. How much time do you need to pull those numbers for me?"

"Half an hour should do it unless something urgent crops up."

"Send them to me when you have them. I won't be back in today."

She stands. "You're on soccer duty again this afternoon?"

I flick my wrist to check my watch. "Yes, and I won't hear the end of it from Alessandra if I'm not there by four, so I need to leave now if I'm going to have time to stop in on Jack first."

As we're heading out of my office, she says, "By the way, I'm not sure what you said to Lorelei, but I sent her the schedule for the next couple of weekends, and she sent me back an email saying thanks, no arguments. Totally not what I expected after she sent your butt plug back. Smooth work."

It might feel like smooth work to Jessica, but getting Lorelei to do what I want her to do is proving a challenge. "She'll be ready to leave at lunchtime tomorrow?"

"That's the time I mentioned in the email. She didn't say anything to the contrary."

We'll see. The thing I'm learning about Lorelei is to expect the unexpected. She has a way of surprising me, which isn't something I prefer. But with her, I'm growing to love.

I enter the bar on Willow Street and scan the building looking for Jack. I texted him after I left my office to find out where he is. It didn't surprise me to learn he's here as this is the bar he and I frequented when we were younger. He's seated at a table with six empty glasses in front of him.

Jesus.

"Ashton." His lazy smile lights up his face when I reach the table. Sweeping his arm through the air, he indicates for me to join him. "You want a drink?"

I take the empty chair across from him. "Really? This is the answer to your problems, Jack? Please tell me my friend is smarter than this."

Glancing at the empty glasses, he says, "It's a good answer, don't you think?"

"I wasn't referring to the alcohol."

He frowns. "What then?"

"Jessica."

"Ah," he murmurs, leaning back. "She told you I called her last night?"

"Yes. And I'm telling you now that you need to leave the past in the past. It's been five years since you two broke up. Why all of a sudden do you want to bring it back up with her?"

"We never did get closure. I thought it was time to try."

"Closure? Fuck, do you think she needs that now? If she

ever needed it, five years ago would have been good. But you didn't stop and think back then. You just moved on to the next woman, never looking back to see how broken Jessica was. She worked through all of that and got the closure she needed. So if you need it now, you find it on your own without her."

Annoyance flashes across his face and he reaches for his glass of whisky. After he drains it, he says, "It's this new shrink you've got me going to. She's forcing me to face the shit in my past that still haunts me."

"Jesus, Jack, leave Jessica out of it. You've got a lot of other shit in your past, focus on that instead."

He takes that in like he always does. Jack's a good listener, but he doesn't always process things the way I imagine he will. This time, however, he nods and says, "Okay, Ashton, we'll play this your way. I'll leave Jessica out of it."

I scrub my hand over my face.

Thank fuck.

"When are you seeing the psych again?"

"Tomorrow."

"Have you told her you're drinking heavily?"

"I told her I was working on cutting back."

"You need to work harder at that." My patience with him is wearing thin.

He scowls at me. "Perhaps I should cancel my appointments with her and book in with you?"

"What you should do is start taking this seriously. Mixing alcohol with your medication is a fucked-up move and you know it."

"I do, but I'm getting a little sick of hearing what I should be doing from everyone. I'm quite capable of living my own life and making my own decisions."

I stand to leave. Being with him while he's in this mood is

only making me angry. "Are you? Because it doesn't seem like it to me."

As I stalk out of the bar, I dig deep not to lose my cool. I don't understand Jack's behaviour. This isn't something new in our friendship, but it's something I'm growing tired of. Watching my best friend unravel like this is hard. I thought getting him to Australia and finding him the psychological help he needed would be enough. It seems this time it isn't. And not knowing how to fix a situation isn't something I'm good at. I always know how to fix problems.

25

LORELEI

"I'VE DECIDED I LIKE ASHTON SCOTT," SIENNA SAYS to me over drinks at the bar down the road from the Willow Street building late Thursday afternoon.

"What's he done to earn your approval?" Images of him from last night flash through my mind as I wait for her answer. Him sitting in my kitchen in his pinstripe suit; him passing me a cupcake; him telling me how it was going to go down between the two of us. I hardly slept after he left. Instead, I tossed and turned, replaying our conversation over and over in my head, wondering how to proceed. In the end, I decided to play along with him. He can have my body, because I want that as much as he does. My heart, though, will just wait and see.

She sips her daiquiri. "I dropped my nephew off at soccer and Ashton was there coaching again. In my opinion, any man who gives up his time to help kids is a man worth knowing."

My heart melts at the mention of Ashton coaching kids.

When I don't say anything, she nudges me. "Well? Don't you agree?"

I sigh. "He came to see me last night."

Her eyes widen. "You've gone all day without telling me this news? You better start talking and spill everything. Do not leave any detail out."

"For a start, he's a stubborn, bossy man—"

Her eyes twinkle as a grin forms on her lips. "Which is *exactly* what you need."

I take a long sip of my wine. I decided alcohol is definitely needed tonight while we discuss Ashton. Although I haven't talked to Sienna about him today, I invited her to the bar after work with the intention of going over every little detail with her.

"I'm not so sure that's exactly what I need, but I have decided I need sex with him again. The man sure knows how to do that."

"Do you think that's all he wants?"

"I don't think so. I'm pretty sure he's looking for more from me. Before I started to get to know him, I would have told you he was a player and just wanted sex going by what I'd read about him, but he's going to a lot of effort if all he wants is my body."

Her grin softens. "Yes, if a man like Ashton just wants sex that would be easy to come by." She drinks more of her cocktail. "You're going to ease up on him and play nice, then?"

I scrunch my face at her. "Whose friend are you anyway? I always play nice. Sometimes I just want to play my way rather than someone else's. And Ashton wants to call all the shots, too, so we do seem to clash a little. I'll try to compromise, but easing up on him would be bad. I think he's used to always getting his way, and he needs to learn that if he wants to be with me, that won't always happen."

She laughs at that. "Oh, boy, you two.... I'm looking forward to this."

"Anyway, we're doing this resort development together,

and he's booked us into a few resorts over the next couple of weekends to check them out. So you and I need to go over my wardrobe."

"Jesus, does he have a brother? I need a man like Ashton who just takes charge. I'd have no problems with being bossed around and taken to resorts."

"Lorelei!" A deep voice jolts me out of the conversation with Sienna, and I glance up to find Jack coming our way.

I stand and hug him when he puts his arms out. "How are you, Jack?" He's been drinking, which sparks my concern. I hardly know him, and yet I'm invested in his health and happiness. I'm not sure how he did it, but he's managed to draw me in.

Without answering me, he turns to Sienna and pastes a million-dollar smile on his face. I bet that kind of smile is what helped make him famous. That, his talent and his ability to charm. "You must be Lorelei's friend who I've heard so much about."

Sienna lifts a brow. "Really? Who from?"

He grins. "You got me there, gorgeous. I haven't heard about you, but that's an error we need to fix. How about the three of us leave so we can spend some time alone getting to know each other?"

Sienna cocks her head. "You're propositioning us for a threesome?"

Jack throws his head back and laughs. It's a genuine, belly laugh and it looks good on him. When he finishes laughing, he says, "Fuck no. You don't seriously think I'd try to screw my best mate's woman, do you? And I'd never sleep with her best friend either. I might fuck a lot of shit up in my life, but I'm smart enough to know not to do either of those things. I simply meant let's have a conversation and get to know each other that way." He leans closer to her and lowers his voice to add, "I need to get out of here, though, because it's starting to get busier and I've had some fans harassing me."

"You don't travel with security?" Sienna asks.

"Usually, but I haven't bothered with it this trip. I should sort something out."

I move off my stool. "I'm sure Ashton's assistant could hook you up."

His bright expression morphs into a darker one. "Yeah, I don't think it's a good idea to ask her for help."

I frown. "Why not?"

He slides his arm over my shoulders. "Jessica and I aren't in a great place at the moment. I need to reserve my conversations with her for more important matters." Glancing at Sienna, he asks, "Now, are you ladies in?"

She nods. "Yes."

The smile returns to his face as he looks between the two of us. "What's your name, gorgeous? I'm going to need it if you and I are going to spend time together."

She gives him her name and he says, "Sienna. Fucking beautiful."

As the three of us leave the bar, chatting and laughing, I can't help but notice that Sienna is hanging off every word he says. I hope he makes good on his promise not to sleep with her. She doesn't need Jack complicating her life.

26

ASHTON

My eyes meet Lorelei's as I enter my living room after soccer practice. She's sitting with Jack and her friend on the sofa, laughing at something he's just said. Her laughter dies on her lips when she sees me, but the smile remains.

"Ashton," Jack says, seriousness replacing his fun demeanour. "How was soccer?"

I drag my gaze from Lorelei. My earlier anger with him is still there, but it's dulled a little. We have the kind of friendship where we don't tend to hold onto arguments. "The kids did great. The parents, on the other hand, leave a lot to be desired. It's a good thing Aly wasn't there today. She would have found an argument to involve herself in."

"Malcolm was there instead?" Jack asks.

"Yeah." My eyes lock onto Lorelei again. "Have you three had dinner?"

She shakes her head. "You got cupcakes?"

Sienna frowns. "Cupcakes?"

"Yes, they seem to be one of Ashton's ways of bribing people," Lorelei says.

I raise a brow. "And they seem to be one of Lorelei's ways of coping when she's trying to avoid something."

Jack stands and holds his hand out to Sienna. "That's our cue to leave, gorgeous. Come, I'll give you a tour of Ashton's home."

Sienna does as he suggests, leaving Lorelei and me alone. She stands as I make my way to her, and I take in the black pants and white sleeveless blouse she's wearing. Her cleavage is on full display thanks to the fitted blouse that dips low in the front.

When I reach her, I run a finger lightly across her collarbone. "You look beautiful today, but for the record, I prefer you in a dress."

Her eyes hold mine. "For the record, I don't care."

My lips twitch, but I hold back my smile. I trace a line down from her collarbone to her cleavage before slipping my hand inside her blouse and her bra to cover one of her breasts. Her nipple hardens as I massage it with my thumb. "I can imagine how much you don't care, but I'm making it clear that when I pick you up tomorrow, I want you in a dress."

She steps closer and slides her hand into my shorts so she can take hold of my cock. My breathing slows as she wraps her hand around it. "I've decided how you're going to fuck me first tomorrow." My dick is hard as hell listening to her dirty talk. Not to mention the fact she's making plans for sex. I was clear last night with what I wanted to happen between us, but I still wasn't sure how long it would take for her to come around.

"How?" I demand, letting go of her breast so I can undo her blouse.

Stroking my cock, she says. "I want you to fuck me on the balcony. I'm going to face the beach while you take me from behind. You're going to make me scream out your name while you give me an orgasm that will exhaust me. Then we're going to have a spa bath together where you'll kiss me forever, because kisses are my downfall, and get me so ready for you that I'll be begging you to fuck me again. Which you'll do in that spa bath before carrying me to the bed so I can recover in time for dinner." She squeezes my cock harder, increasing her pace before continuing to detail her fantasy. "You'll take me to an amazing Italian restaurant where I'll tease your cock all night so that you can't wait to get me back to the room and fuck me until I pass out." Pressing her lips to mine, she murmurs, "And then the next day, I'll wake you up reverse cowgirl style, and we'll start all over again."

Fuck.

Without any warning, I lift her up over my shoulder and carry her to my bedroom. She squeals her surprise but doesn't fight me. When I deposit her on the floor in my room, I slide her blouse off and undo her pants. "I see you've spent some time today fantasizing. Just so you know, though, I've already put some thought into how I'll fuck you tomorrow."

As we remove each other's clothes, she says, "I bet you have, but for once in your life, do you think you could relinquish control?"

Pulling her to me, I take hold of her face with both hands. "I don't relinquish control ever, Lorelei, you should know that." I brush my lips across hers. "However, there are parts of your fantasy I like, so I could be convinced to swap some of my ideas for yours."

She places her hands on my chest. "Just so you know, I never bother trying to convince people of anything, especially not men. Either you're with me, or you're not. This is a take-it-or-leave-it kind of deal."

I let go of her face so I can reach a hand down to her pussy. Circling her clit, I say, "It's not a take-it-or-leave-it kind of deal and we both know it." Pushing a finger inside her, I growl. "We also both know that once I get you inside that resort room, you'll do anything for my cock." She's so damn wet that I easily slide another finger inside and reach deep. When she gasps and digs her nails into my skin, I move my mouth to her ear. "I'm pleased to see you've reconsidered our relationship."

Her eyes glaze over as I bring her closer to orgasm. "I have. But you need to know something else, Ashton."

I dip my mouth to her neck to taste her skin. "What?"

She reaches for my cock. "I've decided I'm all for compromise, and that you need to get on board with that if this relationship is going to go anywhere."

I drop to my knees and run my tongue from one end of her pussy to the other. "I'm listening. What kind of compromise are you willing to make for me to continue this? Will you wear a dress tomorrow?"

She moans as I lick her again. When I stop, she threads her fingers through my hair and grips it hard. "Yes, I'll wear a damn dress. Just keep doing that."

I give her what she wants, working her closer to the edge.

Kissing.

Licking.

Sucking.

Stroking.

I deliver pure ecstasy, and when I know I've worked her into a frenzy of desperate need, I stop and stand, kissing my way up her body. Taking her face in my hands again, I say, "I can make you come. Right now. I'll fuck you like you've never been fucked. But in return, you're going to have to agree to me having full control on the weekend. And that's a take-it-or-leave-it deal." Pushing my cock against her, I growl, "Are you with me or not?"

She's in such a state of desire that I know she can hardly

think straight, but she manages to process what I've said. Wrapping her hand around my dick, she says, "I don't need this to come. I'm quite capable of getting myself off."

"Take it or leave it, Lorelei. You may be able to orgasm without my cock, but I can guarantee you it'll be nothing compared to what I can give you."

"I want you to compromise."

"No."

She pumps my dick in her hand. "Give me something, Ashton."

I kiss her, tangling my tongue with hers. "I will. My cock."

Her mouth claims mine in another kiss. This one is demanding, bruising almost. It reveals her need for what she's asking of me. "I want more than that. I'm not a woman who will be happy with just that."

"What do you want, Lorelei? Tell me."

We're nearly there.

"I told you, I want you to comprom—"

"No," I growl, "tell me what you *really* want. You said you want more than just my cock, more than just sex. What is it you need?"

Come on, baby, don't let me down now.

She stills.

Blinks.

And finally realises where I've been leading her.

Leaning her body into mine, she loops her arms around my neck. "You're a smart man, Ashton."

"That is true."

She shakes her head. "And arrogant, too."

"Guilty as charged." I run my hands over her ass, pressing her even harder against my body.

"You know what I want."

"I want to hear you say it."

Her hands move up into my hair at the back of my neck,

and she pushes my head so my face dips to hers. Kissing me, she moans into my mouth, "I love how your mind works. Even when you're one-upping me, I love your intelligence. But I'm going to need you to give me the occasional win. And some days I'll need the control, not of you, but of the situation. You're so powerful and driven, and you just charge on in and take over. You can't consume me, Ashton. Because you will if I let you. I want you so damn much that I'm worried I'll get lost in that. I need some space every now and then. Can you give me that?"

"I can give you anything, Lorelei, so long as you give me what I want."

She stills again. "What do you want?" she asks quietly.

"I want you to explore this relationship with me. I want you to not pull away every time you feel like I'm consuming you. I want you to talk to me when you feel like that."

Her grip on me tightens.

When she doesn't reply straight away, I wonder if she's going to run again.

And then her body relaxes, and a smile teases her lips right before she presses those lips to mine. *"That's* how you compromise. I knew you had it in you."

"You'd be surprised what I'm capable of for the right woman." I move my hands to take hold of her hips. "Now, I want you on that bed, on your back with your legs spread wide." When she opens her mouth to speak, I place my finger against her lips to silence her. "No negotiations, Lorelei. I'll consider your suggestions for tomorrow, but tonight, you do what I say."

I've done all the compromising I'll be doing tonight. What Lorelei doesn't need to know is that I've never once in my life given a woman this much.

27

LORELEI

"WHAT TIME IS HE PICKING YOU UP?" SIENNA ASKS over the phone on Friday night.

I balance my phone between my cheek and my shoulder so I can free my hand and close the suitcase I've just finished repacking. "We were supposed to leave at lunch, but Jessica called to change it and said he'd be here at five."

"Is it weird he's late? Ashton doesn't strike me as a man who would be late. Especially not for this."

Her thoughts echo mine. It's just after six and I haven't heard from him. The nerves that have been swimming in my belly all day are only intensifying with every passing minute. I finish zipping my suitcase closed and take hold of my phone again. "Yes, it's weird. I tried to call him, but his phone has been engaged. Jessica's phone has also been busy."

"Something must have come up at work."

"That's what I'm thinking." I pad into the lounge room and sink into the couch. "Tell me what you've got planned for the weekend."

"I'm hanging out with Jack. He called me today after making me friend him on Facebook last night and then begging me for my phone number. We're going to take a drive up to Nelson Bay tomorrow."

"Is this like a date?"

"God, no. Jack might be hot, but he's not a guy I want to date. I think he'll be a lot of fun to hang out with, though."

"Why wouldn't you want to date him?"

"Are you serious, babe? Would you? The guy has some major baggage. I checked him out online last night and he's into everything from what I can work out. Drugs, alcohol, women. No way would I go near all that. Plus, I don't want to date a movie star that every damn woman in the world wants. And just on a side note, do you know just how famous he is? I had no idea."

"Well, I know he's won a couple of Oscars." Sienna and I don't follow celebrity news. We could run into the most famous celebrity in the world and neither of us would know.

"He's one of the most sought-after actors in Hollywood at the moment. They paid him something like fifteen million for his last movie."

Before I get a chance to reply, a knock sounds on my front door. I practically jump out of my seat. God, Ashton has me eating out of his hand. "I've gotta go, Sienna. Ashton's here."

"Go. Get your dirty on, and don't forget to do that thing to him I told you about." I'd opened up to her this morning at work about feeling self-conscious with dirty talk. That led us to a conversation about sex, and Sienna has given me a heap of ideas on how to blow Ashton's mind.

"Oh God, if I manage to pull that off, *I'll* be the one who should get an Oscar." I don't consider myself a prude when it comes to sex, but the thought of doing what she suggested causes a rush of nervous energy to swell in my stomach. I'm not sure I have the confidence to pull it off with Ashton.

"Lorelei, that man is hot for you. He's going to love anything you do to him. You've got this."

I smile as I walk the short distance to the front door. "Have I told you today how much I love you?" She never fails to say just the right thing when I need it.

"No, I don't believe you have."

Laughing, I say, "I love you. But I need to hang up on you now."

"Call me the minute you can and give me all the goss." With that, she ends the call and I open the door to Ashton.

He stands on the other side staring at me through eyes that tell me he's had a rough day. "Sorry I'm late," he says, and in those words, I hear just how rough his day has been. Ashton is off, and I suspect something is very wrong with him.

"What's happened?"

He doesn't answer me straight away, but rather, rubs the back of his neck while keeping hold of my gaze. Then he says, "There's been a fire at one of my building sites in Perth." He pauses for a beat and when he continues, his voice is thick with emotion. "Three of my guys died in it."

I swallow down the sick feeling his news causes and try to find the right words to say to him. Nothing comes, though, and I feel useless. In the end, I go with: "I'm so sorry, Ashton."

"I have to cancel our plans for this weekend. I'm going to fly to Perth instead and get to the bottom of exactly what happened."

While I agree this is the best thing he could do, disappointment floods me. I'm surprised by how deeply I feel it. I didn't realise I was this attached to going away with him, but clearly I was. Nodding, I say, "What time do you fly out?"

He checks his watch. "In about four hours. It was the earliest we could charter a plane."

Reaching for his hand, I gently pull him inside. "That

means you have enough time for me to make you a coffee and to listen to whatever you need to talk about."

He hesitates for a moment. It's unusual to see Ashton hesitate, but then again, I've not seen him like this at all. Ashton is always sure of himself; this is a whole other side to him. Finally, he nods and allows me to lead him inside to my kitchen.

I busy myself with making coffee while he remains silent next to me. I know his eyes are on me, because every time I glance his way, he's watching. When he doesn't speak, I stop what I'm doing and give him my full attention. "This has really shaken you up, hasn't it?"

"Yes." He rakes his fingers through his hair and blows out a long breath. "This kind of thing doesn't happen on my developments. I hire the best construction crews and we have the best safety procedures in place. It shouldn't have happened." His words are a little disjointed, as if he's trying to piece it all together in his mind as to how it could have occurred.

"They haven't been able to give you any answers yet?"

He shakes his head. "No. It's why I want to head over to Perth now—so I can make sure they hurry up with those answers." His voice softens when he adds, "And to speak to the men's families."

The fact he wants to see those families touches me. "I like that you want to do that."

His forehead creases in a frown. "You sound surprised."

I nod, going with complete honesty. "I'm only starting to learn all your intricacies, Ashton. What I know of your business style so far is that you're extremely driven to achieve your goals, you don't seem to have a problem with pushing your way into a deal, and that you're very arrogant about it all. This is a new side to you I'm seeing tonight. One I like."

His face is impassive while he listens to what I say, to the point where I'm not sure how he's taking it. But I've never held back with him, and I won't start now. If we've got any chance at a relationship, we're going to need full honesty.

When I finish speaking, he slowly moves in front of me. This brings back memories of the night he made me come in my kitchen, and a wave of desire unleashes through me. "Promise me you'll never stop being so damn honest with me," he says, his voice husky as hell.

My breathing grows shallow as his eyes drop to my chest. I never want the way he watches me to change. Ashton could spend a whole week with me without talking and I'd never beg him to utter a word so long as he looked at me the way he is right now.

I place a hand on his chest and slide it up over his shirt towards his shoulder. He's wearing another one of his suits. He seems to have so many of them. Today's is a dark blue suit that he's teamed with a white shirt. No tie, which I love, because his top button is undone, treating me to a glimpse of skin.

"Honesty is all I have for you, so it's a good thing you like it so much," I say as my hand moves over his shoulder.

He places his hand on my ass. Bending so his mouth is close to my ear, he says, "You wore a dress for me."

Every inch of me sparks with lust. His voice guarantees that. When Ashton is pleased, it vibrates not only from his body but also through his voice. I sway closer to him. "You told me to."

His hand glides slowly down my bottom to my leg so he can take hold of it and wrap it around him. The red dress I'm wearing isn't fitted, allowing him easy access to whatever he wants. He runs his hand back up my thigh and around to my ass again. Approval flashes in his eyes. "I should tell you to do things more often," he growls as he lifts me up onto the kitchen counter. Spreading my legs and lifting my dress, he drops his gaze to my bare pussy. I knew that wearing no panties tonight would be a good idea; I just didn't realise *how* good.

I grip the back of his neck. "You don't need to get any bossier than you already are."

His eyes flick back up to mine. "Lorelei, you have no idea how bossy I am going to get. I've been taking this far too slowly with you."

My tummy somersaults in a million different directions. I'm not sure I want to know just how bossy he's going to get. What I *am* sure of, though, is the fact I like the idea of him trying to boss me around more. And they are the most confusing thoughts I think I've ever had in my life.

Before I get a chance to say any of this, he lifts my dress over my head and drops it on the floor. "I didn't come here to fuck you tonight," he murmurs, his voice drifting off as he dedicates his attention my body.

"No?"

Stilling, he finds my eyes again. "No. I was going to phone to cancel, but I couldn't do that to you after making you wait for me. I only intended to stop by quickly to fill you in. To be honest, what happened at work killed the hard-on I had all morning while I thought about you." He catches my mouth in a kiss, and then adds, "I should have known I can never resist you. That it only takes one glance at you and I'm hard as hell even when I didn't think it possible."

I curl my hands around his neck and pull his lips to mine. This kiss is much deeper than the previous one and lasts for so long I begin to wonder if we'll ever stop.

I'm drowning in it.

In him.

Every look.

Every word.

Every touch.

Everything he says and does draws me further under the Ashton Scott spell.

Our kiss ends but just gives way to another one soon after. Our desire turns into a desperate need, and while we frantically free his cock and find a condom, neither of us seem ready to let the other's lips go.

When he's ready for me, my arms and legs circle his body and hold on tight. Ashton growls out, "Fuck," as he enters me, and I drop my head back while his cock slams into me over and over. Every muscle in my body works hard while I cling to him and fuck him back.

I've never had sex this rough.

This primal.

It's as if he's lost himself in the act.

His mouth is all over my neck and then so are his teeth.

Grazing me.

Biting me.

Marking me.

His pace picks up the closer we move to orgasm.

And then his fingers dig into my skin as his body tenses and he roars out my name. It sends me over the edge, tumbling into wave after wave of pleasure.

I'm the one lost now.

Lost in bliss.

I'm not sure I ever want to leave his arms again.

Ashton may have finally fucked everything out of me he ever wanted to.

"Lorelei," he says as he cups the back of my head.

I find his gaze. My thoughts are a tangled mess, but I come up with: "God, you never told me you could fuck like that."

His lips twitch. "If I knew you liked it rough, I would have given you that from the beginning."

"Oh, God," I mutter, trying to catch my breath.

He pulls out and helps me down from the counter. "Rough appears to bring out your dirty girl."

I bite my lip as I stare up at him. Ashton's the best-looking man I've ever laid eyes on and I can't help but stare at him sometimes. I wish he wasn't leaving. I wish he could stay with me all weekend and fuck me like that over and over. "If only you knew the thoughts running through my mind right now."

"You're not going to tell me those thoughts, are you?"

I smile. "No. It'll give you something to think about all weekend. When you come home, you'll be so—"

He cuts me off as he spins me around so his body is pressed up hard against mine. With his arm around my waist, fingers digging into my flesh, and his mouth to my ear, he growls, "When I come home, I'll be so fucking hard for you that I'll take you over my lap and fucking spank those thoughts out of you."

My legs turn weak.

He really does have me under his spell now.

"You should hurry home," I whisper.

His fingers dig into my skin harder. "I will. And when I get back, you should be ready to block a day off in your diary for me. We'll have a lot of catching up to do."

Something Ashton doesn't realise is that I would block off as many days for him as he wants. That's how far under his spell I am.

28

ASHTON

Entering my hotel room after my mid-morning run, I kick my shoes off and collapse into a chair. Sucking back as much water as I can from my drink bottle, I take a few moments to catch my breath after taking the stairs rather than the lift. The run did me good. Cleared my head after little sleep and a crappy meeting with the heads of my construction crew. They weren't able to give me much information, so I've pushed them harder to find out what the hell happened.

Flicking my wrist, I check the time on my watch and convert it to Sydney time. It's almost two thirty there. Picking up the phone, I call Lorelei.

She takes so long to answer that I'm almost convinced she's not going to. When she finally does answer, she's breathless. "Shit," she mutters, right before a loud clattering sound cuts her off.

Chuckling, I say, "Are you okay?"

Silence for a beat, and then in a cranky voice she grumbles, "Bloody hell, I just dropped my phone and the glass shattered."

"I can have Jessica organise a new phone for you."

She's silent again for a moment. "Thank you," she says softly.

"You don't need to thank me, Lorelei." She sounds so stressed. I'll do anything to take that stress away.

"No," she says and then pauses briefly. "I'm not thanking you for offering to get me a new phone, which by the way I can organise myself, but I really appreciate the offer. I'm thanking you for not chastising me for dropping it in the first place or for not having it in a case to prevent it from breaking. I appreciate that even more."

I sit up straight. "You're clearly speaking from experience." The thought of anyone chastising her irritates the hell out of me.

"Yes."

"Who?" I demand.

She exhales. "It doesn't matter, Ashton. Can we forget I even said anything?"

"It matters to me. Who did that to you?"

"You're not going to let this go, are you?"

"No."

"It was one of my exes, Dean. Don't get me wrong, he was a good guy, but sometimes he made me feel useless. Like I was a woman who couldn't fend for herself and who needed a man to swoop in and save me."

My chest tightens with anger, but that's probably more because this conversation is bringing up childhood memories I'd rather forget. My father treated my mother that way. I hated watching her shrink under his reprimands and belittling. I swore I'd never treat a woman that way, and I never have.

"I hope to God I never meet that man," I say as I grip my phone harder. "Promise me that if I ever say anything that makes you feel useless, you'll tell me. I never want to make you feel less than the amazing woman you are."

Silence again. And then she says, "Sometimes you just say the exact right thing, Ashton Scott. If you were with me right now, I'd have my hand in your pants, wrapped around your cock, and I'd be ready to do anything you want."

"Fuck, woman," I mutter as I stand. "Have you been practicing your dirty talk this morning?"

"What can I say? You inspire me."

"How about I inspire you to FaceTime me and show me what I'm missing?" My hand is already wrapped around my cock.

"Oh, God, no!"

"Why not?"

"Because you need to give a girl notice about these kinds of things. My hair isn't done, my face is a mess, I don't have good clothes on—"

"Well, the clothes can come off, so that's not an issue."

"I don't even know what underwear I've got on."

I frowned. "Does it matter?"

"Yes, it matters! It's Saturday and I'm having a lazy day at home with no chance of you swinging by, so I probably put on my everyday underwear. There's no way I'm stripping for you with that on."

I stroke my cock, closing my eyes as I grow harder. Hell, I don't need to FaceTime her to come; this conversation will get me there soon enough. Listening to Lorelei in a fluster over her underwear is like verbal porn.

"Did you just groan?" she asks.

I chuckle, not sure if I did or not because I was that carried away with thinking about blowing my load while she talked. "Possibly. I'm jerking off to your underwear talk so keep going."

"Fuck," she mutters. "I need to get in on this."

This time I groan loudly. The thought of Lorelei touching herself almost makes me come on the spot, but I slow it down, wanting to continue getting myself off while she does the same. "Touch your clit, Lorelei, and tell me when you do."

I hear her sharp intake of breath, and a moment later, she says, "I'm touching it."

"Good girl. Now take your finger and suck it. And then rub it over your clit again. Over and over until I tell you to stop."

I continue to stroke my cock, but I do it slowly, wanting to draw this out.

"Oh, God...." Lorelei's voice filters through the phone, stirring my desire for her.

"Are you wet for me? Slide your finger through your pussy and tell me how wet you are."

She's practically panting when she says, "I'm so wet that you could easily slide three fingers inside me, Ashton."

Jesus fucking Christ.

I suck in a long breath and squeeze my cock hard as I sit back in my seat.

"Do it. Fuck yourself with three fingers."

Her breaths are ragged now, too. I can hear them through the phone. Just as ragged as mine. She doesn't speak again; the only sounds I can hear are her breaths coming faster and her moans as she brings herself closer to an orgasm.

"Are you fucking yourself?"

"Yes. Oh... fuck... I'm going to come," she says breathlessly. "Oh, God...."

The sound of her orgasm fills my ears, and I pump my dick faster in an effort to come with her. A moment later, cum spurts over me and I groan loudly again.

I've had phone sex before, but I've never come so quickly from it in my life. This is fast becoming my experience with

Lorelei—sex with her is better than I've ever had it with anyone.

"I think we should FaceTime tonight," she says, catching my attention again. "I'll be ready for it then."

I love her enthusiasm. "I've got a dinner to go to with some of my guys here, but I'll make sure I'm back by nine. Be ready for then. And Lorelei?"

"Yes?" Her voice is so fucking sexy when she's just come.

"Be ready for a long night."

29

LORELEI

My back arches off the bed as I come for the third time tonight. Gripping my phone with one hand and the sheet with the other, I say, "I need a break, Ashton. My vagina is so sensitive I think it might explode if I touch it again any time soon."

We've been FaceTiming for an hour and a half, mixing orgasms in between laughter and conversations about our lives. It's been amazing, but I'm honestly not sure I can go on much longer. He's wearing me out.

His smile appears on my phone and he says, "No more orgasms, but I'm not ready to hang up yet."

I position one arm underneath my head on the pillow and hold my phone up in front of me with the other. "Okay, tell me how you're going with the investigation into the fire. We haven't talked about that yet tonight."

His smile disappears. "I learnt some disturbing news today. It seems the three guys who died had been shooting up in the bathroom when the fire started, and that's why they died. Everyone else followed standard safety procedures, but these guys weren't where they should have been, so at first, the foreman didn't realise they were still inside. It wasn't until he was counting heads that he realised they were missing, but by the time the firemen got inside, they were dead."

"That's awful."

"Telling their families will be awful."

I sit up and hold my phone in both hands. "You're going to tell them? Wouldn't that be the foreman's job, or the police's?"

He runs his fingers through his hair. "I'm going to do it. These men worked on my building. I feel a responsibility to their families."

"You're a good man, Ashton."

He's quiet for a moment, the mood still sombre. And then he says, "I'm just doing what any boss would do."

I shake my head. "No, I'm not sure they would. I think a lot would pass the buck."

His phone sounds with a text, and I wonder who it could be at this time of night. It's late in Perth but super late in Sydney. One thirty in the morning here to be exact.

He checks his text and then says, "What are you doing tomorrow?"

"I haven't got any plans. Why?"

"Alessandra could do with some company at a soccer game. You up for it?"

"Sure. Just text me the info and I'll go hang out with her. I really like your sister." I try to stifle a yawn, but he sees it.

"You should go to sleep, beautiful."

My tummy flutters when he calls me that. I can't deny that I like it. "Yeah, I should. I don't want to, but I will."

"I'll be home tomorrow night. I'll take you out to dinner."

I smile sleepily. "Sounds good. Call me before you leave so I know what time to be ready for."

We end the call and it doesn't take me long to drift off. I'm fairly sure my dreams tonight will consist of Ashton doing dirty things to me, because it's what I'm waiting for from him tomorrow.

Alessandra raises her glass and clinks it with mine. "Here's to girlfriends who get you through hard times." With that, she downs half her glass of wine.

It's almost six on Sunday night and she's been at my place for two hours drinking wine and laying her heart out for me. I arrived at soccer just after three thirty to find her and Malcolm arguing. He suggested I take her home, and I'd agreed, but on the way, she said she didn't want to go home. Instead, she purchased two bottles of wine and asked me to bring her here.

I sip my wine. I'm still on my second glass because I really didn't want to drink, but she'd insisted I should. "What time is Malcolm coming to pick you up?" I don't mind her staying, but I'm concerned she's going to write herself off before he arrives.

"He'll be here around six thirty," she says as she narrows her eyes at me. "You haven't told me about your past boyfriends yet. You need to spill."

"What do you want to know?"

Her eyes sparkle with mischief as she drinks more wine. "Everything! But I especially want to know if you always go for men like my brother."

I laugh. "God, no. I've never dated a man like Ashton."

"Okay, but you've dated, so tell me—who was your great love? The one who got away who you never thought would."

This isn't something I want to discuss, so I shrug and say, "None yet. I haven't met my great love." It's not really a lie. I'm not sure I have met him yet.

Her forehead crinkles. "Really?"

"Really. I've met my fair share of assholes and guys who think they can get away with treating me like crap. And sure, there's been some guys who I thought could become more, but none of those relationships eventuated into something amazing. So, I'm still looking."

She lifts her glass to her mouth. "Don't you think some days that life would be so much easier without men in it?"

Laughing, I nod. "Yeah, but then they take their dicks out and show us how good life is with them in it, and we wouldn't have it any other way."

She collapses in a fit of laughter and soon we're both laughing so hard we start crying. I'm not sure why, but I'm guessing it's the wine mostly. It's at that point there's a knock on my front door.

I answer it to find Malcolm standing on the other side. He gives me a smile and I'm instantly reminded of how much I liked him this afternoon when we met at soccer. Although he and Alessandra spent a lot of that time arguing, I'd been impressed with the way he didn't lose his cool with her. He fought fairly, and when he knew they wouldn't be able to resolve their differences, he'd made the suggestion that she go home. And he hadn't made it with a nasty, belittling tone; he'd remained calm and treated her with respect.

"Lorelei," he greets me.

I return his smile. "Hey, Malcolm. Come in."

"I've got the kids in the car, so I won't come in, but thank you."

"Oh, of course," I say, turning to call out for Alessandra. She's right behind me, though, so I snap my mouth closed and step aside so she can exit. As she does, I don't miss the way Malcolm watches her with devotion. Anyone can see how much the man adores his wife. I can't understand why Alessandra even doubts it.

"You ready to leave?" he asks.

She nods before glancing at me. "Thank you for putting up with me this afternoon. We should do this again soon. There's a new day spa opening next week and they sent me two invites. If you're free, I'd love you to come."

"I would love that." And I truly mean it. I've loved spending time with Alessandra, and on top of that, relaxing at a day spa is one of my favourite things to do.

"Good. I'll call you tomorrow to organise it."

We all say our goodbyes, and I watch as Malcolm places his hand protectively on the small of her back to guide her to the lift. I truly hope they can sort out their problems, because I can tell they both love each other so much. From everything Alessandra told me that afternoon, I know she'll be crushed if they can't work through it.

Closing my apartment door behind me, I lean against it briefly. Partly to steady myself, because the wine I drank made me a little tipsy after drinking on an empty stomach. And partly because my heart hurts thinking about love and all the problems it can cause.

Pushing off the door, I leave those thoughts behind and head into the kitchen to grab a drink of water. Ashton will be here any minute to take me to dinner, so I need to hurry and find something to wear. I'd planned on taking my time getting ready for him, but now I'll be lucky if I have ten minutes to spare.

A knock on the front door makes me curse. There goes my ten minutes.

I yank the door open and blurt out, "I know I'm not looking sexy yet, but if you give me—" I stop talking when I realise the man standing in front of me is not Ashton.

"Lorelei," he says, and my heart starts beating rapidly at the voice I haven't heard for five months.

The voice that used to wrap me in love.

The voice I thought I'd grow old with.

I sway a little and reach out to grip the door. My thoughts are a mess of confusion. Is it possible I'm imagining this? I haven't seen him in months, but I was just thinking about him during my conversation with Alessandra. Maybe I imagined him into existence.

When I don't say anything, he steps forward. "Lorelei, are you okay?"

I stare into his beautiful green eyes. "What are you doing here, Boston?"

He can't be here.

I can't do this now.

Before he can answer me, a commanding voice speaks over us. "That's what I'd like to know, too." Ashton stands next to Boston, every inch of his body demanding an answer to his question. We've not talked about Boston yet, but knowing Ashton and his dedication to knowing everything about the people in his life, I wouldn't hesitate to believe he knows exactly who Boston is to me.

Suddenly, I'm not sure if it's the wine causing my light-headedness or the two men standing in front of me who both cause my heart to flutter and who both confuse the hell out of me because of my feelings for them.

30

ASHTON

I'm staring at Boston fucking Haynes and trying to figure out why the hell it's taken him a week to turn up on Lorelei's doorstep. I know everything there is to know about this man, including the details of his relationship with Lorelei, but I'm wondering what kind of man leaves it seven days to visit the woman he still loves when he returns to the city where she lives.

Because he does still love her; that much is clear. It's obvious in the way he's looking at her and also in the way he's glaring at me.

"Who the fuck are you?" he demands.

I take a step closer to him to fill him in on just who the fuck I am, but Lorelei stops me when she quickly inserts herself between us. I take great fucking pride in the fact it's my chest her hand lands on, not his. And also in the fact it's my eyes she searches for first, before turning to face him.

"I thought you were in the States," she says. Her words sound more like a question than a statement, and her voice wobbles with confusion.

Boston eyes her hand on my chest. He scowls as he meets

my gaze, but that scowl disappears when he looks at her a moment later. "Amber was in a car accident so I've come home to help her out for a while."

Amber is his sister, and the car accident he mentions has left her unable to run her business or her life. I know this, too, because Jessica is a fucking rock star at her job. Amber owns a chain of stores that sells guitars. She also runs a school that offers guitar lessons, and a recording studio. She's the best in the business in Sydney and it's a smart move to call her brother home, because the music world is also his world. Boston will be able to smooth over any problems caused by her absence.

"Is she okay?" Lorelei asks. Her tone rises with concern and she grips my shirt. I know from Jessica that she was close to Amber. Sliding my arm around her waist, I pull her against me in an effort to comfort her.

Boston's jaw clenches when she easily moves into my embrace, and I work hard not to show my sense of victory. I'm an asshole—I want to claim Lorelei as mine in front of him so he knows, without a shadow of a doubt, that she isn't his anymore. But I keep a tight leash on the asshole in me and simply hold her. I remain silent while she finds out what she needs to know from him.

"Besides a broken leg and arm, and some cuts and bruises, she's fine. But she needs help with her business, and at home, so she asked me to come help her." He pauses for a brief moment before adding, "I'd been planning to come back anyway. To see you." I don't miss the way he says those last two words, and my body tenses while I fight the growl of disapproval working its way through me.

Lorelei's body tenses, too, as she says softly, "Boston...." Her voice drifts off and she doesn't finish that sentence, but even a fool could work out that she's not convinced seeing him is what she wants.

Boston draws a long breath and exhales sharply while he runs his fingers through his hair. I get the impression this definitely isn't going the way he planned. "Can we talk, Lorelei? Just the two of us."

Over my dead fucking body.

I step forward, keeping Lorelei in my hold but moving in such a way that she ends up further away from Boston than I do. "The time for you and Lorelei to talk has long passed. And besides, she's busy tonight; I'm about to take her out to dinner."

The scowl returns to his face at the same time as his shoulders square. "I still don't know who the fuck you are."

"Ashton Scott. And the only relevant thing you need to know about me is that Lorelei is mine now. So—"

Lorelei cuts me off when she wiggles out of my embrace. "What Ashton is trying to say is that we're dating now," she says, with a hint of annoyance as she glares at me for a beat. "And in answer to your previous question, I don't think we have much to talk about, Boston. I'm going to check in with Amber, but you should go now."

Boston's gaze shifts between Lorelei and me. He seems unsure of his next move, which only proves to me that he is not the man for Lorelei. If he were, he'd know exactly what to do in this situation. And that sure as hell wouldn't be to fuck around trying to figure out what to say or do.

Finally, he says, "I'm not giving up here, Lorelei. I want you back." He moves close to her and whispers something in her ear that I can't hear.

The combination of his hands on her body while he speaks, and his mouth so close to her face causes a level of possessiveness I've never known to surge through my veins. Unable to stop myself, I bark, "Take your hands off her, Haynes."

He is slow to react, which infuriates me. When he

finishes speaking into her ear, he pulls his face away, but as he does this, his lips brush across her cheek. His eyes meet mine, and in them I see the challenge he's laying down. He may infuriate me, but in no way do I view him as an equal here. Lorelei is mine; Boston Haynes has no chance of winning her back.

"Please don't do that," Lorelei says to him as I reach for her. I have no idea what she's referring to, but what I do know is that she easily moves into my hold again.

Boston doesn't reply to her, but rather he glances at me and says, "Don't get too comfortable, Scott. Lorelei might be yours for now, but she was mine for three years. We've only been apart for five months. That's not long enough for her to have fallen out of love with me."

I'm about to tell him exactly what I think of that when Lorelei pushes out of my arms and mutters, "Oh, for God's sake, you two can have this pissing contest without me." With that, she stalks inside her apartment, slamming the door after her.

After the door slams closed, I glare at him. "You don't think five months is enough time for a woman to figure out who she wants in her life? Tell me, have you heard from Lorelei since you left?"

His jaw clenches again, but he doesn't answer my question.

"I thought so." I move towards the door and turn the handle to enter Lorelei's apartment. Looking back at him, I say, "Don't come back here, Haynes."

A moment later I'm inside her apartment and he's out of my sight. In a perfect world I'd never see him again, but I know he'll be back. Lorelei Winters isn't the kind of woman a man gives up on easily.

"Lorelei," I call out as I walk down the hallway in search of her.

She runs into me when she exits her bedroom in a rush. Eyes wild, she places both hands on my chest to steady herself and says, "Just so we're clear, I'm not anyone's property, Ashton."

My arms circle her as I back her up against the wall. "I never said you were." I ignore the way she pushes against me in an attempt to separate us. There's no way in hell I'll allow that. Right now, the only thing on my mind is making sure she knows I'm not going anywhere.

"You may not have used those words, but you did everything except throw me down on the floor and show Boston that I'm yours."

"I don't need to throw you down to prove to him that you're mine. The man's not blind, Lorelei. Everything about the way you are with me shows him that."

"Well, you don't need to rub it in his face."

"He needs to know where you stand, and that is beside me."

She presses hard against my chest, still trying to move out of my hold. "Yes, but I can only imagine what you said to him after I left, and I bet it was something to do with reminding him that I didn't choose to marry him. I don't want you to do that. I've already hurt him enough."

Marry him.

That information was not in Jessica's notes about Boston Haynes. It's the kind of knowledge I would have preferred to have because it slants this situation in a new light.

Her ex will need to think again if he's planning on convincing Lorelei to agree to marriage this time. She might not be my property, but she is most definitely mine. And I always keep what's mine.

31

LORELEI

I DROP MY KEYS ON THE KITCHEN COUNTER AND turn to face Ashton. We've just arrived back at my apartment after he took me to dinner at one of my favourite restaurants. Looping my hands around his neck, I say, "Thank you for dinner."

He watches me in the way he does when he wants to discuss something important. His eyes hold that glint that tells me whatever it is, he won't let it go until he's gotten what he wants from me. "Why didn't you marry Boston Haynes?" he asks as his hands slide around my waist and settle on my ass.

He surprised me when he didn't bring the subject up over dinner, but I'm not surprised he's doing it now. The possessiveness he exhibited earlier when Boston arrived at my front door seemed extreme, so I've been waiting for him to broach the subject again.

"It's a long story. One we don't have time for because I'm about to get naked." I may have been waiting for him to ask me about Boston, but it's the last thing I want to get into with him now.

"Lorelei," he says, his tone issuing a warning. "I don't care how long the story is. I want to hear it."

I sigh. "No, you don't. You just want to know whether Boston is a threat, and I can tell you he's not."

His eyes flash with determination. "I'm aware he's not a threat, but until you start talking, neither of us are getting naked."

I inhale a deep breath and stall for one last moment, needing it to gather my thoughts. This conversation needs to be approached with care. Exhaling, I say, "Fine, but just remember it was you who asked for this." I attempt to move out of his hold, but he refuses to let me go. Raising my brows, I pull a face to signal my irritation, but still he doesn't budge. I'm not sure why I'm being so weird about this, except for my concern that if even *I* can't fully explain my decision not to marry Boston, how can I expect him to understand? And how then can I convince him that I don't want Boston in my life anymore?

A look of frustration crosses his face before he bends to my ear and says, "I have half a mind to take you over my knee."

The last time he mentioned this kind of thing, I was turned on. This time, I'm annoyed. It's one thing to spank dirty thoughts out of me; it's another to use it to get this kind of information. My eyes widen as his gaze meets mine again. "You wouldn't."

His nostrils flare. "Try me, Lorelei."

I straighten and drop my arms from around his neck, resting my hands on his chest. "I was with Boston for three years. I thought he was the man I would spend the rest of my life with, but when he asked me to marry him, I couldn't say yes. I didn't know why, but it just didn't feel like the right thing to do at that time in our relationship. We didn't break up, though, and he said he'd wait for me to be ready. That lasted for three months until the day we had a huge fight. A couple of weeks later, he moved to the States for work, and I haven't heard from him since."

Ashton watches me intently, his mind clearly working fast to process all that. "Why did you say no?"

I press against his chest, and he surprises me by finally letting me go. Taking a step back, I say, "I told you, it wasn't the right thing for us."

"No, you said you didn't know why. You've had time to figure that out now." He pauses for a beat. "What was the real reason?"

I stare at him for a long few moments. He stares right back, pinning my gaze to his. The man just doesn't give up. Always pushing me to give him my truths that I don't want to share with anyone. It's one of the things I both love and hate about him. "I have this fear of losing people," I say softly. "So sometimes I push them away before I have the chance to lose them."

"That may be so, and I don't doubt it because you've tried repeatedly to push me away, but it's not the full story here."

I frown. "I'm not lying to you, Ashton, if that's what you're trying to say."

He shakes his head as he closes the small distance between us again. Placing his hand under my chin, he tilts my face to his. I can't help but notice the way his eyes have softened. "You're not lying to me," he murmurs, "But are you lying to yourself?"

If everything about him right now didn't scream his genuine care for me, I would push him away and tell him where to go. But there is none of his bossiness or dominance in sight. Instead, it's like he's truly trying to help me see something. So I run with it and attempt to explain myself to him. "I'm not lying to anyone. I've spent time analysing this.

Losing Mum at such a young age kinda screwed me up, and I still haven't conquered that demon."

His hand snakes around my waist, and I lose the ability to breathe for a moment when he says, "If you hadn't conquered that demon, we wouldn't be standing here having this conversation. Your walls are high, and you did your best to keep me out, but here I am breaking them down brick by brick. And as much as you try to keep me out, and as much as we fight over that, you're not going anywhere, and you know that." His lips brush my ear when he adds, "There's something I'm giving you that Boston never could. And I'm betting it's the one thing you really need from a man."

His deep voice commands every one of my senses. He is all I can see, hear, touch, taste, and smell right now. The world doesn't exist when he has me like this. And that scares me because I never want to give anyone that kind of power over me. So I do my best to take some of it back. "You're right, my walls are high. But the reason they're falling down is because *I've* decided to let them. I don't want to keep pushing people away." I shoot him a sexy smile as I trail my finger down his chest. "Boston is in the past. You are my future. Now, can we please stop talking so we can start getting naked?" Getting naked is much easier than continuing this conversation, especially when my gut tells me Ashton is right about this.

32

ASHTON

SHE'S FUCKING KILLING ME HERE. I WANT TO KEEP pushing her to open up to me, because everything about this fucking Haynes situation is telling me there's more to it than just her need to control the losses in her life. But fuck, maybe I'm imagining something that isn't there at all. Maybe I'm the one off base here. It wouldn't fucking surprise me. Lorelei has me by the goddam balls, in a way that no other woman ever has.

I take in the smile she's giving me—the one begging me to fuck her—and I struggle to think straight. For the last couple of hours, I've been going over and over the fact Lorelei said no to Haynes's marriage proposal, trying to figure out why she wouldn't want to marry the man she'd given years of her life to. The reason she's giving me doesn't make sense, and I have a burning need to know the truth. I know deep in my gut that Haynes is back with a mission—one that involves not giving up until he has Lorelei back in his arms. And the one thing I know about winning a war like this is that you need to be armed with every last scrap of knowledge you can get your hands on.

"Ashton?"

Lorelei's voice draws my attention back to her desire to get naked. Wanting to forget all the thoughts plaguing my mind, I lift her into my arms, turn, and back her up against the wall in her kitchen. Her legs wrap around me as I drop my lips to her collarbone. I'm a starved man after not having her for a couple of days. Controlling my urge to rip her clothes off and sink myself as deep inside her as I can is proving almost impossible.

"Mmmm," she moans, angling her head back to give me full access to her neck. "God, how I've missed you."

Those words tip me over. I grip her hair with one hand, pulling her head back further, while snaking my other hand up her body and over her breast so I can wrap it around her throat. Not tightly so she can't breathe. Rather, I apply just enough pressure to gain her full attention. When those beautiful green eyes of hers meet mine, I see the same raw need there that I have for her.

"I'll never forget that first day I laid eyes on you." My declaration catches her by surprise, and a smile dances across her lips at what I say. "I knew then that you were a ballbuster. I just didn't realise it would be mine you'd be busting."

The surprise on her face intensifies as her mouth falls open. "You flustered me so much in that meeting and then you pissed me off. If there was anyone who needed their balls busted, it was you."

I grind my cock against her, needing the friction. Fuck, I need more than that. I need every goddam thing she has to offer. "Well, beautiful, you excel at it."

"You bring out the best in me, Ashton. I have to admit, though, that I wouldn't have thought sharing this kind of information would be in your playbook."

My gaze pierces hers. "Haven't you learnt by now? I don't have a playbook where you're concerned."

I let go of her neck so I can slide my hand under her top, taking pleasure in the way her back arches when my fingers brush her skin.

"I'm not sure about that," she says, unbuttoning my shirt in the sexy way she's perfected. Neither slow nor fast, the way her fingers move over my shirt arrests my attention, keeping it hostage and distracting me from my own goal. "I think Ashton Scott has a carefully considered strategy for everything in life."

I pull her hair a little harder and kiss my way up her neck to her ear. "I do," I growl. "Just not with you." As I admit this, I find her breast under her top and slip my hand inside her bra.

Her hips rock against mine as a moan falls from her lips. "If you're telling me this to get me hot, it's working. I am so ready for you to fuck me."

I pinch her nipple and grind against her. She has no fucking idea what her dirty mouth does to me. "I'm telling you this because I want you to know how I feel about you. This isn't just some fun for me, Lorelei. I'm 100 per cent in this with you. Hell, you could hand me a playbook that would work for you and I'd still not use it, because I don't want to chance fucking this up. Everything I say and do with you is completely honest. I'm not bringing any bullshit to this table. When I say I want you, I fucking want you." I draw away from her slightly to meet her gaze fully. "And when I say you're busting my balls, I mean it. I want you to know that's the power you have over me. *That's* the power I'm choosing to give you."

Her body stills and she sucks in a breath while staring at me for a long few moments. Her lips search for mine once she composes herself, and her kiss almost wipes every thought from my mind. That's what she does to me. Her touch, her kiss, her body, her mind—it all eases something in me. I'm clueless to label exactly what just yet, but I do know there's an ache deep inside that only she can soothe. And I'll be damned if I ever let her take that balm away.

When her mouth leaves mine, she meets my gaze again, our faces close. "I know you're not a strategist where I'm concerned, but just so you know, that kind of honesty will win me over every time," she says softly, her voice a wash of vulnerability.

She doesn't realise it, but that's what I've been looking for. A piece of her own raw honesty that reveals I'm not the only one with my dick swinging in the wind here.

I step away from the wall where I have her and turn to walk us down her hallway. "*Now* we can get naked and you can continue talking dirty to me."

Her mouth spreads out into the kind of smile I'd do anything to see every day. Threading her fingers through my hair, she says, "No, I want *you* to talk dirty to me."

We reach her bedroom, and I throw her down on the bed. Without stopping for even a second, I undo my belt and rasp, "My mouth is going to be too busy to be talking dirty, Lorelei." And if I have anything to do with it, my mouth is going to be busy for most of the night.

33

LORELEI

Thank God for lifts. That's all I can think as I stare silently at the display above the lift door indicating which floor it's currently at. My phone is pressed to my ear while Sienna tells me what she did on the weekend, but I hardly take it in as I wait for the lift and try not to think about how sore my body is.

"Lorelei!" Sienna snaps, and I blink back to attention.

"What?"

"Are you even listening to me?"

The doors open and the five people in it exit, leaving me alone when I enter. As the doors close, I sag against the back wall and let out a long sigh. "Sorry, I wasn't really listening because I can hardly focus today."

She's quiet for a beat, and I imagine her eyes narrowing at me the way they do when she's trying to figure out why I said something. "What's going on?"

Images of Ashton flash through my mind at that question, and I squeeze my legs together as a shot of heat hits me. "Ashton is what's going on. He fucked me so hard and for so long last night that I can hardly walk this morning."

She coughs as if she just choked on a drink. When she recovers, she says, "I only have two things to say to you right now. One, when did you start talking like that? And two, holy fuck! *All* night? And can you really not walk? Like, that's some serious fucking we are talking about. Jesus, I am so jealous of you right now!"

"That was way more than two things. And seriously, if you were me today, you would not be jealous."

"Well now you're just being ungrateful. I don't know any woman who wouldn't want a man like Ashton to keep her up all night, screwing the hell out of her."

I groan. She's right. I loved every minute of it, but I woke up this morning wishing he wasn't quite as good at sex as he is.

The lift reaches the floor I need, and I exit it as I concede, "The man is insatiable, Sienna. I think I need at least three days to recover."

I make my way down the corridor I haven't seen in about six months and try to ignore the hesitation churning in my stomach. Coming here today could turn out to be a huge mistake, but I need to do it for my own peace of mind if nothing else.

"Is that why you're taking the morning off? You were very mysterious on the phone earlier when you called to say you wouldn't be in."

"No, I'm taking it off so I can see Boston and clear some things up with him before they get out of control. The reason I was guarded on the phone was because Ashton was in the bathroom, and I didn't want to chance him finding out what I'm doing."

"So you're keeping this from him?" I can hear the disapproval in her voice, but I block it out. I know what I'm doing.

"I'm not keeping it from him so much as I'm avoiding a potential argument that isn't necessary at this point. I'm going to make sure Boston knows where we stand, and once that's done, Ashton and I can continue on as we were before he showed back up."

"Mmmm, I don't see this going down the way you do."

Before I can reply, Boston's voice sounds from behind me. "Lorelei?"

I come to a stop and spin around to face him. He's been out running and is a sweaty mess. A very masculine sweaty mess with his chiselled muscles on display.

Keeping my gaze firmly on his face, I say to Sienna, "I've gotta go." And then to Boston—"Hi."

I'm a tongue-tied fool standing here staring at him while trying to gather my thoughts. I had expected to arrive at his sister's apartment, spend a good five to ten minutes outside psyching myself up for our conversation, and then walk in there and tell him like it is. Instead, he's caught me off guard, and I'm struggling for words in much the same way I imagine an Olympic sprinter probably struggles for breath after a race.

His lips twitch as if he's about to break out into a grin, but he contains it and simply says, "I'm glad you came."

Oh, no.

No, no, no, buddy.

I'm fairly sure he's misreading this whole situation, and I need to get us on the same page before his thoughts progress any further.

I raise my hand as if to say, "Stop," at the same time that he steps closer to me. Unfortunately, my hand lands on his chest. A moment later, his hand is resting over mine, and he's smiling down at me in a way that tells me he very much thinks there is more to this visit than there is.

Oh, God.

Sienna was right—this is not going down the way I pictured it.

"Boston, I—"

Still smiling, he cuts me off as he grabs my hand and leads me towards Amber's apartment. "Amber has been feeling down since the accident. Seeing you will cheer her up."

"Wait. I need to tell you something," I blurt out, but we've reached our destination, and he interrupts me again.

He unlocks the apartment door and says, "Catch up with Amber first, and then you and I can talk." His eyes lock onto mine and he blasts another smile my way as he adds, "It's so good to be back."

My throat goes dry as concern races through my veins. This is definitely not going the way I imagined.

I sip my coffee and watch Boston silently while he sugars his. I've spent the last hour catching up with Amber and doing my best to ignore the growing dread in the pit of my stomach. Boston sat on the couch next to me while I chatted with Amber, acting like the past five months and a break-up hasn't gone down between us. After I finished with Amber, he suggested we head to the café downstairs so we could talk. I was more than ready to talk and set a few things straight.

"Boston, this isn't what you think it is."

He glances up from his coffee and watches me quietly for a few moments. "What do I think it is, Lorelei?"

"You think that me coming to the apartment this morning means I want to get back together with you. But it doesn't. I wanted to come over and see Amber, and I also wanted to come and see you to let you know it really is over between us."

"It's not over between us. Not by a long shot. I noticed the way you reacted when you saw me this morning." He leans closer and drops his voice. "The way your body reacted to me."

"The only reaction you saw was me being caught off guard." The way he assumes to know what I'm thinking and feeling irritates me. It always has.

"Why did you feel like you had to be on guard in the first place?"

I frown. "*This* is why. You have a way of twisting my words and causing me to get all confused." I pause for a moment before adding, "Don't read more into this than what there is."

"There *is* more to read into here. There always is with you."

"Stop it. There's nothing more here. We broke up five months ago, and I've moved on. You should too. I wanted to say that in a much nicer way to you, but you're not giving me much chance to do that."

He lifts a brow as he settles back into his seat. "You've moved on with Ashton Scott? Do you know much about that man, Lorelei? For instance, the fact that he sleeps with women all over the world and moves onto the next before he's hardly finished with the previous one."

Anger bubbles up from deep within me, as well as a desire to protect Ashton and not allow Boston to trash talk him. "I know more about him than you think. And to be honest, it surprises me that you would stoop so low as to put another man down. There are better ways to convince a woman to take you back than to resort to that kind of behaviour." I push my chair back and stand. "Please listen to me when I tell you that there's no future for us. We had some fun, but we weren't meant to be together forever."

He stands too, a determined look on his face. "I told you last night that I wouldn't give up as easily this time, and I meant it."

"And I asked you to please not do that. I've just started seeing Ashton, and I want to give our relationship a good chance."

"You loved me, Lorelei. You don't just fall out of love with someone in five months."

I stare at him for a beat, trying to decide whether I want to hurt him with a truth I don't think he's considered. I decide the truth is always the best course of action. "There are all kinds of love, Boston, and I'm not sure ours was the soulmate kind. Don't get me wrong, I loved you—I still do—but I don't think it's the kind you want it to be."

He stiffens. When he doesn't respond to that straight away, I figure maybe he's finally taking it in. But then he says, "That's bullshit, and you know it. That's you running from this because you're scared. And Ashton is simply your safe place because you know he'll never ask for what I'm asking for. I'll give you the space to figure this out, but I won't walk away. Not again."

My heart beats rapidly as I watch him leave.

Shit.

I don't think I fixed anything today. I think I just made it a whole lot more complicated.

34

ASHTON

LORELEI'S BEAUTY NEVER FAILS TO CATCH MY breath. When I asked her earlier today if she could attend a party with me tonight, giving her only a few hours' notice, she said yes, but she seemed a little panicked about finding a dress and getting ready on time. I told her it didn't matter if we were late, but in the end, she managed to pull it all off with time to spare. She also managed to pull it off looking more beautiful than I've ever seen her.

Watching her mingle with party guests, I take the opportunity to admire the strapless red dress she's wearing. It hugs every inch of her, ending just above her knees. There's nothing flashy about the dress, but Lorelei doesn't need flash to draw every eye in the room. She manages that all on her own.

Smiling at me as the couple we've been talking to leave us, she cups my cheek and says, "You look deep in thought. What are you thinking?"

I slide my arm around her waist and pull her close. "I was thinking about how much I love this dress on you. And how I'm not sure we'll be staying long at this party."

She moves her hand from my cheek to the back of my neck. Threading her fingers through my hair, she says, "Do you know how much my body aches after you had your way with it last night? I'm not sure I'm up for another round tonight."

I did fuck her hard last night. Sex is one area of a relationship where I never relinquish control, and after our conversation where I admitted the power she holds over me, I'd needed to be back in control again, so I'd used sex to do that. A tinge of guilt hits me, though, that I may have demanded too much from her. And yet, it won't stop me from pushing her for more tonight.

I bend my face to hers, and my lips brush her ear as I say, "Do you know how much I've been thinking about my face in your pussy? Tonight is happening, Lorelei."

She grips my hair as her breath catches. Before she can respond, we're interrupted by Aaron Steele. He's the reason I'm here tonight, so I allow the interruption.

"Good to see you, Ashton," he says, giving me a second of his attention before shifting his gaze to Lorelei. "And who's the lovely lady you're here with?"

Lorelei's body stiffens, and I don't miss the brief flare of irritation in her eyes as she takes him in. Figuring she'll introduce herself, I don't answer his question. Extending her hand, she says, "Lorelei Winters."

That's my girl.

I curb the grin that wants to spread across my face. Steele is the kind of man who thinks women should be seen but not heard. I haven't mentioned him to Lorelei, but I'm guessing, by her reaction that his reputation precedes him.

Steele shakes her hand. "Aaron Steele." Turning to me, he says, "We need to talk."

Lorelei lets me go and says, "I'll be back."

I nod and watch her as she makes her way towards a

woman who she greets with a hug. Steele draws my attention back to him when he says, "Cassia's here tonight."

Jesus, even more of a reason to leave as soon as possible. Engaging in conversation with my ex is the last thing I want to be doing tonight.

I ignore what he said. "What did you need to discuss?"

His brows lift. "I'm surprised, Ashton. I never did understand why you let her go. Cassia Brampton would make the perfect wife for you with her family connections and ability to fit in and know her place in business."

I don't like the tone of this conversation. "If I wanted a woman who *knew her place* in anything, I could find that anywhere, Steele. I'm not in the market for that kind of woman. Actually, I'm not in the market for a woman full stop. I already have one. And I didn't come here to discuss my relationships with you."

"You're serious about Lorelei?" His tone is incredulous, and my displeasure with this conversation intensifies.

I don't want to discuss Lorelei with him, but I feel the need to set him straight. "I'm deadly serious about Lorelei, and I'll ask you not to bring this topic up again. The only thing between you and me is a business deal. I have no interest in explaining my life decisions to you." Aaron Steele is a brilliant businessman, but he's on his third marriage and is well known for being an ass to women. He's not the kind of man I'd ever pursue a friendship with.

Distaste clouds his face. "This will be the last I'll mention it. I think you're a fool for walking away from Cassia and an even bigger fool for choosing a woman like Lorelei. What does she contribute to your life? What do her family connections offer you? A smart man would think about those things when it comes to choosing a wife. By all means, keep her on the side, but never make her more than that."

If Steele wasn't absolutely necessary for a deal to go

through that I need to go through, I would walk away from him and never look back. Instead, I force my anger away and say, "Now that you got that off your chest, let's get back to business."

Thankfully, he lets all talk of women drop, and we discuss what we need to. When our conversation ends about fifteen minutes later, I'm more than ready to get out of here, but Lorelei is nowhere in sight. I begin searching for her, but am frustrated to run into Cassia before I find her.

"Ashton," she murmurs, her eyes meeting mine after they run all over my body first.

"Cassia." I make sure to maintain eye contact. Cassia does not need any encouragement to think I'm interested in picking back up from where we left off.

"How are you?"

I ignore the step she takes to move closer to me, hoping that will be as close as she comes. If the past is any indication, it won't be, but a man can hope.

"I'm well. You?" Fuck, I hate small talk.

Her heart-shaped face lights up with pleasure at my question, and I realise too late it was the wrong course of action to take. "I'm good. Busy, though. You know what it's like. A party nearly every night to show your face at. I've been disappointed not to see you at too many lately, but I know you've been busy travelling. I'm happy to see you back in town now."

I need to end this encounter now. Before I manage to fuck it up any further than I already have. "I'm on my way out, Cassia, so I'll have to cut this short. But it's great to hear you're good."

I step away from her, but she reaches out and stops me, her hand gripping my arm. "We should have dinner one night."

Fuck no.

Turning, I face her again. "No, Cassia. I'm seeing someone." My voice is firm in an effort to convince her she needs to move on.

She blinks a few times, clearly surprised. I haven't dated since we broke up, and she knows I don't easily make relationships official. "Oh," she says, her voice cracking a little.

I remove her hand from my arm. "Goodbye." With that, I walk away, not waiting to see how she processes what I've told her. Cassia didn't handle our break up well, and I still feel some guilt over how it all went down. We were together for four years, but in the end, I realised I didn't stay because I loved her, but rather because I wasn't bored with her like I was with most other women. It was an asshole move to make with a woman who planned her life around me, so as soon as I became aware of the reason I stayed, I left. Cassia deserved more from a man than I could ever give her.

She doesn't follow me, and I manage to exit the room without further delay. Fifteen minutes later, I finally find Lorelei. She's deep in conversation with a guy I know only by reputation, and by the looks of it, whatever they're talking about has her excited.

"Ashton!" she exclaims when she sees me. "Come and say hi to Ryan Shandwick. Do you two know each other?" Definitely excited about something. Every inch of her is alive with it.

My arm circles her waist as I shake Ryan's hand. "I've heard a lot about your developments." He's only been in Sydney for about a year. Prior to that, he was working out of Melbourne. His business has grown fast, and he's been plagued by rumours of shady operations.

Shandwick grins. "Lorelei sings your praises, Ashton, but she doesn't have to—I've been following you and your business for years. Great to meet you, man."

"Ryan's been telling me about the project he's currently

working on—an apartment complex in Bondi," Lorelei says, the excitement still clear in her tone, and I wonder at that. What shit has he been spinning her?

Shandwick's still grinning at me. "We're in the early phase of it, but it's shaping up to be something—" His phone rings, cutting him off, and he says, "Sorry, guys, I need to take this. I'll be in touch, Lorelei."

I watch him for a moment as he walks away. Even if I hadn't heard the rumours about him, I wouldn't trust him. He gives off a vibe, and my gut instinct is to avoid him. I always make it a point to go by that instinct—it's never let me down yet. The fact he told Lorelei he'd be in touch concerns me, but I decide to leave that for a conversation with her later. I've got much more important things on my mind right now.

Shifting my gaze to her, I say, "I'm ready to dedicate some serious time to getting this dress off you."

Her eyes sparkle and she laughs. "Here? Now?"

"I'm easy."

"Okay then," she plays along, still laughing. Reaching her arms around to the back of her dress, she says, "You want me to undo the zip and get you started?"

I tighten my hold on her. "Don't you dare," I growl. "There's no fucking way any man in here is getting his eyes on you."

Her eyes smoulder with desire. "You should take me home, but I need you to know I wasn't joking when I said you wore me out last night. This isn't going to be another long night."

"Don't count on that, beautiful. You'll be begging me for more within the hour," I promise.

"Oh, God," she groans as I lead her outside. "I'm pretty sure you're going to kill me with sex, Ashton."

I watch the slow blink of her eyes as she says this and

take in the way her breathing picks up. I see the rise and fall of her chest, the flush that covers her skin, and the way she bites her bottom lip. Everything about this woman intoxicates me. I wasn't exaggerating when I told her last night how much power she holds over me. What she doesn't know, though, is that I've never given this kind of power to any woman in my life.

35

LORELEI

"Mmmm, good morning," I say as Ashton trails kisses down my stomach. Scrunching my fingers in his hair, I try to stop his progress.

When he looks up to meet my gaze, he says, "You want me to stop?"

"Yes… no… but really, yes. I can't take any more of you at the moment." At the twitch of his lips, I widen my eyes and say, "Seriously! I am sore in ways you can't even imagine. I told you I couldn't handle much more last night, but you just kept on going."

He positions himself over me so our faces are close. "And I heard no complaints from you then. In fact, I recall you screaming out my name a few times. Just so you're aware, that's the kind of feedback that tells a man to keep going, not to stop."

I smack his arm. It could be because of what he just said or it could be the huge smile spread across his face that makes me smack him. Either way, he deserves it. "I'll be sure not to scream in future."

He moves a strand of my hair off my face and drops a kiss

on my lips. "Don't you dare stop screaming." Shifting, he lies next to me on the bed and lazily traces patterns on my stomach. "What have you got planned for today?"

I love this side of Ashton. Fun, playful and a little softer than usual. I wouldn't trade his dominant side for anything, but it's nice to have this part of him as well. "I'm in the office all day. How about you?"

"I've got a couple of meetings this morning, and then I'm spending the afternoon with Jack."

"Have you guys got something fun planned?"

"That depends if you classify golf as fun."

"God no! Don't ever ask me to go golfing with you. Bost —" I cut myself off when I realise I'm about to mention Boston to Ashton while in bed with him. Definitely not something I want to do.

He's silent for a beat. "Lorelei, you can talk about your ex with me. He was a huge part of your life. I don't expect you to never mention him."

Guilt slices through me that I didn't tell Ashton about going to see Boston yesterday. I contemplate telling him now, but I don't want to ruin the easy mood we've got going. Instead, I roll to face him, slide my hand over his waist and down to his ass, and say, "Okay, but at this point, I'd rather talk about you."

His erection presses against me, and he groans. "If you keep your hand on my ass and your body next to mine like this, we're going to have to renegotiate me fucking you."

"Did we actually negotiate that or did I just tell you it wasn't happening?"

"The negotiations took place last night. I won if you recall."

"Oh, so this morning when you tried to have your way with me, that was just you trying to squeeze more out of the deal?"

A slow sexy smile hits his lips. "She's finally learning how I like to do business."

"Let me see if I've got this right? Negotiate hard. Don't ever lose. And get everything you can out of the deal. Does that about cover it?" I make sure to keep my hand on his ass as I throw a leg over his body and press myself against him more than I have been.

"Fuck," he hisses. "You're sexy when you talk business."

I lean forward and kiss him, right before I leave the bed. Looking down at him, I smile. "My turn to negotiate now. I've got two tickets to an advance screening of *Mr Alpha* tonight. I want you to take me. And before the movie, I want you to take me to dinner at Agostino's."

He moves off the bed and joins me. I can't be sure, but I think there's approval in his gaze as he says, "You want me to take you to a chick flick?"

"Yes."

He crosses his arms in front of him. "What do I get out of this deal?"

"Time with me."

His lips twitch. "I can get that whenever I want, Lorelei. You're going to have to negotiate harder for this."

"Maybe you can't get that whenever you want."

"Ah, so you'll withhold yourself from me if I don't agree to this?"

"I might."

He shakes his head. "No, baby, you need to be firm. Hard. You have to stick it to me to win here. Remember rule number two—don't ever lose."

God, negotiating with Ashton is hot. I need to do more of this. Straightening my shoulders, I say, "Okay, yes, I won't agree to see you for the rest of this week if you don't agree to this."

His brows lift. "You won't win if you try to bargain with something unbelievable."

"I'm not!"

He chuckles. "Yeah. You are. We both know there's no way you'll go without seeing me for that long."

His smugness makes me want to fight harder for this. Summoning the firmest voice I've ever used, I say, "I'm telling you right here and now, that if you don't agree to take me to a chick flick tonight, you won't be getting any pussy for the rest of the week."

Heat flares in his eyes. "One night."

I frown. "Huh?"

"If I don't take you to the chick flick, there'll be no pussy for one night."

"Uh, uh. No. One week."

His eyes drop to my lips. "Three nights."

I realise he has no intention of backing down. I should have known he wouldn't go easy on me. Hell, it's one of the reasons why I love spending time with him. He treats me like an equal. But damn if I'm not winning this today.

I run my finger lightly over his lips. "Let's see about that." I drop to my knees and take his cock into my mouth. Slowly. All the way in. And then I take hold of it as I slide it out. After I lick it from one end to the other, I look up and say, "You agree to take me to dinner and the chick flick tonight, and I'll suck your cock right now and make you come."

He grins. "That's how you do it. Deal."

I stand. Keeping hold of his cock, I say, "On top of that, I'll blow you on the way home from the movie if you agree to do whatever I want tomorrow night, too."

His arms snake around me and he pulls me against his body. Our faces are so close and my heart is beating so fast at the raw need and respect radiating from him. Having Ashton watch me like this awakens something deep inside me. Something so erotic and pleasurable that I never want him to stop looking at me like that.

"That's right, beautiful, get everything out of the deal that you can," he says, his voice deep and sexy.

"So that's a yes?"

He kisses me slowly and so very thoroughly. By the time he ends the kiss, my knees are weak, and I'm not sure I would still be standing if he wasn't holding me up. His eyes find mine as he says, "I'll agree to all of that with one stipulation—after we get home, you fuck me all night long again."

I hold his gaze for a long few moments before finally nodding. "Deal." I press my lips to his and kiss him before saying, "And that last bit I agreed to... that's called a compromise. Because sometimes when you negotiate with people, you have to do a little give-and-take. Just so you know."

His arms tighten around me. Not that they weren't already around me firmly, but it's like he's trying to clear every last obstacle between us. Like he's trying to get as close as he possibly can to me. "Fuck, you're something else."

I'm about to kiss him again when my doorbell sounds. "They'll go away," I say, bringing my mouth to his.

"Who would it be so early in the morning?" he asks as I try to kiss him. "I imagine it wouldn't be just anyone."

Shit, he's right. It might be my neighbour looking for help. Letting him go, I say, "Okay, wait here. I'll go see what they want, and then I'm coming back to make good on our deal."

I pull on some clothes and make my way out to the door. I expect to see my neighbour when I open it, but am surprised when I discover it's Alessandra. My surprise turns to concern when I see she's been crying. Her face is puffy and her eyes are bloodshot.

Reaching for her, I say, "What's wrong?"

She allows me to pull her into a hug, but it's like she

doesn't even realise what I'm doing. "I've been trying to call you and Ashton, but neither of you answered your phones." She's so disoriented that alarm slithers through me.

"Aly?" Ashton joins us. "What's going on?"

She lets me go and moves to him. Tears stream down her face as she says, "Mum has had a heart attack. She's in the hospital."

Ashton's face pales as he pulls his sister into his arms and holds her while she cries. Alessandra is completely devastated, and for the first time since I've met him, Ashton appears bewildered. It's the kind of reaction to be expected, but it throws me to see him like this. And when I realise that not only is his mum not well, but that this means he'll have to see his father, I know that life is about to be turned upside down for my man.

36

ASHTON

"AARON STEELE CALLED. HE WANTS TO BRING YOUR next meeting forward to tomorrow," Jessica informs me over the phone an hour and a half later when I check in with her.

Alessandra, Lorelei, and I arrived at the hospital to find Dad pacing the emergency room while Mum was still with the doctors. I took his pacing and concern as a sign that he was worried about Mum; however, it turned out he was more worried about missing business meetings today. I shouldn't have been surprised, but it seems there's still a part of me looking for a father who cares about his wife and family. That was what surprised me the most—that after all this time and everything we've been through, I'm holding onto misguided hope.

"Let Steele know I'm out of the office until further notice. And cancel everything for today. I'll let you know about tomorrow when I find out what we're dealing with here."

She's quiet for a moment. "I think he's ready to negotiate, Ashton. He hasn't asked for any more information after everything I sent him yesterday."

I know what she's not saying. If I don't meet with him, he

may find something else to invest in and walk from the deal. I need him on this one, but more than that, I need to make sure my mother is okay.

"He can wait."

"I'll take care of it all." She pauses briefly. "How's your mother?"

"She's still with the doctors. We don't know much more than we did when we arrived."

"Keep me updated, Ashton." The sombre tone in her voice is something I don't often hear from Jessica. It matches the mood at the hospital.

"Will do." I end the call as Lorelei joins us in the waiting room after stepping out to take a call that looked anything but happy. Meeting her gaze, I say, "Is everything okay?"

Shaking her head, she says, "No. But my problems aren't what matters today. Your mother is all that matters."

"Talk to me, Lorelei. I can't do anything else for Mum at this point, but I may be able to help you." And God knows, I could use the distraction.

She sighs, and it's like she exhales the weight of the world. Her shoulders slump at the same time, which lets me know that whatever she's dealing with is causing her a lot of worry. "It's the Willow Street building. I'm having problem after problem with it, and just when I think I've fixed everything, more issues pop up."

I frown. "How long has this been going on? And what kinds of problems?"

"A few weeks. At the moment, I'm fighting with the insurance company about repairing the roof, and dealing with almost-daily vandalism of the building. I thought it was the work of one of my tenant's exes, but now we're not so sure. He's been out of town for a couple of days so he couldn't have done the graffiti that she found over the weekend. On top of that, I have a florist opening in one of my shops soon, and this morning the shop had been broken into and the walls inside were graffitied. Thankfully I have a handyman who I call on to repair stuff like this, but the bill is adding up each time I have to get him in."

"It doesn't look good to customers either," I suggest. I've come across numerous businesses that have had to close up shop due to a bad reputation from crime in the area. I'm disturbed that Lorelei has to deal with this.

"Right. I've heard that some customers have taken notice, and that does worry me. I need to figure out what's going on and fix it, but I'm at my wits end with it all."

I can hear the frustration in her voice. And it's clear to see the tension in her body. I pull out my phone. "I've got a guy who can look into this for you."

Her hand closes over mine, stopping me from making the call. With a shake of her head, she says softly, "No. Leave it, Ashton. You've got far more important things to worry about today."

"This won't take long to organise."

Her gaze drifts to Alessandra who is sitting alone. "And in that time, you could go and talk to your sister. She needs you." I open my mouth to argue, but she silences me with a finger to my lips. "If I'm still having problems after your mum is better, I'll let you know, and you can help me then."

After my mum is better.

My brain fixates on that comment. *After, not if.* Lorelei's mind works differently to mine. I've trained mine to always consider what could go wrong with any given situation. I don't naturally gravitate towards what could go right. This morning has been no different. I've imagined as many scenarios as I could based around all the outcomes possible from my mother's heart attack.

For the first time in a long time, I feel adrift. I have no control over this outcome. And that terrifies the hell out of me. My mind is scrambling to come up with options. But there aren't any that we haven't already put into action.

Lorelei moves closer. Her hand brushes my arm, and care laces her voice when she speaks. "Ashton, did you hear what I said?"

Before I can reply, my father cuts into our conversation. "Your mother had a lunch she was attending today for the Bright Foundation. I need to call and let them know she won't be there. Do you know the number for the woman in charge?"

I stare at him, incredulous. My carefully contained anger at his behaviour this morning frays. He's been on the phone with business associates since we arrived, unwilling to push his work aside for even a minute while his wife's health hangs in the balance. "No, I don't know the phone number for a woman running a goddam charity. That's hardly in the realm of what I do with my time." He always—*always*—does his best to downplay my business success. I have no doubt that him asking me for the lunch organiser's number is his way of putting me in my place.

His lips flatten. It's the only sign that I've angered him. My father is exceptional at hiding his emotions. This skill is one of the secrets of his business success. "I wouldn't know what you do with your time anymore, son." His voice is low and controlled. He's always so damn guarded.

Neither of us moves. We simply stay where we are and watch each other warily. The tension of the situation has me on edge more than I usually am around him. I'm strung so tightly I know it won't take much for me to snap. And that isn't something I want to do while I wait to find out my mother's prognosis.

In the end, it's Alessandra who moves the conversation forward. She joins us, hands Dad her phone, and says,

"That's Margaret's number. She's organising the lunch today."

His gaze slices to her as he takes the phone. "Thank you, Alessandra."

I track his steps as he leaves us and exits the waiting room. Once he's no longer in sight, I drop my head, scrub my face and mutter, "Fuck."

"Jesus, Ashton, can we just get through today please?"

My head snaps up, the anger I'm trying hard to control unravelling a little more. "The fuck, Aly?"

My tone is too harsh, and she responds to it. The anguish lining her face turns to anger as she lashes out. "For once I'd like our family to let shit go and just be together. Dad's never going to change. He is who he is, so why can't you just ignore whatever it is you think he's saying and just answer his questions for what they are? Life would be a lot bloody easier!"

"Ignore whatever it is I think he's saying…. What the hell do you mean by that?" My fury sparks and I'm unable to hold it back any longer. Unfortunately, I'm taking it out on the wrong person. But that's the story of Alessandra's and my lives—we get messy in the bad blood of our family. We go to battle over the very things we both wish didn't exist, because it's the only way our pain can be heard when neither of our parents are interested in acknowledging it.

"You always have to twist his words and make something out of them that might not even be there. For God's sake, all he asked for was a phone number. All you had to do was say you didn't have it, but no, you couldn't stop yourself from reminding him that Ashton Scott doesn't involve himself in something so lowly as a charity lunch."

"Fuck, you know I didn't mean it like that. And you also know *exactly* what he meant by it. I'm not going to stand around and let him belittle me. Not anymore."

She exhales loudly. "Maybe you read too much into what he said."

"You seriously don't believe that, do you?"

She throws her arms up. "I don't know, Ashton! All I'm saying is, he simply asked you for a phone number. If you could have just answered that question for him, all this other tension may have been avoided."

I can hardly believe what I'm hearing. "Christ, Aly, where is this coming from? You of all people know how our father thinks."

Eyes wild, she doesn't answer me straight away. Her face twists with distress and she wraps her arms tightly around her body. When she does finally speak, her voice is choked with emotion. I hear the tears she doesn't show the world. "What if Mum doesn't make it?" She takes a ragged breath. "I can't live without her. Our family can't survive without her."

Every last bit of anger churning in me retreats, and I reach for her, pulling her close so I can quiet her fears. Not that they ever can be with Aly, but I always try.

My sister is a worrier. She clings to all her fears in ways I can't fathom. Sometimes I think it's easier for her to spend time worrying about everything than actually dealing with the truth.

I hold her tightly and smooth her hair. "Mum's going to be okay, and so are we. And no matter what happens, you and I will always make it. *We* are our family."

Her body is so stiff in my arms that I wonder if anything I say will help ease her concerns. She looks up at me, and I see the anxiety in her eyes and on her face. "I know we are, but I wish it wasn't like this. I wish our family could be more," she says softly.

"I know." Fuck, it's all I ever wanted, too. But my eyes are wide open, and I don't see that ever happening.

Approaching footsteps draw my attention, and I look up to find Dad and Malcolm walking our way. Malcolm's gaze is firmly on his wife. The love and concern blazing from his eyes is clear for all to see. I wonder again how Aly either misses it or misreads it.

"Any news?" Dad asks.

Alessandra leaves my embrace and moves to her husband as she answers Dad. "No, nothing yet."

Malcolm's arms circle her as he brushes a kiss across her lips and murmurs something I can't quite hear. She nods before sagging against him. My sister may be well known for her cool and calm manner in business dealings, but I'm concerned that in her personal life she's an emotional mess. At least she's allowing Malcolm to comfort her.

Lines wrinkle Dad's face as he frowns. Flicking his wrist, he checks his watch. "What the hell are these doctors doing? It's been hours."

I bite my tongue from lashing out at him and turn to Lorelei. "You want a coffee?"

She nods. "Yes, but let me get it. You wait here in case the doctor comes with some news."

With a shake of my head, I say, "No, I need to get out of here for a bit. I may say or do something I'll regret if I don't."

Understanding flashes in her eyes. "Yeah," she murmurs. "I'll come with you."

37

LORELEI

I MOVE FAST TO MATCH ASHTON'S PACE AS HE strides with purpose towards the hospital cafeteria. Anyone else would assume he was on a mission to get coffee; I know he's on a mission to escape his father. Gregory Scott hasn't given me many reasons to like him this morning. He doesn't seem as interested in his wife's health as he does in his business. I can see why Ashton struggles so much with him. And I've also been given a glimpse at the dynamics between Alessandra and her father. I don't know her very well yet, but it's obvious she's desperate for Gregory's approval. And from what I've seen so far, I don't think that approval is easy to achieve.

Reaching for Ashton's hand, I attempt to slow him down. "Ashton, can we walk a little slower?"

He does as I ask but doesn't say anything. However, he grips my hand in a way that lets me know he needs me.

A few minutes later, we reach our destination, and he orders our coffees. I watch him closely, taking in the hard set of his jaw and the tense bunching of his shoulders. His father has him wound so tight.

Rubbing his back gently, I murmur, "I'm sorry you're going through this."

I don't expect a reply because he's intently watching our drinks being made and appears to be deep in thought, but he surprises me when he turns and bends to brush a kiss across my lips. "Thank you for being here with me."

"I wouldn't be anywhere else."

His eyes stay glued to mine while I continue to rub his back. We don't speak, but we don't need words. The silence we share speaks volumes, as does his body language. I'm slowly learning to read my man.

We sit at a table once our drinks are made. Before we have a chance to talk, Ashton's phone rings and he has a short conversation with Alessandra before ending it and standing. "They're giving Mum an angiogram and she may need stents. I'm going to head back there to talk with her doctor."

I pass him his coffee and then follow him as he walks to the waiting room. This time I don't ask him to slow his pace. I know how desperate he is to talk with the doctor. His mission is interrupted, though, when a blonde woman calls out his name and runs towards us just before we arrive at our destination.

"Fuck," he mutters, coming to a stop. When she reaches us, he greets her, "Cassia."

That name causes my stomach to knot with apprehension. Cassia is the woman he was with for years.

She moves closer to him and places her hand on his forearm. The way she touches him and then rubs his arm is intimate, and I stiffen.

Looking up at him with what appears to be genuine concern, she says softly, "I'm so sorry to hear about your mother. I came as fast as I could."

I blink as I swallow hard.

She came as fast as she could? She makes it sound like he wants her here. Maybe he does. I don't know anything about the relationship they have now. Perhaps they are still friends. I could kick myself for not knowing this, because now the knot in my stomach is tightening and making me feel stressed. Or anxious. *Or jealous.*

God, I'm jealous. I don't do jealous. It's not something I've ever really experienced while dating. Probably because half the time I'm trying to keep the guy I'm dating at arm's length. But I'm feeling it right now with Ashton and Cassia. The way she's touching him is too much for me. I want to rip her hand off his arm and tell her to back away from him. *Away from my man.*

Where the hell are these thoughts coming from? This is not the day for them. Not while Ashton is worried over his mother. I attempt to lock them down tight and not let them out. I'm sure there's nothing to worry about, anyway. Ashton has made it clear how much he wants me, and he's always been honest, so I trust him.

Without waiting for Ashton to respond, Cassia goes on. "How is she? What have the doctors told you so far?"

It's after she asks these questions that she shifts her gaze to take me in. She inspects me with a fine toothcomb, and by the end of it, I feel like I don't meet any of her criteria for being worthy of her attention because she doesn't acknowledge me in any way. She simply turns her gaze back to Ashton and waits for him to answer her questions.

"We're on our way back to speak to the doctor now," he says, shrugging his arm away from her. His cool tone does wonders for the knot in my stomach, and I take the opportunity to stake my claim.

Sliding my arm around his waist, I say, "Hi, I'm Lorelei."

Ashton's arm snakes across my shoulders and he pulls me close. I take it as a signal to Cassia, and I guess she does too because she stares at his arm for a long moment before meeting my gaze again.

"Cassia," she says, her voice icy. Looking back at Ashton, she says, "I'll come with you."

Ashton's jaw clenches. "There's no need. And besides, it's just family."

I secretly cheer on the inside and instantly feel like a bitch. Maybe Cassia really just wants to check on Ashton's mother.

However, when she moves even closer to him and touches him again, I know her visit here today is all for Ashton. And when she speaks, I know every word of it is for me. "Ashton, Kendall and I are like family. You and I might not be as close as we once were, but your mother and I are closer than ever. She would want me to be here. Please let me come and wait with you for more news."

He opens his mouth to reply, but his father joins us and says to Cassia, "Good, you're here."

Cassia steps away from Ashton and turns to his father. "I'm so sorry to hear about Kendall, Gregory. I was just saying to Ashton that I'll stay with you all through this awful time. The Scotts are family to me."

Gregory nods and indicates for Cassia to follow him. With a catty smile thrown my way, and a squeeze of Ashton's hand, she goes with Gregory, leaving me staring after her feeling like everything just changed in the blink of an eye.

And that damn knot in my stomach has morphed into what feels like a million knots.

38

ASHTON

"Why is Cassia here?" Alessandra asks a few hours after the doctor confirms that Mum is okay. They're giving her stents, after which she'll most likely be in hospital for a few days.

"I have no fucking clue," I mutter, eyeing Cassia with my father. I'm more than surprised at their closeness. He left for a couple of hours and has just returned, and they're huddled discussing something in hushed tones.

Alessandra exhales a long breath while crossing her legs and scrolling through emails on her phone. "I had no idea she was friendly with Mum and Dad. I've not seen her at their house, and Mum hasn't mentioned anything except for the couple of times she said she wishes you two were still together. I didn't take that to mean she'd welcomed Cassia with open arms."

My thoughts drift off while she talks about this. I couldn't care less about whatever they've got going on. What I *do* care about, besides Mum's health, is Lorelei and the issues with her building. She's just stepped out of the waiting room to take another call from one of her tenants. It's the third call today, and with each one I've watched her become more stressed.

"Ashton, are you listening to me?" Alessandra smacks my arm while staring at me, demanding an answer to her question.

I shift in my chair, irritated. "Fuck, Aly. And no, I'm not listening to you because what's the point in dwelling on Cassia and whatever she's doing with Mum and Dad. It doesn't affect us."

Her eyebrows arch. "You're kidding me, right? Cassia is known for manipulating people. Whatever she's doing with them is because of you, so you *should* be paying attention."

"Why? She can't manipulate me into anything."

She stares at me like I've grown another head. "For a smart man, you can be dumb when it comes to women. But luckily you've got me. I'll pay attention for you."

"I have no doubt," I mutter.

She smacks me again but doesn't say anything else on the matter.

My attention is drawn to Lorelei walking our way. I stand to meet her, noticing the worry in her eyes. "What's happened, now?" I ask as I curl my hand around her waist. I've never been the kind of man to engage in public displays of affection, but with Lorelei, I can't help myself. The need to touch her is too strong to resist.

She sighs. "My tenant is consulting with a lawyer about getting out of the lease. She's had enough of all this graffiti and the break-ins. I don't blame her, but the last thing I need right now is that shop empty. It'll be a hard sell leasing it with all the stuff that's been happening."

She's right. I make a mental note to have my guy look into it.

"Do the police have any new leads?"

She shakes her head. "No." Her gaze shifts to my father

for a moment before coming back to me. "I'm really sorry to do this to you, but I'm going to have to leave so I can go and try to sort this out."

I pull her close and brush my lips over hers. "You go. I'll call you later."

Lorelei glances in Dad's direction again, a strange look on her face, and then she nods. "Okay," she says softly.

I frown. "What's wrong?"

With a quick shake of her head, she says, "No, nothing. I'm just worried about you guys, that's all."

"We're good. Don't worry about us."

She says goodbye to Alessandra and then leaves. I watch her go until I can't see her anymore. It's been a shit of a day, but having her by my side has made it bearable in a way I've never known before.

A hand on my arm draws my attention back to the moment, and I find Cassia looking up at me with concern. "Are you okay, Ashton? Your dad and I are worried that you're not taking this very well."

"Cassia, the last time my father worried about me was a long time ago, so I find that very hard to believe. And yes, I'm okay. You don't need to worry about me."

She moves closer to me. "I'll always wor—"

Alessandra rolls her eyes and says, "You can cut the bull-shit, Cassia. The only thing that ever concerns you is your social standing. Don't come here today and use our mother's health as a way to worm your way back into Ashton's life."

"Alessandra." Dad's sharp voice issues a warning when he joins us. "That's enough. Don't talk about things you have no idea about."

My sister's eyes widen as she is chastised. She's only ever chased approval from two men in her life—Malcolm and our father. Malcolm gave it easily. Dad, not so much. I'm guessing that him taking Cassia's side here is like a slap in the face.

I rake my fingers through my hair as I glare at him. "Jesus, Dad, you can be an asshole when you want to be."

His eyes turn cold as his gaze settles on me. "I would prefer it if both my children could use their manners while waiting to hear how their mother's health is. Particularly when we have company."

Anger churns in my gut at his words. "You—"

Mum's doctor interrupts our conversation. "Mr Scott, you can see your wife now."

Dad nods at the doctor. "Thank you." His gaze slices back to me, and with one last icy glare, he leaves us to follow the doctor.

Alessandra shoots up out of her chair and grabs her bag. "I'll be back." She stalks out of the room, leaving me alone with Cassia.

"Your sister always did hate me," Cassia says.

"Hate is an extreme term." This is the last conversation I want to be having today. Actually, I don't want to be having any conversation with her, but it seems I'm stuck.

Her lips flatten in the way they used to whenever we had an argument. "Not where Alessandra is concerned, Ashton, but you were always blind to her when we were together, so I'm sure that hasn't changed. It'd be nice if, for once, you could open your eyes and see things for what they really are."

"Don't push me, Cassia, because you might not like what I see."

Her brows furrow. "What does that mean?" she demands.

"It means that sometimes I intentionally close my eyes when I don't want to see what is plainly there to be seen. You have benefitted from that in the past. Let's not start something we can't turn back from."

She stiffens and lifts her chin, a complete look of distaste covering her face. Securing her clutch under her arm, she throws back, "You think your father can be an asshole, but you don't seem to acknowledge what an asshole *you* can be. You are far worse than Gregory."

The sound of her heels tapping on the hospital floor fills my ears a moment later. It might just be the best fucking sound I've heard all day. What Cassia is doing with my family is a mystery to me, but I have a feeling I'm going to be seeing a lot more of her while my mother recovers from her heart attack. Thank fuck I have Lorelei to stand by my side while I deal with it all. Her presence alone eases tension from my life in ways I never knew someone could.

39

LORELEI

"Here, I brought supplies with me," Sienna says as she enters my kitchen just after seven that night and hands me a bag with the logo of my favourite bakery on it. "Figured you might need them after the day you've had."

It's been the longest day full of stress, so I could kiss her when I rip the bag open to discover two vanilla cupcakes. My favourite. "You are a goddess sent from heaven."

She grins. "I try."

I hold up a mug. "You want a coffee?"

Sliding onto a stool at my kitchen counter, she nods. "Of course. With a side of tell-me-all-about-what-happened-with-Cassia-today."

"Ugh, you had to mention her name, didn't you?"

She clicks her fingers, indicating I need to hurry up. "Spill. And then we can make a plan."

I stop what I'm doing and look at her. "A plan?"

"Yeah, a plan for dealing with bitchy exes. I know you've never had to deal with one before, but I have, so I am the perfect person to advise you on this."

"God, this all sounds awful. I don't think I need a plan. Ashton and I are good."

"It's not Ashton I'm worried about. Cassia Brampton has a reputation. She is not a woman you want to be ill-prepared for."

I take a bite of one of the cupcakes. A huge freaking bite because I need it. I'm starting to feel even more anxious about Cassia than I was this morning. I've spent the day talking myself around on this issue, but now that's all flying out the window.

Sienna takes note of my actions and says, "Okay, you sit and eat cake while I make coffee."

I do as she says. "Make mine strong. I think I'm gonna need it."

We then spend a good hour making a plan for how I'm going to deal with Cassia after I tell Sienna how rude the woman was to me this morning. Mostly the plan involves me remaining confident and not allowing her to make me doubt my relationship with Ashton.

"I'm gonna be there every step of the way cheering you on until she's out of the picture," Sienna says.

I smile at her. "You're always there cheering me on."

"Yeah, but this is going to be so much more. If Cassia Brampton thinks she can waltz back in and mess with my bestie, she's dreaming." The alarm on her phone sounds, and she slides off her stool while reaching for her bag. "Babe, I've gotta go. That hot neighbour dude of mine is taking me out for a drink tonight, and that was my cue to leave so I'm ready on time." She slows for a moment. "Are you okay with all this? Or should I cancel my plans so I can stay with you?"

I shoo her with my hands. "I love you, but you can be a drama queen when it comes to this stuff. Consider me prepped for Cassia. You go and make that man fall for you."

She grins mischievously. "Oh, he has already fallen for

me. That happened when I rescued his dog from imminent death. I saved her from escaping our building and then we spent the next couple of hours swapping life stories. Tonight is our first real date, though, so I need to get myself ready for him."

"Hot neighbour dude has a dog?" Sienna loves dogs. Her last guy hated them, so it was a match made in hell.

A dreamy smile spreads across her face. "Hot neighbour dude's name is Nathan, and yes he does. And can I just say that watching a man love a dog is pure bliss."

"Okay, go get ready. I'm going to spend the night catching up on paperwork and tax."

She pulls a face. "Oh God, that sounds like the worst night ever. Is Ashton still at the hospital?"

I walk her to the door. "I think so. He called a couple of hours ago and said he'd be there for a while and that he may not see me tonight. I was going to head back to the hospital after I finished work, but the doctors wanted only family today."

"I hope his mum is okay," she says as she exits my apartment. Her eyes light up as she adds, "I'll text later to let you know how my date goes."

I laugh. "Something tells me you won't have time to text."

"I can always fit in a quick, sneaky text to you."

With one last grin, she leaves me to head towards the lift. I smile as I watch her go, thinking about how good it is to see her this happy. I'm about to shut my apartment door and go find the paperwork waiting for me when the lift doors open and Ashton steps out.

His eyes meet mine after he speaks briefly with Sienna. They're dark tonight. And they watch me with intensity as he strides towards me that curls hunger through me.

God, how I want this man.

In every way I can have him.

"Ashton," I murmur when he reaches me. A shiver runs through my body when his fingers meet the skin on my arm. No man has ever affected me the way he does. "I thought you'd be at the hospital for most of the night."

He lightly runs his fingers along my forearm before wrapping his hand around it and pulling me to him. Bending his face to mine, he kisses me. It's not a quick kiss to greet me, but rather a deep one that reveals his hunger for me. He takes his time with it, slowly backing me up against the door. By the time he's finished, his hands are cupping my ass and his erection is pressed firmly against me. And I am thoroughly turned on and out-of-my-mind crazy for him.

"I missed you this afternoon," he says, his voice husky with desire. His hands move from my ass, and he slides his fingers through my hair and angles my face up so our gazes meet. The raw need I find in his eyes intensifies my own desire. "I need to be inside you, Lorelei."

I grip his arm. "How's your mum?" I want what he wants, but I manage to sort through my lust-filled thoughts to find this question. It's important. I want to know that she's okay.

"She's good."

His answer is sharp and to the point, and his actions make it clear he doesn't want to discuss this any further, because as soon as the words leave his mouth, he lifts me and carries me inside to my couch.

Depositing me there, he keeps his eyes firmly on mine as he loosens his tie. He wore his suit to the hospital this morning, and even though he's been in it all day, he still looks immaculate. The only thing giving away the fact he's dealing with some heavy family stuff is the tiredness in his eyes.

The room fills with the sound of his tie sliding over his shirt as he discards it. Still watching me intently, he unbuttons his shirt. His fingers move deftly from one button to the next, undoing them, slowly revealing the smooth skin of his chest and abs. I lean back against the couch and enjoy the show of Ashton undressing.

When his shirt hits the floor, he flicks his wrist and beckons with his fingers for me to stand. Those beautiful blue eyes of his drop to take in my body, and when I stand, his hand goes straight to the button on my jeans. He makes fast work of removing them and slipping his hand into my panties.

Cupping my pussy and rubbing his thumb over my clit, he orders, "Take off your clothes."

Ashton is bossy by nature. I know this about him. But tonight it's like a whole other Ashton is here. He's hungry for me, and he's taken control, but he almost seems detached. And if I didn't know better, I would think that all he came for was sex.

I do as he says and a few moments later I stand before him naked except for my panties. I hardly know I'm still wearing them, though, because Ashton's hand covers my pussy rather than their thin material.

His thumb works my clit while he slides two fingers inside me. I'm so wet and ready for him, and I moan as he fucks me with his fingers. When he sucks one of my nipples into his mouth, I close my eyes and place my hands on his shoulders to steady myself.

I lose myself in the pleasure. Time passes in a blur with Ashton in complete control of my body.

When he growls, "Fuck," my eyes flutter open, and I take in the wild look of need filling his features. I'm so close to coming. What I see in his eyes almost tips me over the edge, but before it does, Ashton spins me around, yanks my panties down and says, "Bend over and place your hands on the top of the couch."

When he has me where he wants me, he undoes his belt

and pants. His body moves closer to mine, his cock teasing the hell out of me. "I want to fuck you without a condom tonight," he says as his hands cup my breasts.

It's a statement, but I hear the question in it. I also hear just how much he wants this. His voice is raw with that desire. "I'm clean." I want this too.

His hands move from my breasts to my waist. He grips my hips, and without waiting another second, he thrusts inside me. A primal groan comes from deep inside him, and his fingers dig harder into my flesh as he fucks me with a ferocity I've never experienced in my life.

It's primitive almost.

Wild and untamed.

I love every second of it.

I brace myself against the couch as he slams into me over and over, and when I come, I scream out his name like I never have before. It seems to fuel him, and he thrusts into me harder until he comes too.

"Fuck!" he roars out. He keeps hold of my hips while resting his forehead against my back. "Fuck," he mutters again, breathless.

We stay like that for a while. When he finally straightens, he turns me to face him. His hold on me is firm, like he doesn't want to let me go. And that intensity is still in his gaze.

"Today was one of the worst days of my life, but having you by my side made it bearable. And coming home to you tonight…. Fuck, that was everything I never knew I needed." He stops talking abruptly, like he was going to say something else but thought better of it.

Dropping his lips to mine, he claims me in the same kind of kiss he started this with. I feel every bit of his possession in this kiss, and while I never thought I was the kind of woman who wanted to feel possessed, I can't deny how much I love it. How much I love feeling Ashton's need for me.

And I realise how far I have fallen for this man.

I may even be falling in love with him.

40

ASHTON

I close my eyes and pinch the bridge of my nose. I'm exhausted after the last week of dividing my time between my mother, Lorelei, and work. Work has kicked my ass while I attempt to finalise the deal with Marc Brentley and secure Aaron Steel's investment in the New Zealand resort I'm building. Neither deal is any closer to being finalised.

"Ashton, you look like you could do with a weekend off," Mum says as I hand her the cup of tea she requested.

She's home now, recovering from her heart attack. I've been spending time with her each day so I can see her health improving for myself. The only downfall to this is seeing my father almost every day, too. It has surprised me to find him here each time I visit.

"Jessica's booking one in." I omit the information that it'll be half work, half play while I take Lorelei away to work on the resort we're involved with.

"Good."

I sit on the couch opposite her. "How are you feeling?

258

Really feeling, I mean. Not the bullshit you tell Dad and the doctors."

She purses her lips. "Why must you always insist on using that kind of language? I raised you better than that."

"Stop changing the subject, Mother."

Her shoulders rise as she takes a deep breath. Placing the teacup on the coffee table in front of us, she says, "I'm frustrated that I'm couped up in this house. I feel well enough to resume all my activities, but your father insists I rest. Little does he realise that all this resting is just making me tired."

"No, your heart attack has caused that exhaustion. Your doctor said it can take three months or more for your heart to repair itself."

"Pfft," she mutters. My mother has always been stubborn. "Even so, I should be allowed to do more than sit on this couch and watch television and wait for people to visit me."

We're interrupted by Cassia who joins us. She smiles when she sees me. "Oh, I didn't realise you had company, Kendall. I'm so sorry to intrude."

She's not, though. If she were, she'd offer to come back. Instead, she moves quickly to kiss Mum on the cheek before taking a seat next to me.

Placing her hand on my leg, she asks, "How are you, Ashton? We haven't seen each other for a week, and I've been wondering how you're doing."

I move her hand from my leg. "I'm fine."

"Well that tells me nothing." Her tone is snappy, and I'm not in the mood for that today.

Standing, I turn cold eyes on her. "As far as I'm concerned, I don't need to be sharing the finer details of my life with you anymore, Cassia."

"Ashton," my mother chastises. "That is no way to speak to Cassia."

Keeping my gaze on Cassia, I say, "She understands perfectly well what I'm saying."

Cassia crosses her legs and pouts. "I was just trying to be friendly."

If there's one quality I can't stand in a woman, it's playing dumb. And pouting when they don't get their own way? That is a sure-fire way to turn me off. Cassia didn't engage in much of this while we were together, but she's mastered it since. And it doesn't suit her.

Dropping a kiss to my mother's cheek, I say, "I've got work to do, but I'll stop by after to see how your day was."

She waves me away and shakes her head. "No, don't. I won't be here. I have actually managed to convince your father to take me to the movies tonight. I decided that was something he might agree to because it wouldn't take much effort on my behalf."

"I'll see you tomorrow, then." Glancing briefly at Cassia, I say, "Goodbye, Cassia."

"Don't worry about your mother, Ashton. I'll make sure she has a good day," Cassia calls out as I head towards the front door.

God fucking help me. Why the hell have my parents encouraged a relationship with my ex?

"How's your mum doing?" Jack asks as he enters the kitchen where I'm checking on the dinner I had sent over for tonight. Lorelei's on her way over to spend the night here. I decided rather than taking her out to dinner, I'd organise it here so I can have more time with her alone.

"She's recovering well." I eye the empty whisky glass he places on the kitchen counter and bite my tongue from mentioning it.

Jack still appears to be spiralling, and the more I say stuff about it to him, the further away I push him. That's the last place our friendship needs to be, especially now because he's going to need me more than ever when he finally crashes. But fuck, it's hard to watch someone you love do this to themself.

He pulls an almost-empty bottle of whisky out of the cupboard and pours another drink. "Let me guess, she's being her usual self, defying doctor's orders and thinking she knows best?"

I chuckle. "Yeah, pretty much. Hey, have you got any plans for Saturday? I thought we could take the boat out for the day."

A smile spreads across his face as he downs some whisky. "Sounds like a plan. I'm in."

My phone sounds with a text.

Jessica: Sian just sent a notification that she has three Willow Street buildings ready for you to buy.

Me: Good. Tell her to find more.

Jessica: That was your cue to tell me how happy my text just made you.

Me: If you'd told me she had all of them, then I'd tell you your text made my fucking year.

Jessica: Well since I'm not getting any praise tonight, I'll take a coffee from that Willow St café tomorrow. You know how I like it.

Me: Have my assistant organise it.

She doesn't reply to that, only sends me a gif showing me what she thinks of that idea.

"I'm taking that was good news by the way you're smiling," Jack says.

Glancing up at him, I shake my head. "Not really, but Jessica's sense of humour is out in full force tonight."

"That woman definitely knows how to make a man smile," he murmurs, and I see the moment where he drifts back into old memories.

"Jack," I warn him. "Don't go there."

He throws the rest of his drink down his throat. "So no good news, then?"

"She let me know my real estate has found three Willow Street properties to buy. The news would have been good if the number had been a lot bigger. I'm battling my father for these properties, so I need to make this happen fast before he does."

Jack frowns. "What does Lorelei think of all this? I would have thought she'd be against it."

"This is business, Jack. It doesn't have anything to do with Lorelei."

He whistles low. "And now I understand why my best friend is still single even though women line up to date him. Your head is in the clouds if you think this doesn't have anything to do with Lorelei."

I reach for a whisky glass in the cupboard and pour myself a drink. "When she sees the results of a Willow Street development, she'll understand why it was needed. The businesses on that street are dying while the rest of Sydney moves ahead, simply because no one has bothered to develop it."

His brows arch. "And you really believe she'll sell her building to you for this?"

"It won't matter if she doesn't. I can still go ahead without it. And that will only help her, so she'll reap the rewards of that. There's no way she won't be good with it once I lay it all out for her."

As a knock sounds on the front door, he says, "For the record, I believe this might just be the worst idea you've ever had. If you really want Lorelei in your life, that is. If you don't want her, sure, go ahead because I believe you that it will be good for business. But sometimes, people have to come first, my friend."

I frown. "I agree, and that's why I'm doing this. It'll be good financially for everyone."

He shakes his head at me. "But sometimes other things are more important than cash."

The knocking on my front door grows louder. "I need to get that. Are you joining us for dinner?"

"No, I'm going out for the night."

That thought scares me. Jack out on the town with all the alcohol in the world available to him is a recipe for disaster.

Before I can protest, he says, "Don't stress, Ashton, I'm going out with Sienna. She'll keep me on the straight and narrow."

"Good," I mutter before heading to answer the door.

Finding Lorelei on the other side eases some of the tension from my body. She's been by my side as much as she could be this past week, and has pretty much kept me going when the stress and exhaustion have gotten to me.

Snaking my arm around her waist, I pull her to me. "Do you have any idea how good it is to see you?"

Her eyes light up with pleasure as she loops her arms around my neck. After brushing a kiss across my lips, she says, "Don't judge my outfit, okay? I was running late."

I chuckle as I take another look at her body. "I've got no issue with this outfit. In fact, you should start wearing it more often for me. Have you just come from the gym?" She's wearing the tightest multi-coloured tights and a fitted bra top thing under a jacket. The fact I can see skin makes me more than happy, not to mention that her legs in these tights look fucking amazing.

She presses herself against me with a sexy smile. "You

would say that. And yes, I've just come from the gym, so you need to feed me. I'm starving."

I bend my face to her ear. "No one's going to be eating if you keep pressing yourself against my dick."

Her arms tighten around my neck, and she pushes herself against me again. "I could wait to eat, I guess. Your mad skills more than make up for food."

I run my hands down to her ass and smack her there. "No, I'm going to feed you first, because once I get started on this body, there is no way I'm being dragged from it."

Twenty minutes later, we're finishing up our dinner while chatting over a glass of wine. We've discussed our weekend away that we rescheduled after I had to cancel our last one and have gone over what we want to achieve. Lorelei's filled me in on her tenant issues and the fact she's hopeful they may be resolved soon. And I've updated her on Mum's health.

"So you didn't see your dad today?" she asks as she finishes her glass of wine. My gaze is firmly fixed on her lips as she drinks. I'm imagining them wrapped around my dick later. "Ashton, did you hear what I said?"

I find her eyes again. "I was busy thinking about fucking you, but yes I did hear what you said. And no, I didn't see him today."

Heat flares in her eyes and a smile fills her face. "I like it when you think about fucking me, but before we do that, I want to tell you some exciting news."

"You've decided to stop working so you can spend all your hours naked with me?"

She laughs and leans forward to place her hand on my leg. "Someone's playful tonight."

I lean forward and cup her breast through her top. "No, just ready to be inside you."

"Let's be real, you work too much. You wouldn't have enough time for all that sex."

I slide my hand into her top. "Who said anything about not working? I can multi-task. I would fuck you while I close deals over the phone. Hell, I'd probably be more productive."

She bites her lip and stands. A moment later, she's straddling me and undoing the buttons on my shirt. "Okay, let's be really real, then. You would be bored as hell with a woman who didn't do something with her life. The sex-on-demand would grow old very fast for you."

I reach a hand into her pants and find her clit. Rubbing it, I say, "This is why you're the woman for me. Not only are you beautiful, you're smart as hell."

Her eyes close and she bites her lip again as she moans softly. I could watch Lorelei experiencing pleasure for the rest of my life and I still wouldn't get my fill.

When she opens her eyes again, she hits me with a smile. "Guess what your woman did today?"

I return her smile. I fucking love her calling herself my woman. "What?"

"I agreed to invest in an apartment complex in Bondi."

Alarm bells ring in my head, and I frown. "With Ryan Shandwick?"

She nods excitedly. "Yes! It's an amazing deal. I can't believe I was lucky enough to meet him at that party you took me to and have the opportunity to be involved in this."

Fuck.

I'd meant to look into this, but I got sidetracked with everything else going on.

Before I can say anything, she asks, "Why are you frowning?"

I remove my hand from her pants and place both my hands on her legs. "I don't trust Shandwick."

"Do you know him?"

"I know of him and his reputation."

"What's his reputation?" she demands.

"He's been involved in some shady deals."

Her lips press together. "That doesn't mean this is a shady deal. I went through all the documentation today, and it all looks legit to me. Even the local council is supporting him."

"Fuck, Lorelei, that doesn't mean much. Politicians are as dishonest as criminals. Shandwick must be giving them a kickback of some sort to endorse it."

She straightens, her body tense. "You don't know that for sure. I'm telling you, I went over all the information with a fine toothcomb. I couldn't find anything that concerned me."

I rake my fingers through my hair. "Okay, leave it with me. I'll look into it."

Her eyes widen, and the angry expression on her face tells me I've said something wrong. Moving off me, she snaps, "I don't need you to look into it. *I've* looked into it."

I stand, too. "I know you have, but I've got a lot more experience with this than you, so I'll look at it, too."

She stares at me for a long few moments. Anger radiates off her, and I wonder why she's so worked up about this. When she scoops her bag up and slings it over her shoulders, I'm even more confused.

Moving closer to her, I ask, "Where are you going?"

"I need a moment. Or fifty."

"Where?" I'm hopeful she means somewhere else in this house.

"At my place."

"So you're going home? Because I offered to look into this for you? That makes no sense, Lorelei."

Her eyes flash with wild energy, the kind that screams her fury. "Oh, it makes perfect sense to me. I'm so offended you would think I'm not capable of this. I need some space to calm down."

"Calm down here."

She madly shakes her head. "No, I don't want you anywhere near me at the moment, Ashton."

I attempt to hook my arm around her waist and force her to stay, but she's running on anger and smacks my hand away.

Those wild eyes of hers meet mine. "This is not the night for you to do your usual bossy shit. I'm telling you that I need the night to calm down, and then we can discuss the way you take over without stopping to think about my feelings. I understand that you've got more experience, but *you* need to understand there are ways to say and do things." She pauses to take a breath and then adds, "I can see myself out."

With that, she stalks out of my house, and for the first time in my life, I resist the urge to go after what I want.

I want nothing more than to stop her, throw her over my shoulder and drag her back inside.

I do not want to let her walk out of here tonight. But I'm coming to understand that when Lorelei is angry, she needs a moment. And if I've got any shot at keeping her in my life, I need to step back and give her that. What she'll need to understand very quickly, though, is that after she's had that moment, I'll be coming for her and no fucking way will I be leaving without what I came for.

41
———

LORELEI

Sᴇɴɴᴀ ᴡʜɪsᴛʟᴇs ʟᴏᴡ ᴡʜᴇɴ I ᴡᴀʟᴋ ɪɴᴛᴏ ᴏᴜʀ shared office the next morning. "Babe, you look like you partied all night, got no sleep, and tried to cover your exhaustion with concealer. Tell me you *did* party. With Ashton."

I dump my bag on the table and slump into a chair. After taking a long gulp of the coffee I picked up on the way to work, I grumble, "There was absolutely no partying with Ashton last night. Instead, he upset me, and I left his place early so I could put some space between us. I spent the night thinking about what happened, and only got about an hour of sleep."

Her eyes widen, and she sits next to me. "What did he do? It's not like you to get upset for no reason."

I rake my fingers through my hair, still feeling annoyed and unable to shake it. I fill her in on the conversation that took place between Ashton and me and then ask her, "Do you think I overreacted?"

"No, I don't think so. Ashton can be super arrogant, and it sounds like you reacted to that more than anything else. You work hard on your business, and I'm sure you did your due diligence on this deal, so it would have been like a slap in the face for him to insinuate you didn't."

I sigh. "See, that's where I did overreact. He didn't really insinuate that. It was more like he said he'd look into it because he has more experience, and he's right, he does. I got my back up at the way he just kinda took over and said *he'd* do it. It made me feel inadequate, which meant my ability to think logically flew out the window." I take another gulp of coffee and then groan. "I hate overreacting like this. He probably thinks I'm an idi—"

Sienna cuts me off. "There is no way Ashton thinks anything bad about you. And while it would have been good to be logical, it's not always possible when our emotions take over, so don't beat yourself up. Just reach out to him today and talk it over."

I'm more annoyed at myself now than Ashton. And it's ten times worse being annoyed at yourself than someone else.

A text comes through, and I check my phone.

Boston: I'm doing some work today with Crave. You should come meet them.

Crave is one of my favourite bands, but there's no way I'm going to go meet them. That would send the wrong signal to Boston. I decide to ignore his text, hoping he might take me more seriously.

"Why are you suddenly looking stressed?" Sienna asks.

I hold up my phone. "Boston. He invited me to meet Crave today. I just wish he'd get the message that we're over."

"Crave! Holy shit! I'll go. I wanna get my Jett on." Jett's

the lead singer, and Sienna's had a slight infatuation with him for years.

"Settle down, Jett's getting married. You're out of luck there, babe. What about Van?"

"Ugh, that's right. I keep reading all about the plans they're making for their wedding. Presley this, and Presley that. I wanna vomit at how perfect they seem for each other. But I don't think Van's my type. If I couldn't have Jett, I think I'd have to choose Hunter."

I laugh. "You do know that the stuff you read in those magazines is rubbish, right?"

"Don't burst my bubble, Lorelei. According to what I read yesterday, Hunter is looking for a woman, and he has this thing for blondes. I could totally be who he's looking for. You know I've always had a thing for drummers."

Before I can respond to that, a delivery guy knocks on our door. He's holding a huge bunch of red roses. Glancing between us, he asks, "Either of you Lorelei Winters?"

"Wow," Sienna murmurs. "The man doesn't muck around when he sends flowers."

I take the flowers. "Thanks."

As the guy leaves, Sienna says, "There has to be at least a hundred roses in that bouquet."

I pull the card out of the envelope.

Lorelei, I'm sorry for being an asshole. Please forgive me.

My tummy does somersaults. No man has ever sent me flowers after an argument. It's not so much the flowers that mean so much to me, but rather the fact he's making an effort.

I grab a vase out of the cupboard and arrange them in it.

"I'm going to call him now and talk this through." I don't want to wait for him to reach out. If I could, I'd go to him so we could discuss it in person, but I have an appointment in an hour that I need to finish preparing for.

"No need. I'm here." Ashton's deep voice sounds from the doorway.

I turn to find him coming my way. His eyes burn with determination. I can't deny it—as much as he sometimes pushes me to places I'm not sure I want to be pushed, this fierce drive of his is one of the things I like about him the most.

"I'm just going to pop out for a bit and leave you two alone," Sienna calls out, but neither Ashton nor I respond. He's on a mission, and I'm held captive by it.

"Thank you for the roses," I say softly, suddenly feeling unsure of this conversation.

He comes all the way to me. "I didn't come to discuss flowers, Lorelei. I came to apologise in person. I won't make the mistake of taking over and not thinking about your feelings again." He closes the tiny distance between us and snakes his arm around my waist to hold me close. "But you need to understand that the best way to deal with a disagreement like this is not to run from me."

His commanding tone and bossy words snap me out of the spell I'm under. Pressing against his chest, I say, "I appreciate the apology, but not the directive that went along with it. If I need a time-out, I need it, so don't come here telling me how to deal with a situation."

God, can the man be any more arrogant?

He refuses to budge, not allowing even a small gap between us. His hold on me tightens. "I'm not telling you that you can't have your space. What I *am* telling you, though, is that I don't like leaving a disagreement hanging between us when we're apart from each other. Next time this kind of thing happens, have your time-out, but do it under the same roof. And when you've calmed down, come to me so we can fix it then rather than waiting the night."

It's in moments like this that I wonder about my mental state. One minute I'm irritated with him because of his arrogance, the next, my irritation is completely gone. I often swing between emotions with Ashton, and that's not something I've experienced with a man before. My emotions have pretty much always remained steady when I'm with someone.

Steady and a little boring.

Not a moment with Ashton is steady or boring.

Grasping his shirt, I say, "How do you always get away with being arrogant and bossy?"

His brows lift. "You think I got away with it last night?"

"Well, no, but—"

Ashton cuts me off by backing me up against the wall and gripping my waist with both hands. "No buts, Lorelei," he growls. "I fucked up last night, and I didn't get away with it. I respect you standing up for yourself, but just so you're aware, it was the longest fucking night of my life. I've never wanted anyone like I want you. To not know where your head was at, fucked with *my* head, and I never want to go through that again. Promise me we won't."

My legs go weak at the passion blaring from him, and at his honesty and willingness to lay himself bare like this. Taking hold of his face, I nod. "I promise I won't do that to us again."

His eyes search mine for what feels like forever before he finally lets out a breath that sounds like it's been trapped for a long time. "Thank fuck."

42

ASHTON

"You're in a better mood tonight than you were this morning," Jack says over a drink that night.

He called and asked me to meet him at this bar after work. I could hear in his voice that this was important to him, so instead of arguing about his drinking, I agreed.

I take a drink of the whisky sitting in front of me. "That's because I fixed things with Lorelei."

"Does that mean you told her how concerned you are about the Shandwick deal?"

"No, it means I'm still looking into that. For now, I've apologised and just left it, but I'm certain I'll need to bring it up again soon."

"You really think it's a shady deal?"

"I do."

"I hope you're wrong for Lorelei's sake."

"I'm not wrong, Jack. All I can hope now is that she can get out of it by the time I make her see what's going on."

He throws some whisky down his throat. "I saw Cassia at the café near your work today. Couldn't get away from her.

She went on and on about how good your parents are to her. Are they that close now?"

I squeeze my whisky glass. "Apparently so. She's there every time I visit Mum."

"What's going on with her?"

"I don't know, and I don't want to know."

"Did I ever tell you I don't like that woman?"

I chuckle. "Only every opportunity you got."

He grins. "And you chose never to listen to me. Maybe when it comes to Lorelei you'll listen to me."

I narrow my eyes at him. "I thought you liked Lorelei."

"Oh, I do, and that's why you need to listen to me. I'm concerned you're going to fuck it up with her otherwise."

"How would I fuck it up?"

"Let me count the ways. The Willow Street plans you have. Your need to take control of her and everything she does. There's probably a hundred other things you'll do, but these are the main ones."

"I'm not trying to control her. I'm trying to help her. There's a difference." I ignore the reference to the Willow Street development. We've already discussed that, and as far as I'm concerned, he's wrong.

"We're going to have to agree to disagree, Ashton. But just don't screw things up. I like that woman."

I drink some more whisky. The bar is getting busy as all the suits head out for a drink on their way home from work. I want to discuss whatever Jack brought me here for before it gets too noisy.

"What's going on, Jack? What did you want to talk with me about?"

He eyes me over the rim of his glass and takes his time drinking before he replies. "I'm going back to the States."

Worry hits my gut. "Why?" That's the last place he needs to be now.

"I've found a new manager, and she wants me back there. She's got some scripts for me to read. She also wants me to fix my public image, so I've got a lot of work ahead of me. I need to get back there and start on that."

"What kind of work?" I know exactly what kind of work he means, but I want him to say it so I can bring up my reservations.

"Fuck, Ashton, you know how this goes. Don't give me hell over it."

"Yeah, I know exactly how this goes, Jack. You make appearances everywhere and schmooze with as many of the players as you can. Parties, events, premiers, anywhere you can go. And eventually that leads to drugs and alcohol, and you're right back where you are now, only worse, because you never finished the work you've started here. Why would you do that to yourself?"

Anger flashes across his face. "Because it's my career."

"And here I was thinking you wanted a break from that career. What's changed?" I'm angry, too. But even more than that, I'm worried as hell for my friend. This is the absolute worst move he could make right now, and I'm fairly certain he's not going to listen to my concerns.

"It's what I live for, Ashton. If anyone can understand that drive, I would think it should be you. You live for your work just as much as I do."

"I do understand that, but why can't you take the time to get your health under control before heading back to work?"

He shoves his fingers through his hair, and I notice how shaky his hands are. *Fuck, he's worse than I thought.*

"I need this. I'm going crazy not working."

I lean forward. "You mean you need the attention? Is that it, Jack?" I know I'm being a bastard, but I'm struggling to keep my calm.

He finishes his drink and slowly places his empty glass

down as he stands. The hurt in his eyes is clear to see, and I regret my choice of words. "So I like the attention. I wouldn't be able to do my job if I didn't. But besides that, I want to be back working. I'm lost without it. And fuck you."

He walks out of the bar, and I resist the urge to follow him. It's the last thing our friendship needs right now. Jack might be in desperate need of help where his health and addictions are concerned, but at some point, I have to let him realise that himself. I think we've reached that point, and it fucking kills me to watch him harm himself in the way he is. All I can do now is pray that his fall isn't as hard as I suspect it might be.

"You're so tense," Lorelei says an hour later while she massages my shoulders.

I arrived ten minutes ago, and once she saw how tense I was, she dragged me into her lounge room and ordered me to sit on the floor while she sat on the couch and massaged me.

"Jack's going home."

Her hands stop moving for a moment before she resumes working on my knots. "Why?"

I fill her in on everything he told me. I'm wound even tighter than I was when I spoke with him, and the words fall out of my mouth. It's unusual for that to happen. I've never dated a woman I've shared such personal stuff with.

When I finish, she leans forward against me and glides her hands down over my chest. Her head rests on my shoulder, and she says, "I'm sorry this is so hard for you."

I wrap my hands around her wrists and turn my face so I can catch her lips in a kiss. When I end it, I say, "You should come and sit on my lap and let me work my stress out with you."

She smiles. "That didn't even sound bossy."

I return her smile. "I'm trying."

"You know, I think there are definitely times when bossy suits you better."

"You want me to be bossy, Lorelei?"

"I'm not sure. I'm still deciding. I mean, I don't want to encourage bad behaviour."

Fuck, I love this banter with her. "I'm giving you five seconds to decide. After that, it's bad behaviour all the way."

Her smile turns cheeky, and she moves her mouth to my ear. "Five, four, three, two, one—"

Before she knows what's happening, I move so that she's on her back on the couch, and I'm on top of her. Reaching under her skirt, I find her panties and slide my hand inside. Meeting her gaze, I say, "Is this the kind of bad behaviour you were trying to avoid? I can stop anytime you want. You just say the word."

Her eyes flutter shut as I push two fingers inside her. "Oh God, don't you dare stop."

I have no intention of stopping. Watching Lorelei come is the only thing on my agenda tonight.

Dropping my face to hers, I kiss her while I work to bring her to orgasm. She loops her arms around my neck and grips me there while she kisses me with an urgency I've not known from her.

Fuck.

Her need for me almost pushes me over the edge. I want nothing more than to drive my dick inside her, but I hold myself back so I can make her come first.

Her back arches up off the couch, and she moans as her fingers dig into my neck. My dick grows harder while I watch her head press back against the couch, and when her pussy pulses around my fingers, I almost come too.

"Fuck," I growl. "I love watching you lose yourself."

Her eyes open, and she hits me with a sexy smile. Reaching for the top button of my shirt, she undoes it and says, "I love watching you fuck me. I think you should hurry up and do that."

I scoop my arm under her waist and take her with me as I move to a sitting position with her straddling me. "You know what I think *you* should do?"

Her gaze is firmly on mine, heat blazing from those beautiful eyes of hers. She undoes the next couple of buttons on my shirt. "What?"

I run my hands up her thighs and push her skirt up. "I want to watch you strip for me."

She stops what she's doing with my buttons as her eyes widen. "I've never stripped for a man before."

I hate the hesitation I hear in her voice. Lorelei is a goddess. She shouldn't have any confidence issues. "Good. I'll be your first." I bring my lips to hers and kiss her before adding, "And your only."

She stills as I say those three words. It was my intention to say them, and I'm interested to see her reaction. Taking hold of my face with both hands, she kisses me again. "Your only," she says softly. It's not a question, but I hear the uncertainty.

"Yes, Lorelei, your only," I say firmly. I don't want there to be any misunderstanding here. I'm not ready to say the other three words that would clear any confusion, but there's no doubt in my mind that I want Lorelei in my life forever.

She holds my gaze for a long few moments, not saying anything, just watching. And then she slowly moves to stand in front of me.

I run my eyes down her body, always blown away by her beauty. That she's mine, is everything. I'll do whatever it takes to ensure that never changes.

She finds my gaze and locks onto it as she slowly slides

her top over her head. It hits the floor, but neither of us notice because we're both too engrossed in what she's doing.

Her skirt is next to go. The way she turns her back to me and shimmies out of it while bending over is enough to make me reach for my zip. A moment later, my hand is wrapped around my cock, and I stroke it while watching her.

My breath slows when she faces me again and seductively runs a finger down between her breasts to her panties. She places her other hand to the back of her head and threads her fingers in her hair. At the same time, she begins swaying her hips.

"Fuck, baby," I rasp, gripping my dick harder. "You're a natural at this."

A smile spreads across her face, and she reaches inside her panties. Her hand is hidden from me, but I can see she's rubbing her clit. "Do you want to see my tits next or my pussy?"

Filthy words have never sounded better than on Lorelei's lips. I want nothing more than to drag this out, but I've reached the point where I need her now.

Reaching forward, I curl a hand around her thigh and pull her to me. "I want you sitting on my dick so I can fuck you." I yank her panties down and grip her ass while she straddles me, slowly lowering her pussy onto my cock.

I close my eyes for a moment while she takes me in. "Goddam you are fucking wet," I say when I reopen them.

She grasps my arms. "That's because I've been thinking about you all day. I may have even used my vibrator when I got home from work because I couldn't stop thinking about you."

I'm fucking done at those words. I can't restrain myself any longer. Flicking her bra open, I pull it off and then take hold of her waist. Moving my mouth to her ear, I growl,

"Fuck me, baby. And after you've done that, be ready for me to fuck you in ways you've never dreamt of."

She doesn't hesitate; she fucks the hell out of me. It's hard and it's fast, and I can't get enough of what she's giving me.

We're all fingers digging into skin.

Frantically clawing for release.

Desperately needing each other.

When we come, our bodies are pressed together tightly, arms wrapped around the other, and mouths crushed together in a kiss that goes on forever.

I never want to let her go.

Lorelei is becoming my everything.

My lover.

My confidant.

My weakness.

Time with her is the only thing I crave.

And if I'm truly honest, I am in love with her.

43

LORELEI

"WE SHOULD TAKE MORE HALF DAYS ON FRIDAYS."

Ashton drinks some of his whisky and eyes me over the rim of the glass from across the table. "I'll get Jessica to schedule them in if you're serious."

My eyes widen. "Really? Just like that, you'll change your routine?"

His eyes don't leave mine. "Just like that, Lorelei. You want it to happen, I'll make it happen."

I watch him silently, trying not to show how surprised I am. We left Sydney just before eleven this morning and flew to the Whitsunday resort we're now sitting in having a late lunch. This is after Ashton fucked me the minute we stepped foot in our room, and a long spa bath after that. I only threw my taking-Fridays-off statement out because I'm feeling more relaxed than I've felt in a long time. And I can't think of anything I'd rather do on a Friday afternoon than spend it with Ashton. I never expected him to respond the way he has.

A text comes through on my phone, interrupting us.

Ryan Shandwick: You free for a ten o'clock meeting Monday morning to go over some stuff?

I glance up nervously at Ashton. I'm not sure why, though, because he and I have already had our discussion about this deal. He made his thoughts clear, and I made it clear where I stood. And now I'm moving forward because I'm still happy with the information I've sourced about this deal. But I definitely feel weird about the whole situation after our fight.

Ashton frowns at me. "Everything okay?"

I nod. "Yes." And then I quickly reply to the message.

Me: Yes. Lock it in.

Ashton's frown deepens. "You're not convincing. What's going on, Lorelei?"

I place my phone down on the table and smile at him. "It's just some work stuff. I'm more interested to discuss what we're doing this afternoon." We've got a full schedule planned to check out the resort this weekend, and I'm excited to get started on that. I'm also keen not to discuss Ryan Shandwick this weekend.

He watches me thoughtfully for another few moments before saying, "Jessica managed to get us in for the wine tasting at five. And she also booked us in for the high tea tomorrow morning."

"I freaking love her." Both events had been booked solid, and while Ashton didn't think it a huge deal that we couldn't experience them, I wasn't as sure. We need to know exactly what our competitors are offering so we can ensure our standards are just as high.

His phone sounds with a text and as he reaches for it, he says, "The feeling is mutual I think." As he reads his message, he mutters, "Shit, I have to call my mother."

"Is she okay?"

He dials her number and places the phone to his ear. "Yes. Aly just reminded me that Mum had an appointment with her doctor today, so I want to check how that went—" He stops talking and frowns as he listens to his phone. Then —"What the fuck, Cassia? Why are you answering my mother's phone?"

A sinking feeling hits my stomach. His ex is answering his mother's calls? This causes alarm bells to ring loudly for me. I already feel all kinds of awkward about her and what their relationship is now. This only increases my anxiety over everything.

They have a heated discussion before he talks with his mother. When the phone call ends, he rakes his fingers through his hair and mutters, "Jesus Christ."

I take a gulp of my cocktail. I'm going to need a lot more of these this afternoon. "How is she?" While I want to know how his mother is, I really want to know everything there is to know about Cassia, but I don't know how to ask him. God, why does dating have to be such hard work sometimes?

"Mum's fine. The appointment went well."

I take a deep breath before pushing him for more. "And?"

He throws half his glass of whisky down his throat before answering my question. "For a reason I can't fathom, Cassia is spending a lot of time with my mother. If I know her as well as I think I do, she's after something."

The nerves churning in my gut ease a little. I should have had more faith in my man that he wouldn't keep anything from me. Ashton has been nothing but honest the entire time I've known him, so I'm not sure why I was worried he wouldn't open up to me about this. However, that doesn't ease any of my concern over what Cassia might be up to. Or the way her mere presence in his life makes me feel.

"Like what?" I ask softly.

"I don't know yet, but I intend to get to the bottom of it."

"She must be close to your mum if they're spending all this time together."

"I didn't realise they were this close. They certainly weren't while we were together."

I look away. I'm not sure how I feel about his mum having a friendship with the woman he used to love. And I feel like I need a moment to get my thoughts into some kind of order.

"Lorelei." Ashton's deep voice cuts through my thoughts. "What's going through your mind?"

I turn back to find him leaning forward, watching me intently. Unwilling to answer him until I figure out my thoughts, I say honestly, "I don't know."

"Yes you do. Don't think, just tell me the one thing running through it right now."

God, how I hate it when he tries to force answers from me like this. "I really don't know, Ashton. I need to process it."

"You don't need any time," he says forcefully. "It's written across your face and your body that something has upset you, and I want to know what it is because I don't want it coming between us."

"Fine," I mutter, annoyed at him. "If you want to push this... I don't like that your ex is so bloody close to your mother. It concerns me."

"Why?"

"Why do you think?" *Good God, are all men this unaware?*

"I don't know. That's why I'm asking you." His voice holds nothing but patience, but I sense his impatience with this. Ashton doesn't always have a high tolerance for the workings of the female mind. He's held himself in check with me most of the time we've been together, but I've witnessed it with his sister.

I drink the rest of my cocktail, needing the shot of alcohol. The relaxed state I was in just a little while ago has vanished. Having this conversation with him is hard. We're still walking the fine line between simply dating and admitting stronger feelings, and bringing this up is a whole step closer to me admitting how I feel about him. And acknowledging how vulnerable I am about this.

Placing my empty glass down on the table a little harder than I mean to, I say, "Honestly, you men really need to figure out how to read a woman. Because you seem unable to, I'm going to give you a quick lesson in exes." I pause for a moment, gathering myself, before going on. "When a woman starts dating a man, the last thing she wants to find out is that his ex is still close with his parents, especially his mother. His mother is the person she really wants approval from, and if the ex is still in the picture, it makes her all kinds of uncomfortable and anxious. Will the ex influence the mother? Will the mother be ready to let the hopes she had for the past relationship go? *Will she even like me?*" God, I need another freaking drink now. I can hardly think straight after saying all that out loud.

Ashton remains silent while he processes everything. And then a look of pure determination settles across his face as he moves his chair next to mine. "You have nothing to worry about with my mother, Lorelei. Or with my ex. I'll be getting to the bottom of whatever Cassia has going on, but in case you haven't figured this out about me yet, I'm going to get us on the same page—I have zero feelings for Cassia, and my mother has very little say over who I choose to spend my life with. I would like it if you two become friends, but if you don't, it will not affect our relationship in any way. And as far as the hopes my mother had for my past relationship, I can assure you she had none. She didn't have much time for Cassia, which is why this situation has me confused now. And if I had to hazard a guess, I would say that Cassia is more interested in getting something out of my father than my mother." He leans closer to me, eyes blazing with heat. "Having said all that, you also need to know that it turns me the fuck on to know you feel like this."

I bite my lip as I hold his gaze. "Feel like what?"

He places his hand on my knee and reaches under my skirt, moving his hand up my thigh, stopping halfway up and resting there. It lights my body up to the point where I'm not sure I can breathe properly. "I like a woman staking her claim."

My heart beats so loudly I'm sure he can hear it. "Well, consider this me staking my claim."

His grip on my leg tightens. "I'll sort this out. And next week you'll come with me to meet my mother."

And just like that, Ashton rights everything in my world again.

"What?" I lift my brows at Ashton as we get ready to go out for dinner that night. "You thought I'd just throw a few things in a suitcase and call the job done? A woman needs options when she goes away for the weekend with her man."

He runs his gaze over my clothes I've laid out on the bed in our suite, taking in all the outfit options I've got. "Fucking hell," he mutters, "You've got enough there for a month-long trip."

I ignore that and continue my search for the perfect outfit to wear to dinner. I'm tired from our busy day, but I'm determined not to waste a second of our time here. We might be visiting the resort for work, but that's no reason not to get as much sexy time with Ashton as possible. And I've packed a few outfits that I know will help get him in the mood. Not that Ashton ever needs a reason for that.

The sound of him undressing fills my ears, and I turn to watch as he unbuttons that shirt. It's one of my favourite things to do—watching him undress.

He watches me while he works the buttons, his gaze intense. "Take your dress off."

His bossiness hits me deep in my core and every nerve ending lights with need. I do as he orders, his watchful gaze and commanding attitude owning my every action.

As I kick my dress to the side, he closes the distance between us with determination. Taking hold of my face, he kisses me, his restraint close to breaking point. Ashton can't hide his need, and that's something that turns me on. He makes me feel more wanted than I've ever felt.

When he finally lets my mouth go, he kisses a trail down my neck, his hands on my breasts. In between kisses, he rasps, "Fair warning—you won't be able to walk when we leave this resort on Sunday."

I grip his biceps. "I like these kinds of promises."

Before I realise what he's doing, he lifts me and carries me out to the balcony. I quickly wrap my arms and legs around him while both anticipation and apprehension fill me. *I'm almost naked and he's taking me outside where anyone can see me.*

"Ashton, what are you doing? I have no clothes on." Our room overlooks the ocean and there are people everywhere down on the street. It might be dark, but the resort is lit up. *Oh God.*

He places me down and spins me around so he's behind me, pressing my body against the railing. *The glass railing that hides nothing from the world.* Sweeping my hair off my shoulder, he bends to place his mouth to my bare skin. "You're not naked yet, but you will be soon."

I grasp the railing, almost succumbing to the sensations he's causing, but I can't stop staring down at the people below us. When he moves to unclasp my bra, my limbs turn shaky. I'm not sure I can do this out here.

"Ashton, no. I can't." My words fall out breathlessly and a little unconvincingly. Because if I'm totally honest, there's a forbidden thrill chasing my fear away. I'm torn between being completely aroused by the idea of sex out in the open and nervous about the whole thing.

"Lorelei," he growls against my ear, "You told me you wanted to fuck me in public. Have you changed your mind?"

He's right—I did tell him that. But now it's happening, I'm not sure I can go through with it. "I don't know. It feels wrong with all these people around." *Wrong but so damn good at the same time.*

"It's dark," he says as he runs his hand down my stomach and dips his hand into my panties. "And even if they can see where my hand is, they can't see that I'm fingering your cunt right now." With his free hand, he takes hold of my neck and angles my head back so he can kiss me. His tongue tangles with mine as his fingers reach deep inside me, and I know there's no way I'm saying no to this now. When he drags his mouth from mine, he says, "I want to do filthy things to you out here in front of all these people, but I won't if you don't want me to."

Oh God, I want all those filthy things.

Every single last one of them.

I turn in his embrace and glide my hands over his bare chest. Meeting his gaze, I nod. I want this as much as he does.

"Tell me what you want," he commands in the forceful way he does when he's pushing me to express my desires.

I bite my lip and drop my eyes for a moment, but he tilts my face back up, forcing me to hold eye contact. It's times like this I wish I was more experienced. I wish I had the same level of sexual confidence as Ashton.

"Tell me," he growls again. "I want to know what you want me to do to you and where you want it."

Every last piece of resistance I have to this evaporates when I see the desire flashing in his eyes. It doesn't matter that we're at different levels sexually or that I feel nervous about this; all that matters is we're in this together, and he wants me just as much as I want him.

I take hold of his face and kiss him with all the passion consuming me. It's hot and it grows frantic. There's no stopping this now. "I want you to fuck me out here for everyone to see," I finally admit, panting with lust. *I want that more than anything else.*

In one deft movement, he removes my bra. Bending his head, he takes one of my nipples into his mouth while holding my breast. His free hand slips into my panties again and he finds my clit. I spread my arms out and rest them on the railing. Dropping my head back, I close my eyes and shut out every noise while losing myself in the moment.

Ashton expertly moves me closer to orgasm with every stroke of his tongue and fingers. He edges me there and then pulls back. Over and over until I'm writhing against him and begging for release. It's his favourite thing to do, and he's skilled in ways I've never experienced. But tonight the rush of being in public arouses me to new heights.

Arching my back and threading my fingers through his hair, I beg, "Please... let me come, Ashton."

He stops what he's doing and straightens, eyes coming to mine. "Take off your panties," he orders, his voice all kinds of husky.

I step forward and reach for his belt buckle. Not letting go of his gaze, I say, "I'd rather take these off."

His hand snaps around my wrist. "Do as I say, Lorelei."

Oh God.

I'm not sure I can take any more of his foreplay.

I don't shift my hand. "Ashton—"

He cuts me off with a growl. "Take your panties off and spread your legs. I need to taste you before I make you come."

Although I'm desperate for this orgasm, I can never say no to Ashton's mouth on my pussy, so I do as ordered. He watches me in silence for another long few moments. The intensity vibrating from him increases my anticipation with every passing second.

When I finally do come, it's going to be hard. It's going to shatter through me. And knowing he'll back it up straight away with another orgasm when he fucks me causes my core to clench even more.

He kneels in front of me and kisses my pussy. Slowly and thoroughly. Taking hold of my thighs, he concentrates all his attention on pleasuring me with his mouth.

It's bliss, and if I could, I'd never let him leave my side again. I want Ashton's attention every second of the day.

His hands.

His mouth.

His body.

All of it.

When I'm with him, the world doesn't exist. And tonight is no different. There's only him and me and how good we make each other feel.

I cry out his name when I finally orgasm, my voice slicing through the night air for anyone to hear.

Ashton stands, kissing his way up my body as he finds his way to my mouth. Tasting myself on his tongue is something I find hot. I've never liked it before, but Ashton somehow makes me like everything he does.

"I want you every way I can have you this weekend," he

says as he draws his mouth from mine and turns me to face the railing again.

His hands skim down my body before he undoes the zip of his pants. He then grips my hips and bends his face to speak against my ear. "And this won't be the last time I fuck you out here." He thrusts inside of me as he says that, causing me to cry out again.

I grasp the railing and hold on tightly while he fucks me. This is the hottest sex we've had. And it's on the same scale of wild and untamed as he's been doing it recently. It's as if with every passing day, he's becoming more demanding of me. Rougher in all the ways that draw out my deepest desires. It's as if he can't get enough of me.

His fingers dig into my skin.

His movements grow faster, harder.

And his teeth find my neck as he kisses and bites me.

The pain and pleasure mixed together sends my mind and body into free fall.

I barely know who I am and where I am while he drives into me like this. All I know is that I will never have enough of this man.

"Fuck!" His roar bellows out of him as he slams into me one last time, his hands letting go of my hips and circling me.

His hold is firm, crushing almost, and it wraps me with a feeling of security. I orgasm again and rest my head back against his shoulder, completely spent. *Completely happy.*

"Fuck," he rasps against my ear. "I love you."

The three words we've both been dancing around fall from his mouth. Every sensation coursing through me intensifies at those three words.

I thought I was feeling happy a moment ago, but I didn't know how much happier Ashton could make me with just a few words.

I turn in his arms and smile up at him. "I love you, too, Ashton."

His eyes search mine for a beat. And then his lips crash down onto my mouth and he shows me how much he meant those words. When he finally ends the kiss, he says, "I don't ever intend to let you go."

I stand on my tiptoes and take hold of his face. This man needs to know exactly where I stand. And he needs to know it well. "Good, because if you ever do, I'll come looking for you and remind you of this moment. And just so you know— I don't ever intend to let you go either. You're mine now."

His arms tighten around me. "I was yours a long time ago, Lorelei."

44

ASHTON

"I SEE LORELEI MANAGED TO WIPE ALL THE ASSHOLE out of you on the weekend," Jessica says mid-morning on Monday. "I'm liking this new Ashton."

I ignore her. "Can you call Sian again? I want to ensure she finalises the negotiations on those properties today."

She drops some files on my desk. "She texted me about fifteen minutes ago and said she should have news within the hour."

I lift a brow. "When did texting become the way we do business?"

"The day I took her out on our first date."

I open one of the files from her pile. "Please tell me you don't intend to walk away from her before I finish buying up Willow Street." The last time Jessica slept with someone I did business with, the deal was almost ruined when she ended the affair.

"Willow Street is safe. Now, tell me how Jack was this morning. And how long do you think it'll be before he burns out?"

I close the file and lean back in my chair. "Put it this way,

I've never been so concerned for him. I've asked Josephine to keep a close eye on him. He put on a good show this morning, but I wasn't buying it."

She exhales a long breath, her body sagging. "I kinda hope he crashes fast so he can get the help he needs. God knows what harm he'll do to himself and his career while he's the way he is."

A text sounds from my phone.

Lorelei: You should cook me dinner tonight.

Me: I should do a lot of things for you tonight.

Lorelei: Pick me up from the gym at 6.

Me: With what I have planned you could skip the gym.

Lorelei: Oh I thought you meant you were going to give me a massage. Maybe have a bath with me. Should I start limbering up now?

Jesus. My imagination goes into overdrive thinking about Lorelei readying that body of hers for me. I've got a meeting in five minutes, and the last thing I need is a hard-on I don't have time to deal with.

Me: I'll pick you up at five. Don't text me again today. I have back-to-back meetings that don't require my dick to be hard.

She doesn't text again, but almost instantly, she calls.

"Lorelei," I say with a low warning tone. "Don't—"

She cuts me off, all breathless. "I'm not going to sweet talk your dick. I just wanted to tell you I love this."

"Fuck," I mutter. "You don't have to say anything in

particular to sweet talk my dick. Just the sound of your voice does it."

Jessica's eyebrows arch and a smile crosses her face. "I'll get your files for the meeting," she mouths before exiting the office.

Lorelei's sexy voice floats through the phone. "Oh." It's clear she has no idea the effect she has on me most of the time.

"What do you love?"

"Morning texting with you. Teasing you. There should be more of it."

"Perhaps we could do it earlier in the morning. When I'm not about to walk into a meeting with an investor."

She laughs, and fuck if that doesn't shoot straight to my cock. "There's no fun in that, Ashton." I hear the smile in her voice and know that she intends for this to become a regular thing. "Okay, I'll let you go now. See you at five."

Just as quickly as she phoned me, she ends the call, and I'm left with the kind of need a man would do anything to have his woman take care of. If the meetings I have lined up for today were ones I could easily get out of, I would. I'd cancel them all and demand Lorelei rearrange her day so I could spend it fucking her. But they're not, so I focus my thoughts on work and attempt to put her out of my mind. The fact I struggle with that shows me how deeply she's worked her way into my heart, because not once in my life have I had trouble putting work before anything else. Lorelei is a first for me.

45

ASHTON

"I've loved this week," Lorelei says as she leans in close for a kiss. "Every single minute of it. And just so you know, every Saturday should start the same as today."

"You wouldn't prefer to be woken up by something other than Jessica calling me at 6:00 a.m.?"

She grins. "Well, that part we could change, but I liked that it woke you up and inspired you to do dirty things to me."

My gaze is drawn to the counter of the café we're in. It's the one on Willow Street that Lorelei loves, and the owner is trying to get her attention. "Francesca wants you," I say with reluctance. She's right—this week has been our best yet, and my plan is to spend every second of this weekend with her.

She pushes her chair back and stands. Dropping another kiss on my lips, she says, "I'll get you another coffee."

I reach for her hand. "Don't get side-tracked."

Another smile graces her face. "I like it when bossy Ashton comes out to play."

I track her movements, mindlessly picking up my phone when a text comes in. I've been waiting to hear back from

Jessica, but I'm not convinced even that news can draw my attention from Lorelei for long.

Jessica: Sian has three contracts signed for Willow Street and another two interested. Very interested. I'd say we're confirmed for five now.

    Me: Good.

    Jessica: I love the Scott enthusiasm. It's mind-blowing. Maybe you'll consider throwing a party once we have them all signed.

    Me: Your sarcasm is duly noted.

    Jessica: And there I was trying to be as subtle as you. #Fail

    Me: Enjoy your weekend, Jessica.

I place the phone back on the table and look up just in time to see Boston Haynes enter the café. He heads straight to where Francesca stands at the counter and chats to her for a moment. Lorelei has disappeared while I was texting Jessica, and Francesca motions towards the table where I'm sitting. Haynes's eyes meet mine and he stalls for a beat before striding my way.

"I'm looking for Lorelei," he says when he reaches me.

Relaxing back into my seat, I shrug. "I don't know where she is."

His eyes narrow at me. "Don't be an asshole, Scott. If you two are as tight as you think you are, there's nothing to lose by me seeing her."

"I know there's nothing to lose. I simply don't know where she went." It's the truth, but I also wouldn't tell him if I did know where she was. The less Haynes sees her, the better as far as I'm concerned.

He pulls out the chair next to me and sits, casually dropping his sunglasses on the table. "I can wait."

My relaxed mood disappears, replaced by irritation and the possessiveness I feel whenever I think of him. Unfortunately, he's been on my mind more than I care to admit. I believe Lorelei when she says she's not interested in him, but I want him completely out of her life.

We sit in silence for a good five minutes while waiting for Lorelei to return. I refuse to utter a word and give him the satisfaction of thinking his presence concerns me. And when Lorelei comes our way, I ignore the way he watches her with the kind of look that says he believes she'll be his again. He won't. I'll make sure of it.

"Boston," she says, clearly surprised to find him here. Her eyes dart between us. She seems a little unsure of the situation.

"Hey," he says as he stands and attempts to brush a kiss across her cheek. The fact her hands go to his chest to hold him back causes a swell of triumph in me. Not to mention the confusion written all over him when she does this. That causes a whole lot more than triumph. It damn well makes me want to swoop in and lay my claim. But I don't. Instead, I remain seated, my cool demeanour intact. Boston Haynes needs to know he doesn't concern me at all. Even if that isn't quite the case.

"Why are you here? Is Amber okay?"

"She's fine. I came looking for you because I never heard back when I texted you about meeting Crave. I'm doing some more work for them this afternoon, so I don't want you to miss out on the opportunity again."

Lorelei runs her fingers through her hair, which I've learnt is a nervous habit of hers. "I'm busy today, Boston. Ashton and I already have plans."

The asshole glances at me before looking back at her. "I'm

sure Ashton won't mind you taking some time out to meet one of your favourite bands."

It fucking annoys me that he's putting her in this position. The manipulation tactic he's using isn't one I'd ever use on a woman I care about. I shove my chair back and stand, ready to let him know he's overstepped boundaries here when Lorelei lets loose on him.

"You're right, Ashton wouldn't mind, and he'd certainly never stop me from doing something I wanted, but *I* would mind. And do you know what else I mind? That you would try to manage me in this way. I've told you where I stand with us, and I'd appreciate it if you could respect my feelings."

Boston watches her silently for a moment before saying, "And I told you where I stand, Lorelei. I told you I'd give you space, but I also told you I wouldn't walk away again. This is me not walking away."

This is news to me, and it's clear in the way Lorelei glances nervously at me that she knows I'm wondering when that conversation took place.

"Please go, Boston." Her carefree mood of earlier has also disappeared, her entire body now tense.

He takes a few moments, but finally he nods. Before she can stop him, he kisses her cheek. "I'll be in touch."

We watch him leave, neither of us saying a word. When he's out of sight, Lorelei turns to me, nervousness still clear in her eyes. "I'm sorry, I forgot to ask Francesca for your coffee. I'll go do that now."

Coffee is the last thing on my mind. Not when I can barely think straight due to the overwhelming possessiveness clawing at me. "When did you speak to Haynes?"

"Ashton, let me go get your coffee and then we can talk about this."

"No," I say with force, "We will talk about this now." No

fucking way am I going another minute not knowing about that conversation. I have never done well with people I love keeping things from me, but what I'm feeling about Lorelei keeping something from me twists my gut more than anything ever has before. This will be dealt with, and it will be dealt with now.

46

LORELEI

I'VE NEVER SEEN ASHTON THIS WORKED UP. OR this demanding. And he's been pretty demanding at times. But his forcefulness is at a whole new level.

"I went to see him the day after he came to my apartment." I sound a lot more confident than I'm feeling. My stomach is a mess of nerves. Partly from the way Ashton is watching me and partly because I feel guilty for keeping this information from him. *But mostly from the way he's watching me so intensely.* I can't read him. Well, I know he's upset, but he seems more upset than the situation calls for.

His nostrils flare. "And you didn't think I'd want to know that?"

Sienna warned me I was wrong not to tell Ashton I'd gone to see Boston, but I'd honestly thought it best not to tell him and stir the situation up. I can see now that I made the absolute wrong decision.

"I'm sorry, but I thought if I went to him and made him understand we were over, that I could stop things getting out of hand where he was concerned."

"And do you think that worked?"

God, his voice has turned cold almost. It makes me feel so distant from him. It's a place I don't like to be. "I honestly believed it would."

"So you knew it hadn't?"

"Ashton, don't—"

"I asked you a question, Lorelei. Did you know at the time that you hadn't made him understand you two were over?"

Heat flushes through my body and I tense. His cold manner and hostile tone don't elicit a willingness in me to have this conversation with him. "I don't understand what that has to do with this."

His jaw clenches, and when he speaks next, his words bite me with their harshness. "Judging by your aversion to this question, I'm guessing you did know Haynes—"

"I don't know why you're making such a big deal out of that," I throw back, my own displeasure flaring.

"I don't like things being kept from me, Lorelei. You should have told me you were going to see him in the first place. And you should have come to me with the information that he wasn't taking you seriously."

I cross my arms over my chest. My stomach isn't a knot of nerves anymore; it's a mess of frustration. And defensiveness. I feel like I'm playing catch up with where he's going with this and that I have to be ready to give him an explanation for my every move. "Yes, I should have, but now you know, so I'm not sure why you're getting all worked up over it."

"If I'd known, I would have dealt with it."

My eyes bulge. "Oh my God. So *that's* what this is all about. Your need to always take charge of a situation and to deal with things for me." I uncross my arms and lean forward, as if getting closer to him will make him see the truth in what I'm saying. "I don't need you dealing with this for me, Ashton. I'm completely capable of doing that myself."

"If that were the case, Haynes wouldn't have shown up here today, he wouldn't have taken part in a pissing contest with me, he wouldn't have told you this was him not walking away, and he sure as hell wouldn't have kissed you as he left. You haven't taken care of it, but I will. Once I'm finished with him, Haynes won't step foot near you ever again."

I stare at him, completely stunned. I'm also a little lost for words because not once in my life have I ever had anyone treat me the way Ashton is. While I know he's not detached from his emotions, it's like he's separating himself from them so he can make some calculated moves to get what he wants. He's handling our relationship the way he handles a business deal.

Before I can reply, he checks his watch and stands. "We need to leave if we're going to make the soccer match on time."

We're supposed to be meeting Alessandra and Malcolm to watch Bradley's match today, but I'm not finished with this conversation yet.

I remain seated. "We haven't finished discussing this."

"We have."

"No, we haven't. I've apologised for what I did, and you've had your say, but I don't agree with what you've decided. I don't like the way you're talking to me or the way you're shutting down on me over this. It feels cold."

His face clouds with displeasure. If I thought he was cold before, he's positively arctic now. "I'm not entering into an argument with you over this, Lorelei. I don't want Haynes near you, and I'll do whatever it takes to ensure that outcome is achieved."

I stand so I'm on level ground with him. "Can you hear yourself, Ashton? We're discussing our relationship here, not some business transaction. I don't want to talk outcomes with you. I want to talk about how we can come to a compromise over this. One that makes us both happy."

"I don't see the issue with my way forward. You've said you don't want him in your life, and I'll make that happen."

I take a deep breath, trying to rein my frustration in. He doesn't seem able, or willing, to see this from my point of view. "I don't want you to make it happen. I want you to give me the space to do that on my own. And you told me the last time we argued over something like this that you wouldn't take over again, and here you are doing just that."

"That had to do with your business. This is different. This involves our relationship, and I won't allow anyone to interfere with that."

"It's not different!" He's so infuriating that I can't hold my irritation in any longer. "It all has to do with our relationship because it all has to do with how you treat me. You need to understand that I won't be handled and that you can't assume responsibility for situations that concern me. If we're going to be in this relationship, Ashton, we're going to do it as equals and you're going to have to learn to take my preferences into consideration."

"And you're going to have to understand that some situations call for me to take the lead. Especially when it's clear you can't. Now, we need to get to this soccer match."

With that, he turns and stalks out of the café, leaving me staring after him. I want nothing more than to tell him what an asshole he's being and then to leave him to spend the rest of the day alone. However, I promised him after our last argument that I wouldn't leave a disagreement hanging between us unresolved, so I gather my wits and follow him to his car.

This discussion, though, is a long way from being finished. I'm just getting warmed up.

47

ASHTON

When I imagine Lorelei with Boston Haynes, I can't think straight. It drives all rational thoughts from my mind. I turn into the kind of man I've never understood—the kind who allows a woman to control his behaviour.

Lorelei doesn't know it, but she has me by the balls. Well and fucking truly. She's mine, damn it. I won't stand for another man trying to take her from me. And there's no way in hell I'll stand for him kissing her.

We drove to the soccer match in silence and once we arrived, Alessandra whisked her away from me. Malcolm and I have been debating the dive some shares took overnight, but my eyes have hardly left Lorelei. I have an incessant need to always know where she is and that she's okay. Being with her is unlike any relationship I've ever had. I've never cared about a woman this much or felt as twisted up and distracted before.

"Go, Bradley!" Alessandra calls out, drawing my gaze to the field in time to see him score a goal.

My heart swells with pride, and I'm reminded why I'm here. I manage to spend the rest of the game watching my nephew and keeping all distractions out of focus. *Mostly out of focus.* Every now and then, Lorelei cheers Bradley on, bringing my attention back to her. I can't help but be captivated by the way she has welcomed my family into her heart. Sharing these family moments with her is something I look forward to in our future together.

"What's going on with you and Lorelei?" Alessandra asks as Lorelei and Malcolm leave us to go find Bradley after the match has finished.

"What makes you think something is going on?" Getting into this with my sister is the last thing I need today. Especially when the noise from the crowd is roaring through my head, interfering with my thinking.

"It's obvious to anyone who knows you two that something's going on. Lorelei's distracted and can't keep up with a conversation, and you keep watching her like you're afraid she won't be there each time you look over. I have *never* seen you like this. The Ashton I know doesn't deal in fear. So what's going on?"

"Fuck," I mutter, glancing away from her scrutiny for a moment. If Aly gets involved in this, who fucking knows where it will end up. My sister likes to help when she senses problems between other people. I've always thought of it as her way to avoid her own problems, and she has enough of them to deal with at the moment that I can see her focusing on mine instead. "Can we not do this, Aly? Lorelei and I just need a little time to get our heads around some stuff. We'll be fine."

"Your idea of fine is a lot different to a woman's idea of fine. You really should tell me what's happened so I can help you to not make a huge mistake here."

"I'm not going to make a mistake here. I'm going to sort something out. That's all."

Her eyes widen. "Jesus, this is worse than I thought. No

wonder Lorelei is distracted. Honestly, Ashton, why have you never learnt that sometimes people don't need you to sort stuff out? Sometimes we just want to be left alone to figure it out on our own."

"You're being dramatic, Alessandra. Lorelei simply—"

"Just tell me what happened. When you use the word simply, I know the shit's about to hit the fan. No woman ever wants to hear a man try to downplay a situation that way."

We could stand here for hours arguing over this and I know she'd never cave. When my sister wants information badly enough, she'll never give up the fight. So I give her what she wants and hope to hell she doesn't make matters worse between Lorelei and me. "Her ex is sniffing around and she kept the fact from me that she went to him to ask him to leave her alone. She also kept from me that he has no intention of doing that. We've discussed it today and I've told her I'll take care of the problem."

Her face softens and so does her voice when she says, "Oh boy, this is all new territory for you. I should have known it was something hurtful like this that would cause you to—"

"I'm angry, Aly, not hurt. I don't appreciate information deliberately being kept from me."

"Yes, I know you're angry, but where do you think that anger is coming from? You're hurt by her choices, and it's okay to admit that. You should tell her this is how you feel."

"I've made it clear to Lorelei how I feel on this matter. And as far as I'm concerned, the discussion is finished."

She cocks her head to the side. "So you told her you'd take care of Boston?"

"Yes. Her attempt didn't work. I'll make sure the job gets done."

"Oh God, did you say that to her? The bit about you getting the job done after she didn't?"

I nod. "She doesn't want him in her life anymore. I'm going to help her with that."

"You seriously have no clue about women. You're good at getting them, just not so good at keeping them. You've basically told her you don't think much of her ability to achieve her goal. And that, little brother, is a sure-fire way to upset a woman."

This conversation is pointless and I'm finished with it. Alessandra doesn't know the finer points of my relationship with Lorelei, and I don't have the inclination to explain them to her. Glancing behind her, I spot Malcolm coming our way. Lorelei and Bradley are right behind them, and the smile on Lorelei's face gives me hope she's moved past our earlier discussion.

Lifting my chin towards Malcolm, I say, "They're back, so can we drop this? I've got a handle on the situation."

"I truly hope so, because I've never seen you happier than you are with Lorelei in your life."

My eyes meet Lorelei's as she comes closer. The smile in them disappears. And when she moves next to me and says, "Malcolm has invited us to hang out with them this afternoon and have dinner at their place tonight, and I said yes," I know she hasn't moved past anything.

I frown. "We have plans for tonight." At her request, we're sailing out of Sydney at four this afternoon on a private yacht. We've both blocked out Monday so we can have two nights out to sea with no distractions.

"Cancel those plans, Ashton. We have more important things to do this weekend."

48

LORELEI

I watch Ashton pace his living room as he talks to Cassia over the phone. We left Alessandra's and arrived here about fifteen minutes ago, and they've been on the phone since then. From what I can work out, something's going on with his parents, and Cassia's trying to get Ashton to go over to their house and intervene.

"I've made my position clear, Cassia," he says, ice clinging to his words, "I'm not getting involved. This isn't the first time my parents have argued."

He listens to her response and rakes his fingers through his hair. "Stop. I said no. I'll check in with Mum tomorrow, but I have to go and deal with something now," he says as his eyes find mine.

Deal with something?

I'm just "something" to him?

I turn away from him and walk out of the living room onto the balcony. I'm so angry with him. It's the kind of anger that builds with every passing minute until it reaches breaking point. After everything that's happened today, I'm at breaking point now. I'm not even sure how we made it through dinner at his sister's with this anger between us.

"Lorelei."

I grip the balcony railing for one last moment before turning to him. I don't want to fight, but I won't stand for his controlling ways or his dismissiveness when I take issue with something he does.

His eyes demand my attention. "Are you ready to talk?"

"Yes."

His brows lift while he remains silent. It's as if he doesn't have anything to say and is just waiting for me to get my thoughts out so he can deal with them. His attitude has been off all night, and I'm over it.

"Don't look at me like that," I say as I shiver. The air is cold out here, but I want that sharp bite. It helps keep me focused.

"Jesus," he mutters, "Like what?" His voice and his body language scream his frustration and irritation, and as much as I try to ignore that so we can attempt a conversation, I can't.

"Like you can't even be bothered to acknowledge my thoughts are valid. Like this whole situation is beneath you even dedicating time to sorting out. You've been angry with me all night, and I'm—"

"I'm angry we wasted an opportunity to go away together this weekend. I'm also angry that Haynes is still in your life. But I'm not angry at you."

"Well, it certainly feels like it."

"Look," he starts, but I interrupt him.

"No, not look." I won't allow him to steamroll me again like he did this morning. "We obviously see this entire situation from different standpoints, so I'm going to state mine again. I've already made it clear how I feel, but you didn't listen. This time, I want you to take it in because I don't want to keep having this argument with you."

He doesn't respond to that except to clench his jaw, so I take a deep breath and continue. "I know you're used to getting your own way and being in charge of absolutely everything in your life, but that's not how I see this relationship going. Like I said this morning, we have to be equals in this. Otherwise, I see no reason to be in a relationship with you. Your way of barrelling in and taking over when you think I'm struggling with a situation isn't something I like. I need you to let me work out my own problems unless I come to you specifically and ask for help."

"If you're struggling with something, it's only natural for me to want to help."

"No, it'd be natural for you to *ask* if I need help."

His brows pull together. "Yes, so I'm not sure what the issue is here."

My eyes widen. He seriously has no idea. "The issue is that you don't ask, you just assume."

Irritation flashes in his eyes. "Jesus, Lorelei, you're really going to get upset when I try to help you? That makes no sense."

And there he goes, pissing me off even more. "Why can't you see where I'm coming from?" He's driving me crazy with his inability to comprehend this.

"I don't understand the problem. You couldn't deal with Haynes, so I'll help you with that."

"Oh my God, Ashton, this isn't just about that! This is about so much more than that. For a smart man, you're being dumb about this."

His anger flares; I can't miss it in his eyes and across his face. But before he can respond, his phone rings.

"Fuck," he mutters, checking the caller ID. Then, placing the phone to his ear, he snaps, "What is it now, Cassia? I'm in the middle of something." His tone is harsh, harsher than any I've heard him take with anyone. I pray I never see the day where I'm on the receiving end of that tone.

I turn away from him to face the Sydney skyline. The wind has picked up and I wrap my arms around myself as a chill sets in. I'm not entirely sure if that's from the weather or the way this discussion is going with Ashton.

Leaning against the balcony, I close my eyes and draw in another deep breath. I love being with Ashton, but I'm beginning to have doubts we're a good match. We're both too strong-willed, and while I'm willing to bend, he doesn't seem to even know the meaning of that word.

"Here, you're cold," Ashton says, cutting into my thoughts as he places his jacket over my shoulders.

I secure it around me and face him again. Nodding at his phone, I ask, "Is everything okay?"

He exhales sharply. "I don't know. That was Cassia again. Apparently Mum and Dad's fight has escalated to the point where Mum has started throwing things."

I frown. "Is that usual for your mum?" I'm still to meet her. The dinner Ashton had organised for Thursday this week had to be postponed.

"No. It concerns me."

"You should go over and make sure everything's okay." I don't want him to leave while we're in the middle of discussing our problems, but I don't want him to ignore his mother if she needs him.

He shoves his fingers through his hair again, agitated. "I don't want to leave until we figure this out."

I'm such a mix of emotions right now, and I'm fairly sure he is too, so it would probably be for the best if he left. Some space might give us time to think.

"Go. I'll be here when you get back."

He watches me thoughtfully for a long few moments, as if

he's trying to decide if I really will be here. Finally, he nods. "Okay. I'll be as quick as I can."

"Don't rush, Ashton. We need some time apart." I hate saying that, but it's the truth.

Determination settles across his face as he moves closer to me. His hand sneaks around my waist, and he pulls me to him. His grip is firm, determined, and his tone is demanding when he says, "Time apart is exactly what we don't need, Lorelei. Tell me you'll be here when I get back."

I look up into his eyes, a little breathless at the sudden change in his mood. While I don't love the Ashton who just takes over in some situations, I do like this bossy, demanding one. This is the Ashton who makes me feel wanted rather than just feeling like a piece of property to be owned and controlled. "I already told you I would be."

His eyes search mine. "Tell me again."

I place my hand on his arm. "I'll be here."

He stalls for a few moments before bending to kiss me. It doesn't begin as a deep kiss, more a brush across the lips, but the electricity that is always between us is heightened today. We may be angry at each other, and unable to come to an understanding, but there's no denying how much we desperately want each other or how much we truly want to resolve our differences.

By the time he's finished with me, I'm an achy mess of need. I don't want to be, but I am. I cling to him, pulling his mouth back to mine. I don't want to let him leave. I don't know why I have the sudden feeling that him walking away from this right now is the absolute wrong thing for us, but I do. All I want to do is beg him to stay, but I don't. Not when it's his mother who needs him.

I end the kiss and push him away. "Go," I say, all breathy.

He stares down at me with confusion, which I don't blame him for. *I'm* confused by my mood swings, so I know he must be. He doesn't argue, though. A minute later, he disappears out of my sight, and I wrap my arms around myself again. The chill in the air has intensified, and again, I can't decide if it's the weather or what's going on between Ashton and me. All I know is that my gut is twisting with unease, and I'm unable to fathom why.

49

ASHTON

"Go home, Ashton. Your mother is just experiencing one of her moments," my father says to me when I arrive at their house. He pours a Scotch and adds, with contempt, "I'm not sure why Cassia thought it necessary to involve you in this. It's not like you're part of the family these days."

I ignore his attitude towards me. "Where's Mum?"

"Cassia is putting her to bed."

I have no fucking clue what's going on here or why Cassia is involved, but I intend to get to the bottom of it. Stalking out of his office, down the hall to their bedroom, I reach for the door only for Cassia to open it and slip outside, closing it behind her.

"She's almost asleep," she says quietly, clearly trying to impress upon me that I shouldn't interrupt her.

I scowl. "Move out of the way, Cassia. I want to see my mother."

"No," she says with a firmness that's rare for her. Cassia may have argued with me over many things while we were together, but it wasn't often she took this tone. "She's too upset. Let her sleep it off and then come by tomorrow and see her."

I don't know if it's the fact I had to see my father, or that I'm irritated to find Cassia here, or if it's the turmoil I'm feeling over my arguments with Lorelei today that does it, but I grip her arm and pull her away from my mother's bedroom. When I've got her down the hall, I demand, "What the fuck is going on here, and why does it involve you?"

Her eyes widen at the anger in my voice, or maybe it's at the way I'm manhandling her because that's not my usual style. Yanking her arm from my hold, she whisper-yells, "Don't talk to me like that. I'm just trying to help your parents."

"How?" I demand.

She swallows hard under my scrutiny. "Your mother asked me over for dinner. Everything was going well until she started arguing with your dad. Things went downhill fast, and your mum lost it. I've never seen her like this before. She was screaming at him and then throwing plates and cups. I managed to get her to the bedroom and calmed her down, and I think your dad has calmed down too."

"What were they arguing over?"

She hesitates briefly. "Do you really want to know?"

"I wouldn't ask if I didn't."

Her shoulders slump as she sighs. "Your dad's been having an affair. She found out."

That fucking asshole.

I ball my fists.

"Fuck," I mutter. This isn't my father's first affair. It isn't even his second. At last count, he's had at least five affairs, and that's only the ones I know of. I have no idea how many of those my mother is aware of.

I walk away from her to head back to my father's office, but she reaches for my arm and stops me. "Ashton, don't."

The sound of his car screeching out of the driveway breaks into my thoughts before I can argue with her. Turning back, I meet her gaze. "Why are you spending all this time with my parents?" The question comes out angrier than I intend. Everything's turning to shit today, and I feel unable to rein my emotions in. If I can't confront my father, I'll settle for this confrontation.

Her body tenses. "Is there a problem with me doing that?"

"Yeah, a big fucking problem, Cassia. You and I are not together, so I don't understand your motives. And when I don't understand someone's reasons for doing something, I know deep in my gut that something shady is going on. So start talking and don't leave anything out."

"Ashton, I'm worried about you. You seem so on edge today. Is everything okay?"

"No, it's not. I want to know what the fuck is going on," I bark, feeling a loss of control I never feel.

Her lips flatten. "I don't deserve to be treated this way. I always liked your mum, and when she initiated our friend-ship, I didn't think it would be a problem for anyone. It doesn't affect you in any way. All it does is give her someone to spend time with and share her burdens with. We've grown close, and I treasure her friendship in more ways than you'll understand. I just wish you could be happy that your mum has someone she trusts and confides in. Especially when your father is a bastard to her."

I take all that in and realise I'm being a complete asshole to her when all she's trying to do is be a friend to my mother. She's right—it doesn't affect me in any way.

I rub the back of my neck, taking a step away from her. "Fuck, I'm sorry. It's been a shitty day, and I took it out on you. I appreciate that you're here for Mum."

She watches me silently, the tension easing from her

body. Nodding, she says softly, "Okay." Then, she moves close to me again and places her hand on my chest. "Do you need to talk about it? I'm always here for you."

"No." Talking to Cassia is not what I need.

Before I can stop her, she reaches up and curls her hand around my neck. Pulling my face down, she kisses me.

I pull away from her. "Fuck, Cassia, what the hell?"

Her eyes hold mine, and I see the defiance in them. "You can't tell me you didn't just feel something, Ashton. We've always had something between us, and I think it's time you admitted that to yourself."

Anger at her inability to let this relationship go flows through my veins. I have enough on my plate to deal with; I don't need to add her to the list. "There's nothing between us, and you need to understand that and move on."

Bitterness creeps into her tone as she says, "So that you can continue on with the little fling you're engaging in?"

"This thing between me and Lorelei isn't a little fling."

She hits me with a dirty look before smoothing the scowl lines on her face. Stepping away from me, she says, "You can continue fooling yourself, but eventually you'll see that you and I are meant to be together. I'm not going anywhere."

With that, she walks away from me. The woman is deluded if she thinks for one second that what she said is true. There's no way we'll ever be together again.

Lorelei is in the shower when I get home. I want nothing more than to strip and join her, but I know we aren't in that place today. She can hardly look at me, let alone fuck me. So I lie on the bed and wait for her, doing my best to ignore the way my dick gets harder with every passing minute.

Fuck.

I can't do it. I can't let this divide grow any deeper between us. And the best way I know to stop that is to touch her. The way she responded to my kiss earlier is all the evidence I need to know this. We may have some problems to work through, but I refuse to allow them to come between our sex life.

Pulling my shirt over my head, I drop it on the bed and make my way into the bathroom. Steam warms my skin as I finish stripping out of my clothes. Lorelei's eyes meet mine as I step in the shower, and I suck in a breath at what I find there.

She doesn't want this.

"Ashton," she says. Her voice is soft, but it holds a warning. "I'm nearly finished."

Every emotion I've felt today unleashes itself inside me, but the dominant one is fear. Fear of losing Lorelei. There's no fucking way I will let that happen, so I take charge of this situation before it gets out of control.

Moving toward her, I say, "Don't shut down on me, Lorelei. Not now. Not ever. Just because we've got things that still need to be worked through, doesn't mean I won't touch you. I will always want you, regardless of everything else."

She gasps as I cage her in and take hold of her waist. Hands to my chest, with water streaming down her body, she says, "I can't get lost in you, and I know I will if—"

I put a finger to her lips. "I will make sure we finish the conversation we started earlier, but there is no way I'm not having you now. We need this." God, how we fucking need this.

The sex I've had with other women in the past never meant what sex with Lorelei means to me. With her, it draws me closer. It helps me crack her open a little more each time. It reveals pieces of her I can't help but love and want more of. Time together and conversations may help me get to know her, but sex is the key to unlocking that part of her *she* isn't even in touch with. And I will do anything to touch that part of her, because when she surrenders to it, she gives me everything. She hands me her heart and tells me it's mine to keep for as long as I want. And I fucking want it forever.

She pushes harder against my chest, an apology in her eyes. "No, we don't. Sex is the last thing we need right now."

And with that, she moves out of my hold and exits the shower. I'm left staring after her, wondering how the hell we got here. And how the hell I can fix it.

50

LORELEI

I LIE QUIETLY ON MY SIDE OF THE BED AND STARE out the window of Ashton's bedroom. It's just past seven this morning and I've barely had three hours sleep. I know Ashton hasn't slept much either. After my shower last night, we argued again and didn't get anywhere. After an hour of going back and forth, each of us getting worked up, I told him I was going to bed. In the spare room. He fought me over that, and in the end, I agreed to stay in here with him. He'd gone downstairs to his office while I went to bed. It's been a long night of an unbearable silence between us, and I'm not looking forward to today.

The bed shifts as he leaves to go into the bathroom. A moment later, the shower starts, and I let the breath I've been holding out.

I need to find a way to fix this between us, because my heart hurts too much with the way things are going. Maybe I'm expecting too much from him and being too demanding. Having never dated a man like Ashton, I'm not used to dealing with his kind of needs in a relationship. He is who he is, and I didn't start dating him just so I could then try to change him. And after a lot of thinking during the night, I've come to see that everything he does is to help me. It's my insecurities getting in the way, and that is something only I can work on. That's not on Ashton.

I leave the bed with the intent to join him in the shower and call a truce. As I walk past his dresser, though, his phone rings. I know he's concerned about his mother, so I check to see if it's her calling. It's not. My stomach drops when I see Cassia's name flashing on the screen. I know she's probably calling in relation to his mother, but I don't like her being close with Ashton like this again. Not that I think they're close, but the number of times they've interacted recently seems to be increasing.

That makes me nervous.

Unsure.

I know it's stupid, because Ashton has made it more than clear he's over her, but still, I can't shake my feelings.

The ringing stops and a text comes through almost straight away. I know it's an invasion of his privacy, but I read it. I justify it to myself that maybe her message is urgent, but even I don't buy that reason.

I'm snooping.

Spying on him.

And when I read the message, I wish I hadn't.

Cassia: I'm sorry I kissed you last night, but you can't ignore the fact you felt it too. Call me.

With shaky hands, I place the phone down, but another text comes through, and I'm unable to resist reading it. It's like a train wreck I can't look away from.

This message isn't from Cassia, though.

Jessica: Sian has more properties for you. At this rate, you'll be the king of Willow Street.

The king of Willow Street?

I don't know for sure what she means, but I have a sneaking suspicion Ashton is planning something for Willow Street. It was how we met after all, when he came to me trying to buy my property.

Why hasn't he told me?

I place his phone down and find my clothes. My heart races as a million thoughts explode through my mind.

Ashton kissed Cassia last night.

She thinks he felt something.

He's doing a deal that involves my street.

Yes, *my* street. I have a lifetime of memories there and a network of friends with businesses there who want the same for Willow Street that I want—for it to remain untouched.

I force down the sick feeling rolling through me and hurriedly dress. I don't know what I'm doing, why I'm dressing rather than talking to Ashton about this, but I can't think straight enough to change course.

"Lorelei." His deep voice cuts through my thoughts, and my head snaps up to look at him. He's standing in the doorway between the en suite and the bedroom, towel wrapped around his waist, frowning at me. "What are you doing?"

I swallow hard, all the thoughts in my head slamming together causing the biggest mess in there that I can ever remember.

"You kissed Cassia?" I blurt, not caring that I sound

needy. Dammit, this man has me all kinds of crazy over him. I have never in my life acted like this.

His frown deepens as he moves towards me. "What?"

I motion wildly at the dresser where his phone is. "And you're buying up Willow Street?"

He glances at the dresser and reaches for the phone. After reading the messages, he drops the phone on the bed as he walks my way.

His jaw is set hard, his shoulders determined. "*I* didn't kiss Cassia. She kissed me. And for the record, she's wrong— I felt nothing. But I'm not entertaining a conversation about that because as far as I'm concerned, there is nothing to discuss."

I flinch. His words are sharp, and I don't know what to do with them.

He advances closer. "As for Willow Street, yes, I'm purchasing property there, but that was never a secret. You'll recall I tried to buy yours the day we met."

My breathing picks up, the uncertainty I'm feeling over what's happening, a heavy weight on my chest. The things I want to say to him get caught in my throat, and all I manage to get out is: "I didn't know you were trying to become the king of Willow Street."

He scowls. "Don't use Jessica's words on me."

I cross my arms over my chest, almost like I'm trying to protect myself from his ice. "So what's the plan, then? Are you going to buy us all up and bulldoze us so you can extend your empire and cash in?"

"Fuck, Lorelei, now you're twisting this—"

I drop my arms, annoyed at the arrogance rolling off him. "No, I'm not twisting anything. I just want to know what the plan is here. Clearly I need to be ready for it because it's going to affect me."

"It won't."

"How can you say that? Of course it's going to affect me if you develop Willow Street."

"Only in a good way. You'll reap the benefits of what I have planned."

I madly shake my head. "You don't get it, Ashton. I don't want Willow Street spoiled. Why can't you just leave it how it is?"

His nostrils flare as his frustration grows. "You're not thinking straight. Developing Willow Street is a smart business decision. You need to take the emotion out of this."

"You did not just say that to me!" I'm yelling now, every fibre of my being taut with outrage. He's hitting every one of my insecurities I have over the way I conduct business, and I can't hold back my hurt.

He's also going after the one thing I have left of my grandmother—Willow Street—and I will not go down without a fight over this.

Raking his fingers through his hair, he huffs out, "We need to take a step back—"

"No! You need to answer my question. What's the plan?"

The vein in his temple pulses, and I can tell he's fighting not to lose his temper. "A multilevel centre with shopping and offices. There's a lot of support for this, but I don't need your building for it to go ahead."

I shake my head. "Why can't you understand that either way I don't want this to happen? I don't want you to come in and ruin what we have there. It's one of the last parts of this city that remains untouched. You might call it progress, but I call it greedy."

It's his turn to flinch. However, before he has a chance to respond, I grab my shoes and phone, and add, "I don't see the need for it."

"Where are you going?" he asks as I move across the room to the door.

I don't slow down. "Home."

"Lorelei," he says, his voice low and full of objection.

I stop and spin around to face him. Wild energy blazes from me as I throw back, "I need some space. And some time to think."

"About what?"

"About us. I'm not sure I can do this anymore."

He's silent for a beat, his body rocklike and his face a wall of stone. "I'm not letting you go until we finish this discussion."

I stare into those fierce eyes of his, returning the same level of intensity. "You can stand there and throw orders out all you like, Ashton, but this time I'm not paying any attention. If I don't put some space between us, I'm not sure you'll like the outcome of that discussion."

He works his jaw, his eyes searching mine. "I'll give you the day, Lorelei, and not a second longer. I don't like leaving things unresolved."

I force out a long breath. "I need longer than a day."

That answer does not make him happy. "How long?"

"I don't know."

We stare at each other for a few painful moments, each recoiling from the wounds we've inflicted. This weekend has ripped us apart, and I'm not sure where we can go from here.

He drives me home, unhappily, and doesn't force the point when I say no to him walking me in. When I'm safely behind closed doors in the sanctuary of my own home, I let the tears fall.

How did we mess this up so badly?

51

ASHTON

"I've decided I don't like Asshole Thursday any more than I like Asshole Monday, Tuesday, or Wednesday," Jessica says as she dumps a stack of files on my desk early Thursday morning. "And if, as Lorelei just informed me, we're in for Asshole Friday too, I think I might just take tomorrow off work and leave you to live through it on your own."

My head jerks up at the mention of Lorelei's name. "You were talking to Lorelei?"

"Yes, I called her to follow up on setting a date for your next meeting regarding the resort development with Stan."

"And?" Jesus, I'm wound so tight over the argument Lorelei and I had, and the fact we haven't spoken since, that I'm more impatient than usual for Jessica to give me the information I want.

Her lips purse as I bark out my demand. "You know, maybe I should just go home now. This mood of yours is growing old, and frankly, you don't pay me enough to put up with this kind of shit."

Leaning back against my chair, I exhale a long breath and rake my fingers through my hair. "Fuck," I mutter. "I'm sorry."

Her brow arches. "That's the best apology you've got? We seriously need to work on that if you've any hope of fixing things with Lorelei. I can assure you that she'll be looking for more of an apology than two simple words."

"You're assuming I have things to apologise for."

"I may not know what you two argued over or why you haven't seen her for three days but I'd hedge my bets that you *do* have things to apologise for. That's not saying she doesn't also, but Ashton, I know your ways, and I know you can be an arrogant ass, so I'm telling you that you need to think long and hard about whatever went down and figure out what you need to say sorry for. And then form a better apology than the one you just gave me."

I'm in a mood. Yes. I'm frustrated by Lorelei's silence and growing more restless and tense by the day. Fighting my desire to go to her is proving harder by the minute. But Jessica is wrong; I don't have anything to apologise for. Lorelei and I are simply figuring out how to navigate our relationship. If she would stop running away whenever we have a disagreement, we could better work through our issues.

Getting into a discussion with Jessica about my relationship is the last thing on my agenda today, so I shift the conversation back to my original question. "When is the meeting with Stan and Lorelei?"

She eyes me with the look she reserves for moments when she's especially annoyed at me. I wait for another tongue-lashing but it doesn't come. Instead, she says, "Fine, ignore me. But you'll see I'm right. Your meeting is next Monday, and oh to be a fly on that wall. Unless of course you've come to your senses by then and apologised to

Lorelei." As she turns to leave my office, she adds, "I'll be at my desk. If you need me, check your asshole status first, because I don't intend to answer you unless you're nice to me."

I ignore her snark but call out, "What did you mean by Lorelei informing you tomorrow will be Asshole Friday?" I detest using that term, but my need to know what Lorelei said is greater than my aversion to Jessica's phrasing.

She faces me again. "I asked her whether it's likely you two will have sorted your differences by tomorrow. She said no." With that, she leaves me alone with my warring thoughts.

I swivel my chair and look out the window of my office. Usually, the view of the city helps me focus. Today, it offers me nothing.

Lorelei made it clear she wants time to think. I've given her three days. Two days longer than I would have given anyone else. I don't make it a habit of leaving problems up in the air, and I sure as hell don't make it a habit to be dictated to as to when I can call or see someone to discuss an issue. Lorelei is different. I'm in love with her, and for the first time in my life, I'm unsure of the best way forward. She's unpredictable, which I usually appreciate, but in this instance, I'd prefer to know how she'll react if I go against her wishes and refuse to give her space.

My phone rings, cutting into my thoughts.

I put it to my ear. "Aly, what's up?"

"I'm checking in to see if you've fixed things with Lorelei yet?"

"I would have if she'd allow me near her." Frustrated, my words come out harsher than intended. The fact my sister and my assistant feel it necessary to involve themselves in this situation is too much.

"You still haven't gone to see her? Or call her?"

"She told me to give her space. I'm giving her space."

"Holy hell, this is a new Ashton Scott. I think I'm impressed you listened to her."

"Don't be dramatic, Aly. And don't be impressed. I'm about to stop listening to her."

"Oh shit. I think I should come over and make sure you don't screw this up. There's a fine line when a woman tells you to give her space, and I'm fairly sure you don't have any clue what it is. Promise me you won't do anything until I get there."

"I'm hanging up now. Unless there was a reason you called me?"

"*This* is the reason I called you. I want to ensure you don't piss Lorelei off any more than you already have."

"I'm perfectly capable of handling my relationships on my own. I'll call you tonight so we can discuss next week's soccer practice and whether you still need me."

I end the call and immediately dial Lorelei's number.

She answers almost straight away. "Ashton." My name is a soft murmur, not giving me any hint as to her mood.

I get straight to the point. "Where are you?"

Her hesitation is a beat longer than I like. "Why?"

"Lorelei"—it's almost a growl, and definitely a demand —"I asked you a question. Where are you? I'm coming to see you, and we are going to finish the conversation we were in the middle of on Sunday."

She sighs. "I'm at my office, but I'm not ready to talk. I need some more time to get my thoughts together."

I grab my car keys. "No. I'm not willing to wait another minute to see you. I've already waited too long."

"Please don't come here. I'm asking you to give me the rest of this week, that's all. And then I'll come to you."

The rest of this week?

There's no way I can go a week without her.

"A compromise," I suggest. "You give me this, and I'll give you the rest of the week." I pause briefly, trying like hell to contain my emotions. "I need to see you today."

My head and heart are a raging sea of thoughts and feelings like I've never experienced. I need to see her more than I've ever needed to see anyone.

"Okay," she finally agrees, her voice wavering, betraying her uncertainty over this. "Come and see me, but I'm not promising anything."

I'm not looking for promises today. I'm looking for the opportunity to remind her of how she feels when she's with me. I'm counting on that feeling to outweigh any doubts she's having.

She has her back to the door when I arrive, and my eyes are drawn to those sexy-as-hell legs of hers that are on full display thanks to the navy blue dress she's wearing. It barely covers her thighs, and I immediately wonder how many assholes have laid eyes on her today. How many have run their eyes down her legs and imagined their hands sliding up them? The possessiveness that slams into me is overwhelming as I watch her for these few moments. I've never experienced these kinds of feelings before, and they confuse the hell out of me because I don't know how best to deal with them.

I'm out of my depth here. The one thing I do know with absolute certainty, though, is that Lorelei is mine and I need to do whatever it takes to remind her of that.

"Lorelei," I say as I enter her office.

She spins around, caught off guard, and meets my gaze. "Ashton." Her voice holds uncertainty. "You made good time. I wasn't expecting you so soon."

I didn't make good time; I forced it. But thoughts of how I sped here fall away as I take in the way Lorelei is looking at me like she can't keep her eyes off me, and note the way her voice is breathy and soft like usual. *She's still mine.*

"How are you?" I ask as I close the distance between us. She looks tired. She also looks apprehensive about me being here.

After taking a moment to compose her answer, she says, "It's been a busy week. I feel pulled in multiple directions and ready for a weekend off to recharge."

I know she's been busy; I've had James, one of my security guys, keep an eye on her to make sure she's safe, and he's reported back that she's filled every day with meetings and other work stuff.

"What do you have planned for today?"

Her forehead creases into a frown. "Are you asking me that because you want to know or because you want me to cancel my plans?"

"Both."

A fleeting look of exasperation crosses her face. "I told you I need the rest of this week, so please don't do this. I'm already confused about everything. You coming here trying to force me to a decision only confuses me more."

"I know we have things still to discuss, but what is there to be confused about?"

She stares at me like I'm speaking in tongues and then with a shake of her head, she says, "You're clueless as to why I've put some distance between us, aren't you?"

"No, but I'm unsure of this confusion you're experiencing."

Placing her hand on her hip, she throws out, "Okay then, tell me why I need a week away from you."

She's moved from breathy and soft to challenging, and I sense another argument brewing between us. In an attempt to stop that, I place my hand on her arm and say, "Let's pause and start again. How about we go to Francesca's café so we can sit and talk this out?"

Her face sets with determination. "Ashton, no. I'm not getting into this today. You need to go and let me think."

My own determination flares, as does my frustration. "Lorelei, you've had four nights to think. Now is the time to talk. And as far as why you needed time away from me, I understand you needed space for thinking. It's natural for issues like this to come up in new relationships. Extended time apart, though, won't help us work through our problems."

"Now might be the time for *you* to want to talk, but it's not what I need. This is what you seem incapable of grasping —that I process things differently to you, and that I have different ways of working stuff out. I understood that what you needed was to see me today, so I said yes to you coming over. Now, I'd really appreciate it if you could give me what I'm asking for."

The realisation that this isn't going to go the way I'd expected slams into me. And I'm at a loss for how to fix it. The rest of the week without her isn't something I want to contemplate, let alone give her, but I can see that if I don't agree to that our problems will multiply.

"I'll pick you up at seven on Sunday night and take you out to dinner. After that, I'll take you home and we'll talk this out." I wait expectantly for her agreement, and if she refuses to give it to me, I may just resort to extreme measures. This woman has me wound in knots that feel like they're about to strangle me, and there's nothing I won't do to untangle those knots.

She watches me silently for another few moments, unaware that with each passing second, I'm moving closer to tipping point. Finally, she nods. "Sunday night at seven."

I mentally exhale the breath I've been holding all week.

Thank fuck.

52

LORELEI

Sienna narrows her eyes at me when I arrive at her place Friday night. We're having girls' night in with wine, cheese, and our favourite eighties movies. She knows *Flashdance*, *Footloose*, and *Dirty Dancing* are my go-to movies when life gets too hard to deal with, and she always comes through for me with a night like this to talk it out over movies and wine. However, the way she's eyeing me leaves me unsure as to whether I'm going to get my Patrick Swayze fill. She's giving me the look she gives when she wants to ask me all the questions.

"You look worse than when I saw you yesterday morning. What happened between then and now?"

I dump the bag of cheese and crackers I brought on the kitchen counter and sigh. "Ashton happened." We haven't spoken since yesterday, so she doesn't know he stopped by my office.

Her eyes widen. "Oh God," she says, reaching into the fridge for a bottle of wine. "Tell me everything."

While she fills our glasses, I fill her in on the conversation Ashton and I had. By the time I've told her everything, we're sitting cross-legged on her couch and I've already finished my first glass of wine.

"So he doesn't get where you're coming from?" she asks, refilling my glass.

"No." I take a sip of wine. "Do you think I'm being unreasonable? Like, honestly, tell me how you see this, because I'm completely confused as to what to do here. I can't figure out if Ashton and I are too different to make a relationship work or whether I just have to buckle in and do the hard work hoping that in the end, it'll all be worth it."

She drinks some wine before launching in with her thoughts. "Okay, so we can agree that Ashton is probably used to getting his own way and that his nature is to always take charge. He strikes me as a guy who fixes problems, so that's probably what he thinks he's doing with the Boston situation—helping you with something you struggled with. I'm not saying he's right or wrong, just that I think this is how he has always lived his life. It was the same with the Shandwick deal. He wanted to help you. He just handled the whole thing badly."

I nod. "Yes, I agree. The thing I'm wondering is whether he'll ever be able to see what he's doing and if so, whether he'll come to understand that I want to try to take care of things myself first before I ask for help."

Her face softens as she pauses, watching me thoughtfully. "I guess the thing you have to decide is whether you're willing to bend a little more than him in the beginning of your relationship, because I honestly think it may take Ashton some time to get used to meeting you halfway with some of this stuff. And also, while I hesitate to mention this, because I *am* on your side here, I think some of your insecurities are coming into play here. I don't think you can blame this entirely on Ashton."

"Oh God, I know," I agree as I fall back against the couch.

This is another reason I'm all twisted up over this argument with him. I know I've got insecurities a mile long getting in the way. I just don't know how to force them out of the way.

Sienna reaches for some cheese and sips her wine as she thinks about what we've discussed. "You've always been Little Miss Independent, and I don't see that completely changing. And any change you are able to make will be hard for you because it's your default way of handling things. The other thing is this Willow Street development. That kind of stuff is in Ashton's blood, and I don't know if he'll be able to see it from your perspective. I mean, maybe he'll come around a little, but it's not fair to expect him to change that part of himself for you. Just like it's not fair for him to expect you to change your views. All you can do is try to find a middle ground. This is something that's going to take work for both of you. The thing you have to decide is, do you want to do that work for Ashton? Do you think he's possibly the guy you want to build a future with?"

My heart speeds up as I imagine a future with Ashton. This isn't a question I even have to think about; I *do* want to build a life with him.

Sienna cuts into my thoughts. "Tell me your first thoughts you just had after I said that."

"I do want him in my life, but—"

She shakes her head. "No, no buts yet. Those are the things to consider in a minute. First, I want to know how much you want him in your life. Is he the man you'd be willing to fight for, compromise for, and lay your life down for, or is he someone you'd walk away from if the hurdles got too big? Once you know the answer to that question, the 'buts' become the hurdles you need to prepare for, and we'll start figuring them out in advance and work out strategies for how you'll approach them."

A smile slowly spreads across my face. This is one of Sienna's superpowers. She's a list maker, and she always gets through her lists. She just makes things happen. And she never tackles a problem without knowing it from every angle. Me? I have a tendency to get caught up in the "buts." And sometimes I let them stop me from chasing my dreams.

"I want to fight for Ashton. I want him to be the man I learn how to compromise for, and the man I go to the ends of the earth for," I say softly while internally pushing down all the "buts" my heart is trying to throw out, not to mention my greatest fear that even if I give my heart and soul to Ashton, I may still lose him.

I know it's irrational to always fear the loss of people in my life, and over the years I've tried to get past this fear, but it lives deep inside me. It's the reason why I keep most people at arm's length, only allowing a few close. It's also the reason why I've never given myself fully to a man.

"Okay," she says with a smile, "Let's get to work."

I don't know if Ashton and I can come to a middle ground. I don't know if I'm truly capable of letting my independent streak ease enough for a man like Ashton to assert his dominant side, but I know I love him enough to try. That he's given me this week tells me he loves me enough to try, too, because I don't think it's Ashton style to compromise like this. And that is everything to me.

53

ASHTON

"If you ever grow tired of Lorelei Winters, Donna would be a good distraction," Aaron Steele says on Friday night when he finds me at the party he forced me to attend. It's the kind of event I'd usually avoid due to the lack of purpose to it, but Steele insisted he wanted to discuss business with me tonight.

Turning to him, I do my best to remember I need his involvement in the New Zealand deal. If I didn't absolutely need him for that to go ahead, I'd walk away without a backwards glance because I'm pissed off that he continues to belittle Lorelei. Instead, I keep a tight hold on my thoughts as I respond, "I don't know who you're referring to. Either way, though, I'm not interested."

He nods towards a tall blonde woman standing alone staring out the window that overlooks Sydney Harbour. "Donna Stark. She's always discreet. Lorelei would never know."

I clench my jaw as uncharacteristic emotions work their way through me. I've never cared about how the people I work with choose to run their lives or relationships. They could have fucked five women in one night before going home to their wife, and I wouldn't have blinked. Tonight, I'm feeling a whole lot different. Tonight, I want to punch Steele for being a philanderer and for even assuming I'd consider cheating on Lorelei.

Needing to get out of here before I blow this deal with him, I throw the remainder of my whisky down my throat and then demand, "What did you want to discuss with me?"

His eyes remain on Donna as he leisurely takes a drink. "You need to sell those Willow Street properties you've been purchasing. To your father."

Like hell I need to do that. However, I know how this world works, and there's more to this than Steele just telling me to sell. "Why?"

Shifting his gaze to me, he drops the missing puzzle piece. "The New Zealand deal won't go ahead if you don't."

My eyes bore into his while anger builds deep inside me. "You'll back out of it if I don't give those properties to my father? What the fuck has he got on you?"

"Sell, not give, Ashton. And he has nothing on me. This is a simple business transaction. He has something I want, and in return, he wants those properties."

"It'll be a cold day in hell before I sell anything to my father. Find another way to get what you want from him."

His eyes flash with annoyance. "This is the only way, and if you want me to invest in your resort, you'll make it happen."

Donna Stark joins us, interrupting our conversation. Her eyes hungrily roam my body before she meets my gaze. Stepping a little too close to me, she purrs, "Ashton Scott. It's taken us far too long to meet."

My tone is icy as I let her know how I feel about that. "And it'll be a long time before we meet again." Wanting to put some space between Steele and me, I face him again and say, "I'll be in touch." I have no intention of meeting his demand, but I need time to process it and come up with an alternative plan.

Ignoring Donna's shocked expression, I turn to leave.

"Make it soon, Ashton," Steele calls out. "Gregory wants this sale to go ahead in the next week."

Everything he's said tonight has infuriated me, but what angers me the most is that my father has managed to direct Steele's actions and put my deal at risk. There's a reason I distanced myself from him, and the fact he would put business before his son in this way is central to that.

I stalk towards the door to leave the party, but Cassia ambushes me on the way out. "Ashton, wait," she calls as she hurries across the room.

I keep moving, trying to exit before she reaches me, but she closes the distance between us fast. Curling her hand around my wrist, she says, "We need to talk."

A scowl fills my face. "We don't. What *I* need is for you to let me go so I can get the hell out of here."

My words or my tone or maybe both hurt her, and while she tries to cover that hurt, I see it in her eyes and regret being so harsh with her. But I don't make an effort to take any of it back; I'm too angry with my father to think about much more than him.

Instead of letting me go, she tightens her grip. "What's wrong? Why are you so moody tonight?"

I pull out of her hold. "Can we not do this right now, Cassia? I have stuff I need to deal with."

Again, instead of respecting my wishes, she does the opposite and moves closer to me, her body brushing against mine. Running her hand down my arm, she says, "You look stressed and angry about something. Why don't you talk it through with me? I'll get us a drink and find a quiet spot so we can talk. We still haven't talked about that kiss, and I also want to discuss some things about your mum with you. She's not doing so well, and I think she's hiding that from you."

The kiss is the last thing on my mind, but her mention of my mother catches my attention because I've suspected she's hiding stuff from me. After discovering my father is having another affair, she seems to have chosen her usual way of dealing with their problems and has thrown herself into socialising. She's presenting a happy face to the world, and if I didn't know otherwise, I would think she and Dad were happy together.

"We have nothing to talk about regarding that kiss." I silence her protest with a look that lets her know I'm not changing my mind on this. "I'm interested to hear more about my mother, but I don't want to do it here. I'll drive you home and you can tell me what you know on the way."

She smiles, and I know she assumes my offer to drive her home is more than just a way for us to talk. Cassia has always assumed far too much when it comes to me, and she's going to be very disappointed when I drop her off without walking her inside. "That sounds perfect," she murmurs.

I don't bother to correct her assumptions and place my hand on her back to guide her outside. As we're leaving, she reaches her hand up to my neck and slows my movement so she can press a kiss to my lips. It happens so suddenly I don't have time to stop her. When she pulls away and gives me a triumphant smile, I have no idea what it means.

My anger flares and I remove my hand from her back. "Change of plans," I bark. "I'll talk to my mother myself. I don't want to see you again, Cassia. Whatever this is that you think is happening between us, it's not. I've tried to tell you that nicely, but now I'm telling you bluntly—we were done a long time ago and we won't ever be together again."

Her eyes widen in surprise. "You don't know what you're

saying, Ashton. You're all messed up about something and not thinking straight."

"When have you ever known me not to know what I'm saying?" My tone is arctic. She's pushed me too far this time. The last thing I need is for someone at this party to have witnessed that kiss and to get the wrong idea about it.

She stares at me like I've slapped her. "Why are you fighting this? And why are you being so awful to me? I'm just trying to—"

I cut her off, unwilling to listen to another minute of her delusion. "The only thing I'm fighting is your inability to grasp reality. Listen to what I'm saying. This is over." With that, I finally leave this godforsaken party I should never have come to in the first place.

54

ASHTON

THE SOUND OF A RINGING PHONE PULLS ME FROM A deep sleep at 4:00 a.m. Saturday morning. My breathing slows when I see it's Josephine calling.

"Josephine," I murmur groggily, trying to drag myself fully awake so I can be completely present for this call. "Is Jack okay?"

"I hate to be the one to break the news to you, Ashton, but no, he's not okay. He had a public meltdown over something his manager said today, and went on a bender that ended with him trashing a restaurant. His assistant called me, and long story short, he's been hospitalised." She pauses for a moment, giving my mind time to catch up with everything she's said. "He's a mess, and I really think he's going to need you."

Leaving the bed, I begin mentally planning the things I'll need to do in order to get on a plane to LA. "You've seen him?"

"Briefly. But he's been spiralling since he got back and started doing everything his manager told him to do, so I've seen enough to know he's not in a good place."

She doesn't need to tell me that; I already know. This happened faster than I thought it would, and as much as I don't like seeing Jack in this place, at least he can now start getting the help he needs.

"Thanks for the call. I'll be on a plane today."

"You can stay with me if you want," she says, her tone sliding into sexy territory. It's a familiar place for us and one we easily go to knowing there are no expectations for anything more than a night or a few days together, but things have changed for me.

"I'm seeing someone." Josephine knows the significance of that to me. While she's never been strictly faithful to her partners, she understands and respects my stance on cheating. It's not something I ever do or ever condone in my relationships.

I can hear her smile down the line when she says, "I wasn't sure if I'd ever hear you say those three words to me again. Tell me about her, and please tell me she's nothing like Cassia."

"She's nothing like Cassia. Now, if I'm going to make it to LA today, I need to get off the phone and book a flight."

"Yes, you do, but don't think this conversation is finished. I'll be calling Jessica and scheduling in dinner with you while you're over here, and you'll tell me all about this woman then."

I have no doubt that's exactly what will happen because Josephine has a tendency to always get what she wants. Hell knows how I manage to fall into line with her wishes, but I usually do.

We end the call after I find out the details of Jack's doctor and the hospital he's in, and I immediately phone Jessica.

"Please tell me this call at this time is for a good reason and not just because you've decided to hit me with Asshole Saturday too," she says.

I unzip my suitcase and start packing clothes into it. "Jack's in hospital."

She's silent for a moment, and when she speaks again, the sleepiness and grumpiness is gone from her voice. "I'll book your flights, hotels, and cars. What else do you need me to do?"

At a point where I'm trying to push down foreign feelings of inadequacy and powerlessness where Jack's health is concerned, Jessica's certainty of my actions is comforting. I don't understand that emotion or where it's coming from, but I'm reassured by it. I may not feel any control over Jack's wellbeing, and I may feel a sense of guilt over letting him fall, but I will move heaven and earth to be by his side and do everything I can to help him get back up.

I give her the information about Jack's doctor and the hospital before saying, "Research them. I want to know everything there is to know about how they work."

"Do you want me to call Jack's mother or has Josephine already done that?"

I don't have to have asked Josephine whether she's already called Bronwyn Kingsley to let her know about her son. I know she hasn't because there's no love lost between those two. Bronwyn refuses to forget the low point in Jack's life after Josephine broke his heart.

"No, I'll call her on my way to the airport." I don't want to leave that conversation to anyone else.

"Right, you pack, and I'll send you the flight details. And Ashton?"

"Mmm?" My mind has drifted from this conversation to Lorelei. I need to call her and let her know what's happening.

"This isn't your fault."

Her words draw me back, and again I'm reminded of how well Jessica knows me. And again, there's a strange comfort in that. It reminds me of how I feel when Alessandra looks out for me.

"It feels a hell of a lot like my fault," I bark. As my emotions wash over me, I latch onto my anger and resentment that my best friend has to deal with this disorder. It's easier to sit with anger than it is to sit with worry. I don't make it a point to allow fear into my life, but it has always circled me when Jack refuses to take care of himself. Each time he descends into his hell, I worry a little more that this time may be the last. I can't imagine a life without Jack in it, and that will always fuel me to keep pushing to find a way to help him through. Grasping onto my anger drives me forward. It lashes out at my fear and forces it to be quiet. Unfortunately, it means those around me suffer when I take it out on them.

Jessica sighs, knowing this place well. "You can snap and snarl all you like, but it won't change the fact that Jack is in the hospital right now because *he* chose not to look after himself."

I don't want to continue discussing this. What I want is to call Lorelei and hear her voice. "Send me the flight info once you have it. And try not to seat me right near the toilets like you did on the last flight."

"Yep, Asshole Saturday has arrived," she mutters before hanging up.

She spares me the talking to about the fact she won't have much choice about what seat I can get at this late stage, because it's what we do. Well, it's what *she* does. Jessica knows when to give me a little space to lose my cool. She'll always come back and attempt to pull me into line, but it's that five-second freedom she allows, albeit with some snark, that lets me get my frustration out and then begin to come back to my centre.

I make a note to send her coffee vouchers. And to do

better. God knows she deserves that after all these years of putting up with me.

Focusing back on the task at hand, I finish packing and then call Lorelei. It's way too early for this call, but I can't stop myself. At this point, I need to speak to her like I need air.

My call goes to voicemail, so I try again. After three attempts, I leave a message for her to call me back. I then shower and dress, my mind a steady hum of thoughts about how to help Jack. By the time I'm dressed, I've decided I'll stay in LA with him as long as he needs me. I've also decided to stop by and see Lorelei before I fly out. This couldn't have come at a worse time for us, and I need to see her and speak with her before I leave. I need to make sure we're okay or at least have a shot at being okay before I put any physical distance between us.

55

LORELEI

"OH GOD," I MUTTER AS I WAKE UP ON SATURDAY morning. Slowly easing myself into a sitting position on Sienna's couch, I wince. "Oh God, why did we drink so much?"

Sienna surprises me when she answers my question. I didn't realise she was in the lounge room with me. "I blame you. If you hadn't wanted to celebrate your decision to go and see Ashton today and sort things out with him, we wouldn't be here feeling like we're now living in hell."

I squint my eyes in an attempt to see her. She's sitting on the floor near the other couch across from me. Frowning, I ask, "Why are you on the floor?"

She shrugs. "I must have passed out here."

As much as I try not to, because it hurts, I laugh. "We know how to party on a Friday night, huh?"

"Babe, you were the one partying. I was just along for the ride." A grin slides across her face. "And you should drink more. You were hilarious last night, and when you dropped your phone in the toilet and scrambled to retrieve it, I just about peed myself laughing."

I frown again. "I don't remember doing that. Shit, is it

okay?" I glance around looking for my phone, but I hardly have the energy for that, so I wait for Sienna's reply.

She waves her hand in the direction of the kitchen. "I dumped it in some rice. Hopefully that did the trick. All I can say is thank fuck you hadn't already used the toilet when you did it. No way would I have been touching it if you had."

God, I need to go back to hardly drinking. There are fewer hangovers and fewer mishaps that way.

"I need a shower," I say as I move very carefully off the lounge.

My effort to not stir my headache fails and a sharp jolt of pain hits me. When I place my hand to my head and squeeze my eyes shut, Sienna says, "I'm not sure standing in the shower is what you need right now. I'll make you my best hangover cure, and maybe after that, you'll be up for a shower."

I sit back down and open my eyes to look at her. "What's in this cure?"

She's on her way to the kitchen when she calls back over her shoulder, "Secret things, but trust me, they work."

I do trust her, for many reasons, the least not being that she's had enough hangovers to know how to cure one. Sinking back against the couch, I wait for her and allow my mind to drift to Ashton. Sienna helped me work past my hesitation with our relationship, and I'm eager to call him and organise to see him today. I'm finally ready to let go of my fear and step completely into a future with him. However, my hangover needs to ease before I'll call him, so maybe I'll just send him a text first. Well, so long as my phone is working. That thought gets me off the couch and into the kitchen so I can check my phone.

Sienna is reading something intently on her phone when I join her. She doesn't glance up but rather continues slowly scrolling and reading. Whatever it is, it's got her full attention.

I locate my phone that she put in a container of rice, and try to switch it on. The screen remains blank, and after repeated attempts of desperately pressing the power button, I come to the conclusion it's dead.

"Ugh. I'm going to have to get a new phone."

Sienna finally looks at me, a pained expression on her face. "Sorry babe. That sucks."

I nod at her phone. "What were you reading?"

She places it down on the counter and claps her hands together. "Just Facebook. Now, let's get these drinks into you."

Something about her tone or her expression or her body language feels off. I can't quite put my finger on it, but there's something weird there. Before I have a chance to ask her, she shoves two glasses at me. One contains a cloudy looking clear liquid and the other contains what I think must be tomato juice.

"Drink up," she says.

Narrowing my eyes at her, I ask, "Why do you seem so odd all of a sudden? It's like you're trying to push me into something." I pause for a beat. "Oh God, what's in these drinks? You've smashed up some of your strange health pills and sprinkled them in here, haven't you?" Sienna is all about vitamins and supplements, and is always trying to force them on me, but that's something I'm not really into. Especially when I don't know half the ingredients in the pills.

Her lips flatten and she hits me with an exasperated glare. "There're no pills in either of those. They're just straight coconut water and tomato juice."

"Really? You told me your cure was secret, and now you expect me to believe there's no voodoo in here."

She arches a brow. "Voodoo? Seriously? You think I'm so healthy because of voodoo?"

"No, I think you're healthy because you eat well and exercise. I don't think any of your voodoo pills contribute to your health."

Waving a hand at me, she mutters, "Just drink the bloody drinks, Lorelei. And stop banging on about voodoo."

Although my head is aching and I feel awful, I grin.

"Why are you smiling at me like that?"

"Because I love you and the way you care for me." I grin a little harder. "And I find it amusing when you go on about your pills. You do this thing where—"

A loud bang on the door to her apartment sounds, interrupting our conversation. I stare after her when she leaves to go check what's going on. Partly because I'm moving slowly today and am trying to get the energy to drink these drinks, and partly because I'm lost in the thought that everyone should have a friend like Sienna.

I drain both the glasses, pulling a face as I do so. I don't love either coconut water or tomato juice, but I feel bad enough to give them both a go. After I rinse the glasses, I place them next to the sink to be washed properly, and my gaze lands on Sienna's phone. She's left it on, and it looks like she was reading a news article. Reaching for it, I see a photo of Ashton at the top of the article. Right under the news heading, "The Cashton Empire Set To Explode."

Cashton?

I begin reading, trying to figure out what they mean by that. It doesn't take me long to figure it out. Or for my heart to almost stop beating. Not when I see the next photo. A photo of Ashton and Cassia kissing.

"Shit, I didn't want you to see that," Sienna says, coming back into the kitchen. "It's gossip and is probably bullshit."

I struggle to drag my attention from the article. "They're

kissing, Sienna." I finally look up at her. "And it's not the first time they've kissed recently. It doesn't look like gossip to me."

I desperately want to believe her, though. I want to believe that somehow, someone Photoshopped this image to make it look like he kissed her. What I don't want is to have to rethink my decision to continue this relationship with Ashton. It's all beginning to feel like whiplash. And on top of a hangover, it's even harder to think the situation through rationally.

"You need to call him and ask him about it. Don't jump to any conclusions."

Confusion is starting to take over, and my thoughts are running in a million different directions.

He doesn't want her.

He wouldn't kiss her.

This all has to be her doing.

She's manipulating him.

I can trust him.

He's made it clear he wants me, not her.

But then, the one thought that pretty much wipes out all the other ones, surfaces.

Maybe he got tired of waiting for me and decided I'm not worth the hassle.

I stare at Sienna, gulping down the dread consuming me. "I can't call him. My phone is dead and I don't know his number."

"Facebook. Send him a message and tell him to call you on my phone."

Thank goodness one of us is thinking straight.

I log into my Facebook account on her phone and message him. After I hit Send, I glance at Sienna. "I hope he gets that soon. I feel sick enough from the hangover. Waiting for him may just kill me."

"Okay, you're being dramatic. Let's calm down and get some food into you. That should help."

I shake my head. "I can't eat at a time like this." She's right that I am being dramatic, and it's completely unlike me, but I feel more stressed about getting in touch with Ashton than I've ever felt over a man before. I believe in him and his faithfulness, but I need to talk to him and make sure he hasn't changed his mind about us. That's the one doubt lingering.

Half an hour later when he still hasn't replied to my message, Sienna declares, "Enough! We're going to shower and get dressed, and then we're going out to eat. Sitting around here waiting for Ashton is not productive. He'll call at some point. I mean, hell, the man has made it clear how much he wants you. He's definitely going to call."

I hope she's right. After spending last night getting to the bottom of my fears and then admitting to myself just how much I love and want Ashton in my life, I'm counting on her being right.

56

LORELEI

"LORELEI, THERE YOU ARE! YOU ARRIVED AND THEN you disappeared on me," Ryan Shandwick says, his eyes a little too glittery with excitement for me tonight.

I'm not in the mood. I haven't heard from Ashton all day, so I'm feeling anything but excited. On top of that, Ryan phoned me this afternoon and invited me to this party we're now at, and after repeated attempts to say no, I finally caved. He told me it was important for our development for me to be seen here with him. I didn't want to let him down so I agreed to show my face. I've been here for almost an hour and plan to leave very soon. This party is nothing but shallow socialites, showy businessmen, and government officials who I suspect can be bought with enough cash. Not my kind of people. I'm unsure why Ryan thought it important for me to be here.

I gather my strength because I know he'll do everything to convince me to stay. If there's one thing Ryan's good at, it's never giving up and never taking no for an answer. "I'm about to leave."

He reaches for my arm as he shakes his head. "You can't leave. I have some people for you to meet."

Less than a minute later, he's dragged me across the room and we've joined a group of people at the bar. And I'm staring at Cassia Brampton.

This can't be happening.

Why did I agree to come tonight?

Of all the people, I had to run into her.

Ryan cuts into my thoughts when he introduces me to two men, but I fail to drag my attention fully to the conversation because all I can think about is whether Ashton has chosen Cassia over me.

That he didn't call or check in with me today has my confidence in our relationship at rock bottom. Sienna tried to give me a pep talk, but it doesn't matter how often she says Ashton made it clear he wants me; the fact is he kissed Cassia and hasn't called me. Those aren't actions of a man who wants me.

"You look a little ill," Cassia says as she leans in close to me. "Is everything okay?"

She catches me off guard, and I stumble with my reply. "Oh, do I? No, not ill. I'm fine. Well, I mean, I had a girls' night last night and drank a little too much, so maybe I'm still recovering from that."

Goodness, stop talking.

Do not say another word.

Do not engage with her.

I smooth my hair.

This woman puts me on edge.

Jesus.

Stop smoothing your hair.

In fact, just stop breathing.

Right now.

She smiles, and I don't feel like it means anything nice

like a smile normally should. No, Cassia's smile feels like she's calculating something in her mind while talking to me. "Oh, that's good, that you had a girls' night. It's always our friends who keep us going in times like this, isn't it?"

I frown. "In times like what?"

Her smile disappears and she looks at me with sympathy. Pity almost. "Well, it would be unkind of me to bring it up, but now that we're talking about it, I want you to know I had no idea this was going to happen between me and Ashton again. We didn't plan for it or—"

Gregory Scott cuts in to our conversation. "I for one am glad to see my son came to his senses." He greets Cassia with a kiss to her cheek. "Kendall is over the moon. She'll be over to see you soon."

I want to vomit. In fact, I'm fairly sure I *may* vomit.

What is happening right now?

Why are these people so unkind? Talking about Ashton and Cassia's relationship in front of me like I'm not even here.

I want to tell them what I think of them, but my mind is a mess. I don't trust any thoughts in there at the moment, so instead, I say nothing and try to catch Ryan's attention to let him know I'm leaving.

As I do this, Cassia's phone rings and after glancing at it, she looks between Gregory and me. "Sorry to be rude, but it's Ashton. I need to take this." She then answers the phone with, "Hello, darling," and leaves the group.

The room spins and I lose my manners. I've been clinging to them for Ryan, but I can't even bring myself to do that anymore. There's no way I can stand to be around these people a second longer.

Without so much as a goodbye, I turn and practically run to the exit. By the time I'm outside, tears are streaming down my face, and I'm close to being a sobbing mess. I hail a taxi, and once I'm settled in the back, I pull out my new phone. The one I got today to replace my old one. Pulling up Ashton's number, I wait for him to answer. He's about to get a piece of my mind. And it's not going to be pretty. Not if he can't be bothered to at least let me know we're over.

He doesn't answer, and I stare at my phone in disbelief. He can call Cassia, but he can't answer my call? Is this how he has treated all the women in his life? I can't imagine the man I know acting like this, and yet, I can't ignore everything that's happened in the last twenty-four hours.

Oh God.

This really is the end of us, isn't it?

57

ASHTON

THE FLIGHT TO LA FEELS LONGER THAN USUAL, AND I'm exhausted by the time I arrive at LAX. However, that doesn't slow down my efforts to get through customs and out of the airport as fast as I can. The thing that *does* slow me down, though, is Lorelei. Or precisely, the five angry voice-mails from her I retrieve after clearing customs.

The first two messages came in one after the other.

Lorelei: *Seriously?* I was standing right in front of Cassia just now when you called her, so I know you're not busy at the moment. And yet you don't even have the decency to answer my call? It wasn't enough that you kissed her at that party and didn't call or come see me to end things with me? You are so freaking lucky you aren't standing in front of me right now, Ashton, because if you were, I'd kick you in the goddam balls and make you hurt as much as I am.

Lorelei: I mean, I know we weren't in a great place, but you freaking made me feel like I was the only woman for you and that you wanted to work on our problems. I don't get men who can move from one woman to another like you have, but I'm glad this happened before I fell in love with you more than I already am. And your father! God, he's an asshole. Standing there telling Cassia how happy he and your mother are that you're back with her. Right freaking in front of me! You Scott men really know how to make a girl feel unworthy.

The last three messages came in about an hour later, and Lorelei sounds increasingly upset with each message.

Lorelei: I can't believe I dedicated the entire night last night to figuring out my feelings about you. The. Entire. Night. Not to mention the hours I spent thinking about you all week. God, I'm an idiot to have thought we had something special. I was ready to compromise for you, Ashton. Something I've never been good at in relationships, but for you, I was going to try, because I decided you were the man I'd go to the ends of the earth for. And you chose *her*! I have no idea how men are so freaking blind to women like Cassia. She's only interested in your status. I would have given you so much more than she ever will. You have no idea what you're missing out on with me.

Lorelei: Let me tell you something else. I know I can be Little Miss Independent, and that you probably aren't used to dealing with women like me. Women who don't bend to your every freaking demand. But I was willing to put in the work on our relationship and be the one who did more of the bending because I realised you aren't the kind of man who has ever had to bend before. I've never been with a man who takes over like you do, who always tries to fix things for me. And I may not be good at allowing a man to do that, but for you I was going to try! I was going to fight for you. All I can say now is thank God I found out what kind of man you are *before* I did all that fighting.

Lorelei: I am so freaking mad at you right now! And I know I'm going to regret telling you all this in the morning, but I need to get it off my chest. I knew right from the first day I met you that I should stay away. You were so bloody arrogant that day, but I thought I saw something more when you took me out to lunch. And every step of the way, you've shown me a man so unlike the one I'm seeing now. That was the man I love. *That* was the man I saw myself spending the rest of my life with, compromising, bending, and fighting for. And the worst part isn't that I was ready to do all that for you. No, the worst part in all of this is that I now have to figure out how to stop loving you. And that yet again, I've lost someone I love. I hope Cassia can give you whatever it is you want since I sure as hell couldn't.

Jesus Christ, what the hell happened during my flight?

My immediate instinct is to call Lorelei. However, I want to go into this conversation prepared for it. I need to know what caused her, and my parents, to assume Cassia and I are back together. So instead of calling her, I call Jessica.

She picks up straight away. "How's Jack?" Her worry is clear in her voice. And the fact she's still awake way past midnight tells me how concerned she is.

"I haven't seen him yet. I'm on my way to the hospital now. Have you heard anything more?"

"No, but I went to see his mum and ended up spending the day and most of tonight with her. She's more worried about him than she ever has been. Apparently, he was saying some out-there stuff to her while he was here."

"What kind of stuff?"

"That he's tired of his life and of being alone, and that he would do anything to switch his mind off. She mentioned they're things he's said before, but that this time he seemed really lonely and desperate for an end to it all."

"Fucking hell. Why didn't she call either of us?"

She sighs, and I hear her weariness. This is happening to Jack, but we're all feeling it. "I don't know. It felt pointless to ask her now. I'm just glad the worst thing he did in all of this was trash that restaurant. I get the sense things could have been a whole lot worse this time around." She pauses before softly asking, "Ashton, we're going to get him better, aren't we?"

"Yes." I won't accept anything less than that.

"I'll do whatever you need so you can stay over there for however long it takes. Anything. You just have to say the word."

Her promise puts my mind at ease. Jessica is more than capable of handling things, and that will give me the time and space I'll need to dedicate to Jack. But first, Lorelei. "Jessica, what the hell has happened since I left? Lorelei thinks I'm back with Cassia, and I have no idea why."

"Shit, I don't know. I've been offline today while I was with Bronwyn. I'll look into it now and call you back."

After we end the call, I think about what it means for Jessica to be in the dark as much as I am with this. She's never in the dark about anything. It's one of the reasons why she's so damn good at her job; she makes it her business to know everyone else's business. That she doesn't right now tells me a lot about where her head is at with Jack. Jessica plays it cool and gives the appearance of not caring about too many people or very much in life, but she cares very deeply for Jack. Even after everything that went down between them. And this clearly has her worried.

In the time it takes her to call me back, I check the other messages on my phone. A few problems have cropped up with various developments, but nothing that can't be fixed. There is one message, though, that I replay. It's from my father, congratulating me on making the right choice with Cassia and telling me he's looking forward to buying the Willow Street buildings. I've just finished listening to his message when Jessica calls. If I wasn't intent on calling Lorelei and sorting out this mess, I'd call my father and set him straight. Hell will freeze over before he gets his hands on those buildings. On top of that, I also want to set him straight about Cassia and me. And let him know that if he ever makes Lorelei feel worthless again, he'll have me to answer to.

"You're not going to like this," Jessica says, "And let me just say I told you so."

Jesus. "About what?"

"About that bitch you were dating for far too long. I told you she'd play dirty to get you back, and she finally has. Unless of course it was you who initiated that kiss on Friday night and then told the papers to print a story that you were back together. But since I know your dick has eyes for only one woman these days, I'm fairly sure it wasn't you who did all that, which leads me back to I told you so. And by the way, I know you haven't checked social media because of Jack and flying and all that, but seriously, we need to get you up to speed with Facebook some more. You miss out on so much by not being on there very often." She pauses briefly before adding, "Also, why did you not think it necessary to let Lorelei know about that kiss? Honestly, you need to take a course in dating. That could have saved a whole heap of drama here."

Logging into Facebook every damn day is not on my agenda, and Jessica knows that. I've made it more than clear I have no interest in any of the gossip or bullshit that goes on there. But every few months she tries to boss me around about it. And just like every other time we have this conversation, I ignore her. Besides, my mind is busy processing what she said about Cassia, and that is a far more important discussion to be having.

"I tried to call her before I flew out, but she didn't answer any of my calls, and she wasn't home when I dropped by her apartment on the way to the airport."

My intention had been to call Jessica and ask her to keep Lorelei in the loop; however, Jack's mother had phoned me at the last minute, preventing me from doing that. Bronwyn had been distraught with worry over her son, and I'd refused to rush the conversation. She can't fly due to her health, so I'd stayed on the line attempting to calm her down. In the end, the flight attendant had almost ripped my phone from my ear as the plane prepared to take off.

"Do you want me to do anything for you now? Maybe call upon Cassia and rip shreds from her? I wouldn't do this for just anyone, not at this time of night, but I would do it for you."

At any other time, Jessica's snark would make me smile, but not today. Not when all I can think about is making this right.

"I'll let you know if I need anything."

"You're no fun. I'm going to sleep now, but don't hesitate to call if you need me to take care of Cassia or if there's an update on Jack I need to know about."

"Goodnight, Jessica."

We end the call and I pull up Lorelei's number on my

phone. I don't care that she's probably asleep; we need to talk.

She doesn't answer my call so I try again. This happens four times. On my fifth attempt, she answers.

"Ashton, it's late and I'm tired. And I pretty much said everything I needed to say in those voicemails." Her voice wavers, and my anger with Cassia grows. She will incur my wrath over this once I've corrected Lorelei's assumptions. And I will ensure she never comes between Lorelei and me again.

"And now it's my turn to speak, because the story you got is wrong."

Muffled sounds fill my ears, as if she's shifting positions in bed. When she replies to what I said, she sounds more awake. "That's the thing, though, I didn't get any story from you. I didn't hear from you. And now isn't the time to call me. Not when I'm trying to sleep. It's been a long day, and I'm too exhausted to be having this conversation. Goodnight."

With that, she disconnects the call. I immediately phone her back, but when she doesn't answer after three attempts, I decide she's probably switched her phone to silent and has no intention of answering again.

Christ.

I'm already wound tight over this. It'll be hours till she wakes up and is ready to talk. And in the meantime, I'll be dealing with Jack.

It's going to be a long fucking day.

58

ASHTON

I PACE THE HOSPITAL CORRIDOR AND RAKE MY fingers through my hair as I pull out my phone to call Jessica. It's just after 3:00 p.m. here, which is around 8:00 a.m. for her in Sydney.

"Good morning, sunshine," she answers, her flat tone not matching her cheery words.

"I take it you didn't get much sleep."

"You take it correctly. Now, are you calling with a directive for me to go see your lovely ex? Or are you calling with news on Jack, or is this strictly work? Just an FYI before you answer that, I'm in the exact right mood to take Cassia on this morning. You could rest assured that job would be done to your high standards. And I won't even complain about doing errands for you on a Sunday."

I slow my stride and exhale a long, tired breath. The day has been exhausting, and I haven't had more than a few hours' sleep in the last twenty-four hours, but Jessica has managed to ease some of my tension with her humour.

"Jack's exhausted and asleep. I spoke with his doctor earlier, and if everything goes to plan, they'll discharge him in a day or so. After that, it'll be back to regular visits to his psychiatrist for a while." I don't have to explain it all to her. Jessica has been down this path enough to know how it goes. She knows how intensive and crucial this phase of treatment will be.

"Okay, good. He copes better when he's at home rather than in the hospital. Don't let him get away with any of his shit. You know he can be an asshole during this phase."

She's not telling me anything I don't know, but it's Jessica's way of feeling like she's contributing. "He's too exhausted to be an asshole at the moment, but I give it three days and he'll be in full-blown bastard mode."

I can hear her smile when she says, "Sounds about right."

Changing the subject, I ask, "Did you receive my email?" I've emailed through a list of jobs I need her to take care of today.

"Yes. I'm on it. Did you fix everything with Lorelei?"

"No. But I will."

"Because I know you don't check the gossip section of the paper, they printed another piece on you and Cassia today. A lovely double-page spread. And she even went to the trouble of sending them a couple of personal photos of the two of you for it, along with answering some questions. Are you quite sure you don't want me to go see her and set her straight?"

I contain my rising anger. It seems both Jessica and Alessandra were right about my ex. I should have been firmer with Cassia. I won't make that mistake with her again.

"She's on my list to deal with today. Let me know when you've finished those jobs. I may have more for you. And Jessica, thank you for working today." We agreed a long time ago that she would never work on a Sunday. I'm pushing boundaries here, and I appreciate the hell out of her doing this for me.

"I see an extended spa weekend ahead of me. Paid for by my boss."

I smile. "I'll have my assistant book it."

"Okay, go. Hang up. I've got work to do."

I call Alessandra after hanging up from Jessica.

"Do you know what time it is, Ashton?" she grumbles when she answers. "It's Sunday for God's sake. I know you don't have kids, so you won't understand the significance of Sundays, but for us people who birthed little humans, we try to sleep in on Sundays. Please take note of this for future reference. And please tell me you're ringing for a good reason and not just a casual chat."

"That was a lot of words, Aly. Impressive on a Sunday for an exhausted birther of little humans."

"Birther is not a word, FYI."

"It is now."

I hear a lot more grumbling and shuffling, along with Malcolm's voice before she says, "Okay, I'm sitting up. You've succeeded in waking both of us, so hit me with whatever this is about, and then I can lie here and try to go back to sleep while complaining about the asshole who ruined my Sunday morning."

"Have you seen Mum this week?"

"Yes. Why?"

"How was she?"

"How do you think she was after she discovered Dad's having another affair? And didn't you go see her on Monday? I could swear she told me you did."

"I did, but I think she kept her emotions in check while we talked. Cassia told me she's not doing well."

"Cassia? When did you see her? And more to the point, why are you anywhere near that woman? I keep telling you she's bad news."

"I take it you haven't read the papers this weekend."

"No." She pauses. "Why? What's in them? And why do I feel like I'm ten steps behind in this conversation?"

"It's a long story. One I don't want to get into right now because I'd rather discuss Mum with you. Where's her head at with this new affair?" I'm also concerned about how it's affecting her heart. It hasn't been long since her heart attack.

"From what I can work out, she's pretending the affair isn't happening. And I'm pretty sure Dad's still seeing that other woman. Mum's still really tired from the heart attack, but she's thrown herself back into the social circuit as if there are no issues with her health. I'm worried about her, and I think you should go see her and try to talk some sense into her. She listens to you far more than she listens to me."

Dad *is* still seeing the other woman. I had James confirm it. And knowing my father's history of cheating, my mother's anguish over it won't cause him to end the affair. As much as Mum likes to think it does, her pain means little to him. He can't keep his dick in his pants.

"I'm in LA, Aly. I can't go see her."

There's silence for a beat, and then her shriek fills my ears. "Oh my fucking God! That bitch! Wait, why did you kiss her?"

"I presume you just saw the news."

"Yes, but don't even bother answering that last question. I know she must have manipulated this somehow. Oh God, how's Lorelei? Is she ready to wring Cassia's neck? I bloody well would be."

I fill her in on everything that's happened. While it's the last thing I want to talk about, it's a good distraction from my worry over Jack, and besides, there's no way Alessandra is letting me off the hook with this conversation.

"I bloody told you so," she says after I finish giving her all the information.

"Yes, you and Jessica both," I say dryly.

"So you're coming home to fix things with Lorelei, right? I mean, you could always go straight back to be with Jack."

I grimace. I'm conflicted over this, because I want to be here for Jack, but I also want to do exactly what Aly has said. Deep in my gut, I know which choice I'll make, and it'll be Jack. It has to be Jack at the moment. All I can hope is that Lorelei and I are strong enough to survive Cassia's dirty tricks.

Before I can answer her, she mutters, "Shit, I have to go. The kids are up and running through the house, and I don't think Malcolm is in the house at the moment."

"I thought he was right beside you?"

She sighs. "You have a lot to learn about marriage and parenthood, little brother. I'll call you later."

The phone goes silent at the same time as two nurses rush past me down the corridor, reminding me of where I am. Bringing it all back to me that my best friend is in this hospital fighting for his life. Because from what his mother told Jessica, that's exactly what he's doing.

I put aside all my current problems and walk back to Jack's room. Whatever I'm dealing with pales in comparison to what he's going through. My phone call to Lorelei can wait.

He's still asleep when I enter the room, so I take a seat next to his bed and stare out the window while I think about everything he's going through. Jack's exhausted like he always is after a manic high, and I know it will take him a few days to be ready to do anything more than eat and sleep, but we did manage a brief conversation before I slipped out of his room earlier. And while he didn't give much acknowledgement that he knew I was there, I told him I'd be with him every step of the way.

"What's on your mind?"

I blink at the sound of Jack's voice and turn to face him.

He's barely awake, but clearly enough to know I'm thinking about something.

"You."

His eyes open fully and I suck in a breath at the vacant expression I see there. *He's got so far to go to get better.* "What's on your mind besides me? I can tell there's something else."

"This isn't stuff you need to worry about, Jack. You've got enough to deal with at the moment."

He rolls onto his back and scrubs his hand over his face. "I've got a head full of shit I don't need to be thinking about, Ashton. Give me something to take my mind off it for a minute."

Resting my elbows on my knees, I lean forward and push out a long breath. I'm running on fumes, and my thinking is beginning to suffer from lack of sleep. I'm not sure whether sharing my problems with Jack will be good for him or not, but I know him well enough to know he won't let this go. And that he really does need a break from his thoughts.

"Cassia has caused issues for Lorelei and me, leaving Lorelei with the impression I'm going back to Cassia."

Staring up at the ceiling, he says, "How bad is it?"

"Let's just say I sat through five angry voicemails from Lorelei while she told me she hopes Cassia can give me what I'm looking for. She then refused to talk to me on the phone."

He looks at me. "So, bad."

I nod.

"When are you flying home to fix this with her?"

Frowning, I shake my head. "I'm not going home."

He watches me silently for a few moments. "Don't stay here on my account. I don't want that shit on my conscience." And here's the moody bastard who always shows up in times like this. A little earlier than I'd expected.

A nurse interrupts us, and I leave the room so she can do

what she needs to do. It's perfect timing, because when he gets in this kind of mood, he goes looking for a fight. And as much as I try not to be provoked, Jack knows which buttons of mine to push.

I head down to the cafeteria and grab a coffee, trying to wake myself up. Lorelei's on my mind, and although it's barely nine in the morning in Sydney, I can't stop myself from calling her. I need to have this conversation. I need her to know she's misunderstood everything.

She answers on the third ring. "Ashton, it's early." Her tone is frosty, but I don't blame her. I'd be furious if I was in her shoes.

However, I need to take charge of this conversation to ensure I get my point across. "I'm going to tell you what happened and you're going to stay quiet and listen to every word I have to say. Are we clear?"

That gets her attention, and her frosty tone turns fiery. "You don't get to boss me around anymore, so—"

"Lorelei," I growl, "You need to stop fighting me and listen. There's a hell of a lot more to this than you know."

"I'll tell you what I *do* know, Ashton. I know I've seen photos of you with Cassia. I know I've spoken with Cassia who you called while I was right there. And I also know your father announced his pleasure at the news. What could you possibly have to tell me that changes any of that?"

I'm both pissed off at what's happened and turned on by her reaction to it. Lorelei has finally laid her cards on the table. She wants me and is willing to fight for me. And she's jealous as hell over Cassia. While I don't like the fact she's hurt by that jealousy, it shows me she's completely in this relationship with me. Now I just need to get her to listen to me.

"Jack has been admitted to hospital. I've flown to LA to be with him. That kiss you saw between Cassia and me? That was all her doing. I didn't instigate it, and I sure as fuck didn't want it. I have no idea who's responsible for printing that story, but as soon as I find out, they won't have a job. And as for me calling Cassia, that was bullshit. She was obviously trying to make you jealous."

Silence. And then—"Oh... Oh God, I'm so sorry about Jack. Is he okay?"

This is one of the reasons why I love this woman. Although she's upset and hurting, she's more concerned about Jack than herself right now. I can't name one woman I've dated who would have responded in this way.

"No, but we're doing everything to help him be okay."

She turns silent again, so I say, "I tried to call you before I left, and when I couldn't get hold of you, I stopped by your place, but you weren't home. I—"

"I dropped my phone in the toilet," she blurts. "That's why you couldn't get hold of me. It wasn't working. And I was at Sienna's." Her voice softens when she continues, "I'm sorry I left those voicemails. I honestly thought you'd chosen Cassia over me."

"We need to get one thing straight, Lorelei. I will never choose Cassia again. *Never*. I love *you*. And if anything like this ever happens again, you need to wait until you've spoken with me before making any assumptions."

"Well, you can see why I made those assumptions, right?" There's the Lorelei I know—always arguing with me.

"Yes, but this could have all been avoided if you'd just waited for me to call."

"I *did* wait. You didn't call."

"Are we going to sit here and spend the day arguing over this?"

"Could you maybe tell me you at least understand how I jumped to those conclusions?"

Truth be told, I *could* sit here and argue with her all day.

I'd rather not, though, so I give her what she's looking for. Hell, I'll give her anything she needs at this point. "I understand how you jumped to those conclusions. I'm going to ensure Cassia never has the opportunity to put you in that position again. I promise you I will deal with her. And as for everything you said in your voicemails, you've got it right that I'm not used to dealing with women who don't bend to my every demand. You challenge me some days, and you test the hell out of me. But if you *ever* change yourself for me, I will put you over my knee and spank that out of you. Any bending to be done in this relationship will be done by both of us. Not just by you. You will never have to fight for this relationship on your own. I will be right there with you fighting, because I've never loved anyone as much as I love you. You are everything to me."

Her response takes a moment. "You do realise I'm going to be challenging you forever, right? Like, if you think I'm ever going to take it easy on you, you're dreaming. Although, this spanking thing you've threatened a couple of times now *does* sound good, so maybe I could be tempted to ease up a little until you take your hand to my ass."

Fuck.

I've gone from tired to fully awake in less than a minute thanks to thoughts of my hand on her ass.

Before I have a chance to reply, she adds softly, "I love you, Ashton Scott, and I promise never to make assumptions again. And I'm going to fight for us, with you, forever."

59

LORELEI

"I TAKE IT YOUR DAY ISN'T GOING SO GREAT," Sienna says when she returns to our shared office on Monday afternoon. She's been out with clients all day while I've been stuck in the office trying to put out fires. I'm annoyed because I've had to cancel my weekly beauty afternoon at the nursing home.

I drop my pen and lean back against my chair. Sighing, I shake my head. "Do I look that bad?"

She sits across from me, placing her laptop on the table. "Yeah, you really do. Is it Ashton again?"

At the mention of his name, I perk up a little. "No, he's the one thing going right today. It's everything else. Cranky tenants, my shitty insurance company, and Ryan Shandwick. Between them all, I just wanna go home and crawl into bed with chocolate." I don't see my Monday spin class happening today.

"What's Ryan done? I thought you guys were working well together and that things were progressing nicely there?"

"He hasn't done anything to me, but I found out this

morning that one of the major investors pulled out over the weekend. It was Bob Darwin, who I kinda know through my grandmother. They used to do business together, and she always told me he was one of the good guys who could be trusted. Anyway, so I called him and asked why he pulled out. He told me he was bound by confidentiality clauses, but that I should tread carefully with this development. And now everything Ashton said is coming back to me, and I have a sick feeling in my stomach that somehow I missed something, and that I've made a really bad decision."

"Are you thinking of pulling out of it, too?"

I swallow my uneasiness and shake my head again. "It'll cost me so much to do that. I'm not sure if it's the best course of action." I want Ashton to look over this, and I wouldn't hesitate to ask him if he wasn't with Jack. But I don't want to distract him from doing something far more important than looking over my business deal.

"So what's the plan here?"

I stare at her in silence for a moment before placing my head on the table and saying, "I told you—bed and chocolate."

"Okay, so clearly we still need a plan for that. What's going on with your tenant and insurance company? Have they stopped arguing with you over everything like toddlers?"

Lifting my head, I smile at her. "That's exactly what this feels like. And no, they haven't, but my tenant is coming around. There hasn't been any graffiti for a while now, and no other problems, so she seems to have calmed down. Well, mostly. She's still arguing for me to reimburse some of her rent because of the supposed disruption to her business."

Sienna frowns. "Was there any disruption? I don't recall you telling me about that."

"Hardly any. She's just playing hardball, so I'm playing it

back. I've told her what I'm willing to give her, and if she wants to continue arguing, she can take it up with our lawyers. That'll end up costing her more than she'll get out of me."

"I like it," she says with a grin. "Changing the subject, I think we should go out tonight. We could have dinner at that little Italian place we love, and we could make plans for a girls' weekend next month. It's been too long since we've had one, and I'm in desperate need."

"Me too," I agree. "Italian sounds good. And I'm getting chocolate for later." Ashton's ringing me late tonight. Between him and chocolate, and time with Sienna, maybe I'll feel less stressed over everything.

A knock on the glass wall of our office drags my attention from thoughts of chocolate. Turning, I find Boston entering.

"Hey," he says. "Is now a good time?"

I hesitate with my answer, unsure how to proceed. The last time I saw him, he caused a huge divide between Ashton and me. And while I didn't easily see it from Ashton's point of view then, I do now. Ashton doesn't want Boston in my life any more than I want Cassia in his, so I need to make my ex understand my future is not with him.

Walking towards him, I say, "Now is a very good time for us to talk."

He reaches for me, his hand curling around my wrist. It's a familiar move; this was how he used to greet me when we were together. That, and a kiss. "Yeah, I wanted to come over and make sure you're okay."

I pull my arm out of his hold. He's obviously seen the papers over the weekend, and I'm getting the sense he's maybe using this as a way to draw me closer to him. Whatever he's doing, I'm not into it. "I'm fine, Boston. Don't believe everything you read in the paper."

My tone is cool, and he doesn't miss the chill. His

eyebrows pull together as he says, "I don't, but I'm not sure how a kiss can be anything but a kiss, Lorelei."

"Oh, with Cassia Brampton it can certainly be something other than a kiss. Trust me. But I don't want to discuss that. I want to discuss what happened the last time we saw each other."

He nods, and I'm struck by the expression on his face. It's not the kind of expression a man wears when he knows he's about to be given news he won't like. No, Boston seems assured. Confident. He appears to truly believe it's only a matter of time before we get back together. I'm going to have to be extremely firm with him today.

"Let's go grab a coffee while we talk," he suggests.

Sienna joins us, her purse in hand. "I'm gonna give you guys some space." Eyeing me, she adds, "Just message me once you're finished."

As she exits the office, I give my full attention back to Boston. "We don't need to grab a coffee to discuss this. There's not much to say except that I don't want to see you again."

He looks at me with confusion. "You don't mean that. We've got history that means something to both of us. I should never have left after that fight we had, but I think we both needed that time so we could realise we belong together."

I don't like hurting people, so it is hard for me to say what I need to say to him. But I have to do this for Ashton and me. "Boston, I don't love you. I'm sorry if that hurts to hear, but it is the truth. I thought I said no to marrying you because I was afraid of losing you, and while that was true, I understand now that it wasn't the full reason. I couldn't marry you because you weren't the right man for me. I know that now because I've met the right man. Being with him is completely different to being with you, and the reason for that is because I love him with every piece of myself. I've tried to hold some of myself back from him because that's what I do with everyone, but the fact he's managed to open me up in the way he has tells me everything I need to know. Ashton is my soul mate."

Boston stares at me in silence for a long few, painful moments. I feel good that I've been honest, but at the same time, it's painful for both of us. Finally, he says, "I knew you kept some parts of yourself closed off, but I also thought you loved me enough that you'd eventually share them with me. I guess I was wrong about that. You didn't love me enough."

The ache in his voice hits me in the gut. He's not right, though. The problem wasn't that I didn't love him enough; the problem was we weren't meant to be together. It doesn't matter how much you try to love someone and make it work with them if they aren't the one for you. Love is always hard, but with your soul mate, it's the kind of hard that even when you're exhausted by it, you still cling to each other in the dark of the night. Maybe not physically, but always emotionally. You don't fight simply to prove a point; you fight to hold onto the love you share. And when you're separated, your heart is unbearably heavy. The fact I never experienced these things with Boston is how I know I'm right.

There's no point trying to explain all of that to him. He's not in the right place to hear it now. My hope is that he finds his soul mate and comes to understand all this for himself.

"Goodbye, Boston," I say, my voice choking up a little, because as right as this decision is, it's still hard to close a chapter of my life.

His lips flatten as he watches me with disbelief. But he doesn't fight me on this. Instead, he nods. "I hope he can give you what you want."

Boston Haynes walks out of my life for the second time. This time, though, I know with every fibre of my being that it's the right thing for us. For me. My future is with Ashton. I have never been surer of anything in my life.

~

"You're awake early," I say when Ashton calls me just after 9:00 p.m. "I wasn't expecting you for another hour or so." It's four in the morning where he is.

"I didn't sleep well. Jack wasn't good last night, and it's been playing on my mind. Tell me about your day."

I haven't been able to stop thinking about Jack, and I want to ask Ashton about him, but I get the feeling that's not what he needs right now, so I leave that for another time. "Sienna and I went out for dinner. We planned a girls' weekend next month. And then I came home and ate way too much chocolate." I omit the part about Boston because I want to warm up to telling him that. We've only just gotten past the Cassia debacle, and while I know we still have things to discuss from our previous fight, I want to give us a little time and space to ease into that.

"Is there such a thing as too much chocolate?"

I smile. "This is why I love you. You understand chocolate the same way I do."

"You only love me because of my chocolate addiction?"

My smile grows. I love it when Ashton is like this. "I didn't know of this addiction of yours. I have to say I approve. What's your favourite kind?"

"You didn't answer my question."

Leaning back against the pillows on my bed, I wiggle into a comfortable position. I'm hoping this is going to be a long conversation. "Well, there are a *few* other reasons why I love you, but chocolate has to move near the top of the list. I feel like you'll understand and still love me when I'm older and my hips are carrying some of that chocolate."

"Do you want to know what I love right *now?*"

"What?"

"The fact you're already thinking about growing old with me."

My tummy flutters. "I'm thinking about a lot of things where you're concerned."

"Switch to FaceTime. I need to see you." The fun, flirty tone disappears from his voice, replaced with that bossy tone of his I love.

I do as he says, and a second later, he appears on my screen. My tummy does a whole lot more than flutter at the sight. My man is hot. Between his bare chest and his sexy, messy bed hair, I wish he wasn't a continent away.

His gaze moves over me. The heat in his eyes is undeniable even through the phone. "Fuck I miss you," he growls, meeting my gaze again.

I'm fairly sure where this is going after those four words, but Ashton surprises me when he says, "I shouldn't have reacted the way I did when I found out you'd gone to see Boston. And I sure as hell shouldn't have told you I'd take care of him."

I don't for one second let go of his eyes. "I saw Boston today. I told him I'm in love with you and that I don't want to see him again." My voice grows more serious when I add, "And I made it clear, in no uncertain terms, that my future is with you."

He takes all of that in, but he doesn't comment on it. Instead, he says, "I don't want to fight with you over Willow Street, but—"

I cut him off. "I was silly about that, Ashton. Of course

Willow Street won't remain the same forever. If it's not you who develops it, it'll just be someone else. So while I hate to see it change, I'm not going to argue with you anymore about it. And besides, I think my insecurities came into that far more than they should have."

He frowns. "What insecurities?"

I feel stupid admitting all this to him, but I know that if we've got any hope of building a strong relationship, I have to share these parts of myself with him. The parts I'm not confident about. "I believe in allowing my emotions into my business decisions, but at the same time, I have a lot of self-doubt around that, because I don't see many other successful business people do this. When we argued over your plans for Willow Street, you told me to take my emotions out of it, and that hit all my insecurities at once. I reacted to that more than anything."

He shifts off his bed and stands, giving me a view of even more skin. "It's my nature to take charge, so that's not going to change anytime soon. But I will work on assuming control whenever I sense you have a problem. And as for the way you choose to do business, I'll make an effort not to be an asshole about my thoughts on that."

I try not to, but I laugh. At his enquiring look, I say, "I love you for saying all that, especially the bit about you trying not to be an asshole. I mean, I don't see that happening easily for you, but it'll be fun watching you try."

The thing I truly love in everything he said is that he didn't make promises he knows he can't keep. He acknowledged he can be an ass, but he knows himself well enough, and respects me enough, not to promise me the world and then only give me half of it.

"If you were here right now, I'd—" he starts, but someone knocking on my door drags my attention from him.

Moving off my bed, I say, "Gimme a sec. There's someone at my door."

"At this time of night?"

"Yeah, weird. It's probably Sienna. She's seeing this guy at the moment who's playing it a little too cool for her. She's all over the place about it, because she really likes him and isn't used to a guy who disappears for days at a time."

I reach the front door and open it. Jessica stands on the other side.

"I'm going to hang up on you now," I say to Ashton as I usher his assistant inside. We've not met yet, but I've seen her online, and those photos do not do her justice. Jessica is a stunningly beautiful woman.

"Who is it?"

I'm not sure if I should tell him. I get the sense that this visit may just be between Jessica and me. I'll wait and see what comes of it before deciding. "A friend. I'll call you when I wake up. I hope Jack is doing better today."

We end the call, and I say to Jessica, "Hello. Come in."

I follow her into my lounge room, wishing I walked with as much confidence as she does. She's a tiny woman, not much more than five foot by the looks of it, but even from this small amount of time with her, I can tell she commands a room when she enters. It's in the way she stands straight, head up, and the way her eyes don't give you the option of looking away. Not to mention her impeccable style. Everything about Jessica from her Louboutin shoes to her little black dress to her perfectly manicured nails to her flawless skin to her diamond jewellery screams confidence.

She sweeps her gaze over my couch and says, "I love it. That red is gorgeous." Then, turning to me, she gets down to business. "Sorry to come over late. Actually, no, I'm not sorry, because what I have to give you is something you're going to want."

What she says grabs my complete attention. "Do you want a drink or are we just exchanging info here?" I've always gotten the vibe that Jessica is all about getting to the point and getting things done without small talk, and I'm definitely getting that same vibe tonight.

"Hmm," she murmurs. "What do you have?"

Her answer surprises me, but I'm hoping she does want a drink, because I want the opportunity to spend some time with the woman who Ashton trusts and respects so much. "Pretty much nothing except tea and coffee. I can tell you, though, that the coffee is divine. It's this amazing blend to die for. Although, you may not want coffee at this time of night."

A smile fills her face. "Oh, honey, I will drink coffee at any time of the day or night. You had me at 'to die for.'"

I can't put my finger on what exactly causes it, but suddenly I feel completely at ease with her. There was a softening or something when she made the decision to stay for a drink.

I return her smile and head into the kitchen to make coffee. Jessica follows me, taking in everything I own. Usually, I don't like it when someone does that, but with her, it feels okay. It doesn't feel like she's judging, but rather just taking an interest in what I choose to fill my home with.

"Oh I adore this cookbook," she says, picking up my favourite Thai recipe book. "My copy looks as used as yours." She smiles as she flicks through it, and glances up at me. "I probably have just as many food splatters in mine."

I'm not sure why, but I didn't picture her as someone who spends time cooking at home. I sense a lot of hidden layers to Jessica.

A text comes through on my phone.

Ashton: Mars bars are my favourites.

I grin, loving that he remembered that question of mine. Loving that he's been thinking back over our conversation after it ended.

"From your grin, I take it that was Ashton," Jessica says.

I nod as I quickly send him a reply.

Me: Cherry ripe for me.

Me: PS I'm totally adding Mars bars to my list of things I can bribe you with.

Ashton: There are things far more effective than chocolate for that.

I place my phone down and meet Jessica's gaze. "Sorry about that. Now, how do you have your coffee?"

She slides onto one of the bar stools and rests her arms on the kitchen counter. "Milk, no sugar, please." After a slight pause, she says, "I've known Ashton for a while now, and I've never seen him date anyone as perfect for him as you. I've certainly never seen him engage in text messaging with a woman like he just did with you."

I stop what I'm doing and say, "You just made a really shitty day a pretty freaking great day. Thank you for telling me that."

She opens her purse and pulls out a piece of paper. Handing it to me, she says, "This may make it even better."

I read what's written on the paper and then look up at her. "Whose schedule is this?"

Her brows lift slightly and she gives me a conspiratorial

look. "Cassia's. I thought it might come in handy if you wanted to pay her a little visit."

I do want to do that. I want to make it perfectly clear to her that I'm not buying her bullshit anymore, and that Ashton is mine now. I just wasn't sure how to find her. Not only has Jessica given me a detailed list of Cassia's schedule, she's also listed out addresses for me.

"So I know you're Ashton's assistant and all, but honestly, I'm thinking of stealing you from him."

"Honestly, no one could steal me from Ashton, but if he doesn't stop with the Asshole Mondays, I may need to reconsider that."

I like her even more now, knowing her loyalty to my man. "What are the Asshole Mondays?"

She wiggles on her chair as if she's settling in to tell me a story. "We have so much to catch up on, girl," she starts. We then lose a couple of hours talking about everything under the sun, and by the time she leaves, I know I've found a new friend.

Cassia Brampton is the quintessential mean girl. I've used Jessica's list from last night to track her down at the gym this morning and am watching her treat a woman awfully. They appear to be friends, and yet Cassia has spent the last few minutes telling the woman she needs to change hairdressers because hers clearly has no idea how to style hair. She also shared her dislike of the outfit the woman is wearing. I'm standing close, waiting for my opportunity to speak with Cassia, and as she finishes giving her opinion on the clothes, she sees me. A smug look settles across her face. I can't wait to wipe it off.

Moving away from her friend, she comes my way. "Lorelei. I wasn't aware you're a member of this gym."

God, this woman is something else. Snobby as well as conniving. Two of the absolute worst traits a woman can have.

I straighten my shoulders. "I'm not. I came to see you so we could get our stories straight."

She frowns, but even it's fake. "I'm sorry. You lost me there. What stories?"

I want to slap the superior expression off her face. And I'm not a violent person. Cassia brings out the worst in me.

"The story you've told yourself and the world about being back with Ashton. Honestly, I'm not sure how you live with yourself and your lies, Cassia. We both know that kiss was engineered for your gain and to make me doubt Ashton. The thing you clearly don't understand about Ashton is that when he wants something, he gets it. And he wants *me*. Not you."

Her brows lift. "The thing you don't understand about Ashton is that he grows bored easily. You'll be replaced soon enough, because trust me, there are enough women out there banging down his door. I don't know another man in this city more wanted than Ashton Scott."

I smile. It's as condescending as I can make it. "Yes, he told me how bored he was with you. I guess that's to be expected with shallow bitches." I take great pleasure in her shock. "He's also told me he wants to grow old with me. Did he ever tell you that?"

The look on her face leaves me with no doubt as to the answer to that question. Before she can reply, I say, "I thought so." Taking a step closer so I'm in her space, I lower my voice and say, "Back off bitch, because you do not want to be on the receiving end of me fighting for my man. And make no mistake, I may be a kind and giving person, but when you come after something that is mine, I will go to battle for it. And Ashton is mine."

I don't wait for whatever she has to say to that. I'm more than happy with the way her mouth is hanging open and the way her shoulders have slumped. That's what I came here for today. She may have had the smug look of satisfaction on her face when I arrived, but I'm the one leaving with it.

60

ASHTON

I ENTER MY HOTEL ROOM JUST AFTER SEVEN ON Monday night. It's been a long day at the hospital with Jack, and after not sleeping so well recently, I'm exhausted. And pissed off at my inability to get hold of people I want to speak with. These time zone differences frustrate the hell out of me sometimes. My mood isn't helped by the distance Jack seems to be keeping from me. His doctor advised me late today that he's almost certain he'll be sending Jack home tomorrow, and I'm hoping once he's back in his own surroundings, he'll open up to me.

Stripping out of my clothes, I take a hot shower, letting the heat work its way into my aching muscles. I haven't managed to hit the gym yet, and I don't have time to get a session in now because I've got dinner scheduled with Josephine. After dinner, though, I'll spend at least an hour there, trying to work both these kinks and my irritation out.

As I'm wrapping my towel around my waist after the shower, my father returns my call from earlier today.

"Ashton, I take it this call is to discuss the sale of the Willow Street properties."

"It isn't. It's to discuss my relationship with Lorelei."

That catches him off guard, and he turns silent for a few moments. "I thought that was over. That you'd come to your senses and were back with Cassia."

"You thought wrong. I have no intention of ever getting back with Cassia, and every intention of marrying Lorelei."

"You're a fool. Cassia has a lot more to offer you than that woman."

"She has nothing to offer me, but then, I'm not getting married for social connections. I'm not you."

"You watch your mouth, son. I married your mother because I love her."

"That's bullshit and we both know it. And if you love her, you wouldn't fuck every social-climbing bimbo out there."

My father almost never loses his cool, and today is no different. He doesn't react in any way other than to say, "I presume you don't plan on selling me those Willow Street properties. I haven't heard anything from your assistant."

He's changing the subject like he always does when I challenge him over something he doesn't want to discuss. And just like every other time this has happened, I don't waste my breath on pursuing it, because it won't get us anywhere.

"You presume correctly."

"Steele will back out of your development. Do you have anyone ready to replace him?"

"That's none of your concern." I don't have anyone, and if Steele does back out, I'll lose millions, but there's no fucking way I'll ever let my father know that.

"I have a proposition for you. If you agree to marry Cassia, I'll walk away from Willow Street."

With that, everything starts to fall into place as to why Cassia has become so close to my parents. I wouldn't be surprised if she's been in on this plan with my father all along.

I grip my phone harder. "Cassia has fooled you. Whatever you think she brings to the table, I can assure you she doesn't. And if you think I would entertain for even a second the idea of marrying a woman simply to negotiate a business deal, you don't know me at all. I would walk away from every last cent I have before I would ever marry for that reason. And one other thing—if you ever treat Lorelei the way you treated her the other night, I will make it so you wish you hadn't."

Stabbing at the phone, I disconnect the call, angrier than before our conversation. That my father and my ex have been conspiring to end my relationship with Lorelei, causes the kind of fury I don't usually experience. I can deal with the business bullshit he's pulling, but the minute they started messing with my relationship is the minute they will both come to regret.

Unwrapping the towel from my waist, I finish drying off and throw it on the bed. I then find some clothes to wear to dinner and get dressed. Josephine will be waiting for me, but I have a phone call I need to make first.

Cassia answers almost straight away. "Hey! I'm sorry I haven't returned your calls today. I've been busy with—"

"I don't give a fuck what you've been busy with, Cassia. I didn't call to discuss that."

"Oh," she says, and I can hear the shock in her voice. She's not used to me talking to her like this, but she's going to have to get used to it if she wants to keep pulling the stunts she's been pulling. "Okay," she continues, tentatively, "What's up?"

"You know what's up, so stop playing games with me. I'm calling to discuss our relationship and how it will proceed from here on out."

"Ashton, I—"

I can already hear her mind ticking over, trying to figure

out how to bullshit her way out of this, and I'm not enter-taining any of it. "Do you remember those shares of your family's company that I own? The ones I bought when your reputation was on the line because of the shit your father had gotten himself into?"

"Yes. Why? Where are you going with this?"

"I saved you back then because I cared about you. You've taken that care and you've crushed it to the point where I don't want anything to do with you again. On top of that, you hurt the woman I love. No one does that and gets away with it. If you ever so much as look at Lorelei the wrong way, I will dump every last one of those shares. If you ever kiss me again, I will dump those shares. And I will make sure the world knows I did it because they're a bad investment. No one will touch them again, and your family will lose every-thing. *You* will lose everything you care about." I pause before adding, "Are we clear?"

My father thinks marrying Cassia and me off is a good idea because he believes her family is wealthy. What he doesn't know is it's my money keeping their company afloat these days. Old money doesn't last if it's not looked after properly, and her father made one too many bad investments.

I don't miss the venom in her voice when she responds. "You're late to the party, Ashton."

"What party?"

"The one where your girlfriend ambushed me at my gym and made a scene in front of everyone. She's already threat-ened to take me down if I keep chasing you. It seems you two are made for each other."

I can't deny the pleasure I feel at the thought of Lorelei taking a stand against Cassia. This is a clear sign that she's fighting for us.

"You didn't answer my question," I push her. I'm way

past ready to end this call, but I need to ensure we're on the same page first.

"Yes, we are fucking clear. And let me just say what an asshole you turned out to be. I'm glad to be rid of you."

"I haven't changed. I was always an asshole. The difference is that only certain people bring it out in me, and you turned out to be one of those people."

I end the call and exhale a long breath. Thank fuck that's done. Now I can focus my attention on people who matter to me.

Ten minutes later, I walk into the hotel restaurant and search for Josephine. She waves at me from a table near the window, and I make my way over to her.

Standing, she greets me with a hug and a kiss to my cheek. Holding my arms, she says, "God, you look good. You get better looking every time I see you."

The same can be said for her. She's a beautiful woman, but Josephine's beauty comes from the way she moves with ease. With a laugh and flick of her long, blonde hair, she can catch the attention of every man in the room. She modelled throughout her teens and twenties, and has always had the kind of confidence that draws people in.

I smile. Just being in her presence helps settle me. She has that effect on everyone she meets.

We sit, and after I order a bottle of wine, I ask, "How have you been?"

She leans back against her chair and crosses her legs. "Really good. I can't believe it's been a year since we've seen each other. I've mostly been busy with the agency. And doing some travel." Her eyes sparkle as she adds, "And love. I've been trying to find that too. You're going to have to share your secrets with me about how to do that."

This surprises me. Josephine has never wanted to settle

down. She's a free spirit and likes to share herself. "How's that going? Any candidates?"

She opens her mouth to speak, but quickly closes it. A few moments pass before she finally shares with me, "Jack and I tried again for a little while. I'm guessing he didn't tell you."

That doesn't surprise me. While she broke Jack's heart once, and he swore he'd never go there again, he's impulsive. My friend lives life in the moment and goes with the flow. If he's feeling it, he follows it, without thinking through the consequences.

Our wine arrives and I drink some while eyeing her thoughtfully. "He didn't. Although I'm assuming it ended amicably this time, I'm wondering, did you cheat on him again?"

She whistles lowly. "That's harsh, Ashton."

I arch a brow. "Not really. It is your signature move after all."

Taking a sip of wine, she nods. "Fair point. But no, I'm a reformed cheater. I'm serious about wanting to find someone to spend my life with. Jack realised he didn't want to be that man, so we parted ways. And yes, it was amicable."

"Really? *He* ended it?"

"Of course he did. He's in love with another woman." She leans forward, her eyes boring into mine. "Surely you know that?"

"Fuck," I mutter. *Jessica.*

"Does he have a shot with her still?"

I drink some more wine. "If you're asking me whether she still loves him, the answer is yes. But as for whether he has another chance with her, the answer to that is I doubt it."

"That's a shame."

I need to change the conversation. Jack's my best friend, and I want to see him happy, but I feel protective over Jessica.

I don't want to even consider them together again. Their relationship was wild and intense, and it broke both of them. And although Jack was the one who cheated, I know there was more to that than him just screwing another woman. I know it stemmed from the darkness that haunts him, and *that* isn't a place I want him to go back to ever. So I divert the conversation, asking Josephine about how her modelling agency is going, and we enjoy a long, lazy dinner catching up. And for the first time since I arrived in LA, I briefly escape the worry clouding my mind.

61

ASHTON

I REMEMBER THE DAY I DISCOVERED JACK WASN'T quite as happy as I thought he was. We were seventeen and in our last year of school. Jack was the guy everyone gravitated to. He was always laughing and causing the best kind of chaos. Teachers wavered between pulling their hair out over him and encouraging his enthusiasm in class. Not that Jack loved school or learning; he just loved being around people and being the centre of attention. Until the day he didn't.

That day hit me square in the chest. Winded me. Seeing my best friend go from smiling and laughing to pushing everyone away and wanting to lock himself in a dark room caused me to worry about someone in a way I never really had before. For the first time in my life, I felt fear.

I've always worried for Jack, but I haven't experienced that same level of fear again until now. *Until this time.* I'm having trouble sleeping and I'm not running at full capacity. Wrapping my head around what's happening with my friend is a struggle, because ever since I arrived in LA, he's shut me out. He may have engaged in a few conversations with me, but I know him like the back of my hand, and he's shut down on me.

Jack's doctor allowed him to leave the hospital today, four days after he was admitted, and we arrived home at his Carbon Beach home about two hours ago. He headed straight for his bedroom while I watched him walk away, unsure how to get him to open up. This isn't a feeling I'm familiar with, and it's messing with my head. His doctor advised me to simply be there for him, making sure he's taking his medication and attending his therapy sessions. "Simply being there" for loved ones isn't my strong suit, so this is a learning curve for me. I'd much rather force a positive outcome, but force isn't what's called for here.

"Ashton."

I glance up from where I'm sitting on Jack's back deck overlooking the ocean, and find him watching me. "Did you get much sleep?" Fuck, I feel like I'm making small talk with my best fucking friend.

He walks my way and takes the chair next to me. It's a warm summer day, and yet he's wearing black sweatpants and a grey Henley. In true Jack style, he ignores my question and asks, "When are you going home?"

I follow his gaze to the water. "When I'm convinced you don't need me anymore."

"I don't need you, Ashton. Go home."

"Whose opinion is that, Jack? Yours or your doctor's?"

His lips pull into a flat line as he looks at me. "I'm taking my pills and seeing my shrink. If I need anyone else to talk to, I'll call Josephine. Go home. I know you have much more important shit to take care of than me."

The fact he only mentions one friend who he'll call if he needs someone strikes me. Jack knows more people than he could ever list in a day, and yet when it comes down to it, how many of them would be there for him in the middle of the night when his mind is fucking with him? This Holly-wood life is something else. And, not for the first time, I'm wondering whether it's good for him anymore.

It's my turn to ignore him now. "Your mum told Jessica that you seemed desperate for an end to everything when you saw her recently."

His shoulders tense, alerting me to his discomfort with this topic. But, surprising me, he doesn't shut down. "You're asking whether I contemplated ending my life?"

The air in my lungs feels clogged. I want to avoid this discussion just as much as Jack does, because I'm not sure what I'll do with his answer. "Yes," I force out.

He exhales a long breath and scrubs a hand over his face. "No. But yes."

Jesus, what the fuck does that mean? "So that's a yes, then?"

His eyes bore into mine, and I see the depth of despair he's living with. It fucking slices through me. *Why can't I just fix this for him? I need to find a way to get him better.* "I don't believe in suicide, but that doesn't mean it doesn't come for me."

There's my answer, and it's not the answer I wanted, but it's the one I knew deep in my gut he would give.

"Okay, so that shit you just said about me having more important stuff to take care of back home? Don't ever say that to me again." I'm running on worry and anger, and my words rush out on a heated breath. "We've been friends for decades, Jack, and there's no way in hell I'm sitting this out."

He returns my anger, and it's the first time in days I've seen this level of emotion from him. I take it as a good sign. "This is going to be messy, Ashton. *I'm* messy. My mind is blacker than it's ever been, and to tell you the truth, I don't know how the fuck I'm going to drag myself out of this shit this time. I don't even know if I want to." His brows lift.

"That honest enough for you? Is that what you've been hanging around waiting to hear?"

Finally.

"It's a great fucking starting point, Jack." I stand. "I'm going to make us lunch now, and then we're going for a walk on the beach."

"Really? This is how this is going to go down? You're going to take charge and run my life?"

I nod, feeling more like myself than I have in days. "Yeah."

Jack's doctor told me he needs routine, so I'm going to give it to him. Day by day, hour by hour, I'm going to be by his side, helping him, annoying him, frustrating him, pissing him off, and anything else he needs to get back to a good place. We're going to do this together.

I manage to convince Jack to watch a movie with me after we take our walk on the beach. After it ends, around 5:00 p.m., he heads back to his bedroom, but not before I tell him we're ordering Thai for dinner. It's my way of letting him know I expect him to eat, because I'm fairly sure if I leave him to his own devices, he'll skip dinner and not leave his room again until morning.

I've just made myself a coffee and logged in to check my emails when Jessica calls.

"So, it's Asshole Wednesday here, because Ryan Shandwick has fucked Lorelei in the ass, and let me tell you, she won't be getting any joy from it," she says before I can get a word in. It takes a lot to get Jessica furious, but by the way her words are coming out in an angry torrent, it seems Shandwick has managed that.

"What's happened?" He's shady, but so far we haven't been able to find something to convince Lorelei of this.

"The Herald is breaking a story tomorrow about the high levels of corruption in the State government, and their main focus is the development Lorelei's tied up with. From what I know, they'll be splashing photos of her with the politicians from a party she attended recently. Shandwick used that night to introduce her to them while using her grandmother's reputation to help sway their approval for this development. He's also thrown a lot of cash their way, but the fact he's really pushed Lorelei as the face of it all will ensure this hits her harder than him."

Fuck.

"I'll take care of this. Is there anything else I need to know about?"

"Yes, as a matter of fact, there is." The anger in her voice eases, and I hear what sounds like satisfaction. "I dug up some dirt on Shandwick for you. It seems he has a thing for underage girls, in particular, the daughter of one of his business partners. I've emailed some photos to you. Have fun with that, and you're welcome."

We end the call, and I open the email she sent. Jessica really is a rock star when it comes to her job. This is exactly what I'll need to help get Lorelei out of this mess.

I search the contacts in my phone until I find the one I need. The editor of *The Sydney Morning Herald*. I've had him on my list to call since one of his reporters published that story about Cassia and me, but I've been busy with Jack. Now he can help me with two things.

"Ashton Scott," he answers the phone, a smile in his voice. "It's been a while since we've spoken."

Robert Carmody and I enjoy a friendly relationship. Mostly because I help him out when I can, connecting him with people in my network. Today, that friendly relationship may end. The smile in his voice will certainly disappear.

"Robert, I've got a problem I need your help with."

"Go on."

"You're printing a story tomorrow that features Lorelei Winters and Ryan Shandwick. Is that correct?"

"Yes."

"It needs to be rewritten. Lorelei Winters has nothing to do with Shandwick or that development."

"That's not what our sources are telling us. I've got photos and emails confirming everything."

"Your sources are wrong. Just like they were wrong about Cassia Brampton and me over the weekend. That article was a complete fabrication, and I'm less than impressed you would run it without confirming information with me first."

"We had photos, Ashton. And Cassia confirmed it. Just the same as we have with this article. Photos and confirmation from some reputable people." His voice turns firm when he adds, "I'm not pulling it."

"Yes, you are. Otherwise, you and I are done. And since my contacts are invaluable to you, I know how much this will affect you and the paper."

That quietens him for a moment. "I'm guessing the stories I've heard about you being tied up with Lorelei Winters are true, then. I have to say it surprises me that you would put a woman before business, because these kinds of threats you're making don't sit well with me, and I'd hate to see how that affects *you* down the track." His anger bleeds through the line, but nothing he says convinces me I'm taking the wrong course of action.

"Rewrite the article and take Lorelei's name out of it completely. And while you're at it, fire that reporter who wrote that trash piece. I never want to see her name on a byline again."

His fury is evident when he snaps, "There's going to come a time when you need me, Ashton. When that time comes, don't fucking call."

The line goes dead, and I immediately key in the number Jessica emailed me for Shandwick. He answers almost straight away.

"Shandwick."

"Ryan, it's Ashton Scott. We need to have a little talk."

He confuses my meaning and says, "Great! I've been trying to get in touch with you for a while now. I have a development—"

"I know all about your development, Shandwick, and I'm not interested. However, I *am* interested in discussing your relationship with your business partner's daughter. Does he know you've been screwing her for three months?"

"Fucking hell," he splutters, "What the fuck are you talking about?"

"I'll cut straight to the chase. Lorelei's pulling out of that development, and you're going to make it known that she was in fact never involved in it to begin with. I don't care what the fuck you have to tell people, but if you don't want me to send the photos I have of you with this girl to anyone, you will make it crystal fucking clear that Lorelei's name was incorrectly associated with you. Am I understood?"

"I've heard all about the way you conduct business, and now I know it's true—you're a piece of fucking work, Ashton," he seethes.

"The thing you haven't heard is that when it comes to those I love, there isn't anything I won't do. So believe me when I tell you I will ruin you if you ruin Lorelei's name."

"You don't think *I* could ruin you first? I have a large network that—"

I cut him off again. "Do your best. I'm not concerned. Now, unless there's anything you're still confused about as to my expectations here, I'm ending this call and never want to hear from you again."

"Fuck you," he mutters before hanging up on me.

I have no doubt Shandwick will do everything I've said. He would be ruined if those photos got out, and he knows it. And as far as his threats against me are concerned, I'm willing to take that chance.

I scroll through my contacts and find Marc Brentley's number. I've been slowly formulating a plan to fight off my father's demand to sell him the Willow Street properties. It involves Brentley, but it's risky because he won't appreciate the negotiation, and it may end up backfiring. However, I now have another reason to take this path, so I call him.

"Ashton," he answers, "I have you on my list to call today. How are we placed to finalise this deal? I'd like to make an announcement soon."

This is what I'm banking on. "I'm ready to sign off on it and invest another hundred mill, but there are some stipulations to that."

"What kind of stipulations?"

"Two things. First, the Willow Street development I've heard you're in bed with my father on. Walk away from it and get him to also. Convince him to leave those properties with me. And secondly, I want to bring Lorelei Winters on board. She'll be my partner on this. We'll sign off on it this week, and when you make the announcement, I want her name with mine."

"You know I fucking detest this kind of manipulation. And I have to say I'm surprised you're engaging in it. I didn't think it was your style at all."

"It's not. But on this deal, it is."

"Lorelei Winters obviously means something to you."

"She does."

"I don't like to mix business with personal, Ashton. You

bring her in, you're responsible for keeping personal issues out of this. I won't tolerate it."

"Consider it done."

He turns silent for a few moments before finally saying, "We have a deal, but this is the last time you negotiate in this way with me."

It's the last time I'll negotiate in this way with anyone if I can help it. I'm as against this kind of thing as he is. But for the first time in my life, I've found a reason to do it.

As we finish up the call, Jack's voice sounds from behind me. "Well, that's something I never thought I'd ever hear."

I turn to face him. "What?"

"You allowing personal shit to influence your business decisions. I have to say I'm impressed. How did Lorelei convince you to agree to that?"

"She didn't." I'm the one who has to convince her now. A conversation I'm not looking forward to having.

He joins me at the table where I'm sitting, placing a mug in front of him. I'm not sure what he's drinking, but I hope like hell it isn't whisky. That's the last thing Jack needs right now. "Is this another situation where you're taking charge and she just has to deal with it?"

I grimace. "It is, but for good reason." I then explain everything to him.

When I've finished, he takes a drink and rests back against his chair. "I've never seen you in love with a woman. It's about fucking time." Cocking his head to the side, he adds, "You should invite her to stay."

"I'm not sure that's the best thing for you right now."

"Why?"

"You need routine and space to recover. Having Lorelei around may hamper that."

"No, having her around may help give me that space I need." He sits forward again, resting his elbows on the table.

"You're here trying like fuck to make sure I don't do some-thing crazy, and while I appreciate that, having you in my face 24/7 *will* drive me crazy. I know I need you around, but if Lorelei's here, she'll help fill your time, meaning you won't be all over me."

I know he's right, but I'm still hesitant to agree. And as much as I want nothing more than to see Lorelei, I don't want anything to get in the way of Jack's recovery.

"I'll think about it." I'm not sure I will, though.

"Please do." He smiles. It's the first one I've seen since I arrived. "Besides, I like hanging out with her. She'll probably help me just as much as you will." He then throws the rest of his drink down his throat and stands.

Watching him walk away, I call out, "What was in that mug, Jack?"

Glancing back at me, he says, "Whisky."

It's in the lift of his brows as he says this that I know it wasn't whisky. It's also the first inkling that we've got a good shot at getting him better, because it signals the return of his humour.

62

LORELEI

It's only Wednesday and I'm already over this week. The situation with my tenant has escalated to the point where I'm sure we'll need to go to court to settle our dispute. And I've discovered I don't like Ryan Shandwick quite as much as I thought I did. We've been emailing back and forth about something I'm not completely happy with, and he's growing increasingly more condescending towards me. I arrived at the office just after eight this morning, and in the hour since then, his replies have come through thick and fast. And rude. However, he hasn't replied to my latest email, so something must have come up, dragging him from his computer. I'm relieved for the reprieve and decide to take a break.

I leave the office and head outside to grab a coffee. I've just taken my first sip when Ashton FaceTimes me.

"Hey you," I say, happy to hear from him. I've decided being separated from him is the worst thing. I miss him so damn much.

"We need to discuss something, and I want you to hear me out before you say anything." No greeting, no small talk.

Whatever he wants to discuss sounds serious. The expression on his face confirms this.

"Okay, but you're making me a little nervous here. Is everything all right?"

The expression on his face doesn't change, but something flares in his eyes. It's hard to know what it is through the phone, but he looks like he has the weight of the world on his shoulders. "I received a call today, alerting me to the fact the Herald will be running a story about government corruption tomorrow."

"Okay," I say, confused as to where he's going with this.

"The story was going to focus on Ryan Shandwick's development and the government officials he's bribed." He pauses for a moment. "Lorelei, they were zeroing in on your involvement because Shandwick was using your grandmother's name and reputation to get approvals through. The paper was going to ruin your name."

Things start to fall into place as I listen to him, and suddenly it makes sense why Ryan pursued me for this deal. God, I've been an idiot, blind to his motives.

"When you say 'was,' what do you mean?"

"I pulled some strings to get your name removed from the article. I also called Shandwick and told him you're no longer part of his bullshit."

I frown. "What does that mean?"

His nostrils flare as he says forcefully, "It means that development is going ahead without you. Your name will no longer be attached to it."

And my reputation is safe. That's the part he doesn't mention. It's also the thing he's worked hard to ensure.

Before I can thank him, he continues, "I've also spoken to Marc Brentley to let him know you're coming on board with the development I'm working with him on. You can invest the money you would have invested with Shandwick. If you agree, you'll be my partner in this. He'll make the announcement later this week. If you don't want—"

I cut him off. "I love you."

I know exactly why he's done this, and I love him even more for it. Ashton has effectively made sure my name is attached to something that will propel my business forward, because anyone that Marc Brentley gets in bed with is someone everyone else wants to be in bed with. Any whiff of bad publicity I may still receive from the Shandwick deal will be overshadowed by this one.

His expression tells me he's not completely convinced I'm on board with all this. "You're not ready to cut my balls off?"

I shake my head. "No, your balls are safe." Smiling, I add, "You must really love me." I can only imagine the strings he had to pull to achieve all this, and I know they wouldn't have been easy strings.

"Lorelei, I've never loved anyone like I love you. There's nothing I won't do to keep you safe and happy."

I'm so glad I can see his face right now. The love he's just told me he has for me blazes from his eyes.

"I miss you so much. How long do you think you'll be in LA?"

"A couple of weeks at least, maybe more."

It's not what I wanted to hear, but I knew to expect it. And my respect for Ashton only grows knowing he is choosing his friend over everything else. "Thank God we have FaceTime. I'm calling you tonight so you can talk dirty to me."

Heat flashes in his eyes. "Wear something sexy for me." He glances away from the phone for a beat before coming back to me. "I have to go. Jessica will send you all the info you need about everything we've discussed."

"Thank you, Ashton," I say softly. "I know we've had

problems with me not being able to accept your help before, but I really appreciate it on this."

After we finish the call, I think about how much has changed in such a short time. I truly am okay with Ashton having taken charge of this for me. Mostly because I know there's no way I could have achieved everything he has, but also because I felt the shift in his attitude. He hadn't expected me to be happy with his actions, which shows me he's listened to everything I've said regarding our argument. It's the listening that means the world to me. It makes me feel heard. And that's a great place for us to start our future together from.

Just before lunch, Ashton's father visits my office, venom shooting from every pore of him. I've found Gregory Scott to be an intimidating man on the best of days; this is a whole new level.

"I've just been on the phone with Marc Brentley, and it seems you've got your claws into my son," he fumes, smoke practically billowing from him.

I square my shoulders and work hard to maintain my cool. There's no way I'll allow this man to talk down to me. "And how is that, Gregory?"

His eyes widen, and I guess my icy tone and question don't impress him. *Screw him.* "He's thrown an unfathomable amount of money at Brentley to get him to walk away from a business deal with me."

I don't know what he's talking about. "What does that have to do with me?"

"I'm yet to get to the bottom of it, but I know it has to do with you. Brentley and I were developing Willow Street, and since you own a building on that street, I can only assume

Ashton is trying to keep you from being forced to sell." He stabs his finger in the air at me. "Make no mistake, no one fucks with me and wins. You will live to regret this, and so will my son."

My thoughts are swirling with confusion as to why Ashton has done this. It makes no sense to me. But those thoughts are for later; right now I have to deal with his father.

"My grandmother always taught me if I don't have anything nice to say, I should walk away. Well, I don't have anything nice to say, and since this is my office, you need to be the one to leave."

"Oh yes, the almighty Pearl Winters. She always did think she was above half of us in Sydney. She thought she could save those who shouldn't be in business in the first place. Well let me tell you, she didn't manage to save my loser brother. She wasn't as good as she thought she was."

I'm so stunned by the poison coming out of his mouth that I'm momentarily lost for words. And then they all come out in a rush. "I don't suspect anyone has ever told you what an asshole you are. I imagine they all live in fear of you and what you could do to them if they were honest. Well, I'm not that person. You are a goddam asshole, Gregory. Between the way you treat your son and daughter, and the way you just spoke about your own brother, I'm surprised anyone has anything to do with you. But I guess money talks, and that's the only reason why anyone speaks to you." I take a step closer to him, angrier with each passing second as I think about the man he is. "Money doesn't talk to me, so I have no interest in ever speaking to you again or trying to win your favour. And as for Ashton, I don't have my claws in him, but he does love me, and when you love someone, you do things for them like he's done for me. You wouldn't understand that because I'm fairly certain you've never loved anyone in your life."

He glares at me, his face turning red with fury. "Are you quite done, Miss Winters?"

I shake my head. "Not quite." Pointing at the door, I say, "You need to walk yourself out of here and never come back."

With one last filthy look, he stalks out of my office, leaving me shaking with anger and disbelief. I make myself a cup of tea and drink it slowly, calming down, before calling Ashton.

"Lorelei," he murmurs, his pleasure at hearing from me evident in his voice.

Ashton's pleasure is everything to me, because not only does it cause my own to flare, it helps centre me, reminding me I'm not alone in this world. I'm connected to him now. *I'm his.*

"I just had a visit from your dad. Did you know that my grandmother knew your uncle?"

He doesn't answer straight away. When he does, his tone is sombre. "I knew he rented a shop from her, yes. Why? What did my father want?"

I'm surprised we haven't talked about this yet, but I remind myself we're still getting to know each other. "He came by to tell me he's not pleased I have my claws in you and that I won't get away with making you ruin his plans for Willow Street. What's going on, Ashton? He was furious in a way I'm not sure I've ever seen a man be furious."

"Fuck," he mutters, "I'll sort this out with him. I don't want you worrying about it."

"I don't want you to sort anything out for me. I'm just wondering what's going on, because this was all news to me."

He switches us across to FaceTime, which is good; being able to see his face makes me feel closer. "The deal I struck with Brentley involved Dad as well as you. I don't want him developing Willow Street, so I made sure that wouldn't happen. I don't know why he assumes that is your fault."

"Why do you and your father want Willow Street so much?"

"Willow Street was such a huge part of my Uncle Victor's life. He owned the furniture shop you mentioned to me once, and taught me far more about life and business than my own father did. Victor went through a bad time and lost the business when I was seventeen. My drive to develop Willow Street comes from that. He had a vision for the area, and I want to bring that vision to life."

Everything I've thought about Ashton bulldozing Willow Street comes into focus, most of it now being questioned. This is a whole other side to him that he's not shown me before. A side I really like.

"Is that why your father wants it too?"

He shakes his head. "Fuck, no. He and Victor didn't get on. They were complete opposites, and my father hated me having anything to do with his brother. But Mum encouraged it, thank God. Dad probably wants it so he can knock down the shitty memories he must have over Victor, and the fact he drove him to ruin."

Goodness, Ashton's father is worse than I thought. "How did he do that?"

I watch as he sits on a couch. Once he's settled, he answers me. "I never knew that your grandmother's Willow Street Fund helped struggling businesses until you told me about it. I didn't know she'd helped Victor. I'd always assumed Dad had lent him cash and helped him in some way. Once you told me how the fund works, I realised Dad didn't lift a finger to help his own brother. And when the business went south, Dad did nothing. Victor started drinking after that and eventually drank himself to death. And my father just stood by and let him."

My heart hurts for Ashton; that he had to live through this. And I'm seeing things in a whole new light—the things he does that stem from what he's lived through.

"I'm sorry that happened to your uncle and to you. Victor was an amazing man, and he touched my life in many ways."

He rakes his fingers through his hair and exhales. "Yeah, he was."

Watching him think about his uncle and what he went through makes me miss him a whole lot more than I already do. I just want to wrap my arms around him and comfort him, because this seems to have affected him. And it's not often Ashton appears to be affected.

"I miss you," I blurt, unable to stop myself.

His eyes lock with mine. "You need to get your ass on a plane to LA." It's one of his growly orders, and it hits my core.

God, how I need to do that.

"You're busy with Jack," I start, but he cuts me off.

"Jack wants you here, too."

"Really?" That makes no sense to me.

"Yes, really. He thinks you'll give him some breathing space by taking my attention away from him all the time."

I laugh, understanding where Jack's coming from. "Let me guess, you're being Bossy Ashton, telling him what to do all the time."

He ignores that. "I want you on the first flight out tomorrow morning."

And there's his bossy ways I can't deny I love. "I might have things on that I can't reschedule," I throw out, just to draw more of his bossiness out. I have nothing I can't or won't reschedule for him.

"I'll book the flight myself and send James over to drag you to the plane if I have to."

I smile. "I'll see you tomorrow."

"Good," he growls, and I can tell from the way he says it and the way he's looking at me that he needs to see me just as much as I need to see him.

63

ASHTON

I fight the crowds at LAX on my way to wait for Lorelei. Fuck, I'm impatient today. I need her with me, by my side.

Once I reach my destination and work out I've probably still got some time to kill before she arrives, I call my father. I've been waiting for the right time, thinking over everything that's happened so I can express exactly what I want to him.

He picks up quickly. "It's almost midnight, Ashton. Your mother is sleeping."

Like he gives a fuck about my mother sleeping. But I don't bring that up because it's not the reason for my call today. "I learned something interesting about you last night. Something that pissed me off enough to make me consider telling someone what I know about that construction site accident from ten years ago that you were tied up with."

"Son, you don't want to take that journey with me." His voice is hard. Cold. Just the way I remember it from all the times in my life when he let me down.

"Oh, I think I might, Dad. Especially if you continue fucking with Lorelei like you have been."

"What do you think you know?" He's fishing to see if I do indeed know about all the things he's been doing behind the scenes.

As he asks this question, I see passengers making their way through the gate Lorelei will be coming through, and I search for her while continuing the conversation.

"You paid someone to continually vandalise her Willow Street building and cause her no end of grief so she would sell that building to you. I've had one of my guys looking into it, and he sent me the proof I need to take this further if I wish."

I hear the clink of ice and the sound of him gulping down what I presume to be scotch. "What the fuck do you want from me, Ashton?"

"I want you to leave Lorelei alone. Stop the vandalism, stop dropping by to see her, stop threatening her. Never fucking go near her again. If you do, I'll make sure everyone knows it was you who signed off on that building years ago even though you knew it had safety issues. If that gets out, we both know the outcome." It would bury him.

I spot Lorelei, my gut tightening as my gaze lands on her.

He hisses his disapproval. "When did you get so willing to play dirty?"

I make my way towards Lorelei, my eyes firmly holding hers. "You taught me well, Dad."

"No, I didn't. If I had, you wouldn't let pussy get in the way of good business sense."

I reach Lorelei and slide my free hand around her waist, pulling her close. Her mouth curls up in a smile and she presses a quick kiss to my lips right before I say to my father, "The little that you did teach me was lacking, but I've found a woman who's teaching me the important things."

"You've lost your ever-loving mind, son."

I rest my hand on Lorelei's ass. "Maybe, but I'm a lot fucking happier without it. Do we have an agreement?"

"We do. But if any of this gets out, I will tear you both down, piece by fucking piece."

I smile at my woman, hardly hearing a thing my father is saying. I'm certainly not letting any of it affect me the way it used to. "Give my love to Mum."

I end the call, shove my phone in my pocket, and slide my hand through Lorelei's hair to take hold of her before claiming her lips in a kiss that clears all other thoughts from my mind.

"Fuck, it's been too long since I've had you," I say when I pull away.

She presses hard against me, her hands gripping my shirt. "Take me home."

I don't miss the heat in her words or the need that matches my own.

My woman wants me as much as I want her.

It takes us just over an hour to drive to Jack's place, in which time Lorelei doesn't remove her hand from my body. She moves it between my leg, my arm, my chest and my face. And she kisses me whenever she gets the chance. In the past, this kind of behaviour from women irritated me. With her, I can't get enough of it. By the time we arrive at Jack's, I'm hard as hell for her.

Grabbing her suitcase from the boot, I pin my gaze to her. She's biting her lip watching me, and her expression leaves me no doubt she's imagining me naked and inside her. "Jack's out for the morning, which means you and I have a date that involves no clothing." I don't even care that she's tired from travelling; I can't wait another second for my fill of her.

Her smile lights up that beautiful face of hers. Not even long-haul travel interferes with Lorelei's beauty. "I need to shower first."

I shut the boot and walk to her, every fibre of my being blazing with my need. It's electric and unlike any sensation I've ever experienced. Being without the woman I love for over a week has turned me into a half-crazed man, desperate to get my hands and mouth on her. "We'll start in the shower."

Her eyes burn with desire as she signals her agreement with a nod. I lead her inside and into our bedroom that over-looks the Pacific Ocean.

She drops her bag on the bed and stands in front of the floor-to-ceiling window. "Oh my God, this view is amazing!"

I move behind her and run my hands down over her hips and ass and then around to the front of the pants she's wear-ing. Hooking my fingers in the waistband, I slowly lower them while speaking against her ear, "After our shower, I want you naked in front of this window with your lips around my cock." Her pants hit the floor and I remove her panties. Pushing her body against the window, I growl, "After you make me come, I'm going to slam you up against this glass and fuck you harder than I've ever fucked you."

She moans, and it's the sweetest fucking sound I've heard in weeks. Christ, I might not make it into the shower.

As I move my hand towards her pussy, she covers it with her hand and says, "Shower, Ashton. I'm not fucking you while I'm this dirty."

I hold her in place, refusing to allow her out of my hold just yet. "I don't care how dirty you are. It's been almost two weeks since I've had you."

Another moan falls from her lips as she rests her head

against my shoulder. The way her body sways against mine, coupled with that sound almost makes me ignore everything she's saying and slam inside her.

I drop my hands and step away. "Okay, go. I'll be in there in a minute." I want to give her some space to get clean so she's ready for me, but I also need a moment of my own.

I need to slow myself down. After our separation, my desire to have her in my life in every way possible is intense. For the first time ever, my attention is focused more on a woman than on my business. And while there's not a flicker of doubt in my mind that Lorelei is my future, this is all new territory for me.

Where I once was guarded and cautious, I'm ready to throw that caution to the wind. I'm ready to make this relationship the centre of my entire life, whatever that entails. This exhilarates me more than anything has in a long time. So in an effort not to overwhelm Lorelei, I need to slow myself down.

I leave the bedroom and walk out to the back deck and let the sun warm me for a few minutes. My gaze sweeps over Jack's property, taking in the pool to the side and the beach the house backs onto. He's had this place for about five years, and I've always loved coming to it because the ocean calms me. It was that same calming effect that convinced me to buy my Hawaiian property. And it's working on me now. After five minutes, I'm ready to join Lorelei in the shower.

As I enter the bathroom, I pull my shirt over my head and drop it to the floor. Lorelei has her head back while she washes her hair, and my eyes take the same path as the cascading water down her naked body. My dick is already hard for her, but this sight only intensifies that. A few moments later, my clothes are off and I step into the shower with her.

She runs her hands over her hair, forcing the water away

from her eyes, and moves close to me. Placing her palms to my chest, she briefly drops her gaze to my abs before looking back up at me and saying, "I don't want to be away from you for this long ever again."

I back her up against the tiles. "That won't happen. I'll make damn sure of it."

Not wasting a second, I claim her lips and kiss her.

Fuck.

These lips.

This body.

This woman.

I know deep in my gut I can't do this life without her. I got this far on my own, but I don't want to take another step forward without her by my side.

She wraps a leg around my body, and then the other. I lift her at the same time and hold her up against the wall. "Fuck," I rasp, "I wanted to take my time with this, but there's no way in hell that's happening."

Clinging to me, she begs, "Don't take your time. I need you inside me now."

I thrust inside hard, and her moan fills the air.

Jesus.

How did I go so long without her?

Pulling out, I thrust inside again.

I'm like a fucking savage in the way I take what I want.

I don't even stop to make sure Lorelei is getting what she needs.

I can't.

Desire drives me to lose all connection with anything but my raw carnal need to fuck her.

To claim her.

I don't think.

I just feel.

And hell, this is the best damn feeling in the world.

"Oh God," Lorelei pants, gripping me harder.

Her fingernails dig into me.

Her hips move faster.

Her cunt squeezes tighter around me.

"Fuck!" I roar, slamming into her one last time.

We come together, and when we're done, I find her lips again and kiss her. This is a deeper, slower kiss. Less frantic. And much longer.

I linger there, not ready to drag my mouth from hers yet. I want to savour this moment. It's the moment I make a decision I've been grappling with. One that will completely change the course of my life. And I want to remember it along with the way Lorelei's kissing me—like she wants to stay in my arms forever.

When I finally pull away, I find her gaze. "I love you."

She smiles. "I love you, too." Her smile deepens. "And I *really* love it when you fuck me like that."

That makes two of us.

I trail a finger down her cheek. "I have something for you."

Her eyes light up. "What?"

"It's in the kitchen." I pull out of her and let her go. "It'll get you through the next few hours while I dedicate time to this body."

"Ooh, food! You know me so well."

We finish showering, and I dry her off. After wrapping towels around both of us, I show her where the kitchen is and nod at the counter where I've left a bakery bag for her.

She glances around the large kitchen as she reaches for the bag. "Jack doesn't mess around when he chooses a home, does he? His place is amazing." She eyes the beach through the window. "And that view is to die for. I see a lot of time in the sun in my future."

I rest my hip against the kitchen counter and reach my

hand out to place it on her ass. "Jack certainly likes his comforts, and this place is full of them. It's the complete opposite of the farmhouse he owns in Australia."

As she opens the bag, she glances up at me. "Jack owns a farmhouse?"

I chuckle at her surprise. "Yeah, it's out in the middle of nowhere. Near Grafton. He's had it for about three years, but he doesn't spend much time there. Still, when he does, he roughs it."

She's only just listening to me now because she's discovered what's in the bag. "Oh my God, you are the bomb," she gushes as she pulls a cupcake out. Before I can get a word in, she's taken a huge bite, and her mouth is full of cake. Cream decorates her lips. *Fucking perfect.*

"I have chocolate, too, but that's for later."

With arched brows, she presses her body to mine. "What kind of chocolate? And do you plan on licking it off me?"

"Fuck," I growl. "You're killing me here."

She snakes her hand around my waist. "Good, because I can't even put into words what you're doing to me."

I reach into the drawer where I stashed the chocolate. I had to search hard in LA for this.

When she sees the Cherry Ripes, her fingers dig into my skin. "Dead. That's what you're doing to me. How did I get a man as amazing as you?"

I trail my fingers along her collarbone and thread them through her hair behind her ear. She thinks she's the one who got lucky, when I know *I* was the lucky one. "Don't let the chocolate sway you. I'm still the asshole I was last week. But you make me want to be a better man."

And I will be.

For her, I'll move mountains to be the man she needs me to be.

64

ASHTON

"I saw Lorelei's Instagram last night. You finally got your head on straight," Alessandra says to me over the phone two weeks after Lorelei arrived in the States.

I stretch my legs out in front of me as I watch Lorelei and Jack in the pool. The last two weeks have been hard for him, but having Lorelei here has helped. Much more than I imagined it would.

Lorelei has made it her mission to give my friend the female attention he desperately needed. Not the kind he gets from starlets looking to move up the ladder or from fans who push themselves on him or from women chasing a man with cash to fund their lifestyles. No, Lorelei has spent time simply sitting and talking with him, walking on the beach with him, and watching his favourite TV shows with him. He's slowly started coming out of his room more often, and I credit that to her. She's been the female friend he craved but never seemed able to find. And I've taken a step back and given them that time together, because I could see they both needed it.

The time I've looked forward to with Lorelei has been at

night. We've spent hours getting to know each other's deepest desires, fears, dreams, goals, hurts, and joys in life. In fourteen nights, we've slowly peeled back each other's layers. We've laid ourselves wide open, ready to live our lives together.

"You spoke to me yesterday, Aly. What's changed since then?" I don't bother with Instagram, so I have no clue what she's referring to.

"She posted a selfie of the two of you out at dinner. There, I've just messaged it to you. Take a look. You'll see what I mean."

I check my messages and find the photo. "What am I looking for?" It's a photo of Lorelei and me smiling at the camera. I'm not sure what Alessandra's seeing that I'm not.

She sighs. "God, you men are so slow sometimes. Look at how happy you both look. That smile in Lorelei's eyes tells me you've manned up. And honestly, Ashton, I've never seen you look happier." Her voice softens as she adds, "I'm really happy for you both."

I look closer at the photo, noting the things she mentioned. I *do* look happy. What I can see in myself more than that, though, is peace. Contentment. And Lorelei is breathtakingly beautiful in her happiness.

"How are you and Malcolm?"

"Hmm, where shall I start? We're okay, but he's still as infuriating as he's ever been about some things. I mean, yesterday he had the hide to tell me my driving is getting worse. Can you believe that? I never tell him what I think of his damn driving. Oh, and he also said something about the diet I'm on. He regretted that a lot last night, let me tell you."

I reach for my drink. "What did he say?" I can't imagine Malcolm ever saying anything mean.

"Oh, something about the carbs being far too low in his

opinion. The man has no idea what it takes to shift just a few kilos."

"Aly, he loves you. He doesn't want you to starve. There's no way he meant that in a bad way. You need to stop reading so much into the stuff he says. We're men. We don't have a hidden agenda. If we say the carbs are too low, we mean the carbs are too low. We don't mean you're bad at choosing a diet or anything else you might conclude after thinking about that one statement for hours." I take a sip of water. "Are you two still seeing the therapist?"

"Yes, and she says the same thing as you about men and what they say. I find her as infuriating as Malcolm sometimes."

I chuckle. My sister is in one of her neurotic phases at the moment, but I had a conversation with Malcolm two days ago in which he shared with me that things are slowly improving between them, so I'm relieved about that. "Lorelei will be home tomorrow. Promise me you'll keep an eye out for her while I'm still here. I don't want Dad or Cassia getting near her again."

"Cassia's keeping a low profile, but trust me, if that bitch goes near Lorelei, she'll have me to deal with. And as for Dad, have you spoken to Mum today at all?"

"No."

"I think she's left him. She rang me from the Sofitel and told me she's staying in the penthouse and charging everything she can to Dad. I really feel like she might be having a mental breakdown, you know? Like, not in a bad way, but in a 'fuck him and his whores' kinda way. I'm all for it." She takes a breath. "Anyway, I'll pick Lorelei up from the airport and look out for her. How long do you think it'll be until you come home?"

I process everything she's telling me, making a note to check in with Mum. I'm more than happy at the idea of her leaving Dad. "Probably a week or so. Even if I just come home to take care of some stuff and then fly back to stay with Jack again. Maybe I'll convince him to come for a quick trip with me."

Lorelei leaves the pool and comes toward me. Her skimpy white bikini that barely covers anything is plastered to her skin with water. I struggle to take my eyes off her breasts, and my dick grows hard as I watch her. Truth be told, she could wear a sack and I'd grow hard.

"I have to go," I say. "I'll get Lorelei to let you know her flight time."

"See you when you get home," she says and disconnects the call.

Lorelei slides onto my lap on the sunlounger as I place my phone down. She lies on top of me, soaking me, and presses her lips to mine. After she's done kissing me, she says, "Who were you talking to?"

I move my hand to her ass, hooking a finger under the edge of her bikini bottom. "Aly. She's going to pick you up from the airport tomorrow."

A lazy smile fills her tanned face just as the sun hits it. "I know I have to go home, but I don't want to. I want to live here in the sun with you forever."

Better words have never been spoken to me before, but I groan because, with every passing second and every word she says, I'm finding it harder not to flip her over and sink myself deep inside her.

I smack her ass. "I'm going to get a drink. You want one?"

She wiggles on top of me. "Am I causing you some pain?"

"Fuck," I hiss. "If you do that again, your ass is going to get spanked."

Heat flares in her eyes. "I told you I'm all about that spanking." At my pained expression, she pushes up off me.

"Okay, okay, I'm off. My ass is safe from your hand. And I'll get drinks. What do you want?"

Jesus. Now all I can think about is my hand on her ass.

"Make it something strong. I'm going to need it," I mutter.

Her laughter floats through the air as she exits the pool area. Lorelei is no longer the woman who's shy about sex toys or fucking me in public. She knows exactly how to work me up, and she doesn't hesitate to play dirty when it suits her. *Exactly how I like it.*

Jack lifts himself out of the pool and comes to sit on the sunlounger next to me. Drying himself off, he says, "I'm going to miss that woman."

I eye him. He has some life back in his eyes, which is a relief. He's taking his medication religiously and doing everything he's been told to do to get better. I'm under no illusions, though—his recovery is going to take time. He's having a good day today, but we never know what tomorrow will bring. All we can do is keep on putting one foot in front of the other.

It's a lesson I'm taking note of, because the process is so far removed from how I've always lived my life. I set goals, tackle each step, and achieve what I set out to. And I use sheer force if I have to. But this journey Jack's on is showing me that sometimes, sheer force isn't enough. Sometimes, a whole lot of patience and faith is required. I'm also learning that cash can't fix everything. We need to be surrounded by people as well. And without them, the shit cash can buy means very little.

I glance at him. "You should come home with me when I go. Just for a quick visit, and then we'll come back here."

He considers that as he shakes the water out of his hair. "Maybe."

I didn't expect such an easy answer, but then again, by

tomorrow he may be dead set against the idea. His moods swing daily.

My phone rings, and before I can pick it up, Jack does. "Hello, gorgeous," he answers it, and I know from his tone it's Jessica.

They have a quick conversation, after which he hands me the phone and says, "I think I *will* head back to Sydney with you for a while."

I take the phone, trying not to think about Jack being in love with Jessica. Placing it to my ear, I say, "How are we travelling with Steele?"

"He signed off on everything. It's all going ahead. That's not what I'm calling about, though."

"Oh?"

"Sian has more Willow Street properties for you to purchase. I've emailed the info, so when you get a chance to look at it, let me know if it all looks good and I'll make it happen."

"Is that all of them, then?"

"Almost. Just three more after these."

"Good."

"That's the best you've got? This was a fucking nightmare to put together. I'm looking for a little more than good."

"Once we have all those properties, you'll get free coffee for life from Francesca. I'll see to it." Francesca's coffee has become her favourite.

"Where most assistant's get a bonus, I get free coffee. Go me."

"Goodbye, Jessica."

I end the call and track Lorelei's movements as she exits the house to come back outside. Jack's voice interrupts my thoughts about what I'm going to do to her later. "I'm surprised you're still buying up Willow Street. How does

Lorelei feel about that? And for the love of God, tell me she knows. Tell me you learned your fucking lesson."

I turn to him. "I'm still buying them, and I have a feeling she's going to like what I plan for the street."

"Oh fuck," he says at the same time, Lorelei asks, "What am I going to like?"

I pull her onto my lap. "Nothing you need to be concerned with yet. I'll tell you when the time is right."

My hands on her skin distract her. "Okay," she agrees, pointing at her back. "You should give me a massage."

Jack sits next to me shaking his head while I do as my woman has requested, and I'm struck by the thought that I wouldn't change my life for a second. Even though the last few weeks have been challenging, and Jack has been going through hell, we're all still standing. And we're doing it together.

I'm exactly where I'm supposed to be.

65

LORELEI

IT'S BEEN TWELVE DAYS SINCE I'VE SEEN ASHTON, and I can hardly contain my excitement to see him today. His flight got in early this morning and he went straight home to shower before coming to see me at my office. I wanted to meet him at the airport, but he insisted he had something he had to do before seeing me. It was all rather cryptic, but I didn't argue with him. Well, not for long.

I've just made a coffee when his deep voice sounds from the door. "Lorelei."

The way this man affects me is something I've never experienced before. I've fallen in and out of love a few times, and I've had many crushes, but none of that comes close to the way I feel about Ashton.

I love him at a much deeper level. One I can't quite explain even to myself. My love is all-consuming. It's fierce and soft, and intense and gentle all at once. Unhurried but also frantic and desperate. And above all else, it's unconditional. Never again will I walk away from an argument and tell him I need space to figure out if I want to be with him. I want to be with Ashton forever.

He enters my office, and I can't stop my gaze from dropping to take in his dark blue suit. Good God, the man can wear a suit.

When he reaches me, I place my hands to his chest and slide them under his jacket. "Hey." I greet him with a smile.

Desire races through my veins from the intensity he watches me with. It's not even ten in the morning, and I'm ready to get naked with him. As much as I love that suit, I'd love to take it off him even more.

His eyes search mine for a few moments before he finally gives me what I want—a kiss.

Snaking a hand around my waist, he pulls me close as his mouth crashes down onto mine. This isn't a gentle kiss to say "I'm happy to see you." It's a bruising, claiming kiss that says "I fucking love you and never want to be separated from you again."

It's exactly the kiss I crave.

When he lets my mouth go, he keeps his hands firmly on me and rasps, "I hope you've blocked the day off."

My knees go weak. God, how I've missed his bossiness. There's nothing quite like being loved and wanted by Ashton. "Yes, I'm all yours for the entire day and night."

"Good. I have plans for later, but first I want to take you somewhere special."

I'm intrigued as to where he wants to take me, although it does surprise me that he doesn't want to get me naked first. When I arrived in LA the other week, he hadn't been able to keep his hands off me.

"Okay, I'll just grab my bag and lock up."

He waits patiently, keeping his eyes on me the whole time. There's something in his mood that I've not experienced with him before. It's edgy and wired, and it's rubbing off on me. My excitement grows as I try to figure out where he wants to take me.

When I'm ready to leave, he ushers me out to his car and drives me to our destination. I'm surprised when he pulls into a car park outside my building on Willow Street.

Lifting a brow questioningly at him, I ask, "Why are we here?"

"There's something I want to show you," is the only answer I get before he exits the car and comes around to open my door.

I step out and let him take hold of my hand so he can guide me. We walk down the street towards Francesca's café, and I see her watching us approach. As we draw closer, she smiles at Ashton, and it's a knowing smile that makes me feel like I'm the only one here who's not in on something.

"The table is ready for you," she says to him.

He nods at her. "Thank you." He then leads me to a table in the back of the café that has been decorated with a beautiful tablecloth and flowers.

Glancing around the café, I note it's empty, which is unusual for this time of the morning.

As he pulls my seat out, I ask, "What's going on, Ashton? Why are we here?" God, I hope he's not about to tell me something I don't like. *Is that why he's on edge?*

Nerves flutter in my tummy, and I do my best to hold myself together.

He sits across from me. "It was either bring you here or take you to the McDonald's where we went that day after the soccer match."

I frown. "I'm lost. What do you mean?"

His eyes burn with intensity again. "I mean I wanted to bring you to the place where I first decided to make you mine. Looking back, I couldn't quite decide if that was at McDonald's or here. Since Willow Street is so important to you, I chose here."

The nerves in my tummy turn into butterflies as I realise

why he's brought me here. Or at least, why I *think* he's brought me here.

I'm still trying to get my thoughts in order when he continues, "Before I met you, I had a clear plan for my life. I knew exactly where I was going and I knew how to get there. I thought I knew everything." His eyes demand my complete attention. "Turns out I didn't quite know everything." He reaches into his suit jacket pocket and pulls out a piece of paper. Placing it on the table, he slides it across to me. "My father taught me to approach my life the same way I approach business—with little emotion. Life is a challenge to be conquered, and everything in it is something to be owned. I win one battle, and then I move swiftly to the next. I forgot along the way what my uncle taught me about allowing passion to guide me and about getting my priorities right. And then I met you, and you changed everything."

I can hardly breathe.

The emotion blazing from Ashton is causing my heart to beat so fast. I have no idea what's on the piece of paper he's given me, because I'm waiting for him to finish speaking before I read it. And I'm not sure where he's going with all this. I thought he was going to propose to me, but this doesn't feel like a proposal.

I stay quiet while he continues, "I told myself I wanted Willow Street because it made good business sense. And it did. But there was so much more to it than that. I just wasn't willing to see it for anything more than business, because without my work, what purpose did my life have? Lorelei, you've opened up my world and reminded me of the parts to myself I buried a long time ago." He nods at the paper. "Open it."

"Ashton," I start, all flustered and confused as to where he's going with this.

He cuts me off, all bossy, "Open the letter, Lorelei."

My hands shake as I do what he says. Whatever this is, it feels momentous, like it's going to change something in my life.

Once I have the letter opened, I read it, and stunned doesn't even come close to describing my reaction. If I thought my heart was beating fast before, it's practically leaping out of my chest now.

My head jerks up and I meet his gaze again. "Oh my God...." No more words come. Ashton has stolen them all.

The letter is from his lawyer. It details that Ashton and I are now the owners of every property on Willow Street. Equal owners. It highlights the fact that I have an equal say in any development of Willow Street, and that without my consent, no development can go ahead.

Ashton stands and comes around the table to where I am. He kneels and pulls a blue box from his pocket.

My chest squeezes with love.

Taking hold of my hand, he says, "I don't want to go through life without you. I want you by my side. Challenging me. Pushing me to be a better man. I want you to pull me back when I forget my way. I want to raise children with you, and chase my passions with you, and grow old with you." He lets go of my hand and opens the box for me to see the exquisite diamond ring inside. "Lorelei Winters, I love you. Will you marry me?"

Tears fall down my cheeks as I nod. "Yes." I'm a mess of emotions as I scramble off the chair and throw myself into his arms. Taking hold of his face, I continue nodding like a mad woman. "Yes, I will marry you, Ashton Scott." My lips crash into his and I kiss him for the longest time. I don't ever want to stop kissing this man. He is my everything.

When he finally manages to end the kiss, he blasts me with the smile of his I love. The one I can't get enough of. I love Ashton's intensity and his passion, but when he smiles at me, I feel I'm home.

As he slides the ring on my finger, I say, "Are you sure you know what you're doing with those Willow Street properties? You know I won't make it easy for you to do what you want with them, right?"

His smile doesn't leave his face. "I'm counting on it, baby."

Oh God.

This man.

He stands, bringing me up with him, and pulls me close. "You know I won't make it easy for you either, right?"

I hit him with a sexy smile. "I'm counting on it, baby. Oh, and one other thing?"

He arches a brow, questioningly.

"I'm gonna need that butt plug back."

I can do all the things he asked me to in his proposal. I can challenge him, and push him, and raise children with him, and chase our passions with him, and grow old with him, because loving him is the only thing I want to do for the rest of my life. He thinks I changed everything for him and opened up his world. What he doesn't know is that he *gave* me the world. And I'm going to hold tightly to him forever.

EPILOGUE

"Daddy," Dana says, wrapping herself around my leg, "Mummy said you need to help me get dressed for the party because we're late now."

I reach down and pull my daughter into my arms. Her red hair shimmers in the afternoon sun that streams in through the window of our Hawaiian home. She and I spent far too long outside this morning, and when we finally came inside, Lorelei gave me the look that tells me I'll be the death of her. On a normal day, she wouldn't have cared how long Dana and I stayed out swimming and playing on the beach, but today she had things she wanted me to do.

Touching her nose, I smile. "Have you chosen your dress for today, princess?"

She grins and nods. "Yes, but Mummy said I can't wear it."

I force down a chuckle. Of course Dana has selected something Lorelei said no to. My daughter is as stubborn as my wife. And while I often go to bat for Dana, there's no way in hell I'm going against what her mother has said about this dress. Not when Lorelei's hormones are all over the place

437

after the birth of our third child less than three months ago. My balls are worth more to me than that.

"How about we choose another dress together?"

Her little face scrunches into a frown. "No! I wanna wear the purple dress!"

I walk us from my bedroom to hers and deposit her on the floor. "You've hardly worn the blue one I bought you. I'd really like it if you picked that dress."

She stares up at me while I search for it, her big green eyes blinking while she tries to decide. Finally, she says, "Okay," but it's drawn out like she's not quite convinced.

I pull the dress from the closet and lay it on the pink Barbie blanket that covers her bed. The blanket Alessandra bought when she also bought her a million other Barbie products. Spoiled doesn't even cover the way my sister loves my children.

Sitting, I motion for her to come to me. "I'll help you get dressed, and then we might have to find Auntie Aly to do your hair."

Her eyes light up. "Yes!"

Dana is a fidgety four year old, so dressing her takes a lot longer than it should, but I make it a point to remain patient with her always. I will never be my father and rush my children or push them away.

I've only just managed to do up the last button on her dress when she starts jumping up and down, a look of pure joy on her face. Following her gaze, I find Alessandra standing in the doorway, a huge smile on her face. The joy in her eyes matches that in Dana's. These two share a special bond.

Entering the room, Aly spreads her arms for Dana to run into, and lifts her up. "Hello my beautiful girl. I see Daddy helped you choose a gorgeous dress." She eyes me and adds, "And it's one I know Mummy will love."

Dana's little arms fling around Alessandra's neck. "Daddy said you will do my hair. I want a braid."

"Do we have any magic words today?" Aly asks.

Dana nods. "Please!"

"Okay, how about you find your brush and hair tie, and I'll do a braid. And Daddy can go and help Mummy with Autumn."

"Are you good here?" I ask.

"Yes, you go help your wife." As I head towards the door, she calls out, "Oh, and if you see my darling husband, please tell him it wasn't me who put that dent in our rental car while I was out today. I found it in the carpark like that."

I frown. "Why do you want me to tell him?"

"Why wouldn't I?" At my puzzled expression, she adds, "You know he thinks I drive around all day trying to find cars to crash into. Well, this time it wasn't my fault, and if that news comes from you, I've got half a chance of him listening."

I shake my head. My sister never fails to amuse me. "He's hardly going to pay attention to anything I have to say about it."

She turns Dana around and brushes her hair while muttering, "Honestly, you men. Just trust me. I know my husband."

"I know your husband, Aly, and I also know you. And I think we all know you're just trying to avoid having to tell him about the dent."

Waving her hand at me dismissively, she says, "Either way, please tell him. And also, Mum just arrived. With Marty. I thought you said he couldn't make it?"

In the eight years since Mum left Dad, she's dated some interesting men, Marty being the most interesting. He's not the kind of man I would have chosen for her, being that he's somewhat impulsive and a little too free-spirited for me, but

I can't deny he's made her the happiest she's ever been in her life.

Alessandra is not a fan. Marty is too loud and crude for her.

I shrug. "It was always a maybe."

She purses her lips. "Well, if he starts telling those filthy jokes he loves, I'll be having something to say about it. I cannot stand another night of his vulgar mouth. I just can't fathom what Mum sees in him."

I can. He's the complete opposite to our father, and I'm convinced that's what she sees in him. And for her happiness, I'll put up with a few rude jokes here and there.

Checking my watch, I say, "You girls have ten minutes, and then I want you downstairs."

Dana wiggles on the spot, her smile fixed on her face. She's been looking forward to this party all week. She certainly takes after her aunt with her love of parties. "Yes, Daddy!"

I head into Lorelei's and my bedroom before I go downstairs to find her. I have a gift I want to give to her before the party is in full swing.

I've just entered the walk-in-robe and slipped the gift into my pocket when Lorelei's hands slide around me from behind. "I know this is your birthday party, but I really want everyone to go home so I can have you all to myself," she murmurs.

Turning, I grip her waist and push her back against the mirror. Dipping my face to her neck, I kiss her there and then along her collarbone. The strapless dress she's wearing always draws my mouth to her skin.

"It was your idea to throw a party," I say as I make my way to her lips.

She reaches for the top button of my shirt and flicks it open. "Well, it doesn't technically start for another ten minutes. That's long enough for me to wish you a happy birthday."

"Who has Autumn?"

She flicks the next button. "Jack. You know how much he loves babies. Seriously, his wife needs to give him another child."

"I don't see that happening any time soon. He was lucky to get one out of her."

Her hands move deftly down my shirt, unbuttoning it. Dropping her gaze to my body, she presses her hands to my abs and bites her lip. "I swear you get hotter with every passing year."

It's not what she says, or that she touches me, it's the way she bites her lip that causes me to spin her around and grind my cock against her. Sweeping her hair to the side, I growl against her ear, "If I didn't think one of our family members was likely to walk in on us, I would bend you over and fuck you so hard you'd have trouble walking out of here."

A moan escapes her lips. "No one's going to walk in."

We both know that's a lie. Our family lacks boundaries when it comes to privacy. Between my sister, mother, and Jessica, one is bound to come looking for us if we disappear for too long.

I kiss her neck. "I have a gift for you."

"So no sex? I mean, I'd settle for your mouth on my pussy."

Fuck.

My wife loves to drive me wild by slipping in dirty talk when I least expect it. She tells me it's my fault. That I taught her well when we first started dating. I tell her she's perfected the art over the years and that she can ease up now. To that, she always laughs and carries on.

I pull out her gift and hand it to her. "If you continue

teasing me tonight, there will be no spanking for you later." These days I don't threaten to spank her; I threaten not to. I always get what I want after that.

She turns around and pouts. "You're no fun."

"Open your present."

She unwraps the gift, muttering, "Still as bossy as ever"— her mouth falls open—"oh my God, this is beautiful!" Pulling the necklace from the jewellery box, she spends a minute reading what's written on the two interlocking hearts before looking up to find my eyes. "Thank you, it's perfect." One heart has our names engraved on it, while the other heart has the names of our three children.

The love shining from her hits me fair in the chest, causing my heart to squeeze. I love Lorelei more now than ever. Some days the feeling overwhelms me, and today is one of those days.

Taking the necklace, I lift my chin at her. "Turn around."

She does as I say and scoops her hair out of the way so I can fasten the necklace around her neck. When I finish, she faces me again. "I think I'll keep you."

I arch a brow. "There was never any possibility you wouldn't. And if it ever crosses your mind, I'm having no part of it."

She quirks her brow. "You'll just boss me into staying, I expect."

"You know me well, Mrs. Scott."

Taking hold of the hearts, she says, "What if we have another child?"

"Is that on the cards?"

"Well, maybe. I'm not sure I'm ready to stop yet."

I pull her close. "You know where I stand on this. I'm more than happy to have a soccer team of Scotts." I brush my lips over hers. "I have something else for you."

Her eyes light up. "What? You know I love surprises."

"I've been working with Jack on something for a few months now, and this week it was all finalised." I pull my phone from my pocket and show her an image I've saved. At her questioning look, I explain, "It's the logo for a new fund he and I have established to help children with their education. We're kicking it off with ten million dollars, and we want you to head it like you do the Willow Street Fund."

She peers closer at the logo before looking back up at me, her eyes glistening. "The Pearl Winters Fund?"

I nod. "Yes. You've told me how your grandmother helped children at her church, and how she believed strongly in an education for every child. Jack and I want to work with you to continue that legacy."

We always said we'd give back once we made our millions. We always said we wouldn't become our fathers.

While Lorelei is processing this news, Dana and our two-year-old son, Mason, come running in. "Mummy! The party is starting!" Dana exclaims excitedly. She tugs at her mother's clothes while Mason wraps his arms around my leg.

My wife is watching me with wonder. It's the kind of look a man lives his entire life for.

When neither of us respond to Dana, she tugs harder at Lorelei's clothes. "Mummy! Why aren't you and Daddy coming?"

Lorelei reaches down and pulls Dana into her arms. "We're coming in a minute. I promise. Daddy's just telling me something."

"What is he telling you?"

Lorelei meets my gaze again, tears streaming down her cheeks. "He's telling me about something amazing he and Uncle Jack did."

Our kids wriggle and cling, but I'm completely focused on my wife as she pulls my mouth to hers and kisses me. When she's finished, she says, "I don't even have words for how much I love you. You, Ashton Scott, are the very best man I know, and I am blessed to be your wife. I'm blessed to stand by your side and share your life."

I tighten my arm around her. "All of this is because of you, Lorelei. You've shown me how to love and made me want to be a better man. This is me being a better man."

She kisses me again, grinning through her tears. "That thing I said about keeping you?" At my nod, she continues, "You won't ever have to boss me into that. I am yours forever."

ABOUT THE AUTHOR

Dreamer.

Coffee Lover.

Gypsy at heart.

USA Today Bestselling author who writes about alpha men & the women they love.

When I'm not creating with words you will find me planning my next getaway, visiting somewhere new in the world, having a long conversation over coffee and cake with a friend, creating with paper or curled up with a good book and chocolate.

I've been writing since I was twelve. Weaving words together has always been a form of therapy for me especially during my harder times. These days I'm proud that my words help others just as much as they help me.

www.ninalevinebooks.com

facebook.com/AuthorNinaLevine

instagram.com/ninalevinewriter

amazon.com/author/ninalevine

bookbub.com/authors/nina-levine

goodreads.com/ninalevine

ALSO BY NINA LEVINE

Storm MC Series

Storm (Storm MC #1)

Fierce (Storm MC #2)

Blaze (Storm MC #3)

Revive (Storm MC #4)

Slay (Storm MC #5)

Sassy Christmas (Storm MC #5.5)

Illusive (Storm MC #6)

Command (Storm MC #7)

Havoc (Storm MC #8)

Sydney Storm MC Series

Relent (#1)

Nitro's Torment (#2)

Devil's Vengeance (#3)

Hyde's Absolution (#4)

King's Wrath (#5)

King's Reign (#6)

The Hardy Family Series

Steal My Breath (single dad romance)

Crave Series

Be The One (rockstar romance)

Billionaire Romance

Ashton Scott

Risk

Keep up to date with my books at my website.

ACKNOWLEDGMENTS

Ashton Scott has been a labour of love for over two years. What started as a fun project for me to work on in an effort to find my writing mojo again turned into a serial that many of you guys followed along with and supported me in. Thank you for that support and encouragement. It truly did inspire me to finish this book, especially after Mum passed away and I wasn't writing very much. I knew you were hanging for more Ashton, so I continued writing him.

For my Levine's Ladies, there were quite a few of you girls who really made a point to check in each Monday with me and let me know you loved that week's episode. That meant the world to me. I'd love to thank each one of you here, but I'm afraid I might miss someone and I would hate to do that. But you girls know who you are - thank you!

Jodie, I know I say this all the time, but really, for this book, it is truer than ever - I could not have made Ashton and all these characters who they are without you. Remember those Monday nights two years ago when E had ice-skating and

Mondays were a mad blur of getting the episode finished, beta read, formatted, emailed out etc etc. They were hectic days for me, but you made them fun and achievable. And remember that Monday at like 10pm when you rang me and said "Umm, no you can't send this one out, it isn't good" and then I had a mental breakdown (okay, well maybe I'm exaggerating a little ;))... I love you more for being honest with me each time rather than letting me think something is up to my standard when it isn't. Yes, even that Nash chapter you made me rewrite when I didn't want to do any more rewrites. Even that time! But I digress... thank you for all your hard work on Ashton. You truly are a goddess <3

Becky, you know I love you. Like, a freaking lot! You come through for me every single time. And your edits have taught me how to be a better writer. But let's not get too excited, I still suck at commas and ellipses and compound whattaya-callthem... ;) #DontEverLeaveMe Thank you <3

Dana, I didn't write that scene you wanted, but I did name one of Ashton's girls after you. Thank you for your support, babe <3

To all my readers, thank you for reading my books. Some of you have followed me from bikers to rockstars to bartenders to tattoo artists and now to billionaires. I love that you get my humour and my Aussie ways! I never planned to write all Aussie characters because I didn't think readers worldwide would embrace them, but I am so glad I did, because I found you guys to love them <3

To my bloggers, reviewers, Levine's Ladies & Team Levine - thank you for all of your support. For reading and reviewing. For sharing my books with your friends. For mentioning my books in your book clubs. For forcing my books on your mum and sisters... lol, just kidding ;) (but secretly, many of you have told me that you do, so thank you!). Just, thank you. I so appreciate every share and every word of encouragement <3

To my family & friends, thank you for giving me the space to stare at my computer for many hours on end. Also, for giving me a few hours at each deadline to cram the words in. ;) I love all of you.

Printed in Great Britain
by Amazon

It was a bad start to my week.
Or shall I say, *he* was a bad start to my week.
ASHTON SCOTT.
PRESUMPTUOUS, ARROGANT ASSHOLE.
He barrelled into my office and demanded I sell him my property.
I said no. Never.
He said everything is for sale.
He also said he always gets what he wants.
Well, Ashton Scott can kiss my ass. He's not getting this.
There's one problem with that.
The man *just doesn't give up*.
And now he's decided he wants me, too.
HE'S SEXY AF.
HE WEARS A SUIT LIKE NOBODY'S BUSINESS.
And his bossiness turns me on in ways I can't even understand.
But I'm not going down without a fight.
Or at least, I wasn't...
My fight is what Ashton loves the most.
OF COURSE IT IS.
SEND WINE.

ISBN 9780994585820

90000

9 780994 585820